PROTECTING
WHAT'S YOURS

EVE STERLING

ISBN 13: 979-8-88896-594-8

Book Cover by Eve Sterling

Edited by Roxana Coumans

First edition 2023

For every woman who thought that she couldn't be enough.

TRIGGER WARNING

Please note that this book contains strong themes of infertility with the female main character. It also contains minor themes/mentions of drug and alcohol abuse, violence, and child neglect. Please be aware that this book contains scenes of a graphic sexual nature and may not be suitable for readers under the age of eighteen.

Playlist

True Love (feat. Lily Allen) – Pink
Kings & Queens (Acoustic Cover) – Zero
Vigilante Shit – Taylor Swift
Bang Bang – Kurt Hugo Schneider, Max S, Sam Tsui
Most Girls – Hailee Steinfeld
Million To One – Camila Cabello
Sit Still, Look Pretty – Daya
Breakfast – Dove Cameron
Never Be The Same (Acoustic Version) – Jonah Baker
Hey Stupid, I Love You – JP Saxe
Maybe Don't (feat. JP Saxe) – Maisie Peters
Baby – Madison Beer
Someone You Loved – Lauren Spencer Smith
Angels Like You – Miley Cyrus

CHAPTER ONE

BIANCA

There are those people that come into your life and change every-thing. You meet them and their presence has such a profound impact that they can't help but make you a better artist. A better person. They are a trusted advocate that nurtures your strengths and helps you make necessary changes to reach your goals without stifling your creativity. They support you while simultaneously pushing you to new heights. Yes, there are definitely those people out there.

And then there's this bitch.

"So, you're saying it lacks passion?" Keeping my voice on an even keel is difficult when I'm trying not to beat someone over the head with a canvas.

"Passion, maturity, whatever you want to call it." Margot waves a hand dismissively at my painting sitting on the easel near her desk. "Frankly Bianca, it might as well be a child's finger painting for all the thought that's gone into it."

Finger painting? *FINGER PAINTING?*

I keep the screaming in my head since it's a much better idea than unleashing on my boss. She's sitting at her desk, thick red framed glasses perched on the tip of her hawkish nose, and drumming her fingers like she's impatient for me and my finger painting to get the hell out of her office.

Margot Gault is the owner, operator, and director of The Gault Gallery, and the woman currently tearing down a painting that I'm pretty proud of. At least I *was* proud of it.

When I got this job three months ago, I was beyond excited. I'd been working towards this my entire life. All those classes as a teen, the studying obscure artists, grueling projects in college, and now I was finally where I was supposed to be. Sure, it was just a gallery assistant job for now, but my foot was in the door. With *the* Margot Gault no less. Sure, I'd found documents in her office listing her real name as Maggie Gershowitz, but as Kermit the Frog once said, that was none of my business.

Margot was famous for nurturing young artists and bringing them to the forefront of the Seattle art scene. I had this fantasy where she would see my work, recognize my brilliance, and like magic, my art would be shown amongst the best of the best. I just had to bide my time.

I'd spent months dedicating my every waking moment to this gallery, and this is all the feedback I get from her? Don't get me wrong, I love my job. Even the minutia of updating inventory in the computer gives me a rush. Working in this world was all I've ever wanted to do.

Margot would sweep in and out of the gallery every day, dazzling us with tales of discovering new talent or lunches with established artists she had booked for exhibitions. I was in awe of this tiny woman in her fifties, her hair cut into a severe black as night bob, and lips painted crimson. Her shrewd eyes always enlarged and owlish behind her thick red glasses. If I'm being honest, I'm still in awe, even after she just caused my dreams to come crashing down into tiny pieces all around me. You'd think the least she could do would be to give me something constructive to work with.

"What do you suggest I do to improve?" My teeth clench and I have to make a concentrated effort to relax my hands that have balled into fists at my sides. I can take this as a learning experience at least. After all, Margot knows what she's talking about.

She lets out a heavy sigh. "Bianca, I can't tell you how to make your art. You must do that yourself. If I told you what to do, it wouldn't be your art anymore, it would be mine. Just keep working at it. I'm sure you'll eventually stumble upon something that gives you the genuine passion to create."

I swear to God, if I had anything in my hand right now, I would throw it at the wall. Could she possibly be any less helpful? I'm asking her for advice and she can't even give me that? So much for being taken under the wing of the great Margot Gault.

It takes a real effort not to snatch my painting from the stand and stomp out the door, slamming it behind me. I'm half Italian and half Irish. I've got this fiery temper thing down pat. But since I'm not a child and am in no mood to look for a new job, I just say, "Thank you for looking at it, Margot. I appreciate your time."

She turns her back to me and starts going through the paperwork piled high on the credenza behind her desk, effectively dismissing me. I calmly take the painting I've worked weeks on down from the stand and start to make my way out of her office.

"Bianca, when you find your muse, come back and show me."

I just nod and close the door ever so softly behind me. A twenty-two-year-old who can't control her temper is not a good look. I make my way down the metal industrial staircase and head into the tiny break room that I share with the other gallery staff. The room's barely large enough to hold our outdated coffee pot, table with three chairs—because Margot insists there's beauty in odd numbers—and a little shelf of cubbies that would look more fitting in an elementary school than the hottest art gallery in Seattle.

Before shoving my painting onto one of the empty shelves, I take a moment to study it. Sure, it's probably not the best piece I've ever produced, but calling it a finger painting is a bit extreme. This thing took me weeks to work on. My fine arts degree has an emphasis on painting, and I work in several different mediums, however my subject matter tends to focus on people, whether that be portraits or scenes where they are the focus.

This painting is a portrait of my mother that's done in yellows and blues, her face mostly obscured by her flowing hair. I've been feeling a disconnect from her the past four years, ever since I moved to Seattle for school and stayed after I graduated. Luckily, she's finally decided to move here and I'm excited to get to know her on a more adult level, not just as a child and her mother.

I honestly thought I would impress Margot with my piece. I mean, I'm not naïve enough to think that she was going to fall all over herself and offer me my own exhibition or anything, but I did expect a few encouraging words, maybe an offer to review my other work. Instead, I got finger painting.

I quickly wrap the canvas in a long piece of parchment paper and slide it onto an out of the way shelf so that I can get it home without damaging it, though I guess that wouldn't be the worst thing. Maybe a tear at one edge would make Margot think it was more interesting.

I smooth down my black dress over my wide hips before making my way back out to the main floor where Jenna is standing at the front desk, phone pressed to her ear.

"Of course, Mrs. Clemens," she says into the phone. "I've got your name down right here on our list. You shouldn't have a problem at the door. We're all looking forward to seeing you at the exhibition next week."

When she hangs up the phone, I shoot her a look. "You realize we don't actually have a list for next week, right?"

She gives me a wide smile. "You know that, and I know that, but Mrs. Clemens doesn't." She gives that high tinkling laugh that always brings a smile to my face. "But it makes her feel special and the more special she feels, the more likely she is to buy something."

PROTECTING WHAT'S YOURS

I shake my head and let out my own laugh. "Sometimes you're scary, Jenna. You're going to be the top gallerist in this city in no time."

She lets out a dreamy sigh. Jenna isn't an artist like me. She's here because she loves art and wants to be the person who discovers new artists and introduces them to the world. She basically wants to be Margot, but with better hair. "A girl can dream. Speaking of dreams, what did Margot say about your piece?"

I let out a groan and can't suppress my eye-roll. "Well, there isn't a chance Mrs. Clemens will be buying my piece at next week's exhibition. The phrase *finger painting* was tossed around."

Concern furrows her brow. "Maybe this just wasn't the right piece. You're a great artist, Bianca. Margot will see that someday and even if she doesn't, you know she's not the only gallery in town."

"I know, but she's the best. Besides, if she says it sucks, I'm inclined to believe her, even if it was a little harsh. She said I need to find my muse and I guess she's right. I've got to find something I'm really passionate about."

"Something or someone." She wiggles her brows suggestively at me and I can't help but smile.

"I don't think that kind of passion is my problem."

"Well, I know I could use some inspiration of my own. We need to go out soon and meet some guys before my lady bits fall off from disuse."

"I don't think that's possible. Besides, weren't you dating that guy from your Yoga studio? What happened to him?"

"Christian? He's long gone. Every time we were going to have sex, he wanted to stop and stretch first. I mean, who does that?"

"You're kidding." I laugh, picturing their naked stretching sessions. "We definitely need to go out soon. I heard there's some new band playing at Vinnie's. We should check it out."

Before we can solidify any plans, the gallery phone rings and Jenna grabs it, greeting the caller in her deceptively sweet voice that never

5

lets on she's a shark when it comes to art sales. I email the artists scheduled to participate in next week's event and remind them that their pieces need to be here three days early so we can set up.

The rest of the afternoon goes by slowly. A few people wander in off the street, but they're just browsing. We're open to the public, but most of our business comes from shows and by appointment. However, I always enjoy any chance I get to show people around the gallery and talk about my favorite thing, art.

By the time I've locked up and driven back to my neighborhood, I'm exhausted, my feet hurt, and I'm still a little pissed about my earlier meeting with Margot. Once I finally pull up to the house I share with my roommates, I can see that Violet's beat me home and already parked in our tiny driveway. I can't even be mad. I'm usually the first one home and Hollie and Violet are the ones forced to participate in the Hunger Games, otherwise known as parking on Blum Lane.

Each side of the street is packed with cars and I'm less than thrilled about the prospect of walking half a mile while lugging this canvas in my four-inch heels. There's a tiny spot in front of the house next door to mine, but I can tell my car isn't going to fit. If this was a week ago, I wouldn't have given it a second thought and just crammed my car in there. Unfortunately, the house that's stood empty for months has finally sold and I really don't want to give the new neighbors a bad impression by blocking their driveway.

With a little prayer to the parking gods and a sigh, I hit the gas and circle the block. After my third go around, I've had enough. I just want to drag my *finger painting* inside and have a glass of wine... or twelve. I'm not bitter at all.

The tiny space in front of the neighbor's house is calling out to me, tempting me like a siren luring a sailor to his death. Hopefully, my consequences won't be quite so dire.

Pulling my car into the tiny space, I move as far forward as I can, practically kissing the bumper of the car in front of me. I check my side mirror and let out a groan of frustration. It looks like I'm hanging over the driveway just the tiniest bit. But it's really not that much and who knows what day the neighbors are actually going to move in. Plus, I'll be gone again first thing in the morning. They'll never even know I ever so slightly encroached on their space.

It takes a few minutes to gather my belongings, including my canvas shoved down into my tote, and lock the car. My shoulders actually loosen a little with home in sight. A glass of wine and complaining to my best friends is definitely in order. Then it's right back to the easel to start over from scratch.

"Ma'am."

I don't bother turning and looking to see who's calling out because as far as I'm concerned, I look nothing like a "ma'am". I just keep marching down the cracked sidewalk, careful not to trip in my heels.

"Ma'am. Excuse me." This time the voice is sharp with annoyance and coming from directly behind me. Quickly spinning around, I find a man impatiently trying to get my attention.

Hello there. I quickly take him in all the way from his well-fitting jeans to the tanned and muscled forearms that are crossed over his chest and land on his face that's all sharp angles. There's even a lock of blond hair falling perfectly across his forehead that has me itching to reach for my paint brush.

This guy is hot. Like scorched earth hot. Well, he would be except for the sour expression on his face. It's a mixture of arrogance and annoyance. In fact, his entire aura is giving off an air of superiority. Add that to the fact he apparently called me ma'am—twice—and my hackles are up.

"It's Miss, actually."

Proving himself to be the dick I immediately pegged him as, he continues like I haven't said a word. "Ma'am, your vehicle is parked across my driveway."

Ah, this must be the new neighbor. Well, so much for making a good impression. Unfortunately for him, I'm not some pushover. If this guy thinks he can boss me around without even a simple please just because he's hot, he's got another thing coming.

"It's barely hanging over the edge." I try to cross my arms across my chest to mirror his stance, but the bag holding my canvas is in the way, so I just come off looking like a crazy woman who doesn't know what to do with her hands.

"I'm going to need you to move your vehicle."

"Do you have a moving truck coming or something?" I look over his shoulder and try to see if there are movers pulling up, but don't spot anything. However, I do take notice of a nondescript sedan already pulled into his driveway, under the archway next to the house.

"The movers are already gone, so if you'll just move—"

"It looks like your car is already parked in your driveway. Do you plan on going somewhere?"

He looks a little surprised that someone is pushing back at him and that makes the corner of my mouth tick up in a bit of a smug smile.

"No, but that's not the point."

"Look, I really don't see the issue here. The parking on this street sucks, as you can see." I tilt my head at the plethora of cars squeezed into too few spaces. "There's plenty of room for you to get your car in and out, and I'll be gone again first thing in the morning."

There's a slight tick of annoyance in his jaw that makes me want to smile all over again. "Can't you just park in your own driveway? Do you even live around here?"

"Actually, I live right there." I indicate behind me with my thumb while trying not to drop either my purse or tote. "So, hi neighbor. As you can see, our driveway is already full. If I could park there, believe me, I would."

He lets out a groan and mutters. "You've got to be kidding me."

At this point, I'm getting a little exasperated. My bumper is seriously barely hanging over into his driveway. It would take me forever to get back into my car and go find another space.

"It's only over by, like, two inches. You'll be fine. Now if you'll excuse me, I've had a long day and would like to—"

"I'm going to need to see your driver's license."

"Uh, no." My head rears back in surprise. "Why would you want to see that?" Who the fuck does this guy think he is?

"I want to see if you need corrective lenses because if you think that's two inches, you've got a problem. That's two feet at least."

I can feel my body start to heat and I know I'm about to snap. But is that my fault? This dude is being totally unreasonable. His car can easily make it past mine. He's not even leaving, and I'll be gone first thing in the morning. He's purposefully being a dick. Can I really be held responsible for what comes out of my mouth next?

"If you think that itty-bitty overhang is two feet, then I feel *very* sorry for your wife." I casually scope out his hand and don't see a ring, but nowadays that doesn't mean a thing. This is a family neighborhood after all, and I can count the number of single people living here on one hand. "You men are always exaggerating length." Should I have said that to our brand new hot as hell neighbor? Probably not. Do I give a fuck? Nope.

His eyes widen in surprise for just a moment before they narrow in on me and his lips turn up into a smirk. Alright, not what I was expecting.

"Well, I've never received any complaints, Sparky." Ugh. Gross. I mean, I know I brought that on myself, but still. I hate a man that's hot and knows it. Then the nickname finally registers with my brain.

"*Sparky?* That's a dog's name. Are you calling me a dog?" The smirk remains firmly planted on his face and I can hear my voice raise an octave uncontrollably. I don't want him to know how much he's getting under my skin, but I think that ship has sailed.

His eyes slowly rake my body from the top of my head down to the tips of my heels, then back up again. I resist the urge to cover myself with my hands at his assessing gaze. It's not like I'm ashamed of how I look. Let him see what he can't have. "Nope, you're definitively not a dog."

I've had enough of this conversation and there is no way I'm moving my car. It appears that we're at an impasse, so I decide the only thing to do is leave.

"Look, I'm out of here. If you're so upset, call the cops. I'm sure they'll be right over here to talk to you about your super important parking issue. Have fun waiting."

With that, I spin on my heels and start stomping towards home. I only make it about two steps before I hear that damn sexy deep voice from behind me. "If I call the cops, I guarantee they'll come, Sparky."

I roll my eyes and look back at him again. "Oh really? You got a little buddy on the force that helps you give tired, hard-working women parking tickets outside their own homes?"

"Technically, it's outside *my* home and no, I don't have a buddy. I'm a detective with the SPD. One call and I can have Parking Enforcement here in five minutes." He pulls a badge out of his pocket and shoves it towards my face like it's supposed to mean something to me.

"How do I even know that's real? You could have gotten that anywhere. I'm pretty sure I can buy one of those things off Amazon right now and have it here in two days, free shipping and everything." My head tilts to the side as I study him, trying to think of my next move. He's probably lying. But if he's not, how much trouble can I get in? "If you're really a cop, show me your gun."

He's no longer smirking at me, and I take that as a victory. I can see the muscle on the right side of his jaw tick again, and I want to laugh. I know I shouldn't goad him anymore, but he's just asking for it. "Come on, pull it out. What's wrong, Detective? Don't get all shy on me now."

"I can't just pull my gun out and wave it around in public." He's talking through clenched teeth and what was once a little tick in his jaw has turned into a pulsating artery that's running down his neck. A very thick neck that disappears into his polo shirt that seems to strain against broad shoulders and a muscular chest. Shit, am I getting turned on by fighting with this guy?

"See, I told you guys are always exaggerating. I'm out of here. You can come get me when the real cops show up." Before I make it halfway to my door, I stop and turn back around to find him standing in the exact same spot, absolutely fuming. I guess he isn't used to people not doing what he wants. Well, tough shit. While giving him my sweetest smile, I say in a voice so sugary it could give you a cavity, "Oh, by the way, welcome to the neighborhood." With that, I take the last few steps, fling open the door and slam it behind me.

Chapter Two

Carson

Who the fuck was that?

As the tall beautiful woman who just went toe-to-toe with me over a goddamn parking space walks away, I can't help appreciating the view.

I should stop looking at her ass. I *need* to stop looking at her ass. The second I saw her from the side, strutting down the sidewalk in that tight black dress that's hugging some of the most magnificent curves I've ever seen with a pair of fuck me heels, I knew she was going to be gorgeous. Her skin is a tanned, almost caramel color and she has this long brown hair that cascades down her shoulders and reminds me of the color of chocolate. I fucking love chocolate.

When I called out to her and got her to turn around, I was stunned by her face. A woman with a body that belongs in a Renaissance painting can't have a face like that. It's not fair to the other women in the world. For just a second, her dark brown eyes looked heated as she took my measure, but then turned cold when they landed on my face.

It didn't matter how attractive she was; she was still breaking the law. I mean, it's a minor infraction, but it's also just plain rude. She said her car was hanging over into my driveway by two inches. It is clearly closer to two feet. Yes, I can get out of the driveway as long as I'm careful not to scratch either of our cars, but that's not the point. The point is that it's still an infraction and frankly, it's a safety hazard. What if I had to leave quickly? There are reasons we have rules and laws. They keep everything in order. They keep us safe.

There's something about my next door neighbor I find beguiling. I can feel my cock half hard in my pants and it pisses me off. Being a cop means that I'm basically in the business of heated exchanges and I've never had a reaction like this to arguing with anyone before. Especially someone so obviously flippant about following the rules.

There's movement in the window of the house she just disappeared inside, and I see a young woman, about the same age as my little spitfire, with long black hair peeking out the window. She's quickly joined by Sparky, who has the audacity to give me a little wave. From the look on her face, it might as well be the middle finger.

I've stood here like an idiot long enough and I really don't have time for this. I turn and head back to my newly purchased home. No, I won't call parking enforcement on her. That's a dick move, even for me. I'm just not used to people not doing what I say. The badge usually makes them hop-to, though I'm not one to abuse the privilege the badge can give me. I'm rather disgusted by those cops that flash it around for anything from free food to getting out of a speeding ticket on the highway or even using it to pick up women. No, I just like things to be in order. Under control. That's what I use my badge for.

When I get inside my new home, I look around and am happy with the progress I've made. It took me hours, but most of the boxes are now unpacked and everything is in its new designated place. How I've accumulated so much stuff I'll never know. But then again, it's not only my stuff anymore, is it?

I check the clock and figure I have some time to finish unpacking the kitchen boxes before chaos rains down on me once again. Besides, the work will help keep the curvy beauty next door off my mind where she's been since the moment I saw her walking down the street.

By the time a few hours have passed, I'm barely even thinking about the girl next door and there are no more boxes out in plain sight. I wipe the sweat out of my eyes and pull open the refrigerator, hoping to find something to cool me down. It's fall in Seattle, but that doesn't mean I'm not working up a sweat. Going from a tiny two-bedroom apartment in Los Angeles to a three-bedroom house in the Seattle suburbs is going to take some getting used to. I was positive I didn't have enough things to fill the place up but I guess I was wrong considering how much stuff I just unpacked.

It looks like the only two things I have in the fridge are a six-pack of beer along with a case of juice boxes. I'll have to add going to the grocery store to the very long list of things that need to get taken care of quickly. This kind of thing was so much simpler when it was just me. I mean, who cares if I grab takeout every night? Now I need to be concerned about things like balanced meals and packing lunches. I'm not upset about the change the direction my life has taken, but if you had asked me a year ago if apple juice was one of my household staples I would have laughed you right out of the room.

I grab one of the beers and twist the top off, taking a long pull from the bottle. As I look around at the unfamiliar house, I have a rare moment of anxiety. Maybe we should have stayed in Los Angeles, where everything was comfortable and familiar. I could have made it work.

I shake my head at myself. No, it was time to get away from there. Just the fact that Gloria has put us up for the past few weeks while the house went through escrow is a testament to the help I'll be able to get here that just wasn't available to me in LA.

"Carson? Are you in here?" Speak of the devil. Well, speak of the aging and mildly eccentric busybody known as my great aunt.

"I'm in the kitchen, Gloria," I call out. I'm quickly downing the rest of my beer, trying to quench my thirst, when Gloria struts into the room. She's dressed in head-to-toe leopard print, including a beret that she has sitting at a crooked angle on her head. She's topped off her eye melting outfit with starfish earrings as big as my fist. They look heavy as hell and I don't know how they're not ripping right out of her earlobes. That thought makes me cringe a little.

With his hand held in hers in what appears to be a death grip, is my nephew, Oliver. Oliver and I have known each other—lived together—for six months now, and while he's gotten more comfortable around me, he still has bouts of shyness. And strangers? Forget it.

I squat down so that I'm about at his height and try to ignore the fact that I just heard a pop in my knee. At thirty-one years old, I refuse to believe that my body is falling apart already.

"Hey buddy. Were you good for your Aunt Gloria today?" I guess technically she's his great-great aunt, but there's no reason to confuse the kid.

Instead of answering, he just nods his head at me before disentangling his hand from hers and walks into the new den, looking for the television remote. I suppress the sigh I want to let out. He's had a rough go in life and I figure it's going to take some time for him to really open up and become the carefree and happy kid I'm hoping he'll develop into. But the fact that he's been with me six months and only says the occasional sentence or two is starting to be cause for concern.

Six months ago, I didn't even know Oliver existed.

My father used to be a cop working for the Los Angeles Police Department. He was a doting and attentive father that loved his wife and children fiercely. We were the only thing that could compete with his love for his community and the people that lived there.

When I was eighteen, he was killed during a routine traffic stop on the side of the road. He pulled some guy over for having a busted taillight. He had just planned to give him a warning and let him go on his way. Well, it turned out that man had several warrants out and rather than go back to jail, he shot Dad four times in the chest before taking off down the road, leaving him there to die.

I had always wanted to be a cop, and my father's death just solidified that for me. I wanted to make him proud, so I worked hard, joined the academy, and rose through the ranks until they assigned me to the Gang and Narcotics Division of the LAPD. It wasn't an easy job by any stretch of the imagination, but it made me feel closer to my dad and I felt like I was making a difference.

While Dad's death had given me focus and direction, it seemed to do the opposite with my mother and sister. Mom started drinking her days away, but it was my sister, Molly, that seemed to take it the hardest. She was only twelve when Dad died. At six years younger than me, we didn't have a lot in common. I tried to be there for her, but I was a young man wrapped up in my own life and my own grief.

By the time she was in high school, she was involved pretty deeply into the LA drug scene. Going to class was never a top priority for her and she eventually just dropped out completely. I told her if she graduated from high school, I would pay for her to go to college. I pleaded for her to go to a rehab facility I would find for her. It didn't matter what I tried or how much I pleaded, she wanted nothing to do with getting clean or with me for that matter.

Mom was of no help. She should have been in rehab herself. She was hanging onto her job by a thread and one day, when she was driving home from work, she ran straight into a light pole. The coroner said she would have died instantly upon impact. Her blood alcohol level was three times the legal limit. They assumed the entire thing was an unfortunate accident. I'm not entirely convinced she didn't run straight into that pole on purpose, just ready to get back to my father any way she could.

After that, I lost Molly. She was eighteen by then and there was no controlling her. She literally disappeared. By then I was working with the GND and I held my breath every time I entered a trap house, scouring every face, both hoping and dreading I would find her there, but I never did.

At one point, I even hired a private investigator to find her, but he had about as much luck as I did. The only thing he could tell me was that there was a rumor she left town with her dealer and pimp, heading north.

In an effort to block out the pain, I pushed my sister to the back of my mind and doubled down on work. I picked up every shift I could, every piece of overtime I was offered I grabbed. Sure, it gave me a nice little nest egg to be able to buy a house here, but most importantly, it kept my mind off everything that was missing in my life.

Then about six months ago, I got the call.

"Are you sure you want to stay here tonight?" I see Gloria's head swiveling to check out the state of the house. "You know, you boys are more than welcome at my place until you have everything unpacked."

My body gives a slight involuntary shiver at the scores of "gentlemen callers" she has coming and going from her large home. The woman may be in her seventies, but she's certainly living life to the fullest. At least one of us is. Besides, I unpacked all the essentials. There are a few boxes in the corners, but I'll have those sorted out soon enough.

"You've already put up with us long enough, Gloria. Besides, I think it's time for Oliver and me to start getting into a real routine. I've got work in the morning and he has daycare. Are you still okay to pick him up there at one?" It's a Saturday tomorrow and even though I have to work, I don't want to just leave him with Gloria. It's nothing against her. She's great with him and I trust her completely. I just think he needs to spend some time with kids his own age. Learn how to socialize. The counselor at his school said that was important.

"Of course, I'm happy to spend more alone time with my darling nephew." She bends down and pinches his cheek gently, like I've always heard older women do, but never got to experience myself.

17

While I was growing up in Los Angeles, Aunt Gloria always lived up here in Seattle. She was a bit of a party girl and jet setter in her youth, so she was always traveling the world, off to one exotic location after another. Besides that, she and my mom had never been very close. That meant I only ever saw her on the odd holiday here and there. "Maybe we'll grab an ice-cream on the way home, would you like that?" she asks him. That brings a brief smile to Oliver's face before it quickly fades back into his mask of neutrality.

I want to tell her not to spoil his dinner, but one serving of ice cream can't hurt. I'll just have to make something healthy for dinner to make up for it. I really do need to get to the grocery store. Plus, any reaction I get out of him is a good thing and I don't want to temper even that briefest of smiles.

When we first got here and he gave Gloria about the same amount of attention he gave me, I hate to say it, but I was relieved. I thought maybe he hated me and that's why he always seemed sad and never wanted to talk to me. Once he started school two weeks ago, his teacher began reporting the same thing. He seems bright, he does his work, but he's quiet and withdrawn. I need to do something about it but I'm not sure what. His teacher suggested a therapist near the school and I'm starting to think I should call her.

As Gloria gets ready to leave, she gives me a hug first, which I return wholeheartedly. I haven't had much use for physical affection over the past few years and getting this from Gloria has been like getting a little piece of my mom back, at least how she was before Dad died.

She moves over to Oliver and bends down, giving him a squeeze and a pat on the head. "I'll be seeing you tomorrow, young man. Be good for your Uncle Carson."

"Bye." Oliver shyly looks up from beneath his lashes and gives her a ghost of a smile, which makes me grin. Who would have thought that I would get so happy from a single word being spoken by a five-year-old? But any time he gifts us with even the smallest communication, I see it as a win.

With Gloria gone, it's just the two of us and we stand around the freshly unpacked den, awkwardly looking at each other. This isn't the first time we've been alone. In fact, we were alone quite a bit once I picked him up and brought him home to Los Angeles with me. We had three months of staring awkwardly at each other in my cramped apartment. But back then there were always a hundred things to do to keep me busy. There were court dates to make sure all the custody arrangements were worked out, court ordered parenting classes, and a never-ending supply of things I needed to buy to make sure he was happy and healthy. I can't tell you how many parenting books I read in those first few months. I was constantly feeling overwhelmed and like I was hanging on by a thread.

It wasn't that I didn't want to be a parent, it was just that I had never really thought about it. I was so focused on my sister and then my job that having kids just wasn't on my radar. I mean, you'd have to at least be dating someone to think about having a family, right? I hate to say that even before Oliver came along, my social life had been severely lacking. That became glaringly obvious once I realized I didn't have any friends who could come over and watch him for even thirty minutes while I ran to the store. Of course, I had a couple of buddies on the force, but I wouldn't trust them to take care of my goldfish let alone my nephew. I found myself googling things like "can a five-year-old stay at home alone while I go for a run?" In case you're curious, the answer is a resounding *no*.

Thank God for the teenage girl down the hall that would watch him from time to time. However, at this point, I'm pretty sure I've paid her enough to fund her own tech start up.

The lack of support was one of the big reasons I decided to move up to Seattle when Gloria offered to lend us a hand. Well, that and the fact that I was involved in an ugly drug case that went wrong and cost someone their life. That was the final sign I needed that it was time to move on to a different city. I could get a little help from family and the job here was less dangerous, which was important now that I had someone depending on me. Of course, Seattle isn't some crime free mecca, but it's a hell of a lot safer getting my detective shield here than it is working gangs and narcotics in Los Angeles.

"So..." God, why did I open my mouth when I didn't know where it was going? It's just with the mostly quiet kid, I sometimes find myself trying to fill the void with chatter. "I set up most of your room. There are a few boxes left but we can unpack the rest tomorrow when I get home from work." That gets me a shrug. I don't really blame him, unpacking doesn't sound very exciting to me either. "How about I order us some dinner and we can watch cartoons until it gets here?"

He just gives me a shrug and climbs up onto the couch. I pick up my phone to place an order with the healthiest restaurant I can find while he fiddles with the remote.

I'm reminded again of just how much I have absolutely no idea what I'm doing. Sometimes I get so angry at my sister. Angry that she never told me he existed. Angry that she let her life spiral out of control and left me and this little boy all alone in the world. No, I never expected Oliver, but I love him just the same. He's the one good thing in my life and I'll do everything I can to make sure he's a happy and healthy little boy. I know that I'm going to have to let go of my anger and resentment for Oliver's sake, but it's something I'm still working on.

After we eat and I finally get Oliver to bed and asleep, I head to my own room to get ready for bed. The muscles in my back and neck are sore from moving boxes and furniture all day and a nice warm shower is just what I need.

Before heading to the restroom, I pause for a second at the window and lift the blinds so I can take a peek at the house next door. Not in a creepy way. I just want to see if I can see her... through her window. Okay, that sounds super fucking creepy.

Most of the curtains on the windows are drawn and the lights are off. I don't spot either her or the black hair girl that was in the window earlier. I gently put the blinds back down and go about getting ready for sleep.

Once I'm finally in bed, I do nothing but toss and turn. My thoughts are a mixture of worry over Oliver and thinking about the curvy spitfire next door. I have an uncomfortable half chub that doesn't seem to be lessening and I'm again annoyed at myself for my body's instantaneous reaction to her. The interaction we had wasn't even a good one. The memory of her shouldn't be turning me on so much. After a few hours, I give up resisting and take matters into my own hands... so to speak.

I feel like a perv, jerking off to the girl that lives next door. Hell, I don't even know her name. She's firmly in my mind as Sparky now, being the little live wire that she is. At least I'm finally able to release some pressure.

Just as I'm drifting off to sleep, the annoying rumble of a heavy-duty engine enters my consciousness. I curse and cover my head with my pillow, but it's no use. The rumble persists. I lay here waiting for the car to either drive away or turn off the ignition, but neither of those things happens. After five minutes of waiting, it's pretty clear the driver isn't leaving any time soon.

I drag my ass out of bed and go peek out the front window. There, in front of my house, is a man sitting in a large, lifted truck and from what I can tell, he's staring intently at Sparky's house.

What the hell kind of neighborhood did I move in to?

I grab my badge from the table next to the door and don't even bother changing out of my pajamas before I storm outside. I knock on the window and startle the individual in the cab. He looks about a decade older than me and there's something slightly familiar about him. He also looks like he's about to tell me to fuck off, so before he can say anything I knock on his window again, this time with my badge tapping the glass.

This seems to get him in line pretty quickly. He rolls down the window and asks, "Can I help you with anything, officer?"

"It's detective. And yes, you can. You can tell me what you're doing out here, sitting in your truck at midnight, staring at my neighbor's house."

His face reddens like he's embarrassed about being caught. That doesn't make me feel any better about him being here. "Actually Detective, I own that house. My daughter lives there with her friends. I just wanted to check and make sure she got home alright."

Now I realize why he looks so familiar. This must be Sparky's father. He looks just like her, the same coloring, the same hair color, hell the same nose. It still seems like a pretty thin excuse for sitting out here in the middle of the night though. "Can I see some ID, sir?"

He nervously pulls the card from his wallet and hands it over to me. Dante Moreno. It looks like his address is only be a few blocks away, which could explain why he decided to just stop by. Maybe. "Haven't you ever heard of a phone?" I ask.

"I know, Detective, I'm sorry. It's just that Vi—Bianca, wasn't answering her phone, and I was worried."

Bianca. The name suits her. It sounds both exotic and sexy. It is a little weird that he sputtered the name Vi first. I assume that's the other girl I saw living there, but I'm not sure why he would care about her. In the end I decide it's none of my business and nothing I want to get involved in so I send him on his way, not only because I'm exhausted but also because I feel a little guilty that I just jerked off while thinking about his daughter. However, I'm relieved he turned out to be her father. I don't like the idea of some creep scoping out her house. Well, some creep that isn't me. I really need to get my head on straight when it comes to this girl.

Something they don't tell you when you have a kid is that it takes you three times as long to get ready in the morning. I used to get up and be out the door for work in twenty minutes, freshly showered and shaved. Now, I'm up two hours earlier and lucky if I get to the shaving part. I've got to get Oliver up, which is *not* an easy task—the kid sleeps like the dead—get him dressed, make sure he's had breakfast, and pack his backpack. My days of sleeping in are long gone.

As I'm settling Oliver into his car seat, I immediately notice that Sparky's—I mean Bianca's—car is gone. At least she didn't lie about leaving first thing in the morning. I'm a little disappointed that I'm not able to catch a glimpse of her though.

After getting Oliver safely to daycare, I make my way to the South Precinct. I've been on the job for three weeks now and it's my base of operations. The Seattle Police Department has a severe shortage of detectives at the moment, which was one reason it was relatively easy for me to transfer in with my shield. Looking around the place, you can tell that staffing is off. It's nine a.m. and it looks closer to a ghost town than the bustling precincts I'm used to in the LAPD.

I'm pouring myself a cup of black sludge, that's supposed to be coffee, in the break room when I feel a hand slap my back, almost causing me to spill the cup and carafe all over myself.

"Hey man, how was your first night in the new place?" Rafe asks.

I shrug, setting the coffeepot back down into its holder gently. "It was okay, there's still a lot of unpacking to do but it's nice to finally have our own space. It was great staying with Gloria. She was a tremendous help with Oliver, but we couldn't stay there forever. I want him to get settled into a routine as quickly as possible, you know?"

Detective Rafael "Rafe" Campo, my new partner, nods his head at me. "I can understand that. Is the kid warming up yet?"

I sigh and take a sip of my coffee, then make a face. I can't do it. There's no way I can drink this. It tastes like it's been cooking for three days and somebody added a hefty amount of dirt to it. "Not really. A few conversations here and there. Same as usual."

"Well, I'm sure he'll come around. Now that he's got his own space, things will start to settle down."

"I hope so," I say, while tossing the full cup of coffee straight into the trash.

"Don't worry, you won't have time to drink that anyway. We caught a good old smash and grab out in North Beacon."

"Yeah? Who got hit?" I ask as I make my way through the bullpen to the back parking lot where I know Rafe has his unmarked parked.

"A gas station. Luckily, the owner was in the restroom when it happened, so no civvies were hurt."

"Yeah, but that also means we won't have any eyewitness accounts to go on. And let me guess, their security cameras aren't working."

A wide smile crosses Rafe's face. "Now you're getting it, Detective Turner. Welcome to Seattle."

Chapter Three

Bianca

It's been a long week. A very long week.

I've been running around like a crazy person getting the gallery ready for tomorrow's exhibition. We're showing four different artists and coordinating them coming in and getting their work displayed has been a bit of a nightmare. I'm all for untraditional art, but I don't know how I'm supposed to hang painted and torn t-shirts from our twenty-foot ceiling. Then there's the guy who insists his work be shown in a dark room with only blue tinted lights aimed at his "found art" sculptures. I'm somehow going to have to get temporary walls put up in the gallery to accommodate his requirements. Margot should have looked into this a little further before booking these people together. I guess it's not my job to question, it's just my job to get it done, and get it done, I will. Between the gallery, my friends, seeing my parents, and trying to work on my own pieces, it's been a busy week.

The cold autumn air blows through the backyard and whips the hair from my ponytail around to smack me in the face. I quickly spit out the pieces that have gotten into my mouth and push the rest out of my eyes with my forearm, careful not to transfer the paint on my fingers to my face.

I know I could paint inside right now. Hollie and Violet have never cared where I work, but I love painting outdoors. This is Seattle, so

I need to get outside and enjoy every dry day I can get, even if it's a little chilly and windy.

I dip my brush back into the muted green color I've been using and bring it up to the canvas. Instead of a full portrait, today I've just been concentrating on one enlarged eye filling my canvas. I'm sure it's just a coincidence that the color of said eye is exactly that of the hot jerk that lives next door. As far as I can remember, anyway.

I've been lucky enough to avoid Detective Dickwad—as I've affectionately dubbed him—for almost an entire week and you can bet I haven't parked my car anywhere near his damn driveway. I don't need that kind of grief again. With how much of an arrogant jerk he is, it's beyond annoying that every time I pick up my brush, I seem to paint something that reminds me of him. Strong lips with a hint of a smirk, the profile of a strong jawline, and now a hazel green eye. I could lie and say that I'm painting some rando, but I'd only be fooling myself. He's been off and on my mind all week, much to my chagrin.

To be truthful, I'm not even sure I'm happy I haven't seen him. A little part of me wants to get another look at the man and see if he was as hot as I remember. Though it's probably not worth the attitude I'd get from him. But I can't deny I've peeked out our window a few times to see if I could catch a quick glimpse.

I let out a little sigh and push him from my mind. Well, as much as you can push someone out of your mind while painting their giant fucking eye.

"What are you doing?"

The fuck?! The voice makes me jump and I turn around, expecting to find someone standing behind me with a machete, but the yard is empty. There's nothing but grass and our sparsely filled flowerbeds.

Now, I'm hearing things. Awesome. The stress is definitely getting to me.

"What are you doing?" Okay, I know I heard it that time.

"Hello?" It takes me a moment to notice the movement in the back corner of the yard. There's a wooden fence that separates our house from Detective Dickwad's and in the far corner, two of the slats have come loose. I really need to talk to Dad about getting those fixed, but I keep forgetting and since that house had been empty for so long, it wasn't high on my list of priorities. I'm really regretting it now since there is a tiny light blond head poking through the open space and staring at me.

I tilt my head to the side and examine the tiny human closely.

"Hey, are you spying on me?" I ask with what is probably a harsher tone than is called for. Give me a break. I was surprised.

"Sorry," the little voice says at almost a whisper. "I just wanted to know what you were doing." He looks so dejected that I feel like an ass. Well, great.

Now, it's widely known that I am not a fan of children. Like, at all. I avoid them like the plague... which is something they probably spread. To me, they're nothing more than tiny little demons filled with germs, snot, and sticky hands.

What can I say? Some people are born with that paternal instinct. I was decidedly not. Still, this kid is apparently my neighbor, so I should at least try to be nice. Besides, he sounds like he might cry and the only thing worse than a child is a crying one.

"Uh, I'm just painting. Do you want to see?" I ask with trepidation, hoping he'll retreat to his own yard.

"Okay!" The next thing I know, he's squeezed through the tiny hole in the fence and is stomping towards me directly through the flower beds. I guess it's a good thing Violet didn't get around to planting anything this year.

By the time he gets closer, I've noted he also appears to have hazel-green eyes. I glance at the iris on my canvas and back at him. Yup, there's a definite resemblance. I can only assume that this is Detective Dickwad's son. And that'll put the kibosh on my little crush right there. If I wasn't interested before when he was just a hot jerk, I'm certainly not interested now that I know he comes packaged with a tiny snot machine.

The kid passes by me and comes to a stop directly in front of the easel, standing there silently, tilting his head this way and that, studying the painting like he's really trying to understand it.

After taking his time, he turns to look at me with a hint of curiosity in his eyes. "What's your name?"

"Bianca. What's yours?"

"I'm Oliver."

How do you introduce yourself to a kid? "Well, it's nice to meet you, Oliver. I guess we're neighbors." I stick out my hand for him to shake and he eyes it before lightly sliding his into my grasp and pumping my hand up and down. Yup, sticky fingers. I should have known.

Once we've dropped hands, I resist the urge to wipe my fingers off on my shirt. "So, what were you doing over there?" I ask, indicating his yard with a jerk of my head.

"Playing with my trucks."

Okay, well, I have nothing to relate to that. Suddenly, a thought occurs to me. "Does your dad know that you're here? Is he going to be mad?" The last thing I want is to have another confrontation with that guy. He'll probably threaten to arrest me for child abduction or something.

"I don't have a dad," he whispers. I can't help but let the surprise show on my face, but I don't think a kid as young as him can pick up on that, right?

"Then who do you live with over there?" I ask, now a little suspicious.

"Uncle Carson. Sometimes, I call him Uncle Car." Okay, so he lives with his uncle. That also solves the mystery of Detective Dickwad's name. Carson. Fuck, I wish it wasn't sexy, but it totally is.

"How about your mom?"

"She's dead." His voice is monotone, as if he's stating a simple fact like the grass is green or the sky is blue. He's also staring unflinchingly into my eyes. I'm a little flabbergasted. What do you say to a kid with a dead mom?

"I'm sorry to hear that."

Oliver just shrugs his shoulders at me like it's no big deal, then turns back to the painting. "What is that?"

"It's a painting I'm working on. Do you like to paint?"

"I don't know. I can't remember if I've ever done it." Somehow, that makes me sadder than the dead mom. Painting is such a source of joy for me, and this kid doesn't even know if he's ever done it before?

"Well, do you color or draw?" I ask. He just shakes his head. What the hell is wrong with his uncle? Kids should always have art supplies around, right? Isn't that how they express themselves? I'm pretty sure I was coloring before I could walk or talk. "How about I get you some paper and pencils and you can try drawing something of your own?"

His face lights up and he nods at me enthusiastically. I head over to the small table we have outside that I've stacked with miscellaneous art supplies. Grabbing my sketchpad along with a brand new one and a few graphite pencils, I turn around to hand them over and almost jump out of my skin. The kid is standing not three inches away from me. I put my hand to my chest like it's going to help slow my racing heart. "Jesus, you scared me."

"You'll let me use those?" he asks with a little bit of awe in his voice. Are all kids like this or is it only him? He's a weird mixture of enthusiasm, awe, and a deep sadness that's almost palpable. I'm not sure how to handle him.

"Yup, come on. Let's sit over here." I lead him closer to the center of the yard where the grass is the thickest and plop down rather ungracefully. I never understood those girls who could just flit around place to place with all the coordination and grace in the world. I'm more like a wrecking ball or a bull in a china shop. I blame it on my tall height, large frame, and my general attitude of not giving a shit.

Oliver sits down next to me, so close that I'm a little uncomfortable. I try to subtly scooch my butt a few inches away but give up when he just does the same thing, plastering himself to my side. Taking the new sketchpad, I flip to the first page and hand it over to him along with a pencil.

"What am I supposed to do?" He furrows his brow and squints at the paper with the pencil in his hand.

"Draw whatever you want," I say with a gentle smile. He's taking this so seriously that it's kind of cute and I don't think I've ever called a kid cute before in my life.

"But I don't know how." His voice comes out as a bit of a whine and it almost makes me smile. Almost.

"You don't have to know how. It doesn't have to be perfect. You can draw anything. You could draw that flower over there," I point to one of the few flowers that escaped Oliver's Godzilla like trek through the yard, "or somewhere you've been, your favorite toy, or even something completely made up that no one's ever seen before." He's eying me suspiciously, so I grab my own sketchpad and flip through a few pages before I find what I'm looking for. It's a crude sketch of an enormous bird with eyes way too large for its head and balancing on one long skinny leg that I did one day when I was feeling whimsical.

Oliver's eyes widen as he looks at the drawing. "Okay, I can do that." He immediately goes to work on the blank page, and I flip to a clean one in my book. I decide I might as well sketch this kid out. I paint people all the time. They're my favorite subjects, but I'm not sure if I've ever done a portrait of a child. Maybe for a class at some point, but I don't remember ever willingly doing it. Probably because I didn't want to be around one long enough to observe them.

We're both working away quietly on our own projects when I hear a sniffle come from him. Then another. I look over and he's wiping tears away from his eyes. Oh shit, what did I do?

"Oliver, what's wrong?"

"I messed up!" he practically wails, then bursts into full on tears. Oh no, oh shit. I don't know what to do with this. Where the fuck is his uncle anyway?

"It's okay Oliver, I mess up all the time." I try to gently pat his back, but the move comes off less comforting and more stiff and awkward.

His sobs subside a little and he looks at me with his tear-stained face and for some reason, I get a funny feeling in my chest. I don't like that he's upset.

"You do?" He asks.

"Of course. That's how you learn. Besides, some of my best art has come from making mistakes." He's eying me like he doesn't quite believe what I'm saying. "Plus, if you mess up when you're painting, you can just paint over it. And do you know what you can do if you mess up a drawing?"

He just shakes his head at me, and I give him a little smile. I look down at what he's done so far and there isn't much there yet. Just some shapes and shading which I'm a little surprised by because shading seems advanced for a kid that's... however old he is. "You just do this." I reach over, grab the page, and yank it out of the book with a tearing sound. Then I crumple it up and toss it over my shoulder and give him a smile.

He's looking at me wide eyed and I hope I didn't fuck up. If he starts crying again, I'm tossing him back over the fence for his uncle to deal with. Instead, he lets out a laugh, tears another page from the book and tosses it over his own shoulder. I can't help laughing with him. What can I say? It was cute. Damn it, there's that word again.

"See, now you can just try again," I tell him. With a look of determination on his face, he picks up his pencil from where he dropped it in his distress and starts drawing again while I study him for a moment. It's still not apparent what he's drawing, but it's clear he has something specific in mind. He's not scribbling on the page like I'd expect of a child his age, but making calculated, precise movements with his pencil. I go back to my own work and after about five minutes I've got a decent rough rendering of Oliver's face. I glance back over at what he's working on and am a little taken aback.

He's clearly drawn some kind of room. Maybe a living room? It looks small and there aren't many elements to it. I can't tell if that's because he hasn't gotten to it yet or because the room he's drawing really is that bare. A sofa is against the wall with something coming out of it. Maybe stuffing? There's also a coffee table that's askew in the middle of the room, covered in what appear to be empty glasses and bottles. He's made dark spots all over the floor and I'm not sure what they are supposed to be. There are piles of what I assume are laundry throughout and what looks like a very dead plant in the corner.

This is way advanced. Like super advanced. He shouldn't be able to draw something like this. Even if he told me he had been drawing all his life, which he said he hadn't, there's no way he should be able to draw like this. I didn't produce something with this level of detail and shading until at least middle school.

Besides being blown away by his obvious natural talent, I'm puzzled by the actual subject matter. Did he make this room up? It can't be next door because all these houses have the same floor plans, and it doesn't look right. Maybe it's something he saw on TV. Either way, the room looks barren, cold, and sad.

"Oliver," I say, resting my hand on top of his to still the pencil. "Where is this?" He just shrugs at me and stares unwaveringly at his drawing for a moment before answering, "Home."

I open my mouth to question him further when I hear a frantic shout. "Oliver! Oliver, where are you?" The voice is coming from the yard next door and it's clearly Detective Dickwad—uh, I mean Carson—looking for his nephew.

"He's over here!" I shout back and stand, brushing loose grass off my jeans.

Carson's head pops over the fence, telling me two things. One, he's really fucking tall. And two, he's just as hot as I remember. Damn it.

His eyes narrow in on me. "What are you doing with my nephew?" Well, at least he's still a dick.

"Excuse you. I'm not doing anything with your nephew. He came over here through the broken fence," I point to the space with the missing slats, "and I've been entertaining him since apparently nobody was watching him." His cheeks turn a slight pink. Score one for Bianca. I want to fist pump, but now doesn't seem to be the time.

"I *was* watching him. He was supposed to be playing in the backyard." He levels a stern look at Oliver. "I just fell asleep on the couch for a few minutes." He makes his way over to the hole in the fencing and tries to squeeze through, but gets stuck around his broad shoulders. He keeps pushing and I'm pretty sure he's going to damage the fence further if he doesn't stop.

"You know, there's an actual gate you can walk through." I nod, indicating the gate that opens to the front yard. With a grunt of frustration, he disappears and I can hear his own gate slam before mine opens and he comes charging into my backyard like a sexy angry papa bear. God, what is wrong with me?

"Why haven't you fixed that fence?" he asks accusingly. It's like every time I think he's hot, he has to open his mouth and ruin it.

"Why haven't *you* fixed the fence? You're just as responsible for it as I am."

"You've lived here longer." He sounds a little like a petulant child. He and Oliver must get along real well.

"You do realize you're acting ridiculous, right? What is it with you making mountains out of molehills, anyway?" He frowns at me and then looks over at Oliver, who is standing quietly, staring at the grass.

"Hey buddy, I told you to stay in the backyard. Not cool." Carson's voice is gentle when he talks to him, which slightly appeases me for some reason. At least he's not a dick to his own nephew.

"Sorry, Uncle Car. Bianca was making a painting and said I could look at it."

He turns his head to me and raises his eyebrow. "Bianca, I presume?"

"And you must be Uncle Carson." He looks like he's waging a little war within himself and politeness finally wins out. He reaches out his hand and I slip mine into his. There's an immediate tingle in my fingers that spreads across my palm and up my arm. It's almost like I stuck my finger in a light socket, but gentler. By the wide look of Carson's eyes, I'm guessing I'm not the only one feeling it. It's when his pupils start to dilate that I realize we're just standing here, staring at each other, and holding hands. We haven't even shaken them. I quickly snatch my hand back and take a step away.

He gives me a frown of displeasure but then seems to shake it off and turns back towards his nephew. "Oliver, you're not wearing your watch. I told you that you need to wear it all the time."

"It was tight," he says in a little voice.

"Then you should have told me and I could have loosened it, but we talked about this. You can't take it off, understand? Especially when you're outside."

Oliver looks upset, and that makes my spine straighten. "What's your problem?" I ask. "It's just a watch. So the kid forgot it. It's not like he really needs to tell the time or something."

He turns his gaze back to me, and my body gives a shiver of awareness. Maybe Jenna is right and I really do need to get laid. Fighting with this guy is getting me more turned on than I've been in I don't know how long.

"The problem is that it's not just a watch, it's a GPS tracker. There's no point in having it if he's not going to wear it?"

"Oh, I get it now. You're like one of those helicopter parents who needs to know where his kid is every minute of every day. Jesus, let him live a little."

His eyes flash at me and his teeth clench. Now he really does look pissed. "Is that so? I should let him *live a little*? You sit over here in your safe neighborhood and go to your little job and party with your friends without a care. You have no clue what the world is really like. Well, I see it every fucking day. I know bad things happen to good people. Almost more often than they happen to the bad ones. So if wearing a watch lets me find my nephew if something happens to him, then yeah, I'm going to have him wear it every single fucking day."

I take a step backwards to get away from the vitriol in his voice. Okay, I can see why he wants Oliver to wear it. He's a cop. He's obviously seen some shit. Too bad for him, I'm not one to let things go, especially since he's now insulting my intelligence and lifestyle. Like I don't know there are dangers out there. I just choose not to live my life ruled by fear. I'm opening my mouth to rip him a new one when Oliver, who's been quiet up until this point, decides to speak up. "Uncle Car, you said a bad word."

A smile immediately appears on my face. Did I say I didn't like kids? Because I'm liking this one a whole lot right about now. Carson looks up to the sky like he's asking for some guidance from the great beyond and I hear him mutter, "Fuck," under his breath.

"You said it again," If it's possible, my smile widens even further. Yeah, this kid is okay with me.

Carson takes his hand and rubs it across his face like he's trying to clear his thoughts. "Yeah, you're right, I'm sorry, buddy. I owe the jar two dollars."

"Jar?" I ask, genuinely curious.

He looks over at me and shrugs his shoulders in a way that reminds me of his nephew. "We have a cursing jar. Anytime either of us curses, we have to put a dollar in it." Yikes. I've been told on more than one occasion I curse like a sailor. I consider it a form of self-expression, but then again, I'm not a little kid.

"Hmm, Oliver doesn't strike me as the type that curses." He shoves his hands into the pockets of his jeans and rocks a little on his feet.

"Yeah, I'm pretty sure I've been the sole contributor so far. The good news is that by the time he goes to college, I should have enough in the jar to pay for it." I can't help but let out a laugh. Not a tiny girly giggle that you put on when you're trying to make a guy think he's funny when he's really not. No, this is a full-on belly laugh. I'm picturing him just shoving dollar after dollar into that jar, day after day, and something about that image just sets me off. I'm not sure which I like more, fighting with him or laughing at him.

When I finally calm down, I look over at Carson and his eyes are on me, watching me closely with a little smile on his lips. We're standing there staring at each other again, and I'm not sure what to do about it. Do I look away? Do I shoo him off my property? I'm still thinking when Oliver walks over to me and puts his hand into mine. I'm so taken aback that I almost jerk my hand away, but that would probably come off as rude. "Can Bianca come over for dinner tonight?"

Both of us are looking at Oliver with wide eyes. I guess I wouldn't mind having dinner with them. I mean, I'd like to see more of what Oliver can draw and there's no denying I'm attracted to Carson. But when I look up at him, the look on his face lets me know he's going to deny the request.

I hate being rejected. Even if it's for a stupid dinner invitation I don't even want with a germ ridden kid and a cop I hate. Before he can say anything, I cut in. "I'm sorry, Oliver. I can't tonight. Tomorrow is a big day at work and I have a lot to do."

The kid actually looks disappointed. He frowns and his shoulders sag while he looks at the ground. Now I feel shitty and I honestly don't know why. I don't owe this kid anything. He pulls his hand out of mine and walks over to his uncle. I have to resist the urge to snatch his hand back and I wonder briefly if I'm going crazy. Maybe I'm just hungry. That must be it, I haven't eaten in like... two hours. Okay, so that's probably not it.

"Maybe some other time, buddy." Carson says with a soft smile to Oliver, who glances back at me.

"Sure." We both know we're just saying it for Oliver's sake. Neither of us has any intention of getting together for dinner or anything else for that matter.

"What have you got there?" It's then that Carson notices the sketchpad that Oliver has clutched in his little hand.

"Bianca said I could draw in it."

"Well, I'm sure Bianca needs it. Why don't you give it back to her?" Oliver looks beyond disappointed and hands the pad over to me while I shake my head.

"Oh no, he can keep that. I've got a hundred of those things lying around." Wanting to cheer Oliver up for reasons I don't understand, I continue speaking to Carson. "He's quite talented. You might want to look into signing him up for some classes or something. He's light years ahead of where he should be, and he told me he's never drawn before."

Carson cocks his head at Oliver and gives him a sad look that I don't quite understand before shaking it off and giving him a smile. "Oh yeah? What did you draw?" He opens the cover and flips to the first page with the sketch of the sad looking living room. He immediately freezes. His eyes move over the drawing again and again, but he doesn't say a word.

"You can see all that shading he's done on the couch and in the space under the coffee table? That's super advanced for someone his age. He has a natural talent." Oliver gives me a smile and I smile back at him.

"Did you tell him to draw this?" I've heard Carson annoyed, mad, and pissed off before. This seems beyond that. I look at his face and it's still as stone. But his eyes? His eyes are full of outrage.

"No. I told him he could draw whatever he wanted. That's what he chose. Why?"

He slams the cover of the pad closed. "Do me a favor and stay away from my kid."

My mouth falls open in shock. What the fuck is that about? I haven't done a single damn thing wrong. I was in my own yard, minding my own business, when *his* kid came over to *me*. All I did was give him something to do. Why did that one picture set him off? I'm so flabbergasted that I don't know what to say. I'm pretty sure my eyes are bugging out and my mouth is opening and closing like some kind of demented fish.

He takes Oliver's hand and starts marching back towards the gate he came through, but Oliver pulls out of his hold. He runs back to me and wraps his arms around my leg. Instinctively, I reach down and pat him on the head. I'm not going to take my rage out on Oliver. It's not his fault his uncle is completely insane.

"Thanks, Bianca." He says, giving me another squeeze. I finally get it together enough to look back at Carson, who is standing rooted in place. I see emotion after emotion cross his face that I really don't understand. Anger is certainly there, but there's also confusion, happiness, and hurt.

"You're welcome, Oliver." With that, he detaches himself from my leg and walks back to his uncle. I try to stop, but I can't help getting in one last parting shot. The last word. Hey, it's a flaw, I'm working on it. "You can come over and visit me anytime, kid." Carson doesn't even bother to look at me as they exit the backyard.

This is the second time I've met our new neighbor and the second time we've gotten into some kind of verbal altercation. I'd say that's a rather bleak start. I swear, I don't fight with people like this. I like to think I'm kind and thoughtful with a bit of a rebellious streak thrown in. There's just something about that man that gets under my skin. If how he warned me to stay away from Oliver is any indication, I'd say I'm under his as well.

Chapter Four

Carson

Fuck. Fuck. Fuck.

That did not go as planned. Not that I really had a plan, per se. I just figured the next time I saw Bianca we could have a pleasant, neighborly exchange to fix the terrible impression I'd given her last week. Well, that certainly wasn't pleasant. It wasn't even in the same continent as pleasant.

There's something about her that just pushes my buttons. The more she pushes, the more we argue, and the more we argue, the more I want her. I'd like to say that I didn't jerk off to thoughts of her every day this week, but I can't. I don't understand what's wrong with me. I like control, I like order, and Bianca appears to be anything but.

For a second there, when we touched hands, I felt something crazy. There was an awareness I'd never felt before. It was almost as if the simple touch of our hands woke up my body and every one of my cells was calling out to hers. Like her skin should be molded onto mine. That I should be deep inside of her, not knowing where she ends and I begin. She may have jerked her hand away from me, but I saw her face. I saw the desire in her eyes and the little shiver that went through her body. When she pulled her hand out of mine, for one insane moment, I wanted to snatch it back. If she was feeling even a fraction of what I was, then that was something I wanted to explore. It's too bad she'd just as soon kick me in the balls as kiss me.

I'm certainly not doing anything to help the situation. It seems like every time I'm around her the button she pushes is the one for asshole. It wasn't her fault that Oliver went over to her yard, and I know I was harsh about the GPS tracker. She just doesn't understand the dangers out there. Boogeymen are real. They carry guns. They hurt people. They take kids. I've seen it time and time again, but she didn't deserve my harsh rebuke or my tone. Even after spewing all of that at her, she didn't shrink away. She gives as good as she gets and I like that. So does my cock apparently, judging by the semi-hard bulge in my jeans.

Now that Oliver's safely tucked away in his bedroom, I decide to straighten the kitchen. I recognize that I'm more of a neat nick than most people. I like everything to be just so. If I went to a psychiatrist, I'm sure they would tell me it has something to do with watching everyone in my family spin out and die around me without being able to do anything to stop it. Hence the control freak.

I'm about to sort through the mail that's sitting next to my gun safe on the entry table when I spot the pad of paper Bianca gifted Oliver. Opening it, I look at the drawing again. Bianca wasn't wrong, the drawing is good. Damn good. To be honest, I'd never be able to draw something like this. My drawing skills are closer to stick figure than Salvador Dali.

It's embarrassing that I never thought to get Oliver any art supplies. I want to berate myself, but I know I'm doing my best. I mean, he has a ton of toys and books. I just dropped the ball on the art supplies. Kids need so many things and I'm still learning as I go. If Bianca thinks he needs art classes, maybe I should sign him up. Next time I see her, instead of biting her head off, I'll try asking for recommendations since she seems to know about these things.

I do need to talk to him about this drawing though.

41

"Oliver, why don't you go grab your watch and then come into the living room? I want to talk to you for a minute," I call out to him.

When we're settled on the couch together, I open the pad of paper to his drawing. The sight makes my heart hurt, but he doesn't seem upset at all. "Why did you draw this, buddy?"

"Bianca said I could draw whatever I wanted. Am I in trouble?" He looks nervous and I feel like a major ass for blowing up at Bianca about the drawing in front of him.

"Of course you're not in trouble. I just wanted to talk to you about it. You never talk about this apartment." He just shrugs his shoulders at me. That's been his go-to response whenever I bring up the time before he moved in with me. "Do you want to talk about it?" He was being open and talking to Bianca. He even gave her a hug and invited her over for dinner. To say I was shocked would be an understatement. He seems to have taken a liking to her, and I'd be lying if I said I wasn't a little jealous. I've been with him for months and he's just recently warmed up to me.

I shouldn't have told her to stay away from him. She didn't do anything wrong. I was just freaked out by the perfect rendering of that apartment. I thought she was pushing him to remember things he didn't want to, but if that's what he chose to draw then maybe this is his way of processing things.

"Do you miss it there?" I ask gently.

"Sometimes." Okay, he's actually speaking about it. It might be a one-word answer but at this point I'll take what I can get.

"What do you miss the most?" He tilts his head and squints at the ceiling while he puts some thought into my question.

"I miss my army men."

"You could have told me that, bud. I can get you more army men. Do you want to go do that this weekend?" He gives me a smile and nods his head enthusiastically. His grin is infectious, and I can't help but smile back at him. "What else do you miss?"

"I had a night-light. It was a big circle like a ball and when you turned it on it made the ceiling look like the sky outside with stars and everything." And suddenly, I want to kick my own ass. I'm completely failing at this parenting thing. He doesn't have a night-light right now, he never asked for one. I just figured he didn't need it. He's never said anything to me before. No wonder he keeps having nightmares. I mean, some are going to be unavoidable with what he's gone through, but a night light would have probably helped. I always leave the door to his room cracked open, but that's not the same.

"We'll get you one of those too. You can pick out any one you want." He smiles at me again and it makes my heart hurt. I point over to the lamp that's sitting across the living room. "How about we put that by your bed until we can go get one?"

"Okay."

I almost don't want to ask again but I know I should. "Is there anything else you're missing?" This time he looks away from me and starts kicking his feet against the couch. "You know you can tell me anything Oliver, right?"

He's still not looking at me when I hear his little voice say, "I miss my mom." The air leaves my body in a whoosh. This is the first time in six months he's even mentioned Molly. From what I could see, she certainly wasn't mother of the year but I'm sure Oliver loved her. She was his mom after all. His only parent. I searched for a father when all this went down but there wasn't one listed on the birth certificate. She was in so deep with the drugs and prostitution that she probably didn't even know who his father was.

"It's okay to miss her. I miss her too." That's true. I miss the little girl she was before our dad died and my mom stopped caring about anything but him. When I let myself think about it, it feels like my heart is cracking in two. She was so happy and bubbly as a child. She was smart as a whip too. I remember my parents always bragging about her report card and ribbing me for not living up to the high standards my little sister was setting. But I don't miss who she became later in life. I try not to think about that.

"Do you know what you can do when you miss someone a whole lot?" I ask him.

"What?"

"You can think about all the good times you had together. How happy you were when you were with each other. Then it's like she's right here with you."

Oliver gives me a frown and I can see tears forming in his eyes. I sling my arm over his shoulders and pull him into my side.

"But she's not here with me, Uncle Car. She's gone."

"You're right, she's up in heaven. But you know what happens every time you think good thoughts about her?" I take my hand and put it onto his chest, overlapping his tiny beating heart. "Every good thought goes right in here and that's where she stays. In your heart." Tiny arms are thrown around my neck and he's practically hanging off my body while giving me a hug. I'm so surprised that it takes me a second before I wrap my arms back around him and hold him close to me.

"I love you so much." I whisper into his hair. He doesn't respond and I don't really expect him to. He hasn't told me he loves me yet and I get it, to him I'm just some stranger that took him away from his home. That doesn't matter to me. I take every opportunity I have to tell him I love him. I'm not going to leave things left unsaid with him like I did with the rest of my family.

A few hours later we've had dinner and I'm washing up in the kitchen while Oliver is laying on the floor in the living room with the pad of paper Bianca gave him. I've been watching him out of the corner of my eye and it looks like he's quickly making his way through it. He's filling page after page. I can't really make out exactly what he's drawing from here, but I know that a new sketchpad and a truckload of other art supplies are also going to be on the list of things we need to buy this weekend. Maybe I'll pick up an extra one and give it to Bianca to replace the one she gave Oliver. It can be like an olive branch. Then maybe we can talk for three whole minutes without biting each other's heads off.

I smile to myself now that I have a plan to see her again. After that moment we had in her backyard, I've decided I'm going to peruse this connection I felt. Though I'm not sure if I want to date her or if I just want her in my bed. After all, it's not just me anymore. I can't go bringing someone into Oliver's life just for us to break-up and have her disappear. Maybe we can have some discreet fun between the sheets to get her out of my system. That is, if I can get her to give me the time of day. The only problem is that I have a sinking suspicion a few nights with Bianca won't be enough.

It's a few hours later that I send Oliver off to start his nightly routine when I grab the stack of mail that I'd forgotten about. Most of it is advertisements, a few letters on my 401k with the LAPD, and one letter for the previous occupants that I'm going to have to return to sender. The very last envelope makes me frown. It's a plain white envelope with no stamp and no return address. In fact, the only thing written across the front is my name, meaning it was obviously hand delivered.

Maybe it's a note from one of the neighbors. Maybe it's from Bianca. A small smile pulls up the corners of my lips as I think of her writing me a little note. I wonder if it will be sassy or sweet. Will it be telling me I shouldn't be such an asshole in front of Oliver or will it be a call for a truce?

Smile still firmly planted on my face, I open it up and pull out the single sheet of paper that's folded over three times. My smile immediately fades and turns into a full-on frown when I read the words that are block printed across the page.

YOU RUINED MY LIFE. YOU TOOK MY FAMILY.

What the hell is that supposed to mean? It's almost like something a man would send to the person who stole his wife or something. Well, that's unequivocally not me. It's been so long since I've been in a relationship, I can barely remember her name. But she definitely wasn't married.

It could have something to do with being a cop, but I've been on the job here less than a month. I certainly haven't pissed someone off to the point of leaving me cryptic notes at my home. I'd like to think the entire thing was a mistake but there's my name, written clear as day on the envelope. It's not a threat exactly, though it does border on creepy.

For a second, I consider bringing it into the station and handing it off to one of our forensic experts to see what they can make of it but decide against it. There's no real threat here and I know I haven't earned enough favors yet to be asking techs to work on personal things for me. With any luck, this will be the last time I get a letter like this. I take the note and envelope into the kitchen and fish out a gallon size zip lock bad, sliding them both inside and sealing it. It doesn't hurt to hold on to them and preserve any evidence just in case I end up needing it.

By the time we get home from shopping on Saturday I'm eager to head over to Bianca's. Oliver picked out a sketchpad to replace the one she gave him and I want to get those recommendations on art classes. I won't lie, I'm also looking forward to having a civil conversation with her for once. Fingers crossed.

But when we get home, I see a man in a rumpled suit sitting on the porch of her house. I want to stomp over there and demand to know what the hell he thinks he's doing, but the last time I did that it was just her dad waiting for her to get home, even if he seemed a little cagey about the whole thing.

As I'm fixing lunch for Oliver, I keep glancing out the window at the rather dejected looking man. Shit, maybe she has a boyfriend. Why hadn't I ever considered that? Though wouldn't he be waiting inside for her if he was? Is it some ex-boyfriend? Is he bothering her? He certainly looks like he's been settled in there for quite a while.

I know that I'm feeling irrationally jealous over a woman I barely know, but I can't help it. Besides, I'm just worried about her safety. It is my job after all.

The more I keep glancing out the window at the guy, the more familiar he's starting to look. I know I've seen him somewhere before. After thirty minutes, my curiosity gets the better of me and I call in the license plate on the insanely expensive sports car that's parked at the curb.

What I get back from the dispatcher is a surprising to say the least. The car belongs to Archer Clarke, billionaire hotel mogul. I knew I had seen him before. His face is occasionally splashed across newspapers and magazines. It's usually business related. He doesn't appear to be one of those rich pricks that's always into trouble with drugs, booze, and women. What the fuck is he doing sitting in a suit that looks like it's been slept in, on my neighbors' porch?

I'm just serving Oliver his grilled cheese sandwich—on that healthy bread he hates but I insist on—along with carrots and a sliced apple when I hear car doors slamming outside. I crane my neck to get a better look outside and see Bianca with her short, dark-haired roommate walking up the driveway. When they see Archer Clarke they both freeze and then take up defensive stances. I can't really make out what they're saying, I'd have to actually open the window for that. So this isn't really spying, not if I can't hear anything. I'm just making sure my neighbors are okay, especially since they both look rather annoyed at his appearance on their porch.

Archer Clarke, billionaire businessman, looks like he's about to get on his knees and do some begging. Very interesting. A few seconds later the girls usher him inside the house and I can't deny that my curiosity is killing me. I hope he's not after Bianca. I mean, I get it. She's the kind of tall, curvy, gorgeous woman that any man would be happy to have on his arm... but I saw her first. At least I think I did.

God, she's making me act like a mental patient.

Just as we're finishing lunch, I hear the door to Bianca's house close and watch Clarke hurry to his fancy car and take off, tires peeling on his way down the street.

"Hey Oliver, do you want to go give Bianca the paper you got her?"

"Yeah!" He answers, jumping down from his chair and going to grab the sketchpad sitting on the coffee table. We cut across the lawn and before you know it, I'm knocking at the front door with Oliver at my side.

It's only a few moments before Bianca yanks open the door.

"Archer, I swear we told you—oh! Hey Oliver." She gives my nephew a big warm smile and then turns to me, smile gone. "Detective Di—Carson."

I raise my brow. I wonder what she was about to call me. Maybe it's best I don't find out especially since she's blushing profusely at almost getting caught.

"We're not interrupting anything, are we?" I ask, hoping she doesn't say she's waiting for Clarke to come back.

"Not at all." The three of us stand there staring awkwardly at each other before she finally gives in and invites us inside.

We walk through the entryway and move into the living room that's just like ours. I guess the houses on this street have the same layout. I don't see her roommate anywhere and figure she must be in one of the back rooms.

Instead of immediately giving her the sketchpad like I should, my mouth runs away from me. "Was that Archer Clarke sitting on your porch?"

"Oh, you saw that, huh?" She's giving me a look like she knows I was watching through the window and I can feel my cheeks redden. I can't be fucking blushing, I'm a grown man. I refuse.

"Well, he'd been hanging around for a while. I wanted to keep an eye on him, I wasn't sure what he was doing here. You never can tell about people." That's it, my interest at him sprawled out on her porch waiting for her is purely professional. I was doing the protect part of protect and serve.

She gives me a look like she knows I'm full of shit, then shrugs it off. "He's my roommate Hollie's boss... or boyfriend. Or I guess maybe both. Well, both if she ever forgives him. Now, what can I help you two gentlemen with?"

I don't even try to untangle her explanation. All I got out of it was that he wasn't here for her and that makes me want to smile like a buffoon.

"Go ahead, Oliver." I gently place my hand on his back encouraging him to step forward. He walks over to her, sketchpad in hand, then shoves it out, nearly whacking her with it in the knees.

"What's this?" she asks, crouching down to get on his level.

"Uncle Carson and I got you a new sketchpad since I took your other one."

"Oh, you didn't have to do that," she says looking between me and Oliver.

"I picked it out all by myself," Oliver interjects. He's so proud I can practically see his chest swell.

Bianca gives him a smile. "Well, it's a very nice sketchpad, Oliver. You have excellent taste, but I was happy to give you the other one, you really didn't need to do this."

"We wanted to," I say while rubbing the back of my neck. "It was really kind of you to give it to him. I hadn't realized we were missing art supplies. He's actually been going through the pad you gave him like a madman. It's filled with drawings now and you were right, he seems to be really good. Not that I know anything about art, but he

49

draws better than I ever could. I know you mentioned art classes, so I hoped maybe you would know where I could sign him up for some. Like I said, I know nothing about art, but you seem to know a lot about it, or at least some. Well, more than me. Again, that wouldn't be hard." *Stop. Talking. Idiot.*

Bianca is staring at me with wide eyes probably wondering what the hell is wrong with me and my rambling word vomit. Even Oliver is looking at me curiously. I'm not normally a huge talker.

Finally, she takes pity on me and breaks the silence. "Uh, yeah. Of course, I can recommend some classes. Why don't you take a seat and I'll be right back."

I move deeper into the room and sit down on the couch while Oliver crawls up beside me. I try not to watch her ass as it disappears down the hallway, I really do, but it's no use. The sway of her hips is hypnotizing.

It's only about a minute before she returns, jotting something down on a small notepad. "It really depends on your finances and how intense you want the classes to be. The Y has some classes that are pretty inexpensive, but I feel like they're more exploratory than instructive. There are some more expensive ones with teachers downtown that are good, but I would probably recommend the program for kids out of Branson College. It's taught by art students and it's got a good balance of teaching style and technique. It just depends on what you're interested in." She tears off the paper she was writing on and hands it over to me. I notice with a bit of irritation that she's careful to keep her fingers from touching my own.

I glance at the paper and scan the three places she's written down, feeling a little overwhelmed. "Well buddy, what do you think? Do you want to try art classes?"

"Yeah!" He says enthusiastically. I can't help but smile down at him. This was a good idea, I'm not sure I've seen him so excited about anything that wasn't ice cream. I turn back to Bianca. "Well, it looks like we're sold. So, the one at Branson you think?"

She gives me a big genuine smile and if I wasn't already sitting down, it would have knocked me on my ass. Damn, she's beautiful when she's scowling at me but when she smiles... well, fuck.

"Yeah, I think it would be perfect for him. Call that phone number and ask for Roxy, then tell her that Bianca Moreno sent you. The program has a waiting list but that should let you bypass it. She can call me if she has any questions."

"Really? You'd do that for us?"

"Of course, it's not a big deal." She turns to my nephew. "You're very talented, Oliver. If you like drawing, I can't wait to see what you'll do with paint, or clay, or anything else you choose to try. I'm really excited for you." Oliver jumps off the couch and runs to Bianca wrapping his arms around her legs, almost causing her to stumble back. She gives a chuckle and pats him awkwardly on the head before bringing her gaze back to me and giving me a lopsided smile.

"How do you know about all this stuff? And how do you know the lady at Branson?" I ask, curious to know more about her. This woman who is a sassy spitfire one moment then gentle and encouraging with Oliver the next is an enigma that I can't help but want to explore.

"Oh, I'm an artist. Or at least I'm trying to be." For the first time since I've met her, she looks a bit sheepish and not brimming with confidence. "I just graduated from Branson with a Bachelor's in Fine Arts. I wasn't personally involved in that art program because, you know, kids," she says with a shrug like that's supposed to explain everything. "But a few of my friends were involved so I know a bit about it."

She just graduated? Shit, she's got to be almost a decade younger than me. Another reason I should probably stay away from my fiery neighbor. It's also another reason my dick wants to hear nothing about. "So, what are you doing now? You said you're trying to be an artist."

She finally takes a seat in an armchair across from the couch and before she can say another word, Oliver climbs up into her lap surprising us both. Her eyes snap to mine and it almost looks like she's pleading for help. I can feel the corner of my mouth tick up in a smirk. It looks like Bianca is not the most comfortable person around kids. Join the club, Sparky. Or at least I used to be uncomfortable. I didn't have a choice except to get used to it real quick. I don't offer her the least bit of help while Oliver settles himself on her lap. Her hands are hovering in the air like she doesn't know where to put them, eventually she awkwardly lets them fall to the chair arms and rest there.

"I'm working at a gallery downtown while I try to get my own pieces ready to show. I know I'm basically nonexistent on the scene but I'm hoping my boss will put me in an exhibition by summer. Though I don't know if that's going to happen now."

She mutters the last part, and I raise my eyebrow. "Why do you say that? I'm sure she'd be happy to help you."

A brief laugh escapes her lips. "You obviously don't know her. She basically told me my work was sh—" She looks down at Oliver and decides to change her wording. "Not very good."

"It sounds to me like she doesn't know what she's talking about." She lets out a sardonic laugh this time.

"Oh, that's where you're wrong. Margot Gault is part of the who's who in the art world. A single showing in her gallery could really set me up. She called what I showed her a *finger painting,*" she says using air quotes. I give a little grimace. That seems rather harsh. "Actually, that's where I was coming from when I bumped into you the other day." Now her eyes are narrowing in on me, like I'm bringing back bad memories of her work getting torn to shreds.

I immediately feel guilty. She had a shit day and then I had to go off on her over some stupid parking thing. If she was hoping to make me feel about three feet tall, well, she's succeeded.

"Look, I'm sorry about that," I start. "It had just been a stressful day. I shouldn't have taken it out on you. I apologize."

"And the other day when Oliver was over at my place, and you freaked out on me?" Man, you give this girl an inch. Well, I wanted to clear the air with her anyway so at least she's giving me the opportunity, I guess.

"I was out of line, I'm sorry. Look, I'm new to this whole parenting thing." I quickly glance at where Oliver's sitting in her lap. He's kicking his feet and fiddling with a piece of her hair while looking around the room, paying the two of us no mind. "I guess I just freaked out a little when I couldn't find him and that picture…" How do I explain my worry over what he drew? I certainly don't want to bring it up in front of him. "Well, like I said, I was out of line."

She looks intently into my eyes like she's trying to see if I'm being sincere or not. She must be satisfied with what she sees because she gives a little nod and her lips curl into a tiny smile. "I wish I could say it was all you, but I certainly didn't help the situation. How about a truce?" She says before moving Oliver off her lap and standing up, holding out her hand to me.

A truce is good, it's certainly more than I hoped for when I came over here today. Hell, I half expected her to tell me she was dating a billionaire and that I could shove my apologies up my ass. This is a decided step up.

I raise off the couch and pull her hand into mine, shaking it. Again, there's that spark of awareness shooting through my body like an electrical current. Her body gives a little shudder and I know she feels it too. "You got it, Sparky."

CHAPTER FIVE

BIANCA

"Come on, B. You know you want to."

Jenna's been chirping in my ear about going out tonight for the better part of an hour. I know the reason she's pushing so hard is because she thinks I still need cheering up after Margot's assessment of my painting, and normally I would jump at the opportunity for a night out on the town, but I'm just not feeling it today.

"Don't forget we have work tomorrow. Are you sure you really want to go out drinking all night?" Jenna does an exaggerated nodding of her head, up and down, like I'm an idiot.

"Come on, just a couple drinks, some dancing, and who knows, maybe we'll find some guys to scratch that itch." She waggles her eyebrows at me and I roll my eyes.

"Scratch that itch? You always were eloquent."

"Fine, find some guys to fuck our brains out. There, is that better?" I can't help but let out a laugh. Subtle, she is not.

I always have a good time when I go out with Jenna and it's true that it's been a while for me. I'm not exactly into relationships and have never felt the need for anything more than the occasional one and done I can get from a night out. Sure, I've had a few repeats but the second they start acting like they might want more than a little fun I drop them like a bad habit. I figured out a long time ago that long-term relationships just aren't in the cards for me.

Hollie is still in her hometown with Archer, taking care of her mom and Violet hasn't answered my texts from earlier. I know something is going on with her, she's been acting weird and cagey for weeks. I'm tempted to push her on the issue but she's a quiet and introspective person, I know she'll come to me when she's ready to talk. With both roomies MIA, I don't really feel like sitting at home all alone tonight.

"I promise you'll have so much fun. You totally won't regret it." She bats her eyelashes at me, and I know I'm going to give in. Is this how she puts men under her spell? Because it works.

"Okay, okay. You've worn me down."

"Yay!" Jenna does a little happy dance behind our small reception desk and I quickly glance around, making sure Margot doesn't notice the display of jubilance. Luckily, she's nowhere in sight. It's been a pretty slow day at the gallery so I've mainly been answering phones, cleaning, and following up with clients while Margot has been holed up in her office. She hasn't brought up my paintings again and I'm relieved. I've been working hard on creating a piece she might actually like, but I haven't been able to produce anything I think will be of her caliber yet. I used to think I was an amazing artist, but Margot's reaction to that one painting has really shaken my confidence.

Now, don't get me wrong, I don't think I suck or anything, but for some stupid reason I thought this would all be easier. It looks like it's going to take me a lot longer than I expected to make a splash in the art world. But I'm not giving up. I still create every day and I know that I'll come up with something that's going to blow Margot away.

"Cut it out." Jenna elbows me in the side and I tear my eyes away from the spot outside the large glass storefront I was zeroing in on while spacing out.

"What?" I ask while rubbing the spot on my side. Damn, that girl has bony elbows.

"I know that look, you're thinking your work sucks again."

"I don't think it sucks." How do I explain this to her? "I just thought I was better than this. I guess I thought I would be the exception to the struggling artist cliche. Margot just gave me a dose of reality and I'm working through it in my head. It's no big deal, I've got this."

"Yeah you do," she says. "I may not be a full-blown gallerist yet but I know your stuff is good. If I had my own place, I would definitely show your work, no question."

I know she's not lying. Jenna is brutally honest when it comes to art. If she says she likes my stuff, she likes it. The fact that *anyone* in the art world likes what I do gives my morose thoughts a little bump. This isn't just my dad or my best friends telling me my work is great, this is someone that knows what she's talking about.

I bend down and squeeze her tightly in my arms. "Thanks Jenna. You don't know how much that means to me."

"Well, it's the truth." Her voice is slightly muffled against my blouse so I let her go and she exaggerates gasping for air. "Jesus Bianca, watch out for my ribs next time. We can't go out tonight if I'm in the damn hospital." I just laugh and give her another, gentler, squeeze before getting back to work.

I check my makeup in the vanity mirror one more time while Jenna keeps chattering away and driving down the rain slicked street. Brows? Perfectly arched. Lips? Painted a pouty berry. Cat eyes? Sharp enough to kill a man. I chuckle to myself starting to sing Taylor Swift in my head. Satisfied, I close the mirror and lean back in the leather seat while Jenna whisks us swiftly to our destination.

Hollie and Violet are always teasing me about how long it takes me to get ready and believe me, I know it's a bit excessive. I hardly ever step out of the house without a full face of makeup on, but I can't help it. It's not that I hate the way I look, I actually think I'm fairly pretty. I just happen to love makeup. I figure it's probably an extension of my love to create beautiful things. My makeup is just another piece of art that I've created. It doesn't hurt that it sometimes feels like I'm putting on battle armor. Especially when I'm getting ready to mingle with drunken patrons at a bar all night.

"...and I told him we were coming here tonight so if he shows up then that's got to mean he's into me, you know?"

I quickly tune into what Jenna's saying and feel a little guilty that I've spaced out on her, but this girl can *talk*. If I listened to every word, I'd be dizzy. "Wait, who are you talking about?"

I can see her roll her eyes even though she doesn't take them away from the road. "Michael? The barista at Grind Me? I just spent the past five minutes telling you about him. Girl, you have got to pay more attention."

I grimace a little, feeling bad. She's right, that was rude. "I'm really sorry. I've had a lot on my mind this week. Why don't you give me the TLDR version?"

She lets out a laugh and makes a sharp right that has me gripping the *oh shit* handle above the door. "I've been chatting up the new barista at Grind Me. You know that new coffee place down the street from work? He's super-hot. Like in a total Clark Kent kind of way. If I can get him to take off those glasses, there's totally going to be a Henry Cavill under there."

"The hottest Superman," I interject.

"Exactly!" she shouts, overexcited while I chuckle. "Anyway, I just happened to mention that we were going to be here tonight, and he totally looked like he was paying attention. That means if he shows up that's proof he's into me and I'm going for it. My lady bits could use the fun."

"You think he's going to show up on a Monday night? I thought we were the only ones crazy enough to do that."

"I guess we'll find out if he wants *this* enough." She gives a little shimmy in her seat that lets her boobs shake and threaten to spill out of her top. If Clark Kent does show up, he's going to be putty in her hands.

The car rolls into the parking lot at Vinnie's, a bar slash music venue slash dance club that's not too far from my place. I'm surprised that there's a decent number of cars here for a Monday night.

We make our way across the lot to the squat brick one story building. When I swing the heavy wooden door open a blast of warm air, stale beer, and the sounds of live music practically smack me in the face.

"Awesome! There's a band, I can't wait to get my dance on," Jenna says while making her way to the long scarred wooden bar running across the back wall. While we wait for the bartender, I take a look around. It's a decent size crowd but not a ton of people. I even spot a few out on the dance floor. There's one couple who looks like they're closer to simulating sex than they are dancing and the band's not even playing a slow song.

As I'm scanning the crowd, I can feel eyes on me and it takes a minute to find the familiar face in the crowd. A smile stretches across my face and I shout to Jenna that I'll be right back. I quickly make my way to the other end of the bar and wrap my arms around the man that was watching me. "Jake!"

"Hey, Bianca. Damn girl, you are smoking tonight. Does your dad know you're out looking like that?" I let out a laugh and do several poses showing off my gold dress that scoops low in the front and shows off a generous amount of cleavage, but I feel like the long sleeves balance it out. I give a careful little spin because the skirt is on the shorter side and I don't feel like flashing anyone, at least yet anyway.

"What this old thing?" He just rolls his eyes at me and shakes his head, giving me a deep chuckle. "You better not say a word to him, Jake." I take my finger and poke him in the chest. "I mean it."

Jake Aguilar is the protective older brother that I never had or wanted.

If my brother was a bit of a man-whore.

Not that I judge.

I've known him since he started working for my father's construction company years ago. He started out as a kid doing all the shit jobs nobody else wanted to do and now he runs one of the teams. He's also probably my dad's best friend.

"I won't say a word, I swear." He pretends to lock his lips and throw away the key.

I perch my ass on the stool next to him and look over his shoulder. "Are you here with anyone tonight or are you just going to be leaving with someone?" I ask raising my brow. Jake is hot and always seems to have a gaggle of women around him. He's not quite as hot as Carson, but—ugh, why am I thinking about that jerk?

Anyway, what I'm trying to get across is, if the thought of kissing Jake didn't make me want to throw up in my mouth a little, I would totally hit that, but since it does, he's out of luck. Because of said hotness, he's never hurting for company of the female persuasion and he revels in it. Not that he takes advantage of the women. They all know the score, much like the men that I go home with occasionally. We're both no strings attached kind of people.

"Nah, I'm just here for a quick drink tonight. I'll be heading home soon. Alone."

"What? I don't believe it. Are you not feeling well or something? Do you need a ride to the hospital?"

"You're ridiculous, you know that?"

"I've heard." I flash him one of my sassiest smiles. "But really, what's wrong?"

"Jesus, am I really that bad? You think I can't go out even one night without picking up a woman?"

"I mean, I'm sure you can but I've never seen it."

He shakes his head and gives out a sigh. "Yeah well, I'm turning over a new leaf."

I eye him skeptically. "Really? And why is that?"

"I'm tired of the whole scene. It's turning into more trouble than it's worth. Besides, don't you ever think about finding someone you can spend more than one night with? Maybe settle down?"

I shrug and answer truthfully. "Not really, I'm just not made like that. I'm too busy between work, painting, friends, Dad, Mom—"

"Yeah, I heard your mom was being a real pain in the—" I give him a sharp look making him reconsider his words. "—foot. A real pain in the foot." I'm sure Dad's filled him in on the fact that my mom has recently decided to move to Seattle. The woman can be a bit much, but hey, she's my mom.

"Well, she's moving here so he better get used to it." Just then I feel an arm wrap around my waist and a vodka soda plops down on the bar next to me. "Thanks Jenna," I say giving her a squeeze before I pick up my drink and take a few gulps. "Have you met Jake?"

"I don't believe we've met. Hi, I'm Jenna." She sticks out her hand and leans forward just enough to flash her cleavage at Jake which doesn't surprise me one bit. Like I said, he's hot. What *does* surprise me is the fact that Jake doesn't take the bait. His eyes don't stray from her face, like, at all. Huh, maybe he really is out of the game.

"Nice to meet you, Jenna."

Immediately sensing that he's not interested, her smile turns from predatory to sweet. "You too." Grabbing my arm she turns back to me excitedly, "C'mon, knock that back. I want to dance."

Taking another few gulps until my drink is almost gone, I look back to Jake. "You wanna join us?"

"Nah, I think I'm gonna head home." He takes a couple of bills out of his wallet and tosses them on the bar before getting up and giving my arm a squeeze. "It was good seeing you. Have a good night. Don't do anything I wouldn't do."

"That looks like it's going to be a long list if what you're saying about changing your wicked ways is true," I call after him. Not even bothering to turn around, the only signal he gives that he's heard me at all is the lifting of his hand in a half-assed wave.

Five minutes later we're out on the dance floor, swaying to a rock cover of *Kings and Queens*. I move my body to the sounds and work on releasing the day's stress. Closing my eyes, I sway my hips to the beat.

We spend the next few songs moving to the music until I feel a little bead of sweat move down my back. Gross. I lean into Jenna's ear and have to shout over the band. "I'm going to get another drink!" She just smiles and nods, continuing to gyrate her hips while holding her hands above her head and letting her body roll seductively.

I head over to the bar and lean against it until the bartender gets to me. I'm ranked expert level when it comes to high heels but I've already been standing in them all day at work and the strappy five-inch heels currently on my feet are even taller and thinner than my work ones. My feet are aching but that's the price I have to pay to give my calves some shape and my ass a lift.

As I'm shifting foot to foot a gorgeous little redheaded bartender about my age approaches from across the bar-top. Her hair is in loose curls down past her shoulders and she's wearing a halter top with cherries all over it. I smile at her and the one she returns to me looks fake as hell. I shake it off, figuring she's probably just over this night and ready to head home.

"Can I get a vodka soda, please?"

"Sure thing," she says and swiftly moves away from me to make the drink.

"Hey there, can I buy you a drink?"

The voice is right next to my ear and makes me jump. I take a step back and turn to eye the man that's saddled up to me without me noticing. He's attractive in that clean cut frat boy kind of way that totally would have been my thing freshman year, but that was a long time ago.

"That's okay. I'm getting one already, but thanks for the offer." I give him a polite smile and turn back around looking for the bartender.

"I'll buy your next one then." I turn my head and notice he's edged even closer to my side. I wish I could say he was drunk and that's why he's coming off as pushy, but he looks stone cold sober. That means either he can't read signals or he just doesn't care.

"That's okay, really. I've got this."

"C'mon, don't be like that, doll." Ugh, I hate when men I don't know give me little nicknames they think are cute. At least when Carson calls me Sparky it doesn't come off as sexist. Jesus Christ, I can't get that man out of my head.

"Look, I'm not a doll and I'm not interested. I can buy my own drinks tonight. But like I said, thanks for the offer."

"You don't have to be a total bitch—"

"Hey, Jackson, don't make me eighty-six you and get security over here. She told you to back off a hell of a lot nicer than I would have." I turn to see the tiny bartender has returned with a fierce look in her eye. I'm confident in my ability to take care of myself but I'm also all about females helping females. I just raise my eyebrow at frat boy who I guess is named Jackson and watch as his head whips back and forth between myself and my new friend behind the bar.

He raises his hands in the air in front of him in a placating gesture. "Hey, no harm, no foul. I was just trying to be friendly, Amelia."

"Yeah, well, go be friendly with somebody that's actually interested. Shoo," she says. Making a sweeping hand gesture that tells him to get away from her bar. He mutters under his breath as he turns and walks away.

"Thanks, I appreciate that," I say with a smile.

"No problem." She grabs a cardboard coaster and tosses it onto the bar before setting my drink down on it. "He was out of line."

"So, you're Amelia?" She gives me a nod while she busies herself wiping down the bar in front of her. "Well, I'm Bianca. It's nice to meet you."

"You too." She has a half smile like she's not sure if it's nice to meet me at all.

I take a sip of my drink enjoying the burn of the vodka down my throat. "You know that guy or something? You called him by his name."

She lets out a sigh. "Yeah, you work here long enough and you get to know most of the regulars."

"I haven't seen you here before but I only come in every once in a while."

She nods her head and avoids my gaze while she collects empty beer bottles and glasses. Her next words are so quiet I almost don't hear them over the din of the bar. "So, you didn't go home with Jake?"

I'm confused for a moment until I remember she said she knows most of the regulars and she probably saw me talking to him. I know this bar is close to Jake's place, so he's probably here quite a bit and like I said, he has a reputation for a reason. I let out a laugh. "No way, it's not like that with Jake and me. He's like an older brother or something, I've known him since I was a kid. He works for my dad."

"Oh!" She says with genuine surprise. "Sorry, I just assumed..." Her words trail off like she's embarrassed about what she was going to say but all I can do is laugh. Since she works here, she's probably seen him with more women than I want to think about.

"Don't worry about it. It's a legitimate assumption when it comes to him." She seems to deflate a little so I'm quick to follow up with, "But he seems to be turning over a new leaf. He told me he's done with all that."

63

"Really?" She looks skeptical and I can't blame her. I'm skeptical myself. I look her over again. She really is gorgeous. She's also tiny, like almost as small as my best friend Violet but she seems to have the curves of my other best friend, Hollie. Her hair is a deep shade of natural red that the girls who buy box die could only dream about. Her eyes are big and brown, framed by dark lashes. Sure, she looks like she's younger than Jake, like a lot younger, but I could totally see them together. And judging by how she handled that asshole just now, she could totally keep Jake in line. I wonder if I should play a little matchmaker. I'm about to say something more when a rough voice shouts down from the end of the bar.

"Hey Amelia! You gonna serve some drinks or just gab with your girlfriend all night?"

She rolls her eyes and apologizes before shouting back, "Hold your horses, Mack! And if your security was doing a better job, I wouldn't have to be doing it for them." She turns back to me. "It was nice meeting you, Bianca." Then she flings the towel over her shoulder and struts down the length of the bar like she owns the place.

Yeah, I like her attitude. And she seemed *very* interested in Jake but there's nothing I can do about it right now. I push the interaction to the back of my mind and finish off the drink she gave me before making my way back to the dance floor. I'm surprised Jenna hasn't come looking for me yet, but once I get back over to where the bodies are moving on the dance floor I realize why. She's grinding up on a guy that totally looks like Henry Cavill, if he had glasses and was ten years younger. Huh. I guess she wasn't kidding. And if the way he's pulled her hips tightly against him and his lips against her ear are any indication, I think it's safe to say that Barista Michael is interested.

I smile and head back out to the floor and get near them but not too close to ruin her vibe. I catch her eye and give her that look that asks, "You, okay?" She smiles and gives me a single nod before going back to paying attention to the guy that's wrapping himself around her like some kind of boa constrictor.

I let out a snort and throw my head back before moving to the sounds of the band's cover of *Bang Bang*. I won't lie. This cover band is kind of amazing. I'm having a great time shaking my ass and hips all over this dance floor. A few guys have approached me to dance and I've let them since they've all been respectful and kept their hands to themselves. This was just the night I needed to let loose and stop thinking about the piercing green and hazel eyes of my neighbor.

After a few more drinks and dances, I'm about ready to leave and look around for Jenna who is no longer on the floor in front of the band. I do a quick scan and see her in a dimly lit corner making out with her very own personal Clark Kent.

I smile and head towards her. I clear my throat a few times to get her attention but neither one of them seems to notice me, so I reach in and tap her on the shoulder. She reluctantly removes her mouth from her companion's and I swear I can hear a gross suction sound.

"Hey, I'm gonna head home if you're alright." Her brows furrow and she extracts her limbs from the panting boy that has her pressed up against the wall. "I can take you home."

I shake my head emphatically at her. "Don't worry about it, I'll catch a Lyft home. As long as you're sure you're good?" I eye Clark Kent carefully. I know Jenna can take care of herself but that doesn't mean I don't worry about leaving her with some guy. Though at least she didn't just meet him at the bar tonight.

"I'm totally good." She bites her lip and looks between me and Clark. "Are you sure you'll be okay getting a ride?"

"Absolutely." I smile. "Text me when you get home safe, okay?"

"As long as you don't expect the text until morning," she says with a giggle. I roll my eyes and then turn my attention to the guy that's still wrapped around her, albeit more loosely than when I walked up. I reach out and quickly poke him in the chest, making sure I've got his attention. "Hey, you. Let me see your license."

"Uhhhhh." He looks at me quizzically, but the tone of my voice doesn't allow for any argument. He reaches into his back pocket and pulls out his wallet before taking out the requested card. He hands it over and I inspect it closely.

"Michael Hicks," I read under my breath. I pull my phone out of my tiny clutch and snap a picture before handing it back to him. "If anything happens to my friend, just remember I will find you." He reaches out to take it back, but I pull it away at the last second. "Just so you know, I threatened a fucking billionaire the other day with death if he hurt one of my friends. What do you think I'll do to you if something happens to her?" I gesture to Jenna with a nod of my head before putting the card back within his reach. He takes it, with a now slightly shaking hand and stuffs it back in his wallet.

"You don't have to worry about me, I'll take care of her."

"You better." I narrow my eyes on him so he knows I mean business. I wasn't joking when I threatened to murder hotel mogul Archer Clarke and bury him in the foundation of one of Dad's buildings if he hurt Hollie again. Murdering this guy and getting away with it would be cake.

I pay my tab and head out of the bar. As I step out into the crisp evening air, I'm thrilled that it's not raining. The air smells clean, and it's refreshing after being in the dimly lit and stuffy bar for the past few hours.

I pull up my phone to order a car but see that the closest one is going to take forty-five minutes to get here. What the fuck? We live in a major city, shouldn't there be more drivers? Then again, it is a Monday. I let out a sigh, knowing that I can probably walk home before the car even gets here. I look up to the sky and see a smattering of stars but there isn't a cloud in sight.

I'm not too far from home, besides it's a really beautiful night. I'm not even tipsy, maybe just a little buzzed. I cancel my ride and start my walk down the empty but well-lit street, thinking about the nice long bath I'm going to take to soak my feet as soon as I get home.

CHAPTER SIX

CARSON

I should have been home hours ago. Instead, I'm deep into overtime. The department wasn't kidding when they said they were short staffed. At least it hasn't been anything too dangerous tonight. Well, more dangerous than the usual stuff. We just finished taking a report from a local car dealership that had several vehicle thefts. We told the owner we would do everything we could to find the culprit, and we will, but if this was Los Angeles, those luxury cars would already be in a chop shop or tucked away in a container ship headed God knows where.

We were on our way back to the station, ready to pack it in for the night when we got another call. There was an armed robbery at a convenience store and apparently all the other detective units are busy at the moment. Luckily, the suspect was already apprehended, but it looks like two people were injured. It's our job to head over there, gather evidence, and try to make some sense of what happened so we can prosecute the robber. I barely suppress a groan and just rub my eyes instead. Between interviewing witnesses and talking to the victims, not to mention bagging and tagging any evidence, this is going to take another couple of hours at least.

The only bright spot is that I'll be making as shit ton of money with all this overtime. Thank God for Gloria. I don't know what I would do without her. I should have been there to pick Oliver up from her place five hours ago, instead she assured me I shouldn't worry and he could spend the night at her place.

Guilt floods my brain and heart when this happens. He's my responsibility, not hers. And to be honest, when he's not at home with me, I miss him. It was a rough go in the beginning, both of us feeling each other out, tiptoeing around each other. But over the months as we settled in and got more comfortable, things slowly changed. I never thought it would be possible, but I love that kid and would do anything for him.

I shoot Gloria another text letting her know it's still going to be a few more hours before I can pick up Oliver but when I look at my watch I notice it's well after midnight, there's no way she's awake. I'll have to pick him up in the morning. At least I'm not on until the late shift tomorrow. Or, well, today. Just as I'm scrolling through my earlier conversation with Gloria, trying to reassure myself that she really is okay taking care of him, I hear Rafe let out a curse beside me.

"Fuck. What is this shit show?"

I look up through the windshield as we pull up to the store and my eyes widen. He's not kidding. I don't know what the fuck happened here, but this place is a mess.

As I'm pulling myself out of the unmarked car, I see one ambulance take off, lights flashing and sirens wailing, shuttling its passenger off to the nearest hospital.

There's another bus in the tiny parking lot with its doors open and two EMTs are trying to push a man on a gurney towards it. Too bad he doesn't appear to be behaving too cooperatively. I take a closer look and see that not only does he have blood streaming down the right side of his face from underneath the sterile bandage he has pressed against his eye, but he's also handcuffed to the metal side of the gurney.

Huh. How the hell did he get hurt? Dispatch said he was the one that was armed. As I approach, I can hear the man on the gurney screaming. Not in pain but at somebody across the parking lot.

"You crazy bitch! You almost took my fucking eye out!"

"You're lucky that's all I did motherfucker, after hitting that nice old man in the head with a gun. What did you think was going to happen?"

A shiver runs down my spine and I close my eyes for just a second taking in a deep breath. It can't be. It really can't. My ears are playing tricks on me.

"I want to press charges on that crazy cunt! She tried to blind me! I demand you arrest her right now!" I look over to the uni who's standing next to the suspect. Since he's under arrest a uniformed officer will be with him on the way to the hospital. I notice the rookie trying not to show his smile at this idiot and is shaking his head.

"Just fucking try it you bastard. Everyone saw what happened. If you had just taken your money and run, there wouldn't have been a problem but no, you had to be Mr. Tough Guy and beat up an old man. You're lucky all I did was hit you in the eye, you piece of shit!"

At that, the man on the gurney attempts to leap up and hurl his body across the parking lot, but besides being handcuffed, he's also being held down by several paramedics that are trying to strap him down. "You fat fucking bitch!"

Anger surges through me because, even though I haven't looked in her direction yet, I know instinctively that the woman he's screaming at is Bianca. Every single cell in my body can feel her presence. If he thinks he can get away with calling her that, he's got another thing coming. I take a step towards him when I hear shrieks come from my left.

"Do you want me to finish the job, you piece of trash? Let me go! I'm going to take out his other eye!" Stealing myself, I take a deep breath and turn towards her voice where I see something I never would have expected in my wildest dreams. Right there in the middle

69

of a group of three uniformed officers is my Bianca. Eyes blazing, hair a mess covering her face, and a shoe held over her head like she's about to strike out with it.

The three officers are having a hell of a time holding her back and I can't take my eyes off her. She looks beautiful and wild. Her golden dress has hiked up so it's barely covering her ass and pussy, the shoulder's wrenched down, exposing half her upper arm and it looks like one of her tits is about to fall out of the low scoop of her neckline. One wrong move and she'll be flashing everyone here. Her eyes are full of fire and I can see her chest rising up and down in deep, heaving breaths. Whether those breaths are trying to get herself under control or setting her up to make a run at the man yelling at her, I don't know.

I instinctively move towards her because I don't fucking like all these men with their hands all over her, even if it does appear to be necessary from the way she's trying to break free of them. She's a hellcat right now, and she's going to get herself into real trouble if she doesn't calm down.

Bianca and the man currently getting loaded into the ambulance are still trading insults and before I can get to her, I see the arm holding one of her high heels rear back. Time slows down as her body tenses and her right shoulder and arm catapult forward. She releases the shoe and it goes sailing into the air, tumbling over and over again, headed straight for me. I'm so stunned I don't even bother moving and before I know it, the golden strappy contraption hits me square in the middle of the chest. Even though it didn't hurt I still let a little *oof* sound out. I'm more surprised than anything else. Bianca's eyes are wide, finally catching sight of me for the first time.

"Ma'am, you're under arrest for assaulting a police officer," I hear one of the unis say as he pulls out a pair of handcuffs. I wince because I know she hates being called ma'am.

Bianca looks pissed.

"Don't call me ma'am! And I'm sorry, okay? I wasn't aiming for him I swear. I was trying to hit that asshole who wouldn't keep his mouth shut." As she's speaking, she looks progressively more panicked as her arm gets pulled behind her back. I've never seen her look so nervous or lost. I don't like it one fucking bit.

I jog over to Bianca and the group of officers just as the tall brutish looking one snaps the first handcuff on her wrist. She's not resisting at all and looks like she might be in a bit of shock.

"Back the fuck off," I shout as I'm approaching the small group. The three men stop what they're doing and stare at me. "Officers, there's no need for that." The tall one still has his hands on Bianca and I have the sudden urge to rip them from his body. Trying to reign in the urge I glance at is nametag. "Officer Berger, go ahead and release her."

He looks confused for a second, like there's no reason on earth why I would want to let her go. Even if I didn't know her, she shouldn't be arrested. She threw a fucking shoe that hit me, rather lightly, in the chest. It was obvious she wasn't even aiming for me. It's not a big deal. I'd rather find out what the hell else happened here tonight. Bianca may be a spitfire but this is over the top, even for her.

"Officer!" I bark when he doesn't move fast enough for me. He quickly undoes the cuff that's already on her wrist and Bianca just stands there looking a little lost. It's then I notice almost every man in the immediate vicinity is checking out the disheveled state of her dress.

"Bianca, come here," I practically growl. She looks a little nervous but pushes back her shoulders and strut over to me with the dignity of a queen, even with her bare feet, and one shoe still held in her hand. I would smile if I wasn't so annoyed at those fucking idiots eying her ass.

She's about to bend down and pick up the other shoe that's harmlessly laying next to me on the ground. "No." I say through clenched teeth. Instead of letting her bend over and flash everyone in the damn parking lot, I pick up the shoe and hand it to her before shucking off my jacket and pulling it around her shoulders.

"Come with me," I snap at her. I know it's not her fault I'm on edge, but I need to get her tucked away so I can figure out what the fuck is going on. I spot Rafe over by the entrance talking to another uniformed officer, seemingly unaware of the scuffle that just took place. How he missed that entire spectacle, I don't know.

I take her elbow in my hand and start leading her over to our car that's pulled across the entrance of the lot, blocking traffic from coming in or out.

"Carson?" She asks in a low voice. I know what the question means. She wants to know if she's in trouble. And since I don't know the answer to that right now, I don't bother answering.

When we reach the car, I pull open the back door and take a breath, trying to calm myself down so I don't snap at her again. "Bianca, I want you to sit in this car. Don't move until I come and get you."

"But I was just—"

"Stop," I say with a weary sigh. I reach up and rub the bridge of my nose. "I don't want to hear it right now. Just let me do my job and I'll be back as soon as I can."

A second ago she looked shocked and scared but now she's back to having fire in her eyes and looks like she's about to start arguing with me. It's almost enough to make me laugh. Almost.

"Stay here and don't say a word to anybody but me, you got it?" I stare into her eyes desperately trying to convey how serious I am. After a moment she seems to get it.

She lets out a *humph* sound and mutters "Fine," before lowering herself into the back seat. I firmly close the door, caging her in, happy the back doors don't open from the inside.

I head over to Rafe who is jotting some notes down on the small pad he keeps in his pocket. "Hey man, you got that girl?"

"Yeah, I put her in the back of the car for now until we can figure out what is going on with this shit show."

Rafe eyes me carefully and glances back to our car before looking back to me. "You know her or something?"

I let out a sigh. Apparently my little freak out with the officers touching her didn't go unnoticed after all. I really don't need this as the new guy on the force. "Yeah, she's my neighbor."

"Wait. Are you saying she's the one that gave you a hell of a time about the parking shit?"

"Yes, she is," I grind out. "Can we just drop it for right now?"

A legitimate smile crosses Rafe's face. I knew I should never have told him about my altercation with Bianca. Now it's coming back to bite me in the ass. I choose to ignore that goofy as shit grin on his face and get back to work. "Fill me in. What do we have?"

Immediately he's all business again and flips through his notepad. "What I've been able to gather is that the suspect entered the establishment at about zero one hundred hours with a gun. He attempted to rob the place but when an older gentleman was too slow getting out of his way, he hit him over the head with the butt of his gun and knocked the guy out cold. That was who was in the ambulance we saw speeding off when we pulled up."

I nod my head taking in what he's telling me. "If it's a civvy that got hurt what happened to our suspect? Why is he bleeding?" I look back over to where the second ambulance was parked but see that it's now gone as well, transferring our perp to the closest hospital for treatment. Then it's strait off to jail for him.

"Oh, that's where things get interesting," he says with a grin. "Apparently your girl over there—"

"She's not my girl," I grumble, lying through my teeth. She feels a little bit like mine.

"Whatever man. Well, it looks like there was some kind of altercation between her and the perp. I can't seem to get a straight answer out of any of the witnesses. They all claim their view was obstructed or they were looking the other way."

"What the hell could have happened? This guy is bleeding and has to go to the hospital while Bianca doesn't look like she has a scratch on her. You're telling me they saw nothing?"

Rafe shakes his head. "There were three other people in there and they're all adamant that they didn't see anything after the old man went down. If I didn't know better, I'd think they were trying to protect the girl."

I feel like I've walked into some parallel universe tonight. Maybe I've been on duty too long. We really should have gone home hours ago. I grab the closest officer and make sure he collects any CCTV video the store has. Then both Rafe and I head back to the car where Bianca is waiting. If her fidgeting is any indication, she's not waiting very patiently either. Opening the side door, it's clear she looks pissed again. Awesome.

"You locked me in here," she hisses at me, turning her body so that her feet are out of the car and on the pavement making sure I can't close the door on her again.

"Bianca, it's a police vehicle. All the back doors only open from the outside. It had nothing to do with you." She crosses her arms indignantly under her breasts causing them to push up even higher and I let out a groan before planting my gaze well above her neck.

Rafe and I exchange a look and I give him an almost imperceptible nod as he flips to a new page in is notepad. It's best if he questions her since Bianca and I have a personal relationship. Not as personal as I'd like, but still.

"Miss Moreno, I'm Detective Campo and I believe you know Detective Turner." She glances at me then turns her attention back to Rafe and gives him a nod. I don't know why it bothers me that she's paying attention to him, but it does. I want her eyes on me damnit.

"Bianca, tell us what happened." Both she and Rafe turn back to me. She looks impatient, and he's giving me a look that says *what the hell?* since we both know he's the one that should be doing the questioning. I rub my hand down my face and take a physical step back, giving myself some room to breathe.

"I was minding my own business and that guy just walked in with a gun—"

"Let's roll it back for a second, Miss Moreno. Why don't you start at the beginning of your night."

She lets out a sigh and looks over to me like I can somehow speed this up. She doesn't realize that I'm just as interested as Rafe to hear what the fuck happened tonight.

Realizing she's not going to get any help from me she tugs my coat, still hanging off her shoulders, closer to her body.

"Fine. My friend Jenna and I went out to Vinnie's tonight—" Rafe is just nodding like he knows the place but I'm new here so I can't help interjecting.

"What's that?"

"Vinnie's? It's a kind of bar down on Monument. It's maybe four blocks from here," she answers.

I look around and don't notice her car in the lot. "If it's four blocks away, where's your car?"

She gives me an exasperated look that matches the one Rafe is giving me as well. I know I need to keep my mouth shut but something about Bianca makes me toss my common sense right out the window. It happens every time I argue with her and it's happening right now.

"I thought you wanted me to tell this." She says, voice filled with annoyance. If I don't let Rafe handle this, we're going to have another knock down drag out fight right here in the middle of this parking lot with half a dozen officers looking on.

"I'm sorry, go ahead and continue," I say as evenly as possible.

"As I was saying, my girlfriend and I went to Vinnie's together tonight. She ended up going home with someone, so I told her I'd take a Lyft home."

"What time was this?" Rafe asks.

"Just after midnight I think. It definitely wasn't later than twelve-thirty." He tells her to go on. "I tried to get a car but the closest one was forty-five minutes away and since it was a nice night, I decided to walk instead. I don't live that far. When I passed the store, I stopped in and grab a bottle of water. My feet were killing me, so I kicked off my shoes and held them when I went inside. I know it's completely gross, but it was a foot emergency. Then I was just minding my own business when the front door bursts open and hits me in the arm."

"Who entered the store?" Rafe asks while furiously taking notes.

"The guy they arrested. He was waving a gun around and shouting for all of us not to move which I wasn't happy about because I was only three feet from him. We all just stood there while he started yelling at the cashier to empty the drawer in a bag. He was totally doing it too, nobody was going to argue with the dude with a gun. I'm pretty sure we all just wanted him to grab the cash and get out of there. But there was this older guy, he had to be like sixty-five or seventy, and he was standing at the counter. The guy with the gun started yelling at him to get out of his way but the old guy was like, frozen in place, he looked terrified. I guess he wasn't moving fast enough, so he took his gun and hit the old man over the head with it. The old guy just crumpled to the ground. I'd never seen anything like it, I thought he was dead."

"That was the gentleman they took out of here in the ambulance?"

Bianca nods her head emphatically. "Do you know if he's okay?"

"I'm sorry, I don't, but we'll see what we can find out after we finish up here, alright? Why don't you go on, how did the assailant end up bleeding and why were the two of you in a screaming match when we arrived?"

She takes a deep breath like she's stealing herself to continue then she speaks so quickly I almost can't keep up. "Okay, so, I got pissed. That old man wasn't trying to get in his way, you know? For all I knew that guy had killed him. I was worried he was going to hurt someone else. I mean it was obvious he was totally out of control, right?" She doesn't bother waiting for confirmation from either of us before she continues. "I swear I didn't even know what I was doing until I was already in the middle of doing it. I was just so fucking angry, and I was worried about everyone else in the store, and I was already holding my shoes. There was no way I could walk all the way home in them, I mean have you seen these things?" She holds up the pair of shoes still clutched in her hand.

She's not wrong. Those things have heels on them that have to be at least five inches high and they aren't thick either, I'm surprised she could walk in them at all.

I look over at Rafe and can see he's trying, with what looks like great difficulty, to keep a grin off his face. At this point I think we can both see where this is going.

"Those do look rather difficult to walk in. Go on, Miss Moreno."

"Oh, please, just call me Bianca. Um, anyway so I was a few feet behind him and to the side so I guess he couldn't see me coming. I swung my shoe at him. I just wanted to hit him in the head, I thought maybe I could distract him and he'd drop the gun or just decide it was too much trouble and take off." She wraps her arms around her middle in a protective gesture.

"Well, I guess he must have seen me out of the corner of his eye because at the very last second he turned his head toward me and the heel of my shoe went straight into his eye."

You can hear both Rafe and I suck in sharp breaths. I didn't know she had gotten him in the fucking eye. It takes everything I have not to bring my hand up and rub at my own eye socket. It's only then that I notice the smear of red on the heel of one of her shoes. I don't know how I missed that up til now. We're going to have to bag those for evidence.

It's been a few heartbeats since either Rafe or I have said anything and it's apparent that Bianca is taking that as condemnation of her actions when she spews, "I didn't do anything wrong. It was self-defense, or at the very least other people defense, or old man defense! Is that a thing? Whatever, he could have killed someone and all he got was a teeny tiny stiletto in his eye. Frankly, he got off easy. Not to mention the fact that I threw him a box of tissues so he could stop the bleeding. I'm not heartless. Anyway, I kicked the gun he dropped across the room and while he was rolling around on the ground and screaming at me, two officers pulled up. Man, they got here fast. How did they get here so fast?"

Rafe looks like he wants to burst out laughing but answers her instead, "It looks like as soon as the assailant walked in the cashier hit the silent alarm which alerted our dispatch."

"Oh, that makes sense," Bianca nods her head. She lets out a long breath and her body slumps against the seat like she just used the last of her energy to tell us what happened.

While Rafe has been standing here taking notes and finding this whole thing very amusing, I have steadily been getting angrier and angrier the longer she spoke. It takes a herculean effort not to grab her shoulders and shake her. Nope, I don't do that. Instead, I try to steady my breathing that's gone ragged and close my eyes for a quick second before opening them again and zeroing in on her.

"Give your shoes to Rafe, Bianca."

She gives me a disgruntled look that says she doesn't like me ordering her around.

"Why do I have to give him my shoes? Will I get them back? I love this pair."

"Bianca, they're covered in blood." She looks down at the shoes in her lap and does a little jump in surprise, quickly thrusting them away from her body and straight towards Rafe who calls over an officer to bag them.

"I'm sorry, I didn't realize." I'm sure she didn't. She's been so caught up in adrenaline and what's been going on that she hasn't had a chance to come down, but she's going to crash hard soon.

"Come with me." I grab her hand and pull her from the backseat of the vehicle. Thank God she doesn't bother fighting me. I'm not in the mood.

"Carson, slow down please," she says softly from behind me. I turn around to eye her without missing a step but see that she's concentrating on the ground and where she's stepping. That's when I remember she doesn't have shoes on.

In one swift movement I turn completely, wrap my arm around her thick thighs that are on full display in that dress and haul her up over my shoulder.

She lets out a scream. "Carson, what the fuck are you doing? Put me down right this second."

"You can't walk in this parking lot without any shoes on," I growl at her. I turn to my partner who's watching this interaction with great interest. "Give us a minute, will you?"

He doesn't bother asking me what I'm up to which is probably a good thing because I have no damn idea what the fuck I'm doing right now.

It's then that I notice Bianca is struggling to reach behind her and hold the bottom of her skirt over her ass. Despite her best efforts, the bottom of her plump cheeks are out on display. Arousal immediately sings through my bloodstream. Then I notice all the men in the parking lot ogling her. A deep growl of possession rises from my chest.

I quickly turn around so that her ass is pointed toward the side of the building and start walking backwards. I stare down every man here until they all flinch and avert their eyes. They probably have something to say about me carrying a witness away over my shoulder, but right now I don't give a shit.

I look behind me with a wiggling Bianca still firmly in my grasp and see a small, darkened alley between the side of the convenience store and the closed dry cleaner next door that will work just fine for my purposes.

Once we're shrouded in shadow, I grab onto Bianca's hips and let her body slowly slide down mine until she's standing on in front of me on her own two feet.

"What the hell was that, Carson? You can't just throw me over your shoulder like some kind of fucking caveman."

"Too bad, I already did. Now what the fuck was all that, Bianca?"

"What are you talking about?" she asks while taking a step back like she's trying to escape me. Instead of creating distance between us I merely take a step towards her, stalking my prey.

"I'm talking about you having absolutely no regard for your personal safety," I manage to spit out through clenched teeth. I'm not even bothering to try to hide my anger right now. She needs to see how irresponsible she was. Jesus Christ, she could have been killed several times over tonight and she's acting like it's no big deal.

I don't know why the thought of losing this girl that I've only known a few weeks scares the shit out of me, but it does. I'm not even going to try to fight it right now. I'm too close to the edge of losing all control and I don't like the feeling.

She takes another step backwards until her ass hits the wall behind her causing her eyes to go wide. She's stuck while I'm still advancing on her. "Look, I know it wasn't the smartest thing, hitting a gunman with my shoe—"

I let out a snort of derision. "You think?" I ask sarcastically.

"—but you have to admit that I saved those people."

"You could have been shot, Bianca. You could have fucking died."

I can hear her suck in a breath like the thought is only just occurring to her. She looks disturbed. Good. She needs to understand how unbelievably reckless she was tonight.

"Nothing bad happened," she says significantly more subdued than she was a few moments ago but I don't let up.

"You were lucky, you understand that, right? If you hadn't gotten him in the eye, he could have just turned and shot you dead right there in the middle of the store. And what about the absurd decision to walk home from a bar, by yourself, at one in the morning?"

"Carson, we're not that far from home. I walk home after nights out all the time, nothing bad ever happens. I'm fine." Her telling me she does it all the time is not helping calm me down. "I'm perfectly capable of taking care of myself." And that's what finally sets me off.

I move my body right into hers so that she's pressed firmly against the brick wall behind her. With one hand I snag her wrists and raise them over her head. My other hand settles around her throat.

"Yeah? If someone grabs you like this, can you get away, Bianca? You take care of yourself?" I mock.

"Stop manhandling me! Let me go!" She struggles against me but I just tighten my grip on her hands and put a little pressure on her throat just to show her what I could do if I wanted to. Her pulse is pounding furiously against my hand and I'm not sure if I want to choke her or fuck her up against this wall. Maybe if I'm lucky, I'll get to do both.

"If you can't even get away from me, how do you propose you'll get away from somebody who actually wants to hurt you, Bianca? You can't be this reckless. If you keep acting like this, eventually your luck is going to run out."

She's breathing hard and I realize my chest is heaving to match hers. The look in her eyes has gone from full of defiance to glazed over. I mutter a curse when I realize she's turned on. Her tongue darts out of her mouth and moistens her full lower lip, practically calling for me.

Fuck it.

That's the last thought I have before my mouth goes crashing down onto hers.

CHAPTER SEVEN

BIANCA

You are not getting turned on by this.
You are not getting turned on by this.
Fuck.

My wrists are pinned above my head, there's a hand encircling my throat, and Carson looks beyond pissed. I've never been into hate fucking before but I guess there's a first time for everything.

It's not that I disagree with him. Yes, what I did wasn't exactly safe. I didn't think anything about walking home alone in the dark, but I really have done it before without a problem. I guess that had the unfortunate consequence of emboldening me.

I don't even want to think about the guy with the gun. And I guess that was the problem, I didn't think, I just acted on instinct. I was incensed when I saw him hurt that old man and it was reflexive.

Of course, I could have admitted that to Carson but his know-it-all attitude makes me slightly crazy and want nothing more than to push back. He somehow knows all my buttons, and he's not afraid to push them.

Now here I am, trapped between him and a brick wall. His solid body up against mine. My nipples are hard little pebbles that are straining against my dress and I pray he can't feel them pressed up against his chest.

The look in his eyes is making my stomach flip-flop and my pussy cheer as it drips with arousal. These panties are absolutely ruined.

"You can't be this reckless. If you keep acting like this, eventually your luck is going to run out." He's so furious right now it's hard to hold his steady gaze. I'm tuning back into what he's saying, really I am. But mostly, I just want to climb him like a tree and have him fuck my brains out right here with a parking lot full of cops fifty feet away.

We're both breathing hard. I'm so damn turned on I can't seem to catch my breath. Well, that and the pressure he's intermittently putting on my throat that dumps flood after flood of arousal into my panties every time he squeezes.

He's panting too, and I'm not sure if it's from the rage he's feeling at my actions or if it's something else. It's hard for me to believe he could possibly want me just as much as I want him.

I know he's waiting for a response, but I can't remember what it was he was saying. My entire body is aching for his touch and I'm starting to feel dizzy. Instead, I imagine him kissing me and can't help but run my tongue along my lower lip, wetting it in desperate anticipation.

His eyes flash something I can't read and before I even realize it's happening, his mouth is on mine. This isn't some slow, getting to know you kiss. No, this is a kiss fueled by anger and arousal.

His lips and tongue are on the attack and I'm just doing my best to keep up with the invasion. His tongue swipes into my mouth and wraps around mine then pulls back and his teeth nip at my bottom lip before his tongue enters my mouth again.

Needy little moans are escaping my lips. Any other time this would embarrass me, but not right now. I'm trying to pull my hands out of his grasp so I can run them over his body. The need to touch him is almost as much as the need to feel his touch and it's not a reaction I'm used to.

He wrenches his mouth away from mine and it's only when we're both panting that I realize we were so caught up in each other that neither of us remembered to breathe. Luckily, his mouth isn't gone for long and when it comes back and he's running his lips and tongue down the delicate skin of my neck. Teeth nip at my skin with sharp little bites, then his tongue runs over them like it's some kind of soothing balm. All I can think about is wanting his tongue between my legs.

"Carson." The whine comes out like that of a petulant child, but I can't even bring myself to care as I tug at my trapped hands once again trying to escape his iron grip.

His breath tickles my neck as he says a simple "No" and it makes me shiver with need. Instead, he removes his hand from the base of my throat and slides it down to my breast. At first he gives it a gentle squeeze before following it up with a much harder one that makes me gasp and try to rub up against him like a cat in heat.

I may not have the use of my hands, but I can still feel his rock-hard cock behind the slacks he's wearing. It's poking me in my lower belly and his own hips are making slight thrusting motions against me. I can't help the little smirk that comes to my face when I realize he wants me just as much as I want him.

My mind doesn't have time to gloat though, because his searching fingers have found the hard tip of my nipple through my dress and he gives it a long hard squeeze. It feels like my tits have a direct line to my pussy and I swear I can feel it in my clit.

Suddenly, my hands fall to my sides, free of Carson's tight grasp. I immediately bring them up to his shoulders and try to pull him closer. I realize why he finally let my hands go when I feel his firm, warm hands under my skirt cupping both my ass cheeks my thong has left that bare. He draws me further into his heat and I let out a whimper.

"You're a needy little thing, aren't you, Sparky?" I'd tell him to go fuck himself if I didn't want him to fuck *me* instead. Rather than answering, I lift my leg and hook it around his hip, tilting my own until I finally have my panty clad pussy up against his hard length.

Fuck, I'm going to dry hump him like a teenager in the back seat of a car.

He licks the outer shell of my ear, sending shivers through my entire body, before whispering, "I bet if I touched your pussy right now you'd be soaking for me, wouldn't you?"

"Yes," I gasp. God, he has no fucking idea just how wet I am. I'll be shocked if there isn't a wet spot on the front of his pants where my pussy is rubbing against him.

His hand leaves my ass and the next thing I feel are his fingers just barely grazing my pussy through the thin material of my panties. I know he can feel that they're soaked through and my clear juices are spread messily across my inner thighs. I'd be embarrassed if I could feel anything except unadulterated lust right now.

Desperately wanting to feel him, I reach for his belt buckle but before I can get it undone, he pulls my hands away. "Believe me babe, there's nothing more I want to do than fuck your tight cunt right here, against the wall but we don't have time for that."

The realization that we're in public clears the haze in my brain but only for a moment because that's when I feel him pull my panties to the side.

His fingers run up and down my slit almost lazily. His touch is so light I can't help but buck my hips, trying to get him to touch my clit. He finally relents and runs two fingers from my dripping hole, wetting them further, then running them up to my engorged button. He takes the sensitive bundle of nerves between his fingers and squeezes. I swear to God I can feel my heartbeat in my pussy and I can see stars without looking up to the sky.

He moves the hand that's not exquisitely torturing my pussy and covers my mouth before taking my clit in his fingers again and rubbing it firmly between them. Thank fuck he's covering my mouth because I can't help but let out a squealing noise that turns into a low moan.

I look into his eyes and can see the satisfaction in them. He loves the power he's wielding over my aching body, and I hate it. I don't like being under anyone's control, I just don't have the strength or will to stop it right now.

His fingers move down to my entrance again but this time he doesn't stop at the outside. He takes both fingers and thrusts them inside of me. The feeling is intense pleasure and burning pain at once. I'm so shocked by the sudden action that I don't even have time to scream before my legs give out. Now I'm being held up almost entirely by the grip he has on my pussy and his body pinning mine to the wall.

"Hold on, babe," he whispers. His words and those lips pressed against my ear are enough for me to scramble my hands up to his shoulders holding on for dear life as I get my legs back underneath me.

"Good girl." He continues to thrust inside me over and over again. How can just a few fingers make me feel so full and needy? His thumb is firmly pressing against my clit while his fingers work their magic inside me and I can feel my muscles tense up, I'm so close to coming right here in the dark corner of an alley, and I couldn't care less. I let my head fall back and clunk against the wall, screwing my eyelids shut. All I can do is get ready to be taken by the wave of pleasure that's building inside me.

That's when his hand disappears completely from my pussy. I'm suddenly feeling emptier than I've ever been in my life and my pussy is pulsating between my legs. If a strong breeze were to hit it right now, I'd come.

He takes my panties and pulls them back into place over my swollen and aching lips while I try to catch my breath. His large hand gives me a firm slap between my legs, directly against my protruding clit and tiny waves of pleasure move through my body and make me whimper with need.

"Why the hell did you stop?" I ask accusingly.

He gives me a smirk and I immediately want to slap it off his stupid handsome face. "If I just let you come when you're bad, how will you ever learn to be more careful?"

I can feel my jaw drop as he takes a step back from me, leaving the front of my body cold in the night air. "Are you fucking kidding me right now?" Instead of answering he grasps my dress, pulling it down so that it covers my panties. I smack his hands away in frustration and he lets out a low chuckle before adjusting the bulge in his pants. At least he didn't get any relief either, though that feels like a cold comfort right now.

"Ahem."

Both of our heads snap to the opening of the alley where that other detective who took my statement is standing, and I immediately feel my chest and cheeks heat with embarrassment. How long has he been standing there? God, I hope he didn't hear me begging Carson to let me come.

"If you two are done, we really need to get a move on," he says, his eyes sparkling with mirth.

"We'll be right there," Carson calls back before turning to me. "Give me your phone." My first instinct is to argue with him but I'm too aroused and too tired right now. Instead, I reach into my tiny clutch and unlock it before handing him the phone.

I eye him suspiciously while he types away at it until I hear a buzzing coming from his pocket. He pulls out his own phone to check it and then hands mine back to me. "There, now you have my number. Next time you have the genius idea of walking home by yourself in the middle of the night I want you to call me. You understand, Bianca?"

"I don't need a keeper," I grumble.

"Apparently you do. The second you're not being watched you bring a goddamn high heel to a gunfight."

"What can I say? I'm a trendsetter." I give him the brightest smile I can muster and that seems to irk him because I can see his teeth grinding.

"Let's go, I'll drop you at home. I've got to head back to the station and fill out a mountain of paperwork because of this mess."

I wait for him to start walking so I can follow and instead he bends down, grasps me under my ass and hauls me over his shoulder again like I'm a sack of potatoes. This time his large hand is holding the back of my skirt down. I don't know if I'm thankful to him for protecting my modesty or embarrassed that he's acting like some caveman in front of a parking lot full of people.

I ball my hands into fists and beat them against his back which he notices about as much as he would notice a fly landing on him. "Carson, put me down!"

"Shoes, Bianca."

I let out a sigh because I know there's no way he's going to let me walk through this broken bottle ridden parking lot and let him carry me to the car.

Groaning, I reach over and accidentally smack my phone off the nightstand and across the room. I pull myself out of bed and practically crawl over to it so I can shut off the constant trilling that's piercing through my pounding head.

I didn't get home until almost four last night and then I couldn't go to sleep because I was still on edge from the orgasm I was denied. I ended up pulling my vibrator out of my drawer and making myself come in what must have been record speed but I still didn't feel satisfied. I have a feeling my pussy won't be happy until I get that orgasm that Carson's fingers promised. Well, that's too bad because we're staying far, far away from that arrogant asshole. Sure, that might have been the hottest thing I've ever done, but I'm not going to play his little power games. As far as I'm concerned, my girly bits are a Carson free zone and they'll just have to deal with it.

I should go back to calling him Detective Dickwad.

I drag my ass to the shower and let the warm water relax my tired muscles before getting out and looking at myself in the mirror. I don't have much time before I have to leave for work so I'm going to have to either skip my hair or my makeup. The choice is obvious. I pull my hair up into a sleek bun at the top of my head, making sure there are no wayward bumps sticking out and then set to work on making up my face.

Thirty minutes later I leave my bedroom dressed in an Amber color blouse with my high-waisted, black skirt that falls just below my knees. When I was pulling my three-inch pumps out of the back of my closet, I saw the place where my gold strappy heels used to be and took just a moment to mourn their loss. Admittedly, I did smile a little to myself about taking that asshole down with them.

Violet's sitting at the kitchen table, both hands clasped around a mug of coffee, and staring off into the distance. "Hi, sweetie. You alright over there?" She jumps at the sound of my voice like I've just awakened her from a trance. She looks almost as tired as I feel.

"Yeah, I'm fine. It's just been a busy couple of days," she mumbles. I eye her while pouring myself a cup of coffee and add a shit ton of cream and sugar. Glancing at the clock I see I can spare a few minutes before I need to head out, so I sit down across from my best friend.

"Have you heard from Hollie? I haven't spoken to her in a few days."

"Yeah, I spoke to her last night. It sounds like things are going well. Her mom is already on her way to the rehab that Archer set up for her. Now they just need to pack up her apartment along with Paige's things. She promised she'll be back in time for your birthday party."

I can't believe I almost forgot about my party this weekend. I love a good party, especially when it's for me, but I've been so occupied with work and the asshole next door, I had completely forgotten about it. "I hope you told her she doesn't have to rush home for me. You know I would totally understand if she can't make it. She needs to be taking care of her little sister right now, not worried about a stupid party for me."

Violet reaches across the table and pats my hand. "It's not a stupid party. We *want* to celebrate your birthday. Hollie knows you wouldn't mind if she missed it, but she wants to be here. Plus, I think she's looking forward to letting loose after the stress of the past week. I think she also hopes that a big party will distract Paige. You know her sister never wanted to move here and now she's being forced to."

"Yeah, but that was before she knew she was going to be living in Archer's mansion," I point out.

Violet lets out a soft melodic laugh. "Very true."

I take another sip of my coffee and check the clock again. Margot is a total monster when her worker bees are late. "Oh, have you seen my dad?"

Violet's eyes widen just a little. "No, why do you think I would have seen him?"

Okaaay. Someone is acting a little defensive. "Maybe because you work with him? I was trying to get a hold of him yesterday so I could schedule a dinner with Mom but he didn't answer his phone or any of my texts."

Violet's cheeks turn pink and she fixes her eyes on her coffee mug like it's the most interesting thing in the world.

Huh.

I wonder if this has something to do with the crush she used to have on Dad. I mean, she never explicitly told me she was crushing on him, but she's my best friend. I could tell. But I thought she had gotten over it, she's basically avoided anything that has to do with him for the past six months, plus she's dating Tyler now.

If I thought she still had a little crush on him, I wouldn't be trying to get my parents back together. Well, in front of her at least. No way, she's totally over it. I mean, Tyler is super cute and seems nice. Plus, they have a ton in common. I could always ask her about it, but I don't want to embarrass her. I know she would be mortified if I knew how she felt about Dad.

"Why don't you invite Tyler to the party this weekend?" I ask.

She looks like she's surprised by the suggestion, but I don't know why. "Yeah, maybe," she says distractedly before a soft smile curls her lips. "So, anything new with hot cop next door?"

Now it's my turn to look away. "How should I know? That man is a total pain in the ass, I'm thankful every day I don't run into him."

"Uh huh, sure."

"Don't take that tone with me, Vi," I tease her. "Sure he's kinda cute but he's not my type." I shrug and take my cup to the sink and rinse it out.

"Really. And what type is that? I don't remember you ever being so picky."

"The type with a kid. Besides the fact that I can't stand the little mongrels, men like that are always looking to settle down."

"And that's not you." She says it more as a skeptical observation than a question and I turn my head so she can't see my face. Violet isn't as annoyingly perceptive as Hollie, but she's still my best friend and can read me like a book. I blame it on her literature degree.

Violet walks over and gives me a hug which I return whole-heartedly. She's so small her head barely clears my chest and our hugs always make me feel protective of her.

She grabs her bag from the hallway and gives me a wave as she's heading out the door. "If I see your dad today, I'll let him know you're looking for him."

"Thanks, sweetie." I wave back before she shuts the door. I grab my purse and quickly eyeball the contents, making sure I have everything I need for the day. My hand is on the doorknob when I do my quick check out the window, just like I've done every single day since Carson moved in. I know it's silly to be avoiding him, but I can't help it. He drives me crazy and turns me on at the same time which is a confusing as fuck combination. Add in what happened last night and there's no way I can face him. For just a second, I let my mind flash back to the alley and I let out a groan thinking about how I threw myself at him and practically begged him to make me come.

The coast is clear and just as I'm turning the doorknob there's a flash of movement in my periphery coming from the direction of his house. In a blind panic, I immediately drop straight to the floor and curse when I bang my knee against the hardwood. I know this is ridiculous, but that doesn't stop me from army crawling towards the window.

When I finally make it across the room, I can barely catch my breath. Maybe I should go to the gym once in a while because this is embarrassing. I'm just glad there's nobody here to see it.

Ever so slowly, I raise my head until I'm just peeking over the windowsill. Carson's car is in sight and when I look over to the driver's side there's a pair of moss green eyes staring right at me.

Shit, shit, shit.

I immediately drop back down to the floor like some kind of deranged ninja and realize now I look even crazier than before.

Okay, Bianca. Just. Act. Casual. I quickly bring myself to my feet and dust off the front of my outfit. Gross. One of us really needs to vacuum. I know he's still looking at me. I can feel his eyes on my body like it's his touch. Spying my purse, I lean down and pick it up before saying way too loudly. "Oh look, here's my purse! I wondered where I left it." *Totally convincing.*

I chance another glance out the window and see he's smiling at me with a crooked smirk on his face. He slowly raises his hand and gives me a casual wave. Before I can say or do anything else stupid, I spin around on my heel and walk back into my bedroom where there are no windows facing his place.

CHAPTER EIGHT

CARSON

By the time I finally made it home this morning, I only had time to shut my eyes for twenty minutes before I needed to go pick up Oliver this morning and get him to school. Luckily, I wasn't on again until this afternoon so as soon as I drop him off I'm coming home and passing out.

I spent those precious few minutes of rest staring at the ceiling and trying to imagine what was under that tiny dress Bianca had on last night. My hands might have been all over her, but I didn't get to see a thing. What color were the panties I swept aside to give me access to her dripping pussy? What color are her nipples? Are they a dusky rose or a rich brown mocha? What is that plump ass going to look like when I'm fucking her from behind? That's a good one I'll have to tuck away for later.

I should probably feel bad about what happened last night but how can I when she was so responsive in my arms? I wanted to take her right there, but I wouldn't let some asshole come over and see her in that state. Nope, that's for my eyes only. Now that I know she wants me I don't plan on letting up until I have her in my bed. We might fight like cats and dogs but that apparently just makes the chemistry between us off the charts. I didn't think it was possible for her to be turned on as I was but those little gasps and moans she was making in my ear were a dead giveaway. I want to hear her moan while simultaneously cursing me.

Was I an asshole for getting her worked up and not letting her come? Probably. But I wasn't lying, I wanted her to think about all the stupid and reckless shit she did last night. I was so livid listening to her recount the night's events that I could barely see straight. Hopefully that feeling of needing release will make her think twice next time. I mean, it probably won't but it's at least worth a try. If she keeps this up, I'm going to go prematurely gray.

"Do I have to go to school today, Uncle Carson?" I quickly shift my eyes to the rear-view mirror so I can see Oliver in his car seat and quickly turn my attention back to the road in front of me. He's been a little quiet this morning, but that's not completely out of the ordinary for him, he's a quiet kid.

"Is something wrong? I thought you liked this school." When he doesn't respond I spare another glance to the mirror and see him blankly staring out the window. "Hey, tell me what's wrong. Do you not feel good today?"

"They're being mean to me."

There's a sudden tightness in my chest, this is the first time I'm hearing about someone being mean to him. According to his teachers everything was going well and I've never heard any complaints. He even seemed to be making a few friends. "Who's being mean to you, buddy?" I keep my tone even so he doesn't know I want to beat a five-year-old for being mean to my sweet and kind nephew.

"Elijah and Jacob," he says quietly.

I scrunch my up my face in confusion. "I thought they were your friends." Hadn't he just said that a few days ago?

"Then I told them I didn't have a mom or dad and they made fun of me."

I can feel my entire body stiffen and suddenly I'm squeezing the steering wheel so tightly my knuckles are turning white. I have to make a conscious effort to relax so I can get more information. "What do they say to you?"

He's still looking out the window when he quietly says, "That I must have been really bad if they left me all alone."

There's that tightness in my chest again. "You're not alone, you have me and your Aunt Gloria who love you very much. Even if you were bad, we would never leave you, we can't live without you now. You know your mom didn't want to leave you, right?"

Finally, his eyes meet mine in the rear-view mirror and I can see unshed tears fill his eyes. "She didn't?"

"Of course not, Oliver. She loved you more than anything." At least that's something I know to be one hundred percent true. The first time I had walked through that shithole of an apartment they were staying in, I found his room. Sure, the furniture looked second hand, but it was the only room in the entire place that was clean and well cared for.

After he was first put into my care, the social worker suggested I take him to the doctor to make sure he didn't have anything wrong with him, which is always a possibility with a junkie for a mother. The doctor noted that, while he was small for his age, he didn't show any indicators for fetal alcohol syndrome or any other ill effects from a drug and booze filled pregnancy. She must have gotten clean long enough to give birth to him, and I'll be forever grateful for whatever strength she could muster to do that.

We're only a few blocks away from the school so I pull to the side of the road then turn in my seat so I can face him. "She would be here with you if she could, buddy."

"I don't have a dad either." What am I supposed to say to that? When I'd finally been able to obtain a copy of Oliver's birth certificate, there had been no father listed. Chances are pretty good it was her dealer, but it could have been anyone, really. While anxiously awaiting the courts to grant me full legal guardianship of Oliver, I would sit next to his bed and watch him sleep, filled with worry that some man would pop up out of the woodwork and try to take him away from me. When nobody ever showed up, I had the competing emotions of feeling heartbroken for Oliver and immense relief that he could stay with me.

"I know you don't have a dad but that doesn't make you any less special. You have me and I *chose* you Oliver, out of every little boy in the world. Do you know how happy I am to have you with me?" It's true, it was a whirlwind in the beginning with all the legal issues and trying to get him to trust me, not to mention all the shit that went down with my job. God, it was a good thing we got out of there.

Oliver is watching my face closely as he quietly asks, "Since I don't have one, can you be my dad?"

Oh shit, there's that tightening in my chest again, it's so strong this time it threatens to hinder my breathing. There's only one thing I could possibly say to that. "Oliver, if you want me to be your dad, I would be honored." I blink away the tears that have formed in my eyes before they can spill out and clear my throat.

"What's honored?"

I give him a wide smile. "It means that being your dad would make me really really happy. It's you and me against the world, buddy."

"You and me and Aunt Gloria?"

"Of course, Aunt Gloria, we can't forget about her."

"What about Bianca?" There's a hard lump in my throat that I manage to swallow down. This is one of the reasons I never wanted to bring a woman around Oliver. I didn't want him to get attached then have them disappear from his life like his mom did. How could I have known that he would take such an immediate liking to Bianca? I'd seen anything like that from him. I couldn't do anything to protect him from her. Hell, I couldn't do anything to protect *myself* from her.

She burst into our lives like an out-of-control wildfire, beautiful but dangerous to both our hearts. I know, especially after last night, that I want her in my bed, but maybe there could be something more than that. I won't make any promises to him though. We barely know her and she's an artist. Aren't they supposed to be unstable and flighty? At least that's what I've always heard. I like things I can observe, understand, and control. Bianca doesn't fall within those perimeters.

"We'll have to see about that, okay? Now," I say changing the subject, "are you ready to get to school? I have a few extra minutes and I'd like to talk to your teacher. If Elijah or Jacob say mean things to you again I want you to tell her. It's very important."

"Okay, Dad." *Well shit.* I suck in a breath and rapidly blink to keep my eyes clear before pulling back out into traffic.

Forty-five minutes later I pull back into my driveway, my eyes automatically seek out Bianca's car but it's missing from its earlier parking spot. I didn't really expect to see it there. Not after those gymnastics she did trying to avoid me this morning, but it didn't stop me from checking, just to make sure. She was gorgeous when she was disheveled last night but this morning, with her hair pulled back and her curvy body clothed in that tight blouse and skirt? She was every dirty librarian fantasy every boy has ever had.

I have to remind myself that she literally dove to the floor to avoid me. That's not a good sign. Sure, she was into what we were doing last night but it doesn't mean anything other than the fact we have great sexual chemistry. Like off the charts. But she'd also just been in a life-or-death situation and I know that can make people do life affirming things they might otherwise avoid. Awesome, now I feel like an ass that took advantage of her vulnerable state.

It doesn't matter what last night was; I need to keep Oliver in mind. What if I sleep with her and she started avoiding us completely? Oliver would be crushed. Ever since she gave him that sketchpad and the info for art lessons, every other word out of his mouth is Bianca.

I can't help but smile to myself as I make my way up to the front door. He's got his first art class next weekend and I've never seen him this excited. Not even about ice-cream, and that says a lot.

I'm about to put my key into the lock when I realize there's a white paper shoved between the door and the jam at eye level. Pulling it out, I get a weird feeling, like I'm being watched. I glance over my shoulder but don't see anyone, just a street filled with empty and quiet cars. My name is scrawled across the front of the envelope just like last time. Quickly unlocking the door, I slip inside and make sure I engage not only the lock, but the deadbolt as well. I set the note down on the table and go from room to room, making sure every window and any other point of entry is secure. I'm always good about locking up the house but it's better to be safe than sorry.

I don't have any gloves on me right now, so I improvise by grasping it on the very edge and using a letter opener to reveal the folded-up piece of paper inside. I grab a set of tweezers to pull it out and slowly unfold it. Fetching the first letter from the drawer, I place them side by side on the table.

Yup, those are the same black block letters from the first note.

YOU'LL PAY FOR WHAT YOU'VE DONE.

I slip this letter into another plastic bag and move it to the table near the front door. The first letter was vague and rather harmless if a bit creepy. This one has certainly taken on a more threatening tone. I know it's probably nothing, but it's time to bring Rafe in on this. Maybe he has a connection in forensics that can run prints on them. DNA would be much harder to get, the department has months of backlogs not to mention all the cold cases and old rape kits they're going back and processing. Hopefully, fingerprints will be enough.

I wrack my brain but can't think of anyone I could have pissed off lately. They say I took their family, maybe I arrested their kid? This is going to be impossible without something else to go on. Seattle may have only a fraction of the violent crimes and arrests of Los Angeles but there is still more than enough to keep me busy. This person could be upset about anything.

I don't like that they walked straight up to my front door and left it here. I'm going to have to get an alarm installed. Odds are it's just some crazy person, but I know better than anyone that bad things happen to good people and I refuse to let Oliver get hurt.

"Wait, wait. You did what?"

Gloria gives me a look like I might be stupid for not grasping what she's telling me.

"I dislocated my knee and ripped just a few ligaments." She has two crutches wedged under her arms but manages to a gesture down to her leg that's wrapped in some kind of brace from mid-calf to mid-thigh that's not allowing her leg to bend.

"And how did you do it?" I rub the bridge of my nose hard enough that I can see colors burst behind my eyelids.

She lets out a belabored sigh like she's explaining something to a child. "My gentleman friend, Arty over there," she lifts the crutch in her right hand and waves it in the air to the car idling at the curb with an older gentleman behind the wheel. "Well, he and I were having a bit of an early afternoon delight and Dorothy at the club told us about this new position where you stretch—"

I hold up my hands ready to beg her to stop. I never should have asked. "And you and this Arty are going to take Oliver to your place to watch him tonight?"

"As usual," she says with a smile. I look for Oliver and find him sitting on the porch drawing away in his sketchpad. When she asked me to come outside instead of coming to the door, I should have known something was wrong. I'm shocked she could even get out

101

of the car with that thing, let alone traverse my walkway and the two stairs up to the porch.

I glance back at Artie again who appears to be happily fiddling with the radio in a Chrysler that looks more like a small boat than a car. The man looks old as dirt and can barely see over the steering wheel. I'm not sure I want Oliver *or* Gloria riding with him. Maybe I should ding his license so he has to go back to the DMV and update those tests.

"There's no way, Gloria. You can't be running around after a five-year-old. I'm sure you're in a ton of pain too."

"It's really not bad, Carson." The only tell that lets me know she's lying is that she won't quite meet my eyes. They're pinned to the tip of my nose. She's good, remind me not to play poker with her.

"It's totally fine. Accidents happen. I can call the sitter and see if she can make it last minute." My voice doesn't sound convincing even to my own ears. The only sitter I've found here so far is a senior in high school who I'm pretty sure looks at her phone more than she does my kid.

"That's really not necessary," Gloria weakly argues while I hold the phone to my ear, listening to it ring twice and go to voicemail. Shit.

The strain of standing out here on the sidewalk is starting to show on Gloria's face. I knew she was in more pain than she was letting on. "C'mon. Let's get you back in the car. I'll just call out tonight. It's not a big deal." It's totally going to be a big deal. I just started. I probably only have a few hours of PTO banked. She weakly protests as I help maneuver her, crutches and all, slowly towards the car.

"Bianca can watch me!" Both mine and Gloria's heads snap to Oliver who is pointing to something behind us. If only the Olympics gave out medals for synchronized whiplash.

What I see has me raising an eyebrow in amusement. Apparently, Oliver's yell exposed Bianca trying to sneak past us. She looks like a cartoon burglar taking comically big tip-toe steps and then freezes once they're spotted. Her eyes are wide and she's frozen mid-step, foot floating in the air, ready to move forward. I wonder how long she can hold that pose because she starts to teeter.

Oliver shoots across the grass and latches onto her leg almost sending her crashing to the ground. "Oliver, be careful," I scold. Gloria turns to me with a knowing smile on her face and mischief in her eyes.

"And who is this?" Gloria asks loud enough for her to hear. Bianca glances at the front door of her house and I know she's wondering if she can make a run for it. I guess she decides she won't make it since her head shakes and she makes a slow march over to where we're standing, like she's a condemned man on his way to the guillotine.

"You can watch me tonight, right Bianca?"

"Oh...uh..."

Gloria puts her out of her misery by changing the subject. "Hello, dear. I'm Gloria Edwards and it appears you already know my Great Nephew Carson and my Great-Great Nephew Oliver."

"Bianca Moreno, uh, neighbor to both those guys. It's lovely to meet you." Since Gloria's hands are occupied with clutching on to her crutches for dear life, she doesn't put out her hand for a shake. It hasn't escaped my notice that she hasn't spared me a glance this entire time, and it's making me feel anxious.

"It appears we're in a bit of a pickle, Bianca. Carson is supposed to work tonight and I usually watch Oliver, but I dislocated my knee earlier today and I'm afraid I won't be able to do it today."

"Oh no, what happened?" She asks.

Before I have a chance to stop Gloria or just flat out lie, she's already answering. "A bit of a misadventure with a sexual escapade. You know how that Kama Sutra book can be." She lets out a *tsk* and shakes her head.

Bianca's eyes widen so much I'm expecting her to hoot like an owl right before she bursts out laughing. "Of course. I've only ever tried a few but the difficulty level can be up there. I'm glad your knee was the only casualty." My mind immediately latches on to Bianca working her way through the Kama Sutra, and I get that feeling of irrational jealousy again. It doesn't stop until I picture us wrapped around each other in one of those poses.

"Oh good, you're not stuck up. I like her, Carson," she says to me in a stage whisper that Bianca can absolutely hear. I'm starting to get a headache as they both go back to ignoring me. "I'll let you borrow my book dear. I've gone through and made several notations in the margins. There are quite a few you can indulge in without risk of injury, just stay away from The Lustful Leg unless you have very limber knees."

Fuck. Me. Sideways. Would it be rude to throw a seventy-year-old disabled woman into a car and send it on its way?

Oliver is still clutching tightly at Bianca's leg and I really hope he can't decipher this conversation.

"What's a comma soodra?" I toss my hands up in the air. Well, there goes that. This day is getting completely away from me.

"We'll talk about it later," I tell him, hoping that the five-year-old attention span will work in my favor and he'll completely forget about it. "Now let's head inside and call Uncle Rafe and let him know I'm going to stay home with you tonight."

"But Dad, I thought Bianca was going to watch me." Both Bianca and Gloria are looking at me questioningly when they hear Oliver call me Dad. I'm not going to lie, it gives me warm fuzzy feelings just hearing it.

"It's new. I'll tell you about it later," I let them know. "Oliver, Bianca can't babysit you. That's not what she does."

"But why not?" He's going full on pout now and I know he's getting close to shutting down.

"Yeah, why not?" Bianca's voice sounds annoyed as hell and when I look over at her she's got her arms crossed defiantly over her chest while her heeled shoe is tapping impatiently.

"Well, I just thought it wasn't your thing. You don't seem like the type." How can I explain delicately that she always looks a little terrified whenever Oliver's around and she treats him like an ugly as hell porcelain figurine that she could shatter at any moment?

"Really? And what type is that?" She's got that look in her eyes again. I almost want to smile, but I'm worried she might stab me in the eye with a high heel if I do. I take another glance down at her shoes. At least these look a little shorter.

"The type that doesn't really know what to do with kids?" She asks, raising her head and stiffening her spine. Apparently I'm pushing her buttons and I'm not even trying. I'm attempting to get her out of this for crying out loud. She turns away from me and bends down as best she can in her tight skirt so she's almost at Oliver's height.

Don't look at her ass. Don't look at her ass. Shit, I looked at it. And now I'm remembering how it felt in my hands. I shift uncomfortably from side to side since I'm now sporting a half chub in my pants.

"Oliver, I will absolutely watch you tonight."

My eyes go wide, and my mouth drops open. I'm pretty sure Bianca isn't a kid person, so babysitting is likely the last thing she wants to do with her evening. Besides, do I even want to leave my kid alone with someone I don't really know and whose experience is in question?

I'm between a rock and a hard place here. I really need to work tonight. And just because Bianca may not hang out with kids that often doesn't mean she can't keep him alive for a few hours while I work. Hell, I didn't know the first thing about children, and I've kept Oliver alive this long.

"I won't be home until really late, at least two. I'm sure you have work in the morning."

"Two is fine," she clips out while staring at me.

"Okaaay."

"What time do you need me?" I smile and I'm about to make some cheesy innuendo about needing her all the time but before I can she catches herself. Her cheeks turn just slightly pink and she stutters. "W-what time do I have to be over here?"

I check my watch, cursing how time is slipping away from me. "In about an hour?"

"Sounds great, see you then."

She turns back towards her own home, but before she can take a step Oliver asks, "Can we draw Bianca?"

In a blink of an eye the stone-cold face she was showing me melts away into a brilliant smile and she tussles the hair on top of his head awkwardly. Why am I suddenly jealous of a five-year-old?

"Of course we can, kid. I'll see you soon." She then turns her attention to my aunt. "It was nice to meet you Gloria, you have a lovely great-great nephew."

"Thank you! It was wonderful to meet you as well." It doesn't escape my notice that she left me out of that compliment.

She turns her head to give me a glare that would have a lesser man shaking in his boots. Maybe I should have let her come last night. Next thing I know, her front door is slamming and Gloria is tugging on my arm. I'm surprised because I almost forgot she was standing there with everything going on.

"She's spunky. I like her."

"Yeah, me too."

Chapter Nine

Bianca

"Don't forget to find out how old he is!" Violet calls out before closing the door behind me. I carefully make my way down the two porch steps while keeping a firm grip on the stack of art supplies clutched in my arms. I may not know anything about babysitting, but I figure there's got to be at least a few things in this heap that will entertain Oliver until his Unc—Dad now I guess, gets home.

I shouldn't have let Carson goad me into this. In fact, I should be staying far, far away from him. I even had plans tonight! I was going to have dinner with Mom and Dad but since I agreed to watch Oliver, I had to cancel.

It's probably for the best. Yes, I'm trying to facilitate the rekindling of their connection but I don't think Dad is into it. Most of the reason I even tried to set them up, besides Mom pushing for it, was because he seems so lonely. I don't want him to be alone and I thought that if they loved each other once, maybe they could do it again.

It's probably best that I had to cancel, though I feel bad about doing it at the last minute. But once Carson started acting like he didn't want me to watch Oliver and that I was out of my depth, saying I'd do it was a knee jerk reaction. I don't know what it is about him that drives me so crazy. If anybody else had said I wasn't cut out for babysitting, I would have laughed and agreed with them. There's something about him that just makes me want to put him in his place, especially after he left me so sexually frustrated last night.

At least Oliver is a pretty cool kid. I don't think it'll be too bad to spend a couple hours with him. Who knows, maybe I'll start to like kids after this.

Yeah, it doesn't sound convincing to me either.

I manage to shift all the supplies over to one arm so I have a free hand to knock on the door. They're tilting precariously, so I manage a quick knock before redistributing the weight. Carson opens the door and takes in the pile of art supplies I'm carrying. "Did you leave anything at home?"

"Here, help," I say, ignoring his question and shoving the pile into his stomach. He carries them much more easily than I did and moves them to the kitchen table. I walk inside and close the door behind me, taking a moment to look around. The first thing that strikes me is how clean and organized it is. It looks like there's a place for everything and everything's in its place. I wander over to the mantle of the fireplace where there are pictures lined up way too evenly to be by accident. I smile to myself imagining Carson standing here with a ruler making sure each picture is placed just-so.

There's a photo of a teenage Carson with an older couple and a young girl, I figure that must be his parents and his sister. There seems to be a gap in time between the teenage Carson photos and more recent ones. There are plenty of pictures of Oliver either on his own or with Carson and Gloria. In every photo he looks about the same age he is now which I find curious. Shouldn't he have pictures of him from when he was a baby or a toddler or something? For the first time, I wonder how long he's been with Carson.

His bookshelf seems to be organized by color instead of by author or even genre which, as an artist, I find aesthetically exciting, but I know if Violet saw this she would have a heart attack. What would happen if I took just one book and moved it? Would he notice? Would it drive him insane?

"Why are you staring at my bookcase with an evil look in your eye?"

I quickly turn back to him and give a shrug. "I don't know what you're talking about." I join him in the kitchen where he's jotting something down on a pad of paper. "You really don't have to do this, Bianca. It isn't your responsibility."

I wave my hand at him dismissively. "It's not a big deal, I didn't have any plans for the evening," I lie smoothly. He's searching my face like he's trying to find my lie, but I keep my face perfectly impassive. "So, what are you writing?"

He shakes his head like he's trying to clear it of whatever he was thinking. "I haven't had a chance to feed Oliver dinner. I've left the name of the restaurant along with his order. Pick something for yourself too."

I give an appreciative smile. Since I had been planning on eating with my parents, I hadn't had a big lunch and now I'm feeling just short of ravenous.

"I also have a list of emergency numbers that I'll text you so you can have them in your phone."

"Everything is going to be fine Carson, I can watch him for a few hours without some kind of major disaster," I say with a bit of hurt in my voice that I'm not able to disguise.

"I know, Bianca, really. It's just that when I'm on the job I can't always get to my phone and you might have questions. It's just the numbers for Gloria, my desk at the station, and the number for dispatch. If it's a real emergency, you can contact them and have them get me over the radio."

"It'll be fine, I promise. We're just going to have some dinner, do some drawing or painting or whatever he wants. Maybe watch some TV. You know the usual." At least I think that's the usual for babysitting. At least that's what The Babysitter's Club had me believe.

He chews on his lip a little which I've never seen him do before. I'm sure it's a nerves thing, but it immediately sends me back to the alley last night when he nibbled on my own lip and suddenly an ache appears between my thighs while my nipples harden into stiff points. Thank God I changed into a thick knit sweater so he can't see them through my top. It hasn't escaped my notice that we're both doing our best to avoid talking about what happened which is fine by me.

He's nodding his head while distractedly gathering the things he needs for work. "That sounds good, he'll love that. Just make sure he's in bed before nine. He knows his bedtime routine so just have him start it at eight thirty and it should be fine."

"No problem, we can do that."

Oliver comes rushing into the room, toy truck in hand and yells "Bianca!" before latching himself onto my leg. I can't help but laugh. If I could get another kid to grab onto the other one, walking around would be a great workout. If I was into that kind of thing.

"Oliver, what do you say to Bianca?"

"Thank you for watching me tonight."

I give him a smile, he really is cute. "Of course. We're going to have fun. Look what I brought." I gesture to the pile of things on the table and his eyes go wide.

He immediately moves over to it, trying to pull out a tube of paint. "Buddy, you need to wait until after dinner, alright? Bianca is going to order for you guys and it should be here soon." His little face turns into a pout but he nods and goes into the living room, sitting down with his truck.

Carson turns his attention back to me and for the first time I notice he looks a little stressed. There are circles under his eyes and the smattering of lines he has in the corners seem more pronounced today. "I'm sorry I'm not going to be home until late. I plan on getting here at around two a.m. but you never know, that can always change. Feel free to sleep on the couch, I left a blanket on it for you.

You're also more than welcome to sleep in my bed. The sheets are clean and everything so it's ready for you."

Even though the thought of lying in Carson's bed makes my stomach do little flip-flops and my heart race, I think it'd be best to stay away from anything that has to do with his bedroom. "The couch will be fine, thanks."

He absentmindedly moves to the front door where there's a little safe sitting on the entry table I didn't notice before. After punching in a series of numbers, it opens with a click and he pulls out a big shiny black gun, handcuffs, and a badge. He swiftly attaches everything to his belt. Cop Carson is hot. My mind drifts to all the things we could do with those cuffs before I can stop myself.

Bad Bianca. We are not interested in that type of thing.

He's about to leave but stops and turns back to me. "Just please make sure all the doors and windows are locked the entire time, and don't let him play in the backyard. That's all I ask tonight."

It looks like someone is being a little overprotective but then I remember Oliver and his watch/tracking device and how he schooled me about the dangers out there for kids and understand where he's coming from. "Okay, no problem. I'll lock this place down like Fort Knox."

Kissing Oliver on the head he heads out the front door with a "Thanks again, Bianca," but I just wave away his thanks and tell him to have a good night at work.

Once the door closes behind him I go over and lock the bottom as well as the deadbolt. Then it's just Oliver and me. Staring at each other. "Soo..." I have no idea what I'm supposed to be doing right now. Then I remember Carson said to order dinner.

"Should we get something to eat?"

"Sure."

"Okay, let's see what he's written down here." I scan the paper and the restaurant he says to order from is one I've never heard of before. "Do you like burritos? Because that's what he says is for you."

I'm surprised when Oliver doesn't look enthusiastic about the prospect of a burrito. "They're alright, I guess," he says while fidgeting and looking down at his feet.

Hmm. I pull up the menu for the restaurant on my phone. "Let me check what burritos they have. It looks like there's only one and it's made with a dehydrated green pea tortilla, cultured beans, and macadamia cheese? What the hell is macadamia cheese? You guys eat this?" Okay that sounds disgusting. No wonder he doesn't seem enthused about dinner.

"I don't know, the ones Dad get taste weird. They're not like the ones Mom gave me." I'm not going to touch the mom issue with a ten-foot pole, especially since I don't know what happened to her. I turn back to my phone, scanning the entire menu this time and don't see anything I'm even tempted to try. There's just no way. If I won't eat this crap, I'm certainly not making Oliver eat it.

"I'll tell you what, if you can keep a secret, I'll order us a pepperoni pizza. How does that sound?"

He eyes me like maybe I'm trying to trick him. "With cauliflower crust?"

I can't help but blanch at the thought of ruining my pizza with cauliflower. "No way, regular carb-filled bread crust for us."

He gives me a wide toothy grin that I return. It only takes me a couple minutes to order from the place down the street. "What should we do while we wait?

"Can we play with the stuff you brought?"

"Come over here, let me show you." We sit at the kitchen table and slowly sort through the pastels, charcoal pencils, paints, and anything else I could grab from home.

"What's that?" Oliver asks while reaching for a medium-sized tub with a handle.

"That's modeling clay. You can use it to make stuff and once it dries it hardens and you can keep it. Do you want me to show you how it works?" He gives me an exaggerated nod and a smile. I pop open the container of clay and pull out a sizcable chunk for each of us. I show him simple stuff like how he can roll out a snake or turn it into a ball and he loves it. He tells me about all the things he wants to make, and I let him have at it.

Eventually the pizza arrives, and we move the clay to the side so we can stuff our faces. Even though he asks for a soda, I get him some milk because even I know you probably shouldn't give a child caffeine or sugar before bedtime. Oliver is a relatively calm kid but if I had to chase him around all night while he was on a sugar high I might lose it.

"Oh, Oliver. My roommate, Violet, wants to know how old you are." I tell him while taking another bite of pizza.

"What's a roommate?"

"They're people who live with me. I have *two* roommates."

"I have one too! Dad's my roommate. Who are yours?"

"Violet and Hollie. They're my best friends."

"That's cool. I don't have a best friend."

"Well, you're pretty new here, I'm sure you'll get one." He just shrugs at me and picks the pepperoni off the piece of pizza on his plate. He seems a little upset, so I try to steer the conversation back to safer topics. "You didn't tell me how old you are."

"Five," he says, holding up a greasy hand with all five fingers spread wide for me. "How old are you?"

"I'm twenty-two."

"Wow, that's old." He says it like this is a grave concern for him and I can't help but laugh, especially since his Dad has to be ten years older than me.

"You think that's old? Well, I'll tell you a secret. I'm going to be twenty-three on Saturday."

Oliver's eyes get impossibly big like he just can't believe it and that causes my smile to widen. In fact, I've been doing a lot of smiling with him tonight. "Are you going to have a party?" he asks.

"I sure am."

"Can I come?"

"It's actually going to be a super boring grown up party. There'll be lots of adults and won't even be any kids to play with. Sounds boring, doesn't it?" I don't want him to think that he's missing out on something and there's no way I can actually invite him. I have a feeling that even though Dad is letting me throw it at his house, it's going to be a booze fueled mess of epic proportions.

"If it's a grown-up party, are you going to invite my Dad?"

There's no way in hell I'm inviting Carson for several reasons. The first being, if he didn't like how I handled myself last night I can only imagine how he would flip out if he saw me drunk off my ass, which I very much plan on being. The second reason is that I don't want him around my friends. Specifically, the female ones. Some of those girls are sharks. One look at the blond-haired, green eyed, toned dream boat and they would be all over him. It's not that I'm jealous, I'm just looking out for him.

Shut up, it's true. Kind of.

"I think he's probably working, but I'll check with him," I say to appease him. Gathering up our plates I carry them to the sink. I look at the box with the leftover pizza and briefly consider hiding it so Carson thinks he got that disgusting pea and macadamia burrito.

Fuck it. I grab the whole thing and shove it into the fridge. If he's hungry when he gets home at there will be leftovers for him. Checking my phone, I realize there's at least another hour until Oliver has to start his bedtime routine. "So, what do you want to do now?" I ask, hoping he has some idea.

"Can we watch a movie?"

"Sure." A movie I can do. Sitting and relaxing sounds like a great idea. This is a kid after my own heart. "Do you know what you want to watch?"

"Ratooey." What the fuck is Ratooey? It's not like I'm up to date on the latest kid movies.

"Okay, Ratooey it is. Why don't you sit on the couch, and I'll pull up the movie." I don't see any DVDs lined up on the entertainment unit underneath the large television, so I assume he streams everything. I flick on the TV and stand in front of it, looking at all the different streaming services Carson subscribes to. "If I were a kids' movie where would I be?" I mutter under my breath. I start flipping through Netflix, but when I finally find the kids' section, I can't find anything called Ratooey.

"Bianca! Bianca! Bianca!" I glance back and see him jumping on the couch.

"Oliver, just give me a second to find the movie, okay? Please don't jump on the couch." He plops down on his butt, and I go back to scanning the movies. It looks like Netflix is a bust so I move on to the next one.

"Did you find it, Bianca?"

"Not yet."

It doesn't even take twenty seconds before he's on me again. "Did you find it now?"

I take a deep breath. "Not yet, Oliver." I try to not let the irritation seep into my voice but I'm not sure I'm doing a good job of it. *Where the fuck is this movie?*

"Maybe we should watch something else."

"No! I wanna watch Ratooey!"

I let out a full-on sigh of frustration and move to the next streaming service. Why the hell are there so many of these things?

When I feel something hit my calf, I ignore it until there is another small push against my leg. There are two toy cars laying on the floor next to me. I close my eyes for a second, trying to keep my cool. I think I've gotten myself under control until I hear him call out "Bianca! Bianca! Bianca!"

"Oliver! Cut it out. I'm trying to find the movie *you* want to watch. You need to be patient so I can find this stupid thing." Immediately, I know I fucked up. Oliver's bottom lip trembles, and his eyes fill with tears. I drop the remote from my hands and reach for him but I'm not fast enough.

"Oliver, wait..." but he runs right past me down the hall where I can hear a door slam.

Shit. Shit. Shit.

I knew I wasn't cut out for this and now I've hurt his feelings. Maybe I should call Violet over so she can fix this, she offered to help if I needed anything. I pull out my phone and am about to call her when I decide I made this mess so I'm the one that needs to clean it up.

I genuinely feel awful. He was just being so impatient he got on my nerves, but that's not his fault, he's a kid. I can't expect him to act like a little adult and sit there quietly for ten minutes while I mess with the television, can I?

I head through the hallway to the rear of the house. The first door I open looks like it's some kind of playroom for him. There are plenty of toys—all put away far too neatly for a five-year-old, but there's no bed, and definitely no Oliver. The bathroom across the hall is also empty. The only two doors left are the one at the end of the hallway that I assume belongs to Carson and one to my left that's closed.

I knock on the closed door and gently call out, "Oliver?" He doesn't answer but I can hear him sniffling inside. This might be the first time I actually feel my heart break a little. How on earth did this child become so important to me, more than I ever thought one could, in such a short amount of time? I'm more determined than ever to fix this. "Oliver, I'm coming in." I warn him.

I slowly push the door open, and it takes me a few seconds to see him huddled into a ball in the corner, facing the wall. If I thought I felt awful before, I was wrong. This is much worse.

"I'm really sorry, Oliver." He just goes on ignoring me, sniffling every once in a while. I'm not sure what to say or do but I know I'm not leaving this room until I fix this. Taking a seat cross-legged on the floor I ask, "Can we talk for a few minutes? I promise I won't say anything mean."

He turns his little body towards me, and I see tears streaking down his cheeks and my own eyes fill with moisture. "Can I tell you something about me?" He nods in answer, not meeting my eyes and since that's as good as I'm going to get right now, I soldier on. "I'm not good with kids. In fact, I don't even know any. You're the only friend I have that's a kid."

"You're my friend?" He asks hesitantly, finally looks up at me.

"Of course I am. At least, I hope you'll still be my friend." He looks away again and I let out a sigh. "Since I don't know any kids, I don't always know what to say or do. I'm not good at this. I shouldn't have spoken to you like that. You didn't do anything wrong."

"I didn't?"

"Of course not, Oliver. I was the one who did something wrong. Hanging out with someone your age is all new to me and I'm not always going to know what to say or how to act. I've never even met a kid I liked before, but you're really cool and I would be so sad if you didn't want to be my friend anymore."

"You think I'm cool?" There's a little hopeful tone in his voice that makes me think I might be getting through to him.

"Are you kidding me? You're the coolest! Do you think we can still be friends?"

He uses his little fist and wipes the tears off his face. "Yeah, we can be friends."

"Good. And since you're my friend do you think you can be patient with me sometimes? I might do or say the wrong thing, but I'm trying to learn. If I mess up, will you tell me? You're smart and the only one that can help me with this, and I really do need the help, don't I?"

He nods his head looking solemn. "Yeah, you do."

I suppress a laugh. "Do you think I can have a hug?" He crawls straight into my lap, wrapping his arms around my neck. I squeeze him tightly and talk into his hair that smells like baby shampoo, "I'm so sorry. I was scared you'd never forgive me."

"I forgive you. Sometimes grown-ups mess up. That's what Dad tells me."

"Well, it sounds like your dad is very smart," I say begrudgingly. I guess there's no harm complimenting Carson when he can't hear me. "Now how about we go into the living room, and you help me find that movie you want to watch?"

"Can I sit in your lap?"

"I would totally be disappointed if you didn't."

Once we get back to the abandoned television, I sit on the couch and hand Oliver the remote. He finds the movie it took me ten minutes *not* to find in fifteen seconds flat. In my defense, apparently he was saying *Ratatouille* not *Ratooey*. But who am I to give him a hard time? I still can't say Worcestershire.

We start the movie, and he climbs into my lap, resting his head against my chest and I feel surprisingly content. I'm usually itching to do something, go out and party, paint, drink with my girlfriends. I fill my life with a lot of things but there's nothing I'd rather do right now than hold this little boy on my lap and watch this silly movie. It's a strange, but not entirely unwelcome feeling.

Within twenty minutes, Oliver's breathing has evened out, and he's fast asleep. I slowly pick him up, careful not to wake him, and carry him into his bedroom, placing him on the bed and covering him with his blanket. I straighten up to walk out but as an after-thought bend down and plant a quick kiss on his forehead.

I know we didn't do his bedtime routine like Carson wanted but he's just going to have to deal with it. I already made that little boy cry tonight, I'm not going to stand over him and demand he brush his teeth. Besides, I'm the friend, not the parent. That's Carson's problem.

Once I'm back in the living room, I give a little chuckle and rush over to the perfectly color coordinated bookcase. I grab a book from the second shelf that's navy blue and quickly switch it with a book with a yellow spine closer to the bottom. I couldn't help it, it's just too damn organized, and Carson could use a little chaos in his life. How long will it take him to notice?

I dim the living room lights and let the movie keep playing while I kick off my shoes and stretch out on the couch. It's not exactly comfortable laying here fully dressed in jeans. For a brief second, I consider laying down in Carson's bed but decide that would be playing with fire. I don't know how I feel about sleeping with someone who lives next door to me. Not being able to ghost him after our time is up seems like a bad idea. Plus, once Carson and I ended our little hook-up situation I wouldn't be able to see Oliver again and I don't know if I'm okay with that. I didn't lie to the kid. I really do like him and consider him my friend.

I pull down the soft blanket that's laying across the back of the couch and spread it over me. It's only ten so I should be able to catch a few hours of sleep before Carson gets home which is good since Carson was right, I actually do have to work in the morning. I toss and turn a bit but the couch is comfortable, and it isn't long before I fall fast asleep.

Chapter Ten

Carson

It's been an extremely long evening, especially knowing that I'd be going home not only to Oliver, but to Bianca as well. That was an unexpected benefit of having her watch him.

I told Rafe about the notes I've been getting and showed them to him. He agreed they aren't something we should just ignore since the second one has crossed the line into threatening. He was able to get in touch with a friend in the forensics department who is going to run any prints they can lift off the paper. I can only hope whoever it is has committed a crime before and is in the system. I still need to call and get that alarm system installed.

I pull into the driveway and see that the house is completely dark which doesn't surprise me since it's after two a.m. Both Oliver and Bianca should be fast asleep at this point. I'm a little disappointed because I would have loved to spend some time with her but she probably has work in the morning.

Closing and locking the door behind me, I divest myself of my gun, badge, and cuffs, locking them away in the safe next to the door. I take about two seconds to home in on the sleeping form of Bianca lying on the couch.

I slowly move closer, careful not to wake her up. Bianca is gorgeous when she's awake but shit, there's something about her when she's sleeping. She's stunning. Her features are softened and there's a vulnerability to her she hides when she's conscious. She's snuggled under the blanket I left out for her. It's one that usually sits on the end of my bed, and I know I won't be washing it anytime soon. Her chest is rising and falling in the gentle pattern of her breathing, and I have to suppress a laugh when she lets out a rather unladylike snore. Somehow that makes this picture even better.

I take another few moments to study the dark lashes that rest against her cheeks, the delicate shape of her neck that's peeking out from under the blanket, and her full lips that are slightly parted as she breathes. I do my best not to think about how those lips felt against mine last night. I guess I better wake her up before she finds me standing here, staring at her like some kind of weirdo. Though that's exactly what I'm doing.

"Bianca," I call softly as I crouch down in front of her sleeping form. She doesn't move an inch so I call her name again, a little louder. This time she gives out a combination of a snort and snore, stirring slightly beneath the blanket but doesn't wake up. A piece of chocolate colored hair has fallen forward over her eyes, obscuring her face. I gently tuck the piece of hair behind her ear and say her name again.

With a gasp she bolts upright before I can move back and knocks me onto my ass. She's clutching her chest and breathing hard, eyes darting around the room. "It's just me, Bianca."

"Jesus Christ, Carson. You scared the shit out of me," she says before slapping my shoulder.

"I can see that." I raise up off the ground and offer her a hand. She eyes it for a second like she's considering rejecting the simple offer to help her up, but grabs it and lets me pull her to her feet. "Did everything go okay tonight?"

"Yeah it was fine," she says with a yawn, rubbing the sleep from her eyes and looking downright adorable. Now I know I'm in trouble. "What time is it?"

"Just after two. I got home as soon as I could, sorry."

"Don't worry about it, at least I was able to catch some sleep on the couch." I walk her towards the front door, sorry to see her go, but knowing that she needs to go home and get some more sleep if she's going to function in the morning. That's when I spy the tiny pieces of clay on the table.

"What is this?" I ask, picking up something that looks like a rotund ball with four appendages sticking out of it at all angles and something resembling a rectangle squished on top.

She gives me a wide smile. "I'm very sorry to inform you that Oliver is not quite the artistic genius we once thought. He can't work clay for shit."

"What is this supposed to be anyway?"

"It's a giraffe. Duh." Her voice is completely serious like I should absolutely recognize this lump as the majestic animal. I look at her and can see the amusement sparkling in her eyes.

"If it's a giraffe, then where's its neck?"

"Maybe you should take him to the zoo."

I can't help but laugh at that. In fact, I think I've laughed more in the past few weeks since I've known Bianca than I have for years. "I haven't gotten a chance to thank you for the art class recommendation. I was able to get him into the program over at Branson. In fact, his first class is this weekend."

She claps her hands together in excitement. "Really? That's great! He's going to love it. Just keep him far away from the clay. Very far." She gives me a wink and a smile.

"Well, it's all thanks to you. I spoke to Roxy like you suggested and she said they had a wait list a mile long but since you're the one that sent Oliver to them, they found a spot for him. It seems like you have a lot of pull around there."

She brushes the compliment aside. "Nah, it's just that I recently graduated so I still know a lot of people there."

"Well, she seemed a little shocked you were recommending a kid. She seemed to imply that's the last thing you would ever do."

She just gives me a shrug like it's no big deal. "I'm not really a kid person. They just aren't for me. They tend to get on my nerves more than anything. That's one of the reason's I never helped out with that program. It's only for young artists. I work much better with adults."

"Well, you seem pretty good with Oliver. I can't thank you enough for helping get him in. He's beyond excited, it's the only thing he's talked about for days."

"Like I said, it's no big deal." I can tell she's uncomfortable with the topic of children as she quickly shifts gears. "Oh, there's some pizza in the fridge if you want some." She lets me know while hunting for her purse.

"Pizza?" I raise my eyebrow at her. That definitely wasn't what I'd told her to get for Oliver's dinner.

"Oh, don't look at me like that. There was no way I was going to eat something made with a pea tortilla and macadamia cheese and I wasn't subjecting that sweet child to it either. I mean, really, Carson? *Macadamia Cheese* that's an affront to the cheese gods. It's got to at least be a crime of some sort."

"So, you're saying you're a bit of a cheese lover?"

"You should see my fridge, I'm pretty sure there's more cheese in there than anything else, except maybe wine. The point is, I couldn't in good conscience feed that to him."

"Yeah, I hate that shit too," I admit to her. "But it's what all the books say he should be eating to make sure he grows up healthy."

"Yeah, but are those books concerned about his quality of life? Because carbs and real cheese are some of the things that make life worth living."

I let out a chuckle and prop my hip against the kitchen counter, leisurely observing Bianca standing here in my kitchen in tight jeans, a fluffy sweater that's falling off her shoulder, and hair that's tangled from sleep. I like her here. She feels like she belongs. "I'm doing the best I can, but one book contradicts another and another until my head is spinning."

I can see her face soften and she looks like she's contemplating whether she should bring something up. "Go ahead, I see you have something you want to say," I encourage her.

She's fidgeting a little, shifting her weight from one foot to the other. "I was just wondering how long you've had Oliver. He told me his mom was dead and that he didn't have a dad. How did he end up with you?" Sighing, I rub my hand through my hair. "You don't have to tell me, it's really none of my business. I'm sorry I asked," she quickly adds.

She heads out of the kitchen, but I stop her by placing my hand on her arm. She stills immediately and a little shiver of awareness goes through her that gives my male ego a tiny boost. I like that she's not immune to my touch. "No, I want to tell you." Well, I want to tell her the sanitized version, anyway. She doesn't need to hear about the really bad stuff.

"Oliver was my sister's son. She died about six months ago and we don't have any other family. My dad died when I was a teenager, he was a cop and was killed on the job. My mom never really recovered from his death, and it wasn't too long until she followed him so it was just Molly and me. But she was so young when everything happened and so lost that she spun out of control. I should have been there for her, but I was caught up in my own grief and getting into the LAPD. I didn't do enough."

"That's not your fault, Carson." She walks up to me and gently squeezes my hand. Just her touch gives me the strength to say the rest of it. "That's nice of you to say, but I know I should have done a better job. She got into drugs, dropped out of high school, and the next thing I know she'd disappeared. I tried to find her, I really did. I even used my connections in the department, it was against the rules, but I didn't care. Once those had dried up, I hired a private investigator but he couldn't find anything either. She had completely fallen off the map."

I suck in a breath when Bianca wraps her arms around my middle and holds me close. This might be the first non-sexual, physical touch she's initiated between us. I can't help myself and raise my hand, running my fingers through her thick, lush locks. "It got really bad," I whisper against the top of her head. I don't enjoy talking about this but saying it quietly in the dim light of the night while in her arms seems to give me strength. "I worked a lot of gang and drug cases down in Los Angeles. Every time I walked into one of their trap houses or crack dens, I searched every face looking for her. You'll never understand the competing emotions of both hoping and dreading finding her there.

"Then one day I got a phone call from up in Bakersfield, which is a shit town in the middle of nowhere. Molly died of an overdose. It took them a few days to notify me because they couldn't find any next of kin. That's how I got Oliver. I didn't even realize he existed until then. She didn't even bother to tell me I had a nephew."

"It sounds like she was going through a lot of stuff, I'm sure it didn't have anything to do with you. I bet if she could see how well you're taking care of him she would be so thankful. It's clear he loves you."

"You think so?" I ask quietly. Apparently, all my doubts and insecurities are coming out tonight.

"Absolutely, I could have never done for him what you have. I don't know the first thing about kids and frankly, they aren't exactly my favorite thing."

I can't help but smile at that. "Yeah, I was getting that impression. You don't seem like a kid person."

"I'm definitely not."

"Oliver seems to have taken to you though."

"I guess there's no accounting for taste."

"Nah, he can sense you have a big heart."

125

It seems like this line of conversation is making her uncomfortable, so she switches the subject. "So, what's up with him calling you Dad now?"

I groan, thinking about the uncomfortable conversation I had with his teacher earlier. "He told me this morning that a couple of kids were picking on him because he didn't have any parents. They said they left him because he was bad."

Bianca lets out a gasp and pulls away from me just enough so she can look into my eyes. "Why would they say something like that?"

"Who knows? I'm learning kids can be unbearably cruel for no reason."

There's genuine anger in her eyes when she says, "Why don't you slip me their names? I'll make sure they never bother him again. I've already threatened to kill and bury the biggest hotel mogul in Seattle, what do you think I'd do to a bunch of asshole five-year-olds?"

"You told Archer Clarke you would murder him and dispose of his body?"

She just shrugs like it's no big deal. "He hurt Hollie. I take care of the people that belong to me."

"As a member of law enforcement, I really shouldn't hear about your plans for murder."

"Eh, I'll be okay, I've got a hook-up at the police department now." I just shake my head. Bianca's a little crazy. Apparently, I'm into that now.

"You don't need to worry about the boys, I spoke to his teacher and told Oliver to let me know if they bother him again. That's when he said he didn't have a dad and asked if I would be his."

She's quiet for a beat before she speaks again. "That's really sweet. It's obvious how much he loves you. Do you know where his real dad is?

I shake my head. "No clue, there was nothing on his birth certificate. I'm assuming it was either her dealer or her pimp. No one stepped forward when I was petitioning the court for custody and

Oliver said he's never met him. So, if he wants me to be his dad and to call me that, I'm happy I can be that for him."

The lights are low in the kitchen, but I can still see her smile tilted up at me while my arms remain around her. "You love it, and you deserve it. Like I said, I don't know anything about kids, nor do I really care to, but Oliver is something special."

"Yeah, he is." I'm looking down into Bianca's upturned face and I don't want to talk about Oliver anymore. I'd much rather talk about us. Or better yet, do no talking at all.

"Do you have some time to hang out tonight?" I ask like it's not two thirty in the morning.

"I think I could move some things around and make time for you." Her rich brown eyes are a shade or two darker than they were just moments ago, and her breathing is picking up slightly. "What do you think we should do?"

"How about a tour of my bedroom?" My voice is deep and husky, I know there's no way she can miss the need that's seeping out of it. She's looking a little hesitant and I'm hoping I haven't pushed her too hard too fast. Her silence has me nervous she's going to bolt.

"I don't know, are you going to let me come this time?" I can't help the smirk that comes to my lips just thinking about our moment together last night. Now I'm hard as a rock.

"Since you were so good at helping me out tonight. You'll definitely be coming. The only questions are how many times and how hard."

CHAPTER ELEVEN

CARSON

"That's some big talk, Detective. You think you can live up to it?"

Instead of answering I place my hand under her chin and tilt her head up while I lean down and press my lips firmly against hers. I can feel the warm sensation spread out to the rest of my body and it's only a few moments before I'm deepening the kiss, my tongue slipping into her mouth to tease and play with hers.

Bianca's arms have snaked around my neck and she's up on her tiptoes, pressing her body into me. There are definitely too many clothes in between us. I reach behind her, grab those thick thighs I've been dreaming about, and lift her up while she instinctively wraps her legs around my waist, settling there.

I wrench my mouth away from hers and snap, "Sweater," at her with no instructions. Luckily she gets my meaning and pulls her sweater over her head before tossing it to the floor. Normally, a piece of clothing lying on the floor in the middle of my kitchen would drive me nuts, but I barely notice it. Instead, my eyes are glued to her lace covered tits.

I bury my head in her chest, kissing first one then the other, sucking hard on her skin. I know I'm going to leave a mark and I don't give a fuck. She should have my marks all over her body. She moans out my name and clasps the back of my head, holding my lips right where she wants them. I find the stiff peak of her nipple hidden underneath her bra and draw it into my mouth, sucking hard through the lace. Her gasps only fuel my hunger and I move to her other breast showing it the same attention.

Her hips are rubbing against my middle, grinding against the tip of my cock. If she doesn't stop soon, I'm going to come in my pants. I may not have let her come last night, but neither did I. We're both desperate with need.

I reach behind her back with one hand, the other planted firmly on her ass, and unclasp her bra, setting her tits free. She grabs the fabric and shucks it down her arms, dropping it to join her sweater on the floor. I let out an involuntary groan, I finally have the answer to what color her nipples are. A beautiful light mocha that I want to drink up. I go right back to suckling one in my mouth, playfully swirling my tongue around it before giving it a little bite.

Bianca's moaning is playing on a loop in my ears. "Carson." She whines my name, asking me to give her more without the words. I push off the counter and head down the hallway until we reach my bedroom, all the while never taking my face away from her beautiful tits. Now that I've finally gotten my mouth on them, I don't know if I can let go. It's a miracle I didn't crash us into a wall.

I set her down, letting her body slither against mine so we can feel every inch of each other in the darkened room. I reach over to flip the light on, but she reaches out and stills my hand. "No lights," she says. Sounding a little nervous.

"I need to see all of you."

"Just for tonight." Bianca doesn't seem like the shy type to me but if she wants no lights tonight, then no lights it is. I plan on there being plenty of opportunities in the future where my eyes will be able to feast on her body. Besides, there's a bit of moonlight streaming through the windows that will give me enough light so I won't be fumbling around like a teen in the dark. "You have too many clothes on," she coos at me while reaching up to unbutton my shirt.

129

"You too," I say. She abandons my shirt for the button of her jeans, and I take over practically ripping the thing from my body while she wiggles her tight jeans over her hips. Watching her hips move and her tits sway makes me let out a groan and I can see her a mischievous smile in the moonlight. She's clad in a tiny piece of fabric she calls panties and slowly turns while I unbutton and drop my own pants.

When her back is fully to me, I almost swallow my tongue, realizing my mistake. Those aren't panties, that's a thong. I see the fabric disappear between the full globes of her ass and I realize I want to spread her open and taste her pussy from behind. The thought is almost too much, and I grip my dripping cock firmly through my boxer briefs to stop from coming on the spot.

She looks over her shoulder so she can see me and slowly bends over, dragging the thong down, out from where it's nestled between her ass cheeks, over those gorgeous thighs, and down to feet, ending up in a puddle on the ground before stepping out.

"Come here," I rasp. She walks slowly back to me. Too slowly. I rush to her and slam my mouth down on hers, showing her through my kiss how much I want her. I tease her tongue, her lips, I nip at her with my teeth, all the while cupping those luscious tits in both my hands, softly rolling her nipples between my fingers, letting her gasps and moans be my guide.

My cock is leaking like a sieve and I'm certain I've never been this hard in my life. I've never wanted anyone the way I want this woman who is full of fire and passion, something I realize I've been sorely missing in my life.

Her hands trace the panes of my chest then lower to my stomach, gliding over me, teasing my skin, until I feel her dip down into the boxer briefs I haven't had time to remove yet. Her hand grasps my shaft firmly and I suck in a breath, close my eyes, and grit my teeth. I'm too close to being inside her, I can't embarrass myself now. "You didn't tell me you were packing this much heat," she says with wide eyes that make my male pride inflate. I'm not huge but I know I'm bigger than average.

Before I can respond she gives my cock a few quick strokes, then releases it and moves down further to cup my balls, cradling them in her warm hand. "Bianca," I moan.

"Do you like that, Detective?" She asks, a note of teasing in her voice.

"God, yes," I grind out. She sinks to her knees dragging my briefs with her and my cock finally springs free and almost hits her in the face. The tip is red and dripping with pre-come, more than ready to have her lips wrapped around it. I've decided she's had her fun feeling me up, but it's time for me to take back control. "Do you want my cock in your mouth, Bianca?"

She nods her head and moves forward, ready to wrap her lips around my tip but I quickly grab her hair, holding her back. She gives me the prettiest little pout that makes my blood sing. "You need to beg me for it, baby. Tell me how much you want my cock in that little mouth of yours, how much you want to taste me."

Her eyes narrow and there's a stubborn set to her jaw. I suppress the smile that wants to break free. Of course she was going to resist. I tilt my hips forward and run my tip across her closed lips, coating them in my pre-come. She opens her mouth and sticks out her tongue to taste me, but I jerk back just in time. "Uh-uh. Give me what I want, and I'll give you what you need."

She looks from my angry red cock back up to my face and I'm sure she's calculating which one of us can hold out longer. She must remember I let her go last night without either of us coming because she finally gives in. With a little whine from the back of her throat, while down on her knees, she looks up at me through her lashes and says, "Please Carson, let me suck your cock. I need it, right now. Please."

"Good girl." I push my hips forward again and she immediately accommodates me in her mouth. She's warm and soft and so fucking amazing as she rolls her tongue over my head. Then she starts to suck. I let out a grunt and thrust my hips again while I bury my hands in her hair, almost hitting the back of her throat but pulling away just in time. There will be plenty of other opportunities for her to choke on my cock.

I let her explore, tasting all of me, sucking my shaft in her mouth then taking it out and peppering it with the gentlest kisses from the base to the tip. Her head dips lower and she traces my balls with her tongue, making my breath catch in my throat. "Suck," I command with a moan. For once, she follows orders and draws one of my balls into her mouth, applying gentle suction. Looking down and seeing this vision on her knees in front of me makes me want to thank whatever god sent her to me.

That's when I notice where her hand is. I take a step back and my sack pulls from her mouth with a pop. Bianca reaches for me again and gives a needy little moan. "What are you doing, Bianca?"

Her eyes are clouded with lust, and she looks confused. "Sucking your cock, if you'd just let me."

"Uh-uh, what are you doing with your fingers?"

She tilts her head down and there's a look of surprise on her face like she's just noticed her hand is deep in her pussy. "That's mine, Bianca. I get your orgasms, they belong to me. You don't get to come on your fingers. Would you deny me what's mine?"

I help her up to her feet even as my cock screams at me to let her get back to work. I take the hand that was playing with her pussy, and I show her how wet it is with her own juices. "This belongs to me, baby." I slip her fingers into my mouth and suck them clean. Her flavor hits my tongue, and it's like nothing I've ever tasted before. She's sweet and musk blended together, and I immediately want more. I want to eat her pussy out for hours, getting every last drop of her honey, but I know if I start now I won't be able to stop and I need to be inside of her.

"Hands and knees in the middle of the bed." She looks like she wants to argue, every fiber of her being is trained to rebel against someone ordering her around. I can see in her eyes the moment she decides it's worth it and she scrambles up onto the bed just as I've asked, shaking that delicious ass at me.

I climb up onto the bed behind her and pull her sweet cheeks apart so I can see both her holes. Her pussy is dripping wet and ready for me. I grab my cock and drag it through her slit bumping her clit with each pass before I pull away. She makes that same whining sound that comes from the back of her throat, and I decide right then it's my favorite sound in the entire world.

I take my index and middle fingers and thrust them inside her tight opening, not bothering to take my time, I can see she's ready for it. She lets out a cry of pleasure and pushes back against my hand. I start a relentless pace of finger fucking her while rubbing my thumb across her engorged clit. I owe her a digit induced orgasm from last night and I always pay my debts.

I curl my fingers inside her, searching for that spongy patch of nerves that I know will drive her wild. Her gasp tells me I've found it. "Carson!" she yells. I need her to be quiet, I don't want to wake up Oliver but the sound of my name on her lips is like the sweetest melody I've ever heard.

"You've got to stay quiet, babe or we'll have to stop," I whisper.

She lets out a whimper and nods her head. "Okay, please just don't stop." She looks so beautiful pushing back against my hand, her ass shaking with every movement that I can't help myself.

"Come for me, Bianca. Give me what's mine." I lean down and sink my teeth into that plump ass. Apparently, that was the last bit of stimulation she needed because she shoves her head down into the pillow and lets out a muffled scream while her whole body convulses. Her pussy is squeezing my fingers so tightly I'm worried they're going to break but I keep the pressure on her clit, drawing her pleasure out and watching as her entire body shakes with her release.

Once her body has settled a little, I withdraw my hand and grasp her hips, pulling her back into position. I'm about to plunge deep inside her when I suddenly realize something and still. "Fuck."

"What's wrong?" Bianca asks over her shoulder, rocking her hips, trying to entice me into her pussy. I want to bang my head against the wall.

"I don't have a condom." I close my eyes in frustration.

"What? You're joking, right?"

I open my eyes and look at the incredulous expression on her face. "Believe me, I would not joke about this."

"Don't you have like, a plastic baggie? A trash bag with a zip tie? Something?" I give out a sardonic laugh of the visual of trying to fuck her with a trash bag on my dick.

"Nope, I haven't needed one since I moved here." I take a deep breath and suggest something I swore I would never do. "Bianca, I'm safe. I had a full physical when I joined the SPD and I've never had sex with anyone without a condom."

"Me either," she says, the passion growing in her eyes again at the thought we might be able to continue.

"Are you on the pill?" I ask. I figure someone who has such a strong aversion to kids must be.

"Yeah, something like that," she says quickly, and I send up a brief prayer of thanks to whoever came up with the ring, the patch, the shot, or whatever the fuck it is she's on. I think if I had to stop right now my cock would go on permanent strike.

"We okay to do this?" I want her to be sure, to have no regrets.

She looks me straight in the eye, no wavering, no uncertainty. "Carson, if you don't get your cock inside my pussy and fuck me right now I'm going to scream."

I give her a smile. "Oh, you'll be screaming all right. You better grab hold of something." I grip both her hips firmly in my hands, holding her still, then thrust my cock into her as hard and deep as I can, losing my breath at the intense sensations of both pleasure and pain wrapped around my cock making me dizzy. I'm not sure if it's because I'm not wearing a condom or if it's just because it's Bianca, but I'm leaning towards the latter.

I can't hold back, I don't even give her time to get used to my size before I'm pulling back out and thrusting in again, seating myself firmly inside her over and over. She's moaning and rocking backwards trying to take me deeper.

Pressing my hand to the middle of her back, I put pressure until her ass is in the air and her tits and head are down on the mattress, which tilts her hips and shifts the angle. My thrusts become shallow and fast, and it takes just a moment for her to realize the benefits of this position. "Oh my God, Carson. Holy fuck."

I force my cock over her g-spot again and again while I watch her scramble for something to hold on to beneath me. She finally fists the sheets and holds on for dear life while I increase my pace.

She's chanting my name and I have to grit my teeth to keep from spilling inside her too quickly. I need her to come first. Preferably twice before I find my release.

She's gasping and making a high keening sound into the pillow while rocking her hips against me. I can feel the sweat running down my back as I relentlessly pleasure her cunt. "Carson, I think I'm going to—"

"Come for me Bianca, I want your dripping pussy to come all over my cock."

With two more thrusts she's over the edge, her body convulsing, back arching and pushing her face into the air. She's biting her lip to keep from screaming and I wish we were alone so I could hear her vocalize the pleasure my cock is giving her.

I slow the pace of my thrusting to get myself under control but don't stop completely. Her cunt is still flexing, squeezing my cock and coaxing it to spill my load. "We're not done yet, babe."

EVE STERLING

She tries to push up onto her hands but doesn't quite manage so she just turns her head to look at me. "I can't," she says.

"You can and you will. Remember, your orgasms are mine and I want another." I reach down and wrap my hands around her upper arms, pulling her up so her back is pressed to my front, never letting my cock slip out of her.

"No," she whines at me, exhausted.

"You can do this, baby. Just one more." With that I start grinding my hips against her ass, feeling my cock glide in and out of her tight channel. I grab her tit in one hand and bring the other down to her pussy. I can tell that if my arms weren't wrapped around her right now, holding her up, she would fall forward onto her face. My fingers find her hardened nipples teasing and pinching them while the palm of my other hand rubs firmly against her clit that's beyond sensitive and sopping wet at this point.

My mouth is all over her neck, I can't get enough of the taste of her skin while I drill into her again and again from behind. Bianca is whimpering in my arms and her hands reach behind her to find my thighs where she firmly embeds her nails. Good. I hope she leaves scars. I want this woman all over me just as much as I want to be all over her.

The walls of her pussy start to flutter around my cock and I know she's close. I let go of her tit and grab her chin, turning her face so I can look into her eyes. "You're right there, I can feel it. I need you to come and milk my cock dry." Her eyes are wide and vulnerable, and I realize this might be the first time I've ever seen her with her walls completely down. She throws her head back with a gasp leaving her neck exposed to me. I sink my teeth into the delicate skin where her shoulder meets her neck while squeezing her clit at the same time.

Her eyes widen, never leaving me, and her body shakes with the force of her orgasm. I can see she's about to scream and am able to cover her lips with my own just in time, capturing her screams in my mouth, tasting them with my tongue, savoring them. I feel the

136

wetness leak out of her pussy and slide down my shaft to cover my balls.

The contracting walls of her cunt are too much and take me over the edge with her. Spurt after spurt of my come coats her insides. It's true that I've never had sex without a condom before and now I know why. Coating Bianca's insides in my come, claiming her this way is turning me into some kind of caveman. My brain keeps repeating the same words.

I marked her. I claimed her. She's mine.

Exhausted, I fall to the side and pull her with me, careful to make sure I take all our weight. I can feel my cock slowly softening inside of her but I'm not ready to leave her warmth yet. We're both breathing hard and sweating, but I couldn't unwrap my arms from around her if I wanted to, and I don't. Instead, I nuzzle her ear and her body gives a little tremor.

I reluctantly pull away from her and can feel our combined fluids spill out of her pussy. I go to the bathroom and wet a washcloth with some warm water before making my way back to the bedroom. To my surprise, Bianca is already up and searching the ground for her clothes.

"What are you doing?" I ask.

"I should really go," she won't look at me and I know that moment where her walls were down is over.

"Sit down for a second."

"Carson, I—"

"Just indulge me, please."

With a little huff that makes me smile, she goes back to the bed and sits on the edge. I come up to her and press her shoulder until she's lying on the bed. "I need to clean you up," I say while gently rubbing the warm cloth over her pussy and between her thighs, cleaning up the mess I've made of her.

"I can do that you know," she says with a touch of annoyance. I finish up my job of wiping away the proof of our time together, a little sad that she's no longer wearing my come, and toss the cloth into the hamper across from the bed.

"I know you *can* do it, but I *wanted* to do it." She moves to get up again but I dive onto the bed and anchor her to me with my arm across her chest and one of my legs pinning hers to the mattress. "Just relax for a few minutes," I whisper in her ear. "Don't make me feel cheap."

She gives a little giggle that I can feel in my chest and slaps my arm, telling me I'm crazy but stays right where she is. It's not long before I drift off into a deep satisfied sleep.

Chapter Twelve

Bianca

The campus is filled with students celebrating the end of another semester. They're everywhere I look, chatting with friends, playing Frisbee in the quad, or simply sitting under a tree and reading.

I smile to myself as I make my way towards the dorms, breathing in the sweet spring air. I haven't even been in Seattle a year yet, but it already feels like home.

Not only is it the end of the Spring semester but I'll also be introducing my boyfriend to my dad tonight. I'm nervous because he's the only guy I've ever introduced to either of my parents.

Chris is handsome and popular, girls always stare at me with envious looks when we're out together, but I know he's all mine. In fact, last week we said I love you to each other for the first time. I was over the moon that he felt the same way about me I did about him. It was only then that I told him my most tightly guarded secret. Not even my best friends, Hollie and Violet, know what I shared with him that night. When he told me it was fine, it didn't matter or change how he felt about me, my heart soared.

Yes, he's my first real adult boyfriend and everyone says young love never lasts but I have a good feeling about us. I can picture our future all laid out, going to school, graduating, getting our first place together. I'll work on my art, and he'll get a job at his father's investment management firm. I can barely wait for our future to start.

When I make it to his dorm I slip inside as some other students are chatting loudly and leaving. My afternoon class let out early and I'm coming to surprise him with his favorite meatball sub from Hugo's since he has one last final this afternoon.

When I reach the door to his room, I don't even hesitate to push it open and step inside. But what I see freezes me. Chris is laying on his back and there's a naked blonde writhing on top of him. Her head is tossed back and there's an expression of pleasure on his face. Meanwhile, his hands are all over her tits and he's grunting the name Ashley repeatedly. Neither one of them has noticed my entrance so they just continue on. It's like I'm in a nightmare.

The heavy door behind me slams closed causing all three of us to jump. The girl grinding on Chris's dick, Ashley I presume, lets out a shriek when she sees me and scrambles off the bed, frantically grabbing her clothes that are strewn across the floor, but my eyes are glued to my boyfriend. He doesn't even look guilty, more like frustrated about being interrupted?

He grabs a pair of dirty jeans off the floor and slides them on before running his fingers through his hair in agitation. We're staring silently at each other, neither one of us saying a word.

I think I'm in shock. I know when people find out their significant other's been cheating on them they say they never saw it coming and most of the time. I always thought that was bullshit. There were always signs they just didn't see, or maybe they just didn't want to. But I honestly didn't see this coming. He told me he loved me, we spend all our time together, he's meeting my dad tonight for fuck's sake.

It's only the slam of the door behind me, indicating Ashley's timely exit, that knocks me out of my funk.

"How could you?" My voice is low, calm, and steady, even surprising me. I'm not exactly known for my even temper.

"Come on, Bianca. This thing between us isn't going anywhere. It's not like we're going to get married or anything. You can't have kids,

Bianca. You can't exactly expect me to be exclusive when we don't have a future."

Those words are like a stab to my gut, and I have to make a conscious effort to keep my hands at my sides instead of curling around my middle protectively. I told him I couldn't have kids, and he said it was fine. Now, he's saying there's no future for us? That it's a reason for him to cheat on me?

"If you didn't want to be with me, why didn't you just break up with me?" I will not cry. I will not cry.

He lets out an impatient sigh like he's explaining something to an idiot. "Just because this thing between us isn't going to go anywhere doesn't mean we can't have a good time together. I mean, the sex is great, we're young, there's no reason we can't get each other off."

"So let me get this straight. We can fuck, but when you find someone that can have your children, you're going to drop me and get serious with her?" That pain in my chest isn't my heart breaking. It can't be. It's got to be indigestion.

"Don't act like you're surprised by this, Bianca. What guy is going to want to give up having a family for some girl he met when he was eighteen?"

"But I love you. If we decided we wanted to have kids in the future, we could always adopt." I sound pathetic even to my own ears and I wish I could just stop talking. I told him the thing I was most scared about sharing. He acted like it wasn't a big deal. Now... this.

He scoffs at me. "Don't be so naïve, no man wants to raise someone else's kids when he can have his own." Now his eyes fill with pity as he looks at me. That, even more than the cheating, is what sends me over the edge.

"You want to be friends with benefits. That's what you're saying?"

My voice is shaking with rage, but he doesn't notice. Figures. In fact, his eyes light up with lust. "Of course, I'll still dick you down good."

I almost laugh at that. "Dick me down good? Why don't you go fuck yourself, Chris? That's the only person you fuck well, anyway. If you think I'm going to hang out with you just to perfect my fake orgasm performance, you're nuts."

He looks genuinely shocked, of course he had no idea he never get me off. I wanted him to feel good about himself. I was his girlfriend after all. Plus, I put on a good show.

"You're just saying that because you're mad, baby. You know I make you come harder than anyone else can."

"How should I know? You've never made me come even once."

His face turns scarlet with rage. Apparently I've hurt his male ego. Good.

"You fucking bitch! You're going to be a bitter old hag and alone forever."

"I feel sorry for whatever girl you knock up and gets stuck with your pencil dick and your demon spawn. If you ever get within ten feet of me ever again, I'll make sure every girl on this campus knows just how small the equipment you're working with really is and how you couldn't make a girl come with a road map."

I turn on my heel to leave when I notice I'm still clutching the bag of sandwiches tightly in my fist.

"You'll regret this, you slut."

Instead of replying I chuck the bag at his head and don't bother to see where it lands before walking through the door, though the "Oww" he cries out gives me a good hint that I was on target.

This is what I get for allowing myself to be vulnerable, for trusting someone with my darkest secret. I walk out of that dorm, head held high, tears streaming down my cheeks, and never return.

Standing naked in front of my full-length mirror in the early morning light, I gently run my fingers over the scars that cover my lower abdomen, right hip, and upper thigh. My scars are a physical manifestation of my metaphorical thicker skin. The battle armor I don every day without fail.

As soon as Carson fell asleep, I wiggled out from beneath his heavy limbs, careful not to wake him, and snuck back home. I didn't want him to see my scars, at least not yet anyway. That's why I wouldn't let him turn the lights on last night. I'm not usually self-conscious about the web of marks that mar my body. Sure, I could tell him part of the story and not all the gory details, I've done it plenty of times before with random men I've hooked up with, but somehow it would feel like lying if I did the same thing to Carson.

I don't know why it would feel like a betrayal to him, and frankly I'm not inclined to explore the feeling right now. Carson and I are not a possibility. Sleeping with him was a mistake. I should never have gotten entangled with a single dad, especially one that lives right next door. That was going to make the whole ghosting him thing significantly more difficult.

I force myself to look at the crisscrossing of scars on the outer edges of my wounds and slowly drag my eyes to the large, thick swatch of scar tissue over the right side of my abdomen. Because of an almost religious use of different scar minimizing creams, vitamin E, and visits to a plastic surgeon over the years, the scars are significantly lighter than the angry and puckered red they used to be. Finding a bathing suit is still a bitch though.

It's funny. They look so small and benign yet they're indicative of such a bigger problem. When I got into the head-on car accident with a drunk driver at seventeen, everyone—paramedics, doctors, my parents—thought I was going to die. I was pinned inside the car by jagged and ripped metal running straight through my pelvis. It took them hours to extract me from the car and if it wasn't for that metal somehow holding me together, I would have bled out long before emergency crews could have gotten to me.

Healing was a slow process but eventually the bruises faded. The bones stitched back together. My skin scarred over. The only lasting effect was that my uterus and one ovary were practically obliterated, rendering having children an impossibility for me.

Admittedly, this wasn't life shattering news. I knew from an early age that I didn't want children. I have a clear memory of me at ten-years-old telling my mother I didn't want to have kids. They were annoying, which was pretty ironic since I was one. Still, my mind had never changed, I don't connect with children and don't see the need to bring any more into this world.

But it didn't matter that I had already made that decision because there's an enormous difference between not wanting children and having that choice taken away from you. So I grieved the loss of that choice, something a teenager should never have to do, but I ultimately came to terms with it.

It didn't matter how at peace I was with it though. That same scene with my college boyfriend played out repeatedly with a different lead actor every time. Of course, not every time involved cheating or a flying meatball sub. No, I learned early on to let them know my... limitations long before either of us spoke of love. There were guys who broke up with me right away, those that waited a few weeks to end it so they didn't look like assholes, even though we both knew the unspoken reason, and the ones who thought we should be just friends... with benefits of course.

It was almost funny in a pathetic sort of way. You would think a guy in college would be happy to go at it with his girlfriend like horny rabbits without having to worry about having an accident. Well, there were plenty that wanted to fuck me, but they didn't want anything else.

Eventually, I gave it up all together. There would never be a man that was okay settling down with a woman who didn't want, and almost more importantly, *couldn't* give him a family of his own. That's when I knew I was never meant to share my life with somebody.

Some people just aren't built that way and I'm one of them. I've stuck to my occasional impersonal hook-ups and have been just fine. They filled any longing for physical affection and my friends and family supplied me with all the companionship I would ever need.

The bottom line was that my life worked for me and I didn't need some guy like Carson coming in and messing it all up. I hated that I liked his kid, that I liked him, that it was impossible to escape him when he was so close.

I even feel a little guilty letting him believe I was on birth control last night. And I'm annoyed with myself for feeling guilty. I shouldn't! There was no way I was going to get pregnant, I don't need birth control for that. The end effect would be the same even if he wasn't fully enlightened to the reason why.

No matter how much I try to tell myself differently, last night felt like a big deal. There were moments that didn't feel like fucking. Like we had an actual connection, something bigger than either of us. And that scares the shit out of me.

"Why does the birthday girl not have a drink in her hand?" Jenna yells to be heard over the pulsing beat of the music coming from the living room.

"I just finished my last one," I shout back. It's true, I'm at least three—or maybe it's four—deep in those bright pink drinks Hollie whipped up. Fanning my face, I watch Jenna as she pours me a shot. I'm not sure if it's the alcohol that's making me flushed or the fact that there seems to be an inordinate amount of people squeezed in the house. Dad is going to kill me.

Dad's house is much larger than ours and I convinced him to let me host my birthday party here this year. I promised there would be around fifty people but there's at least twice that number crowding the rooms. Never underestimate the number of artists that will show up for free food and drinks.

"Here drink this," she shoves the tiny glass in my hand and I don't even bother asking what it is before I toss it back. It burns down my throat and clears my sinuses, as expected. There's a drop on my lip and I run my tongue over them to clean it off.

Uh oh. I can't feel my lips anymore. That means I'm well into the tipsy stage and heading straight into drunkville. Oh well, it's my birthday and I'm safe at my dad's house, even if the place looks like it's been taken over by an unruly fraternity.

I wanted a sort of grown-up kid's party and my friends did not disappoint. They have drinks poured into pouches like adult Capri-Suns and there are drinking games modeled after kids' games scattered everywhere.

"Let's go play red light/green light," Jenna grabs my hand and drags me through the French doors into the backyard where there seems to be a spirited game going on. Apparently, if the caller catches you moving on red, then you have to take a shot. I'm all over this. The current caller is swaying and looks like he's lost a few rounds himself.

As soon as a new round starts, we all walk up to the line running across the grass. I look around and see some friends from school as well as a few coworkers from the gallery. There's a guy at the end that looks vaguely familiar, and it takes me a second before I place him as Tyler, the guy that Violet is currently dating. I take another look around the backyard but don't see her anywhere. Weird. Maybe she's in the bathroom?

"Green light!" the caller yells with his back to us. I make the cardinal mistake of taking off at full speed and forgetting that I'm both wearing high heels and a bandage dress that's so tight I can barely walk, let alone run. I make it about three steps before my heel sinks into the soft grass and I go catapulting forward just as I hear

"Red light!" being yelled out. I manage to keep my feet under me, but just barely. Thank God, it would have sucked to have gotten covered in grass stains.

Shots are handed out to myself and three other players that were caught and I down it quickly, not even tasting it this time. Instead of putting my shoe back on I kick the other off to join it in a heap on the grass. This time when it's green light I speed walk instead of running like my life depends on it. It appears to be the right move because I don't get caught on red light this time.

More shots are getting passed around, and that's when I notice an argument down the line from me. It looks like Tyler has taken exception to being told he was spotted moving on red. My smile turns into a frown as he continues yelling at the caller, not letting it go. What the hell? It's just a stupid kids' game. It's not like there's some prize or anything.

Looking around the backyard again I still don't see Violet. Maybe she should get this guy out of here. Then again, if he's being this much of an asshole, I don't want her alone with him. I decide to abandon the game and go to find her just as Tyler seems to get his way, which is probably for the best. The last thing I need is for the cops to get called over some drunken fight.

I scoop up my shoes and put them back on before heading through the doors and weaving through bodies looking for my roommate. I grab a finger sandwich as I'm walking by the refreshment table and quickly gobble it down hoping to soak up some of the alcohol and that it'll help the inevitable morning hangover.

"Bianca!" A curvy blonde bombshell barrels into me and I smile and hug her as soon as I realize it's Hollie.

"I'm so happy you could make it," I tell her. "But I totally would have understood if you needed to stay at home and help your mom."

"Are you kidding? I wouldn't miss your birthday for the world. Besides, there was really nothing else to do there. Mom's on her way to the rehab facility and we packed up Paige's things pretty quickly.

My face crumbles, and Hollie looks at me in concern. "What's wrong?"

"This means you're going to be moving out, doesn't it?" I ask.

"Yeah, hun, it does. There's no room for Paige at our place and Archer offered so—"

"Oh, so you get a billionaire boyfriend and suddenly our little house isn't good enough for you?" Hollie looks momentarily stunned, like she doesn't know what to say. I can't keep a straight face any longer and burst out laughing. "Come on, you know I'm joking." I pull her into a hug and say softly, "I'm really happy for you Hollie, you know that, right?"

She pulls away and looks at me with misty eyes. "Thanks B, you don't know how much that means to me."

"You deserve to be happy."

"You know you deserve that too, right?"

"What are you talking about? I'm happy. Look at these people who are here to celebrate with me." Using the glass of pink liquid in my hand I gesture around the room and a little sloshes out onto my hand.

"I can see that," Hollie says, giving me a tiny smile. I'm not stupid, I know what she's talking about. She wants me to find someone that makes me happy. She just doesn't understand. Even though Hollie and Violet have seen the scars, it would be impossible for them not to when we've lived together as long as the three of us have, I've never told them what it really meant. I didn't need their looks of pity. I had gotten my fill of those from the doctors and nurses. Hell, I could even see it in my parents' eyes occasionally.

Wanting to change the subject I quickly ask, "Have you seen Vi anywhere?"

Hollie averts her eyes from mine and glances around the room quickly which seems pretty sus, but then again, I've definitely moved over the line from tipsy to drunk.

"I saw her a little while ago, she must be around here somewhere," she says.

"Well, I saw her date in the backyard and he was acting like a total douche."

"Really? What was he doing?" She looks concerned and I'm right there with her.

"He was yelling because he lost at red light/green light. And not just yelling, like he was *mad*. His face was turning scarlet."

"Do you think he was just drunk?" She's chewing on her lip in concern.

"I mean, I'm sure he's drunk, aren't we all? But if he's going to act like that at a party with Violet's friends, who he's never even met before..." I trail off, knowing that Hollie will get what I'm saying.

"Yeah, if this is his best behavior, what's he like when he's comfortable and gets upset."

"Exactly," I toss back another mouthful of my drink. When Violet first told us about Tyler, we were excited for her. She rarely dates and he seemed perfect on paper, but this is concerning behavior. Plus, Violet is quiet and sweet, I'm not sure she can handle that dude if he's being an asshole. Let's just say she wouldn't stab him in the eye with a high heel. I can't help giggling to myself and Hollie gives me a weird look. I clear my throat, getting back to the topic at hand, "I just want to make sure she doesn't go home with him."

"I'll keep an eye out for her and make sure she gets a share ride, alright?"

"Who needs a share ride home?" I must be pretty drunk if I didn't notice the large, imposing male walk up behind Hollie and wrap his arms around her middle before nuzzling her neck.

"Violet," she answers him. "Her date is apparently not a pleasant drunk and is causing a bit of a scene outside." They both exchange a look that I don't quite get but who can understand couples and their weird secret languages. I'm glad I've never had one of those. Yes sir, I certainly am.

I think I need another drink.

"You taking care of my girl, Archer?" I let out a giggle because my alcohol-soaked brain thinks it's funny that a man wearing an outfit that probably costs as much as my first car is standing in the middle of my dad's living room with a bunch of twenty-somethings, drunk off their asses.

"I promised I would Bianca, so there's no need to murder me," he says with a smile. I like that he has a sense of humor. Hollie needs that.

"Good, it would be a shame to upset Hollie."

"I agree." He gives her another squeeze and sets his chin on the top of her head, all cute and shit. "Here, I got this for you. Happy Birthday, Bianca."

I frown down at the and the card he just pulled from his pocket. "You didn't have to get me anything."

"I wanted to," he says with a genuine smile. I take the card from him and turn it over in my hand. It's postcard sized and printed on the front is a reproduction of my favorite painting from Soo Kent. It's covered in shades of purple and green blended together to look like large bunches of hydrangeas. I fell in love with the painting at first sight.

"Thank you, Archer, I mean it. How did you know this is one of my favorite paintings? I don't have any reproductions of it so I'm totally putting this up in my bedroom."

He lets out a chuckle. "Hollie mentioned to me it was one of your favorites. But it's not the postcard that's the gift. The painting is going to be delivered to you next week."

I look between him and Hollie waiting for the joke, but they're both just staring at me with smiles on their faces. "Are you fucking with me?" I practically shout because I apparently no longer have volume control.

"No, I'm not fucking with you," he laughs.

"Archer, I work for a gallery. I know how expensive this is, like tens of thousands of dollars. You can't just give it to me."

Is it hot in here or is it just me, I feel like I'm going to pass out. "Full disclosure, it's been hanging in the penthouse of The Clarke San Diego. Do you know how many people have probably walked right by it and not even noticed? I'd feel much better if somebody had it who would actually appreciate it."

I look down at the card in my hand again, feeling slightly stunned. "I know I should refuse this, but I really really want it," I admit to him.

"Good, because it's already being boxed up, so you really can't refuse it." I pull him into a hug, and he seems a little surprised. He's completely stiff for a few seconds before he relaxes and gives me a quick squeeze back. When we pull away, I see Hollie grinning at both of us like a fool.

I hold the card to my chest, still not sure I believe him, but I just want to make sure he understands something. "Just because you're giving me this doesn't mean our bargain is off. You hurt her, you die," I point to Hollie who is rolling her eyes.

"Understood," he says in all seriousness before turning to the woman in question. "Do you want another drink, angel?"

"Yes, please."

"You too, Bianca?"

"Yeah, thanks."

He takes off towards the kitchen leaving us alone again. Well, as alone as you can be in a house crowded with a hundred drunk people. "Your boyfriend gave me a painting."

"You're going to have to get over it, hun. Once that man sets his mind to something he doesn't let it go."

"Oh, I'm not talking him out of it. I'm hanging that thing right over my bed."

She laughs and hooks her arm through mine as we head outside for some air. It's then that I feel my boobs shaking. "Hold on a second." I reach down into the top of my dress, fishing around.

"What the hell are you doing?" Hollie laughs.

My hand wraps around the solid object, and I pull my phone out of my cleavage triumphantly. "Where else was I supposed to keep it?"

I can feel the smile spread across my face when I see the name displayed on the phone.

"Who is that?" Hollie asks.

I shrug my shoulders, playing it cool. "Nobody, why?"

"Uh, because your face just lit up more than when Archer gave you a thirty-thousand-dollar painting!"

I quickly school my features even though it's apparently too late. Damn alcohol.

Her eyes narrow in on me. "That's fine, you can keep your secrets. For now."

"I don't know what you're talking about. If you'll excuse me, I need to use the restroom." I walk away as steadily as I can and am treated to Hollie's laughter following me down the hall.

CHAPTER THIRTEEN

CARSON

"Did you have fun at Aunt Gloria's?"

"It was fine." Oliver is staring out the window watching the street go by.

"Just fine?"

He gives a shrug without looking over at me. "She doesn't have any art stuff. I only had my pencils and the sketchpad I brought."

He's been obsessed with art since Bianca introduced him to it. I know that the class at the college tomorrow can't come fast enough for him. "What if we pick up a few things this weekend so you can keep them there?"

He finally tears his eyes away from the window and looks at me in excitement. "Really?"

"Sure, buddy." I pull into the driveway, happy to finally be home. I quickly glance at the house next door and don't see any lights on. For a house that has three girls supposedly living in it, the place always seems surprisingly empty. Then again, they're young, they're probably out living it up like they should be at that age.

"Can we get a present for Bianca?" I whip my head around to Oliver who's climbing out of the car with his backpack.

"What are you talking about? Why would we get Bianca a present?"

"Because it's her birthday." The way he says it makes it sound like I'm the biggest idiot in the world. Please don't tell me this is a glimpse into how he's going to be as a teenager.

"It's her birthday *today?*" I ask.

He rolls his eyes at me. "That's what I said." Yeah, he's definitely going to be a pain in the ass as a teen.

I open the door and quickly type in the code to the new alarm system that was just installed before closing the door behind us and making sure it's locked. "Well, since you seem to know so much, how do you know it's her birthday today?"

He tosses his backpack onto the kitchen table and climbs up into the chair, waiting for me to get him his dinner. Things are finally settling into a routine and that's letting him feel secure enough to come out of his shell a bit more.

"She told me. She says she's having a party. It's only for grown-ups or she would have invited me."

"Really?" I pour a glass of milk and hand it over to him while I pull the leftovers from last night's dinner out of the fridge. I glance at her house through the window but it looks just as empty as it did five minutes ago. If there's a party, it doesn't look like it's going to be over there. "Did she say where this party was?"

I should feel bad about pumping my kid for information. I *should* but I don't. He just shrugs at me. Some help you are, kid.

"What do you think we should get her?"

"A sketchpad," he says, pulling out his own to draw while I heat dinner. I pull a beer from the fridge, pop off the top, and take a long pull from the bottle before I answer. "We already got her one of those remember?"

"Oh. Then we should get her a ring," I almost spit the beer out all over our dinner. The hoppy liquid went down the wrong pipe and it takes me a minute to stop coughing.

"Why do you think we should get her a ring?"

"Luna from school says when a guy likes a girl, he gives her a ring. We like Bianca," he states matter-of-factly while drawing away, like I didn't just almost die from drowning by beer.

"Well, that's a little different, buddy. That's something a boyfriend gives a girlfriend when he really likes her."

His pencil stops moving, and he stares at the wall, his face scrunched up like he's mulling something important over. "But she is your girlfriend. She's mine too."

I let out a sigh, I really don't know how to get out of this conversation. "Actually, Bianca is a girl that is our friend, she's not our girlfriend." He looks like he's about to argue with me, so I hurry to change the subject. "How about we look for a present after your art class tomorrow?"

His eyes light up at the mention of the class and he goes on and on about all the things he hopes they'll do. Thank God.

Since I couldn't get him from Gloria's until late today, by the time we finish dinner it's time to get ready for bed. He goes through his normal routine that he's learned so well he doesn't need much help from me anymore, and then climbs into bed before handing me the same book about a boy whose best friend is a dragon that he's had me read every night for a week. I think I'm getting to the point where I can recite it by heart.

He falls asleep by the time we're halfway through and I take a minute to just watch him. I never could have guessed in a million years that I would end up with Oliver, but there's something that just feels right. Like he was always meant to be here with me. I may feel lost some of—okay most of—the time but we're figuring things out together.

If my sister could see us, I hope she would be proud. There's a lot of resentment inside me about how she left Oliver and the circumstances of her death, but I know deep down she was a person in an immense amount of pain and I wish I could have been there for her. I know that through my work I've tried to save young women and get them out of dangerous situations. Sometimes it worked and others, like the reason I finally left the LAPD, failed spectacularly. I just hope that if Molly could see us together, she would be happy. I lean forward and give Oliver a kiss on his forehead before switching his new night light on and move the door until it's open just a crack.

The couch creaks just the tiniest bit as I flop down onto it, exhausted from my long day. I flip on ESPN, not even registering what's on. I don't plan on watching, I just want some background noise. Taking a sip of my fresh beer I let my mind drift and of course it lands on my spitfire of a neighbor.

I was thinking about asking her out on an actual date, especially after our night together. There's no denying that we have amazing physical chemistry. Hell, even when we're arguing you can feel the sparks flying. I was going to talk to her about it in the morning, but when I woke up the spot in the bed next to me was cold and empty. She'd slipped away while I slept. If she was actually interested in me, she would have stayed, right? It's not like I forced her out of the house. Hell, she was ready to make a run for it as soon as we were finished. I had to drag her back to bed for a few more moments of her time.

I'm not interested in chasing someone who doesn't want to be caught and I have a feeling that fits Bianca to a T. Maybe it's for the best, it's not just me I have to worry about. There's Oliver too. Unfortunately, he already seems overly attached to her so I'm not sure it matters if we're dating or not. She's just so young and let's not forget how reckless she is. It's probably best that we just stay distant neighbors and forget about that one amazing night together. Never mind that I can't stop thinking about how it felt to be inside her while she made those little whining noises that drove me crazy.

Fuck, and now I'm hard.

I shouldn't be surprised, just the thought of her has been able to get my cock to stand at attention since the moment we met. The other night she was like every fantasy I'd ever had all rolled up into one. It was hands down the best sex of my life. Would I like a repeat performance? Of fucking course. But it isn't just a physical thing. At least not for me. We may fight like cats and dogs, but I like her. There's a connection between us.

Which leads me to my current dilemma. I want to see her, speak to her, but it feels like she's been avoiding me. Again. Now that I know it's her birthday, it couldn't hurt to send a quick happy birthday text, right? She'd probably see through that right away, plus she's obviously out partying with friends. Then again, who is she out with? Is she with a guy? What if she meets someone when she's out? That thought sends a wave of jealousy coursing through my veins and I don't like it at all. I've never been a jealous person before, but apparently Bianca brings out that side of me.

I run my fingers through my hair. I sound fucking ridiculous, like some kind of fifteen-year-old-girl with her first crush. I need to just man the fuck up and message her. If she's busy, she doesn't have to answer. Besides, it's just polite to wish someone a happy birthday.

I pull her contact info up on my phone and stare at the blank screen. Should I just say "Happy Birthday" or should I write out a longer personal message? After I've written and deleted four different texts, I roll my eyes at myself and just type out a quick "Happy Birthday Sparky" and hit send before I can change my mind. She can answer me or not, it's no big deal.

I try to watch the replay of today's baseball game but end up glancing down at my phone every fifteen seconds, so I toss it away from me to the other end of the couch. I refuse to be this pathetic. Which I immediately backtrack on when my phone buzzes and I dive across the cushions like I'm trying to escape a bomb.

Bianca: How'd you know?

Me: Oliver said he needed to get you a present.

I give up all pretense of watching the game and stare at the phone, waiting to see if she'll say something else. Maybe I should have asked her a question to keep the conversation going? Then again, she is at a party. I can't really expect her to be paying attention to her phone.

Bianca: Thats sveet of him. He doesnt have toget me anything

I look at the message for a second. I've never texted with her before so maybe this is the normal type of messages she sends? Somehow, I doubt it.

Me: How much have you had to drink tonight?

Bianca: Lots! Dont worry offiver im not driving.

I let out a groan. Goddamn it. Why does this girl bring out every protective instinct in my body? I'm sure she's fine. She already told me she wasn't driving, and it's really none of my business how much she drinks anyway. I should just put the phone down and get ready for bed. Yeah, that's what I *should* do.

Me: Where are you?

The time between her replies is setting me on edge.

Bianca: At my birtheday party. It's my birthday.

Me: I know. Are you somewhere safe? How are you getting home?

Bianca: I'm perfectly safe. Ill either stahy here or catch a lyft home.

Shit. I'd go pick her up, but Oliver is asleep and she still hasn't told me where she is. At least she's not driving but I don't like the idea of her getting a ride home from a stranger. Sure, most of the time those rideshare services are safe, but that's not always the case. I've seen it happen before.

Me: Don't get in a car with someone you don't know Bianca.

Bianca: uh oh detective dickwad is back

Uhhh is that what she's been calling me? I don't know whether to be pissed or laugh. Since she doesn't seem to be listening to me about her safety *again* I'm leaning towards pissed.

Me: Then you should listen to me. Get a ride home with a friend who hasn't been drinking. Don't ride home with a stranger.

She leaves me on read for quite a few minutes this time and now I'm up pacing the length of my living room. I know without a doubt if I had any idea where she was right now I'd be loading Oliver into the car and going to get her. Like a crazy person. I barely know this girl, I need to let this go.

Bianca: don't tell me what to ducking do

Bianca: not ducking, ducking

Bianca: ducking

Bianca: duck

Okay, I can't help but let out a chuckle at that.

Me: Just tell me where you are and I'll come pick you up.

Bianca: Nope. All good here detective dickwad

Me: Bianca I'm serious.

Me: Bianca?

Me: You need to answer me so I know you're alright.

I don't receive any more messages from her. I hope it's either because she got distracted from her phone or she's on her way home and not that something happened to her. I try to tell myself it's not my problem, this wild girl is not my responsibility. But that doesn't stop the sinking feeling I have in my stomach.

About thirty minutes later, I see a car pull up in front of her place and I run to the window like some kind of puppy eager for its owner to get home. Instead of Bianca getting out of the car, her roommate Violet exits and then enters the house without a backward glance.

I'm sure Violet was with Bianca, I could always barge over there to find out where she is, but I haven't even formerly met her yet. I don't want her to think I'm normally as crazy as I'm currently acting.

It's well past midnight and I should be asleep. Instead, I'm pacing and bouncing between checking my phone and looking out the window. There's no sign of Bianca. I lay down on the couch, hoping that maybe I'll be able to catch a quick catnap. I know if I go back to my room there's no way I'll be able to sleep if I can't hear her come home.

At first, I was having just general anxiety about her being out and drunk and something happening to her. Now, with all the time that's passed I'm starting to get worried for real. Her roommate was home hours ago.

I'm staring at the ceiling when I hear a car door slam outside. Hopping up, I rush to the window and see a distinctly Bianca shaped shadow weaving along the sidewalk. Her ride is already pulling away away from the curb and I don't even think. I open the door and rush outside in bare feet, pajama pants, and a thin tee shirt.

She must hear me coming even in her inebriated state because she turns towards me and a drunken smile lights up her face that almost brings me to my knees. Apparently, I've only been getting small, guarded smiles from her before. This is a genuine and real Bianca smile and I feel almost blessed that she's bestowed it upon me.

"Detective Dickwad!" She yells loud enough to wake the neighbors. I roll my eyes as she takes a step forward and trips on the edge of the grass, stumbling. I quickly grab her arm keeping her upright and look down at her shoes. High heels again.

"Don't you own any shoes that won't cause you to break an ankle?"

"Hey, these shoes are cute. Look what they do for my legs and ass." She turns and gives me a little pose, pushing her ass out a little and I can't deny she's right, but I also know she looks just as good without the heels.

"Where's your coat?" She's wearing some kind of dark green, skintight dress that not only has every single one of her curves on display but is calling for everyone to look at them. I don't like that every man she came across tonight was probably having the same dirty thoughts that I'm having right now.

She looks around her like a coat will just suddenly appear in her arms or on the ground near her. "I guess I forgot it," she shrugs. "I'll get it tomorrow." She walks towards her house and before I can stop myself, I put my hand on the small of her back and steer her over to my place. I just want to watch her and make sure she's alright. She's obviously drunk, what if she gets sick during the night? Sure, her roommate is home, but she's probably asleep by now. It would be better if I just kept an eye on her.

Absolutely. Right. Totally on the up and up.

She rattles on about the party and talking about people I've never met, but she sounds so happy that I can't help but smile down at her. Once we're inside, I move her towards my bedroom.

"Are we going to have sex now?" She asks eagerly, like nothing would make her night better. I let out a groan and adjust the bulge that's been in my pants since she posed for me outside.

"We can't have sex, Bianca. You're drunk."

She gives me that sexy pout that only some women can pull off without looking like a total idiot. She happens to be one of them. "But I wanna, Carson," She whines which just has me thinking about those little noises she made when I fucked her.

Maybe this wasn't such a good idea after all.

"I thought I was Detective Dickwad."

"That's only when you're being bossy," she looks at me with narrowed eyes. "Which is most of the time, actually."

"Come on, you can sleep in here and I'll sleep on the couch."

"But what if I get lonely?"

"You'll be fine," I assure her. She reaches down to pull her heels off and drops her tiny purse on the floor, spilling the contents out. I quickly pick up the few items which seem to consist of several different types of makeup, her phone, a credit card and ID, and some kind of postcard you'd get from a museum gift shop with a painting full of flowers on the front.

"What's this?" I ask. She's now chucked her shoes into a pile in the corner of the bedroom which makes me wince a little. I'll pick them up later.

"Oh, that's my present from Archer." Her face lights up and I don't particularly like that another man seems to have made her this happy.

"He gave you a postcard?" It seems like a strange gift, especially for a man that owns more hotels than I have socks.

She stands up and faces me. Even though Bianca is tall, the top of her head comes up to only my nose when she's not wearing shoes. "Nope," she says before tapping my nose and saying "boop" which draws out an unexpected laugh from me. "He got me the actual painting. He's having it shipped here."

"Is this small artist or something?"

"Soo Kent? Nah, she's kinda a big deal," she laughs. Jesus, he got her a painting from a known artist? I don't even want to know how much that cost. Nothing I get her could even come close, probably even if I emptied my savings.

"And you're still telling me that Archer Clarke isn't your boyfriend?" I ask slowly getting worked up over the fact that he was invited to her party, while I didn't even know it was her birthday.

"Of course not, silly." She stands up and starts fiddling with her dress so I move over to my dresser, digging through stacks of my shirts trying to find something she can wear to sleep in. "I don't do boyfriends."

Well, this is interesting, she doesn't do boyfriends? I mean, I guess that explains why she doesn't have one right now. Bianca is the type of girl you would want to lock down, it never really made sense to me she was single. "What do you mean *you don't do boyfriends?*"

I grab a shirt with the LAPD Cadet logo on it and hold it behind me without turning around, trying to be a gentleman like my father taught me.

"Uh, Carson. Can you help?" Her voice is muffled and when I turn around, I see Bianca has worked her dress up and it's stuck over her head. I try to keep my eyes focused on the dress, I really do, but I'm a guy after all. I can't stop my eyes from quickly sweeping over her body. I've never claimed to be a saint.

She's wearing tiny panties that are nothing more than a scrap of fabric and a strapless bra that seems to defy gravity by holding up her full breasts. Even though her barely clad body is on full display my eyes hone into an area on her lower abdomen and thigh that looks like it's covered in scars. I hadn't noticed them the other night. Is that why she wanted to keep the lights off?

I rush over to her and take over struggling with her dress. I can't seem to get it over her shoulders so instead I pull it back down and see that there's a zipper she neglected. "Here, this will be much easier." I pull the zipper down slowly like I'm unwrapping a present and keep telling myself that she's drunk, we can't sleep together tonight, it wouldn't be right. "Okay, you're set," I let her know once the zipper is all the way down.

She doesn't hesitate to let it pool at her feet and step out of it. I quickly hand her the shirt but not before she's chucked off her bra and thrown it into the same corner as her shoes.

"Get dressed, Bianca," I grind out. If she keeps walking around like that I might just forget all of my good intentions.

She lets out a huff and instead of pulling on the shirt, lays across the bed, spread out for me like a feast. Trying to focus on anything except her tits that now have tight puckered nipples practically begging to be in my mouth, I run my finger over the edge of the scarring. "What's this, baby?" I ask in a low voice. I don't want to scare her off if she's self-conscious about it. Though the thought of Bianca being self-conscious about anything almost seems laughable to me.

She lifts her head from the pillow to look where my hand is, like she can't feel it on her body. "Oh that. It's from the car accident."

"When were you in a car accident?"

"When I was seventeen," she says in a sleepy voice that's slightly slurred. I run my hands over the scared skin. It covers a fairly large swatch of her torso and upper thighs and even though it was dark last night, I'm surprised I didn't notice.

"What happened?" I ask softly.

Her head is back on the pillow and her eyes flutter closed but she still lifts her hand and mimes batting away my question dismissively.

"I was coming home from a football game and got hit by a drunk driver. Not a big deal." Jesus Christ, it doesn't look like it wasn't a big deal.

"How did you get the actual scar?"

She sighs and rolls over pulling the blanket over her nearly naked body. "The car hit me from the side and a bunch of metal tore and kind of stabbed through me, it's fine." Metal *stabbed through her*? How is she pretending like this wasn't a big deal? I've seen accidents that sound much less violent end in fatalities.

"And you were okay?"

She sighs again, like I'm really bothering her with all these questions. She props her head up on her hand and stairs into my eyes. "I was fine. The metal held all the important stuff inside until the ambulance got there. They thought I was going to die, but I didn't. End of story. If you aren't going to fuck me, can I go to sleep now?" She flops back down and pulls the blanket over her head. I'm not sure if it's to hide from my questions or to block out the light.

I close the door then turn off the bedside lamp before sinking down into the bed next to her. As soon as she feels my body weighing down the mattress, she tosses the blanket back and looks at me as I crawl into the bed.

"I thought you were sleeping on the couch."

"I was until you told me about your car accident, now I need to hold you so I can reassure myself you're okay."

"Carson, it happened years ago. I'm fine now."

"Yeah, but I just found out about it so you're going to have to shut up and let me hold you."

She scoots into me and lets her hands travel underneath my shirt. Her hands are warm on my skin and raise goosebumps. "Fine, but if we're going to sleep in the same bed couldn't we fool around just a little?"

Her seductive routine is completely ruined by a hiccup that shakes the entire bed. "Nope, it's time for sleep."

She lets out a huff and turns so that her back is facing me. Still, I can hear her mumble "Detective Dickwad," under her breath.

I wrap my arm around her waist and pull her towards me until her back is against my chest and her ass is nestled against my cock that's currently straining the confines of my pajama pants. I know she can feel my hard length pressing into her when she starts wiggling her ass. I grab onto her hip and still her movements. "Sleep, Bianca." It only takes about thirty seconds for her breathing to even out.

I run my hand back up her middle and hold her to me. It still doesn't feel like she's close enough so I throw my leg over both of hers, anchoring her to the bed. I let my fingers run along the puckered edges of her scars while I bury my nose in her hair, breathing in her scent. If I was a more poetic man, I'd be able to describe every fragrant note in great detail but all I can say is that she's sweet and she's spicy and she smells like she's mine.

I know it's crazy. It's not rational to think I could've lost her before I ever found her. Hell, I don't even have her technically, but she told me she almost died in the same mundane way you would tell someone you got a parking ticket. All the while she had no idea the fear that was creeping in and clawing at my insides. This girl is a fucking daredevil and I don't know what to do about it. It would be so much easier if I didn't care, if she was just some nondescript neighbor. But that's not how I feel. I've only known her a short time, but I already feel more for this woman than I've ever felt for anyone else in my entire life.

She drives me absolutely crazy, but even while she's doing it, I want to kiss her senseless. Half the time I don't know if I want to argue with her or fuck her. I'm completely lost in her and now there's nothing else for me to do except convince her we'd be perfect together.

I know it won't be easy. This woman has walls stretching higher than the Empire State building and I'm pretty sure I'm going to have to knock them down with a sledgehammer, but I've never shied away from a challenge before. Hell, I'd never thought about being a father, but I took in one traumatized little five-year-old boy and it changed my entire life.

If I hadn't of been up for the challenge, I would never have realized I could love another person as much as I love him and I never would have met Bianca. I'm going to make her mine, she just doesn't know it yet.

Chapter Fourteen

Bianca

My head is pounding. I must have had way too much to drink last night. I attempt to bring my hand up to rub at my temples, but it doesn't seem to move. That's when I realize my entire body is being weighted down. I look and see an arm tossed across my chest and a leg with blonde hair over my hip.

Carson.

It's starting to come back to me. We had been texting while I was at the party, he didn't want me to get a rideshare for some stupid reason. When I finally got home, he met me outside and I somehow ended up in his bed. I look down my body again and note that while I don't have a shirt on, I'm still wearing my panties, so it looks like he held out on me again.

His hand is absentmindedly stroking a small circle on my stomach right in the middle of my scars and I squeeze my eyes shut, remembering that he asked me about them last night. Thank God, I wasn't black out drunk or who knows what I would have said. I'm pretty sure I gave him the nice and clean version. Was in a car accident. Got pinned in by some metal. Was saved by paramedics and doctors. End of story. At least he doesn't appear to be disgusted by them.

When people hear my story, they all either react with pity or horror. Hell, sometimes I even get apathy. I've gotten used to all of those reactions. But not Carson. No, Carson wanted to hold me so he could assure himself that I was alright from an accident that happened years ago. From a time when I didn't even know him. How am I supposed to process something like that?

I can feel his chest steadily rising and falling against my back and know that he's still asleep. The light in the room is relatively dim and I wonder if I can sneak out before either he or Oliver gets up.

His arm tightens around me unconsciously as I try to escape. I quietly sigh, trying not to alert him to my attempted escape. I gently grab his wrist and pull it up and away from my body so I can scoot away but that damn leg of his over me as well. What is this man, some kind of spider monkey?

"Morning, Sparky," a mumbled voice says against my ear, making me jump.

"You know I hate it when you call me that," I grumble, letting his arm drop. There's no use in trying to sneak out from under it now.

"No, you don't."

"Yes, I do."

"If you don't want you calling me it, stop being such a little spitfire."

"I don't even know what that means."

He lets out a chuckle from deep in his chest and it sends shivers of awareness through my body. I try to scoot away again so that I don't feel completely surrounded by him but he keeps his grip firm. "Where are you trying to go?"

"Just the bathroom," I lie.

"Liar. You were trying to sneak out of here." Damn it. I hate when he seems to read my mind.

"Well, I have a busy day."

"Yeah? Okay, that's fine." He rolls away from me, and my body immediately feels three times lighter without his limbs covering it. It also leaves me feeling a little empty which I don't understand at all. "I just thought we could get your punishment for last night over with." His hand snakes into my panties and he softly runs his finger up and down my slit.

I can't help but let out a groan and move my hips, trying to get him to dip his fingers inside me. "What are you talking about?" My voice sounds breathy and aroused just from this lightest of touches. He bends his head down and takes one of my hardened nipples into his mouth, causing me to gasp, and applies gentle suction before letting it go again.

"I told you not to ride home with a stranger when you're drunk and you did it anyway." What is this man talking about? How the hell was I supposed to get home?

His finger parts my lips and I know he can feel the moisture there, making me moan. "It wasn't a big deal, I do it all the time."

"That is probably not something you should be admitting to me right now." He starts kissing my neck and my legs fall open, giving his hand better access to my pussy.

"So, what are you going to do? Get me all worked up and not let me come again?" I'm pretty sure that came out of my mouth sounding like a challenge but I really didn't mean it to. The last thing I want is for him to leave me aching right now. In fact, I might just murder him if he tries it and I really don't want to go to jail. Orange totally isn't my color.

His fingertips graze across my clit, finally, but it's not enough. I tilt my hips trying to get him to press harder, needing more. "No baby, today I'm going to make you come again and again until you're begging me to stop."

My entire body shudders at his words and I can feel a rush of wetness leak out of me onto his fingers. "That doesn't sound like much of a punishment," I gasp.

"We'll just have to see about that." He gives me a wicked grin then his hand disappears from my pussy and he's pulling the shirt he's wearing over his head. I let my eyes wander over his chest, the sculpted pecs and grooves of his stomach. This is the first time

I've seen him shirtless in the light and I can't help but wet my lips thinking of running my tongue all over his skin.

He's staring at my lips and growls out at me, "Panties off, Bianca." He doesn't have to tell me twice. I must break the land speed record for underwear removal. I wrench them down my things and kick them off somewhere to the side of the bed. He lets out another one of those deep, masculine chuckles that makes my body shiver in arousal before he sits on the end of the bed and then lies back so his face is staring up at the ceiling.

Before I can ask him what he's doing, he says, "Come over here and straddle my face."

"W-What?"

"I want you to sit on my face so I can eat you out. So get over here."

My entire body lights up with excitement, still I've never sat on anybody's face before. I'm not exactly a delicate flower over here. "I'm too heavy. What if you can't breathe or something?"

He grabs my hand and pulls me towards him, "You're not too heavy and if I can't breathe, then all the better. I want you covering my face with that sweet cunt. I don't want to breathe or taste anything that's not you."

I can't contain the moan that comes out of my throat at the thought of his tongue all over me and pull myself up so that I have a knee on each side of his face as I hover above him. I didn't consider how exposed this would make me feel. With his eyes glued to my pussy I feel incredibly embarrassed and vulnerable. Instead of making any jokes I can see him breathe in deeply, taking in the scent of my arousal which makes me blush.

"Once I taste you, I'm not going to be able to stop so you just hold on. If you can't be quiet, then lean forward and bury your face in the pillow."

I try to gather any bravado I have left in me, so he doesn't know how desperately I want him, but I'm pretty sure my shaking thighs are giving me away. "I still don't see how this is a punishment."

"You will." Then he grabs onto my hips and pulls me straight down onto his mouth. He doesn't waste a second and I can feel his tongue all over my pussy, from my entrance up to my clit which he draws into his mouth and sucks for a moment before releasing it and going back to my tunnel, pushing his tongue inside.

I can't help myself, I start grinding on his face eager for more of him. If I thought that would make him slow down or push me off, I was wrong, it only seems to excite him more.

This isn't some kind of dainty controlled licking of my pussy. This is messy and primal. The noises he's making beneath me are practically obscene as he slurps up my juices. It's like I'm a ripe summer peach he can't eat fast of enough, the juices running down his face.

With no warning my body erupts in ecstasy. My legs are shaking and my back arches as the pleasure runs through me. Carson keeps teasing my clit with his tongue and teeth, drawing it out, making it last longer than any orgasm I've ever had before.

Just as I'm coming down my body is wracked with the second orgasm I didn't even see coming. I want to scream but fall forward and bury my face in the pillow as instructed. My hips are bucking on his face wildly like I'm a rider and he's my saddle. I'm yelling "Fuck, fuck, fuck," into the pillow like it's some kind of prayer.

Once my second orgasm is over my clit gets extremely sensitive and every time he hits it with his tongue my entire body jerks. I try to roll off of him but he wraps both of arms around my legs and holds me right where I am. He leaves my clit and thrusts his tongue deep inside me, fucking me with it relentlessly. I grind against him again, trying to pull him deeper inside me.

Eventually he latches onto my core and begins to suck. Hard. All the while his nose is bumping into my clit, causing little electric jolts to race through me. It's a feeling I've never experienced before. It's like the suction is pulling on my insides. I stop breathing and that's when another orgasm rolls through my body. This time I'm too exhausted to scream. I just moan into the pillow. I can feel a rush of liquid exit my pussy and go straight into his mouth. It should be embarrassing, but I don't have the energy to care.

I try to get off of him again but he takes his hand and smacks my ass hard, letting me know he's not done before holding down my legs again. It's no use, I'm stuck on this wild ride and Carson is in complete control. He's a wild beast and my cunt is his prey.

It takes me a minute before I realize I'm babbling, begging him to stop. "Please, please Carson. No more. I'll be good, I promise. No more." At this point I can't even remember why he's punishing me, all I can feel is a combination of pleasure and a sensitivity that's verging on pain. His full day's growth of beard has been rubbing my inner thighs and pussy raw, only ratcheting up the overwhelming sensations.

It takes quite a while but I'm convinced I have no more orgasms left to give, just when I think he's about to give up, he attacks my clit once again, rolling it with his tongue relentlessly and I'm begging all over again. Now, I'm not sure if I'm begging him to stop or keep going.

He takes my engorged and oversensitive clit between his teeth and gently bites down. I cum so hard all I see is white, or maybe that's just the pillow my head is buried in. All I can do is ride out the waves of pleasure that course through my veins.

When I finally come down from my orgasmic high, Carson releases me. If it wasn't already buried into the pillow, I would have fallen forward onto my face. He gets out from underneath me and gently rolls me onto my back. I can't even speak at this point. I'm just gasping for air and staring up at him.

His face is slick and shiny, covered in me. I should be embarrassed, I really should, but I'm too tired and sated for that. My eyes start to close but Carson lifts one of my legs causing them to fly open again. "You didn't think we were done yet, did you, sweetheart?"

All I can do is whimper. He's between my legs and at some point, he must have shimmied out of his pajama bottoms because all I see is his cock standing almost straight up, red and angry looking, slick with his own pre-cum. "Look at you, you're a mess," he says, staring between my legs. "Do you think you've had enough?" I follow his eyes down to my pussy and see that it looks red and swollen from his efforts. I reach down to touch myself and it's so sensitive I can't help but blanch.

"No. I can't," I beg him.

"You owe me one more," he counters.

I try to muster any defiance I have left in me and tilt my chin away from him. "I don't owe you anything."

He just grins and doesn't say a word as he plunges his cock deep inside me. I wasn't expecting it and my sensitive pussy feels like it's being rubbed raw. I can't tell if what I'm feeling is pleasure or pain. Then he seals his lips against mine and plunges his tongue into my mouth. I can taste myself on his lips, in his mouth, everywhere. I never thought that would be something I would like but with him, it's a complete turn on. He's pounding into me, and my hips are meeting his every thrust.

"I won't be able to last long babe, your pussy was too delicious." His hand moves down, and he places his thumb over my clit applying steady pressure. I can't stand any more stimulation and come one last time. It's not as sharp as the others, more like a warm sensation that flows through my entire body. I gasp for air instead of screaming and hold on tightly to his shoulders, anchoring myself so I don't float away.

"Fuck," he yells sharply and stills. I can feel his cock pulse inside me as I'm flooded with the warmth of his seed. It feels like it goes on for hours but I'm sure we're only clinging together for moments.

Carson collapses onto the bed to the side of me, careful not to crush me under his weight. I can't do anything but try to catch my breath while I stare blankly at the ceiling. I've never felt so satisfied in my entire life. I think he's ruined me. How am I supposed to be with anyone else after this? Each time with him only gets better and better.

He raises off the bed and goes into the bathroom. This time I know he's getting a washcloth to clean me up. When he reemerges, I let my legs fall open, too tired to argue about doing it myself. He gently presses the warm cloth to my core, and I let out a hiss which just makes him chuckle.

"It's not funny," I say, trying to glare at him, but I'm pretty sure I'm too exhausted to pull it off. He leans down and places a gentle kiss on the top of my mound, far from where it's swollen, and for some reason that makes me want to melt.

Get it together, Bianca. We don't get all goofy eyed over some dude. No matter how many orgasms he gives us.

I jerk up and scramble off the bed like it's burned me and start searching the room for my clothes. I find my panties in a little heap next to the bed and quickly slip them on before spying my bra across the room.

"What are you doing?" He asks casually from his spot on his bed.

"Getting dressed," I mumble while I try to squeeze my tits back into this ridiculous strapless bra.

"I can see that. Where are you going?"

"I've got to go home. I've got a bunch of stuff I need to do today."

"You can stay, you know." He says softly, drawing my eyes to him. "I'm going to make breakfast. You're going to eat, aren't you?"

For just a second I want to stay. I want to hang out with him and Oliver on a Saturday morning while I try to choke down whatever healthy crap Carson's made. But it's dangerous to think that way.

"I should really get going." I start searching the rest of the room for my dress. Where is the damn thing? Carson clears his throat and I look over to where he's now standing in the corner of the bedroom, my dress in one hand and heels in the other. "Thanks," I mumble, grabbing them out of his hands.

Once I'm dressed, I rush out into the hallway and through the living room. I've almost made it to the front door when I hear, "Hi Bianca." I come screeching to a halt and turn towards the voice, my heart beating out of my chest. Oliver is sitting on the couch with the cartoons playing quietly on the television.

I place my hand over my pounding heart. "Fuck, Oliver. You scared the shit out of me!" His eyes get big, and I realize what I just said as Carson enters the living room.

"You owe two dollars to the jar, Bianca!" Oliver says in a sing-song voice like catching me cursing is the highlight of his morning.

"Fine," I grumble looking through my tiny clutch, hoping that maybe I tossed some money in there that I forgot about. "C'mon Oliver, nobody carries cash anymore." I give him a frown before I'm struck by an idea and pull out my phone. "Do you take Venmo?" At his blank look I carry on. "PayPal? Zelle?"

I hear Carson's deep chuckle from across the room and shoot him a glare where he's leaning against the kitchen island. "Hey buddy," he says to Oliver without taking his eyes off me. "I'll cover Bianca this time. Pulling out his wallet he moves to the bookcase where there's a jar overflowing with dollar bills. "We're going to have to get a bigger jar."

He stuffs them in before his body freezes. "Um, Oliver. Have you been moving things around in the bookcase?"

"No. My books are in my room."

I can feel the smile stretch across my face as I remember my impulsive book rearranging from the other night. He yanks out the two misplaced books and I can't help myself. "You're only just now noticing? I'm disappointed. I thought that would drive you nuts within five minutes of you coming home the other night."

"You did this?"

"Guilty as charged, officer." I give him a cheeky wink.

"Well, maybe I would have noticed the other night if I hadn't of been so..." he looks at Oliver quickly before looking back at me, "distracted when I got home."

"Bianca, I have my art class today. Are you going to come? Pleeease?" His expression is pleading and I look over at Carson who's busy putting his books back where they belong.

"Don't look at me," he says without turning around. "I'm just a guy organizing his bookshelf."

"It was only two books, Carson."

"Well, it looks different." His tone has a little pout in it and I roll my eyes at his obsessive-compulsive ass before turning back to Oliver.

"I don't know, Oliver. There are a lot of things I need to do today." I can see him physically deflate and feel a tug at my heart. Why does this kid have such a pull over me? I've always done everything I could to avoid children and never given it a second thought. Now this kid wants to drag me to a place where there are going to be even *more* kids and he has me actually considering it.

I mean, truthfully, I don't have that much to do today. I was mostly going to hang out at home and work on some paintings. Of course I was making up excuses to get out of here, I wanted to be far away from Carson who is bringing up feelings I don't care to examine, like ever. I'm just going to chalk it up to orgasm fatigue.

I look at Oliver's downcast eyes and slumped shoulders and let out a sigh. "Okay, I'll go with you."

"Really?" There's hope in his voice that I'm loathe to stomp out.

"Yeah, really."

He cheers and jumps around the living room like I just told him today was Christmas and his birthday all wrapped into one and I can't help but feel affection for him.

"What time do we need to leave?"

Carson checks the clock. "In about two hours. I should probably shower. You know, wash my face." He gives me a smirk that I would very much like to knock off his face if only I was standing a few feet closer to him. Instead, I settle on giving him the finger while Oliver's back is turned, which only makes his eyes sparkle with mirth. Someday I'm going to murder him.

There's a tugging on my skirt and I look down, remembering that I really need to get out of this dress. "Can you help me with my watch?"

"No problem, kid," I take the proffered watch from him and wrap it around his tiny wrist, strapping it into place. "Too tight?" I ask.

He fiddles with it, turning it slightly on his arm. "No, it's good," then takes off down the hall, to his bedroom I presume.

"We'll see you in a few hours?" Carson asks.

I give him a quick nod and walk out the door, thankful that my walk of shame is only as far as next door.

Don't any dads take their kids to this art class?

We're in a medium-sized auditorium on the outskirts of the Branson campus. The room is filled with kids of all different ages, spaced out with their own stations, and there are three volunteer student teachers walking amongst them to make sure they aren't having any issues and offering encouragement. They've set up a small area of folding chairs in a corner for parents to observe and that's where Carson and I are sitting right now. Along with every single mom in the greater Seattle area, apparently. At least I presume they're single from the way they've been eyeing up Carson like a piece of meat.

From the second we walked in the room their eyes have been devouring him, head to toe. Not that I care, I just think it's extremely rude since I'm sitting here with him. Sure, we're not together but they don't know that. Do they realize how desperate they look when they can't stop staring at him?

Carson jolts me out of my thoughts when he wraps his arm around my shoulders and squeezes my arm. "What are you doing?" I hiss.

"Nothing. Just figured maybe this would help you stop staring daggers at some of these women."

"I don't know what you're talking about," I lie, refusing to look at him.

"Sure." Then I feel his lips plant a gentle kiss on the top of my head and I suck in a quick breath as I feel warm all over. I don't really do public displays of affection. Hell, I'm not usually out with guys in the daytime where people could see it. It feels weird and exposing. But it also makes me feel much better when a few of the women give me glares and turn away from us.

"Don't look so smug, babe." He whispers into my ear. I try to twist my face into a neutral expression because I'm sure I looked smug as fuck. I can't help it. He's basically claiming me in front of these other women. I shouldn't like it, but I do.

Instead of answering him my eyes drift back to where Oliver is painting with acrylics on a canvas. One of the student teachers is standing next to him and pointing out something in his painting and he's smiling and nodding. I can't help but smile as well, he looks so happy. Maybe happier than I've ever seen him. Up until this point he's just been drawing. He's filled up several pads with sketches of everything within his sight. He hasn't tried painting yet, but he seems to take to it without issue. I'm sure I could gather up some of my extra supplies and bring them over for him to use. Plus, for my birthday my dad gave me a monthly credit at Dark Arts and Crafts. It's more than I need every month so maybe I'll take him to pick out some supplies he can experiment with.

The ninety-minute class seems to fly by as I watch Oliver paint and ask questions. Before I know it, he's running over to us, canvas in hand.

"Whoa. Slow down, buddy. Let's let this dry," Carson says, plucking the canvas from his hands. We both look at what he's painted and give each other the side eye, trying to hide our smiles.

On the canvas there is a rather realistic scene of a giraffe walking amongst the brush and tall grass of a plain. However, just like with the model he made of clay, the giraffe's neck is short. So short, one might even call it stumpy.

"This is great, Oliver. I love the way you made the bushes. How do you know where giraffes live?" I ask.

"I have a book all about animals." He grabs my hand and starts tugging me towards the door where the rest of the kids and their parents are emptying out of the room. "C'mon Bianca, let's go."

As I dutifully follow behind him, Carson stays at my side and I can't help but whisper to him, "I thought you were going to take him to the zoo."

"I'm going to, but until then I got him a book with pictures. Apparently, he didn't notice their necks."

As we're making our way back to the car Oliver spots a small farmer's market that's doubling as a craft fair and before I know it, we're walking along the stalls of fresh fruits and vegetables dotted with handmade jewelry and soaps.

Oliver's maneuvered himself in between Carson and me and has a grip on each of our hands. Anyone looking at us would think we were a family out for a Saturday stroll. The thought makes my chest tighten and breathing suddenly becomes more difficult. I'm not even sure if it's because that thought makes me happy or scared to fucking death.

Get your shit together Bianca. You're better than this.

"Look at these!" Oliver pulls us towards a stall filled with hand knitted scarves, hats, and mittens. They really are well done, and I run my hand over one of the scarves taking in the yarn's softness.

"Daddy, can I get this for Bianca?"

"Oh, no Oliver. You don't need to get me anything. I'm fine. But thank you for thinking of me."

"But it's for your birthday," he says. "I didn't get you anything."

I'm just about to protest that I don't need anything for my birthday when Carson butts in. "You're right, bud. Is this the one you want to get her?" He points to the scarf I was just touching waiting for Oliver to answer. He nods his head emphatically and Carson picks it up and takes it over to the vendor.

"Carson, I really don't need—"

"Bianca, you're going to have to get used to people doing nice things for you. It was your birthday. We want you to have it."

I can feel awkward at the thought of these two doing nice things for me. Instead of addressing Carson I bend down so that I'm level with Oliver. "Thank you for my scarf. It's beautiful."

"You're welcome." He jumps forward and gives me a hug so big I almost fall back on my ass. I'm able to steady myself and wrap my arms around him returning his hug. When I finally release him and stand back up Carson comes up behind me and gently wraps the scarf around my neck, carefully tucking in the ends and making sure none of my skin is exposed to the chilly wind.

"Thanks to you too, you really didn't have to."

He brushes a strand of hair out of my face and gently tucks it behind my ear. "Of course I didn't have to, I wanted to. You deserve something special." His green eyes are penetrating and I feel like they can see into my soul. I quickly avert my own, fearing he may see too much. I don't know what to say. Between the two of them I feel... cherished. It's a weird feeling I'm not used to. I have plenty of love in my life between my parents and my friends, I'm not discounting them or the special place they all have in my heart, but I've never felt so considered and cared for.

While I'm letting my thoughts fly through my head like fireflies, Carson leans forward and places another kiss on my head, just like he did when we were in class. I close my eyes and let myself feel, just for a second. There's no harm in that. It doesn't have to mean anything. It can't possibly hurt to just take these few hours and feel truly special and cared for, can it?

Chapter Fifteen

Carson

It's been a few weeks now since I decided to lay siege to Bianca's walls and to tell you the truth, I'm not sure how it's going. She hasn't called me Detective Dickwad in a while, so I guess that's progress. The only one my efforts definitely seem to be working on is me. I'm in so deep with this girl I'm not sure I'll ever see the light of day again. She still fights me like a hellcat every chance she gets, and I should probably be ashamed of how turned on that makes me.

I want to give her time to get used to the idea of there being an us, so every chance I get I pull Bianca into our lives. She has dinner with us most nights, runs errands with us, hell, she even picks Oliver up from Grace's on nights when I'm running really late. Grace keeps making not-so-subtle hints that I need to lock Bianca down and all I can tell her is that I'm trying.

She's taken us to a bunch of tourist traps on the weekends, things she said she did when she first moved to Seattle. She claims they're a rite of passage for every Seattle transplant. So we've been to Pike's Place Market, seen the Space Needle, we even took Oliver to the zoo last weekend to see the giraffes. He still insists on making them with stubby little necks though. What can you do?

On the outside you'd think we were a happy couple, hell, a happy family. I've even let her disorder my perfectly ordered life. There's makeup strewn on my bathroom counter, shoes all over the place, sketchpads and pencils covering every surface.

But there are certain things I just can't break through with her. I have my cock in her every chance we can get and truthfully, it's mind blowing. The best sex of my life, hands down. Sometimes it's quick and dirty against a wall or perched on the bathroom sink when Oliver's attention is temporarily diverted. Sometimes it's slow and burning with passion at night in my bed. She's insatiable and I'm more than happy to be the one to satisfy her.

Even though we spend so much time together and fuck practically every day, I've never been able to get her to stay over a full night. Usually she's gone within moments of us finishing. If we fall asleep afterwards, she's always gone when I wake up. Honestly, it's starting to make me feel a little used. I want to wake up with her by my side, in my bed.

She keeps mentioning how happy she is that Violet never seems to be home anymore because she would definitely know something was up between us. I'm not exactly thrilled she's hiding us from her friends. It's riling me up so much that I've almost asked her where her dad is every time Violet disappears, but I shouldn't be the one to burst that bubble for her. That's something those two are going to have to come clean about on their own. Frankly, I'm surprised she hasn't figured it out, which makes me think she just doesn't want to see it.

Then there's the fact that she won't show me her paintings and I don't understand why. Whenever she's here and we're watching TV with Oliver, she's always sketching something out on one of the pads she's left here. She can't seem to keep her hands still, she always needs to be creating. Everything she draws is beautiful and fills me with a sense of awe that she can create something so beautiful, and that's just what she does absentmindedly, I know the paintings she spends hours on would blow me away. But whenever I ask to see them she brushes me off. She won't even work on them over here, she just disappears back to her place. I'm considering sneaking over there one day just to get a peek, but I know if I push too hard she'll run for the hills. I'm trying to get her slowly used to the idea of us being a couple, but it's going more slowly than I'd like.

On top of my Bianca problems, the letters keep on coming. There's been three more and they're progressively getting more and more threatening. Even though I now have cameras outside, I never get a good look at the person delivering them. It's heading into winter and the figure that's been putting them in the mailbox is all bundled up, making him or her a shapeless blob. They're never delivered at the same time or day either so it's useless trying to catch them in the act. The one thing the cameras have caught is Violet climbing into Dante Moreno's truck on more than one occasion which just confirmed my earlier suspensions about their relationship.

Rafe has been trying to help me, but forensics said the paper and envelopes are all clean, there are no fingerprints to be found. I've asked DNA to be run but I know it's a long shot. It takes forever to get results and even if they find something, the person will have to be in the system to get a match.

I've been wracking my brain trying to figure out who would want to threaten me and it's not that I haven't come up with anyone, it's that there are too many people to narrow it down. Maybe not here in Seattle, but I was in Los Angeles long enough to piss off a long list of people. It's impossible to home in on one person unless they slip up and give something away.

I haven't told Bianca, Grace, or Oliver about the letters. I don't want to upset them, especially since it's all been rather harmless so far. Plus, the threats have only been against me, asking how I can live with the guilt, that I ruined their life, and that I'm going to pay. Rafe seems to think if they were going to take some kind of action, they would have done it already and I'm inclined to agree with that assessment. For now, all I can really do is wait, but I'm not a person who likes to just sit around. I'm concerned that if I wait too long, it will put the people I care about in danger.

Instead of dwelling on that, I'm laying in bed with my arms around Bianca while she dozes on and off. It was another evening of me worshiping her body like the goddess she is. I let my hand skim over her breasts, down to the dip of her waist, then the swell of her hips. Her body is perfection and fits against me like it was made for it. I nestle my face into her hair, breathing her in. With how often she's been here I feel like everything I own is beginning to smell like her, yet I still can't get enough.

I'm taking in and treasuring every moment I have her in my arms. I know as soon as she wakes up, she'll be gone. Those are the worst moments of my day. I'm not sure what else I can do to make her realize how good we are together, but I'm not ready to give up. I'm pretty sure that the stolen moments I get with her would be better than a lifetime with anyone else. That thought should scare the shit out of me but it just makes me more determined to make her realize we belong together.

I'm about to drift off myself when I hear a scream down the hall. Bianca and I both jerk straight up and I'm off the bed, pulling on my pajama bottoms before Bianca is even done asking me what's going on.

I race down the hallway to Oliver's room, Bianca hot on my heels and burst through the door, flipping on the light as I enter. For just a moment I'm relieved to see him in bed alone, that nobody has broken in and tried to hurt him. Then my heart clenches when I realize that he's had the nightmare again.

It's been a few weeks since he's had the nightmare that plays on a continuous loop in his sleep. When he first moved in, they were a staple of almost every night. Since we got the night light, they've become less and less frequent. However, it looks like tonight is ending our streak of good luck.

I sit down on the bed and pull a sobbing Oliver into my arms. I stroke his hair and whisper what I hope are comforting words into his ear while he keeps crying.

Across the room, Bianca is standing in the doorway in one of my shirts that she must have pulled on before racing out of the bedroom. She's looking unsure like she can't decide if she should step in and intrude on this moment.

I'm rocking Oliver back and forth, trying to comfort him while his little body is wracked with sobs. "It's okay, buddy. You're here with me. You're not alone. I'm never going to leave you alone." I repeat the words over and over, hoping he understands. His sobs lessen and now he's just crying instead of gasping for air and wailing.

"Is Bianca here?" He asks, his head buried in my neck. I look over to her and instead of the look of indecision I expect to see, her face is a mask of determination. She rushes forward and gets onto her knees next to the bed where I'm sitting with Oliver.

"I'm right here, Oliver," she says, touching his back, so he knows she's right behind him. He releases my neck and slides down onto Bianca's lap wrapping his arms around her.

Her wide eyes look up at me, questioning what's happening, even she can tell this isn't your normal, run-of-the-mill nightmare that every kid gets. I give my head a quick shake letting her know I'll tell her later. She seems to understand and turns her attention back to the little boy in her arms. She starts rocking him and rubbing small circles around his back.

"It's okay, it's okay." After long minutes he finally calms enough to stop crying and pulls away from her. She gently reaches up and wipes the tears from his eyes.

"Was it the dream again?" I ask quietly, already knowing the answer.

"Yeah," he says, giving a little hiccup.

"Do you want to come sleep in my bed?"

"Is Bianca going to sleep with us?" I'm silent, letting her make her own decision, this isn't one I can make for her. If she wants to be here for Oliver, that's something she needs to decide on her own. I hope she realizes how big this is that he trusts her so much, that he derives so much comfort from her presence. I'm worried what will happen if she doesn't. Oliver is so attached to her, and I haven't been able to get her to make any kind of commitment to us. If she breaks his heart, it's going to be my fault.

She doesn't even bother looking at me for a clue as to what she should do. "Of course I will," she says, full of confidence. The relief I feel is almost a physical thing. All my muscles relax and the tension leaves my body. I look at her, holding my new son in her arms, kissing the top of his head, and I'm not sure she's ever looked more beautiful to me.

Rising, I pull him from her arms and carry him back to my bedroom, laying him down on the bed. He scrambles to the middle and gets himself situated under the covers while Bianca and I slide in on either side of him. He turns toward Bianca and tucks his head under her chin. He looks so tiny as I watch her stroke his hair and I rub his back again.

It only takes a few minutes for him to fall back to sleep. He's got to be exhausted from the crying and rush of emotions he just went through.

Bianca kisses him on the crown of his head again and then looks over at me. "What was that?" she whispers so quietly I can barely hear her.

I look back down at Oliver to make sure he truly is asleep and the soft snores emanating from his little mouth gives him away. Sighing, I keep my hand firmly on his back, needing to feel him here with me. How this person who I didn't even know existed a year ago has become one of the most important people in my life is something I'll never figure out.

I answer her in low whispers, "I told you I got Oliver because my sister died of an overdose." She silently nods, urging me to continue. "When she died, she was in a trap house, full of other addicts. When the ambulance arrived, she was already long gone and the coroner came and took her away. There was a police report, but it was cursory. What was there to investigate? She was another addict, dying of an overdose in filth.

"I'm not sure if nobody knew or if they just didn't care, but the police and coroner were never notified that Molly had a son. They didn't know to go looking for him." Her eyes widen in shock, but she still doesn't say anything, letting me continue. I swallow down the lump in my throat thinking of the next part.

"I don't know everything, he won't talk about all of it. But he was alone in that apartment for ten days. When, he ran out of food he went hungry. Eventually he left and knocked on a neighbor's door asking for food. When he told them he didn't know the last time he saw his mom they notified the police who came and had him taken into custody of child protective services. It took them another few days to locate me."

"How could they have left him for so long?" Her voice is shaky, and I see the layer of moisture covering her eyes. I know exactly how she feels.

"Nobody knew he was there, I guess. As soon as I heard, I rushed to get him. Luckily, since I was a police officer, they let me take provisional custody of him until I had it made permanent with the court. He was so small when I got him. I mean, he's still small but you should have seen him the first time I laid eyes on him. I took him to the doctor, and he was suffering from such extreme dehydration and malnutrition that they wanted to keep him in the hospital for a few days." I close my eyes, trying to fight away the memory of those first days with Oliver. How sad I was about losing my sister and how terrified I was that I wouldn't be able to save her son.

When I take a deep breath and focus back on Bianca, I can see silent tears streaming down her cheeks. I've never seen her cry before. I reach out and use my thumb to wipe them away and she quickly raises her hand to her cheeks, wiping them away herself before pulling back and looking at her fingers, seemingly shocked that there's moisture there.

"That's why you're so concerned about getting him to eat all that healthy stuff." It's not a question, and she's right.

"At first, I was just trying to make sure he got all the nutrients he needed after he got out of the hospital, then it became a kind of obsession. Like if I could just get him to eat the right things, he would be okay. I know it's crazy."

Her head shakes back and forth, her brown hair moving in waves over her shoulders. "And his nightmare was about that?"

"He's had them since he came to live with me. In the beginning they were almost every night but lately they've been tapering off. He never tells me all of it, I'm not sure he remembers. But he talks about being all alone and he can't find his mom or me. I know the experience of being left alone in that apartment was traumatizing but the thing is, anything could have happened to him before that too. Molly obviously wasn't in any condition to take proper care of him. Who knows who she had coming in and out of that apartment, what he saw, what happened to him. I try not to worry about it too much, but on nights like tonight, when he wakes up screaming, it's impossible."

"You're doing everything you can. He seems so happy here."

"I'm trying my best, but some days I feel so lost. I'm not sure if what I'm doing is enough."

"Don't talk like that." The tone of her voice is rather harsh but still only just above a whisper, mindful of Oliver sleeping against her. "He's lucky to have you. Without you, where would he be? In some foster home with no one who cares enough to sit with him when he wakes up from a nightmare."

I pointedly look at him snuggled up against her chest, head tucked under her chin and her arms wrapped around his little body. "What about you, Bianca? Does he have you too?" I know what I'm asking her isn't fair, but I'm not concerned about fairness right now. I'm worried about my son who is falling for this woman just as much as I am.

Her deep brown eyes bore into mine, and I see her chewing on her bottom lip. She knows what I'm asking is deeper than if she's just going to be around sometimes. That I want to know if she's going to stick around to be part of his support system. After all these weeks, this is the hardest I've pushed her to make some kind of promise or declaration of her intentions. I won't even bother asking about us right now. I just want to make sure that she's going to be there for Oliver.

"Yeah," she says softly. "He has me too." I'm so relieved that I can't help reaching out to her, lightly stroking her cheek as she nuzzles against my hand. Lying in bed with her, Oliver snuggled between us, is the closest thing to family I've felt since my dad died and I decide right now, I'll do anything to keep this.

CHAPTER SIXTEEN

BIANCA

"Who are you and what have you done with my friend?"

I stand back from the painting I've just hung on the white gallery wall and try to see if it's off kilter. "What are you talking about?" I ask before stepping forward and nudging the bottom corner of the frame to the right.

"I'm talking about you never wanting to go out anymore."

I just shrug and dig back into the stack of canvases that need to be hung today. It's not like this is the first time I've ever turned down a night on the town and I'm sure it won't be the last. "Carson's not getting off from work until late tonight and I promised Oliver I would take him to the park when I get home. They just installed some new play equipment he wants to check out."

"That right there!" she says pointing at me with an accusatory finger. "For someone who is supposed to be single you're sure acting like a married woman with kids." I just shrug her off again. She's probably right. I haven't gone out in weeks. In fact, I don't think I've been out drinking since my birthday last month. It should probably worry me I'm ditching a night out to take Oliver to the park but honestly, it sounds like more fun.

"What happened to you calling kids Satan's spawn and all that?"

"Oh, I still think they are, you should see some of those kids at his art class," I give an exaggerated shudder thinking about how they are always running around like wild heathens and screaming at the top of their lungs. If they're not mouthing off to the teachers, they're being obnoxious to their parents. Not that I can really blame them for that, those moms are like piranhas and Carson is the chum. It's no coincidence that I've never missed one of Oliver's art classes. Not that I have any kind of claim on the guy, I'm just looking out for him. They would eat him alive.

Yeah, it's starting to sound less and less convincing to me too.

"Oliver's not like a regular kid. We're like kindred spirits or something. Did I show you the picture of the rat he drew from Ratatouille?" I reach to grab my phone to show her the pic.

"Yes," she says holding up her hands to stop me. "Yes, you showed me the drawing. He's a good artist, especially for someone his age. Most kids are drawing hand turkeys. Just because he has talent doesn't mean you have to be his mentor or something. You got him into that program."

I'm starting to get annoyed with this conversation. I don't like my relationship with Oliver being questioned. I know it's not exactly traditional, but I like the kid. "Jenna, I like spending time with him. I have fun. Back off, will you?"

"Fine," she says in a playacting tone while handing me a J-Hook to hang the next painting. "There will just be more hot guys for me then." I see her giving me side eye before she continues. "So, what's up with you and the kid's dad, anyway?"

That's an excellent fucking question. I mean, the sex is mind blowing. I've never experienced anything like it. I've tried really hard to keep it on that kind of superficial level, but little by little Carson's been reeling me in, whether he means to or not. I'm starting to have actual feelings for him, and I don't know what to do about that.

At least he hasn't brought up the subject of us being more than just fuck buddies. I don't want to have to tell him I can't have children then have him dump me like all the rest. I think that might be something I wouldn't be able to come back from. Though there is a teeny tiny part of me in the very back of my brain that tells me he might not care. I ignore that voice and shove it away. Every past experience I've had tells me it's a deal breaker.

I'm doing my best to keep walls up between us. We fuck like rabbits, but I've never spent the night with him. That feels like a line, once crossed, I won't be able to come back from. Of course, I spent the night when Oliver had the nightmare but that was different.

It's getting harder and harder to go home every night, whether it's when I say goodbye and see that look in his eyes that tells me he wishes I would stay or when I sneak out of his bed while he's still sleeping. I want to stay there and wake up next to him in the morning. I just know that once I do, my heart is going to be lost for good. This is better.

Jenna elbows me, and I realize I haven't answered her. "Nothing's going on, really," I say with as much nonchalance as I can muster. "He's amazing in bed and we're fuck buddies. That's it."

"Oh, that's it?" She asks like she doesn't believe a word I'm saying which she probably shouldn't.

"Yes, that's it." I say firmly. "Have you ever seen me get all googly eyed over some guy before?"

"Nope, never. That means you're long overdue."

I shake my head at her and try for a change of subject. "What happened to you and Clark Kent, anyway?"

"Oh my god, I can't believe I haven't told you!" I let Jenna go on about her hook-up that seems to be sticking around and I'm glad this seems to have gotten her off the subject of Carson for the moment. He and I are not something I want to think about right now. It feels like our situation is coming to a head and a decision is going to have to be made soon. I'm just not sure I'm ready for that or what will happen when it does.

And what if he doesn't want to see me anymore? Does that mean I can't see Oliver? I think that would break my heart and I'm pretty sure Oliver wouldn't be happy about it either. No, I don't think

Carson is that cruel. When this thing between us ends, I can't see him keeping me away from the kid. At least I hope he won't.

"Can you push me on the swings?"

"Of course." The blanket I brought for us to sit on is covered with the healthy, Carson approved, snacks I brought. Though that didn't stop me from getting us each a little something when the ice-cream truck came around. I mean, I understand where he's coming from with the health food, but sometimes you've just got to live a little.

He climbs up onto the swing and I give him gentle pushes while he yells at me to make him go higher. I can't help but laugh. Was I ever as carefree as this kid is? I'm sure I was at some point, but as you get older things just get more and more complicated and you can lose that enthusiasm for life.

After the swings he wants to go across the monkey bars so I hold him up while his tiny hands move from rung to rung. We repeat this about twenty times and before long my arms are shaking. "Let's head back to the blanket and get something to eat, then we'll pack up and head home."

"Do we have to?" He whines at me.

"Yup, it's getting dark, it's not safe to be out in the park this late." Well, look at that. Carson may be rubbing off on me after all. It could also be that I'm much more concerned about Oliver's safety than I am my own which is an interesting revelation.

We're walking back over to the blanket when I see an older man slumped against a tree near our picnic spot. I grab onto Oliver's hand and pull him closer to me. Thankfully, he doesn't seem to notice the figure wrapped in a heavy coat and a hat pulled down low over his face. He's got to be in his fifties and his hands are shaking while he leans against the tree which immediately says to me he's either a junkie or an alcoholic, either way I don't want Oliver anywhere near him.

Not to be *that* over dramatic bitch, but he gives off sinister vibes. I'm not sure I've ever used those words to describe a person before. Cats? Sure. But never a person.

We have to pass within ten feet of him to get to our stuff. If my car keys weren't tucked away in the picnic basket, I would just abandon everything and take off. Sure, the man hasn't done anything. He hasn't even indicated that he's paying attention to us, but something about him is giving me the creeps, even though I can't see his eyes I can practically feel them on me.

When we're within a few feet of him, I turn my head and blatantly stare at him. I don't want him to think I'm some weakling that's not aware of my surroundings. If he has anything nefarious planned, he should know I'm ready, alert, and waiting for him. I know I'm probably being melodramatic, but I don't want anything to happen to Oliver. Is this that maternal instinct women talk about having? It's got to be, because I feel like I would fight this guy to the death if he got anywhere near him. It's a weird feeling but I'm going to embrace it for now.

Luckily, it doesn't seem a fight to the death is on tonight's agenda. Apparently, my staring has unnerved him as much as his lurking unnerved me. He turns and slowly starts making his way across the park to a clump of picnic tables.

Between Oliver and I, we get everything packed up quickly and I've got him buckled into his car seat within minutes. Before I pull out of the spot I look around and don't see the man anywhere. I knew I was being paranoid, but it's better safe than sorry. God, I'm going to become an overly anxious basket case if I hang out with Carson much longer.

We're back at Oliver's within ten minutes, and I walk him inside the house. I've got my own key now to their place. It's not for some relationship reason or anything, I've just been watching Oliver a lot lately when Carson's been at work. At least I don't think it's some kind of relationship milestone. Come to think of it, Carson didn't really say anything when he handed it to me, but we're not in a relationship so it has to be because of Oliver, right?

Carson's in the kitchen leaning over a pot of something on the stove. When he hears us come in, he looks up and smiles. "How are my two favorite people? Did you guys have fun at the park?"

I'm not normally a person who blushes but whenever Carson pays me an offhanded compliment like saying I'm one of his favorite people, I can't help but feel two burning patches of pink on my cheeks.

"It was so much fun, Dad. Bianca pushed me on the swings and then we went on the monkey bars, and she even got me a popsicle." He's so excited that I don't think he even took a breath through that. I cringe a little at that end part about the popsicle, especially since he seems to be a little hopped up on sugar.

Carson just looks at me with a raised eyebrow and I give him a shrug. "We ate the healthy stuff first."

"I'm making whole wheat pesto pasta for dinner. Are you staying?"

Ugh, why do I feel upset about missing whole wheat pasta? "I can't tonight. I'm having dinner with my mom and we're going to swing by Dad's place and see if he wants to come with us. I'll take a rain check though. Preferably, when you're making real pasta," I tease.

"Buddy, go on into the bathroom and wash your hands, dinner is almost ready." Oliver takes off to the bathroom and Carson sets the spoon down, stalking over to me. Before I can say a word, he's wrapped his arm around my waist and pulled me to him. I can immediately feel my nipples harden through my clothes and heat pool between my legs. How can just having him up against me immediately turn me on so much?

"You sure you can't stay?" His breath is heavy on my neck, and I can feel his tongue trace the shell of my ear, it causes my knees to go weak and I'd probably hit the floor if he wasn't holding me up.

"Are you saying you'd make it worth my while?" I move my hand down to the front of his jeans and palm his heavy length straining to get out. God, I love how hard he is for me all the time.

His hips give a little involuntary surge forward and I give him a squeeze. He looks down at me and I can see those moss green eyes have turned a deeper emerald. "I think it will absolutely be worth your time."

I want to stay, I really do, but I've made plans and I feel like I'm already losing myself in him. I have to keep something else in my life that's not just Carson and Oliver. If I forgo everyone and everything else, what will I have when they're gone?

"I really can't." I reach up with my lips and give him a soft kiss that he immediately deepens. The need is radiating off him and it's penetrating me. I grab onto the front of his shirt, steadying myself. It's only when I hear Oliver's tiny footsteps on the hardwood floor of the hallway that I pull back. His look is smoldering and my lips feel swollen. I know if I don't get out of there right now we're going to end up in the bathroom perched on the vanity again while Oliver watches a movie.

"I've got to go," I reiterate.

"Are you coming over later?" I want to, I really do, but maybe it's best if I put a little space between us. It could do my heart some good.

"Maybe." Well, that wasn't exactly a no, but at least I'm trying.

Hours later I'm sitting in my car, engine off, hands shaking. I glance back towards my house and see that Violet's made it home safely.

Good. I'm not so petty that I want something bad to happen to her but I'm also not ready to go in there and speak to her yet. I need to sort out a few of my emotions first. I pull my phone out of my bag with unsteady hands and quickly type a message.

Me: Are you awake?

It only takes a few seconds to get a response.

Carson: Yeah, I'll leave the door unlocked for you.

I take a deep breath and exit my car, navigating the walkway up to Carson's door. Just when I'm about to reach for the doorknob he opens it.

"Hey, babe." He's smiling until he sees my face. Then he moves forward at lightning speed and wraps me in a tight hug. "Bianca, what's wrong? Tell me."

"I'm fine, really. I'm fine." And I really am, I think I'm more shocked than anything. Though there's a little hurt mixed in there too.

Carson takes my hand and leads me to the couch, sitting down himself before settling me in his lap. I've never been quite comfortable with this position. I always feel like I'm too big for it and it makes me feel exposed, but not tonight. Tonight, I relish the feeling of his arms around me holding me tight. I lay my head down against his shoulder and take a moment to feel his hard solid body holding me.

"Tell me what's wrong, baby." He brushes the hair out of my face and rubs small circles on my back. I slowly start to calm down, my hands becoming steadier. Carson's patiently waiting for me to tell him why I'm upset, and it warms my heart that he isn't pushing me for answers before I'm ready.

When I finally get my thoughts in order, I start to speak. "You know how I was picking up my mom for dinner and we were going to stop by my dad's to see if he wanted to go with us?" I can feel his silent nod against the top of my head so I continue. "Yeah, well, his place has never really been one of those knock before you enter places. I mean, I have a key. I just wasn't expecting..." My voice drifts off thinking about what happened again.

"You weren't expecting what?" he prods gently.

"When Mom and I walked in, Dad and Violet were both half naked, going at it in the kitchen."

There are a few beats of silence before he says. "Oh. So, you've finally figured it out, huh?"

I pull away from him quickly and lean back so I can look into his eyes. I don't see any surprise there and I'm confused.

"You *knew?*" I practically shout and whack him on the chest.

"Well, I didn't have any tangible proof, but I was pretty sure."

"What are you talking about?" I demand.

He lets out a sigh and pulls me back against his chest. "I'm a detective, remember? It's my job to piece things together and see things other people miss.

"A few days after I moved in your dad was sitting outside in his truck well after midnight and watching your house. I didn't know who he was, so I approached him to find out what was going on. I didn't want some man spying on you three. He was your dad, and he made up some lame excuse that he was just checking on you to make sure you made it home alright and couldn't reach you on the phone, except he accidentally said he was waiting for Violet before correcting himself. In my experience, a man only drags himself out of bed to lurk in the shadows and make sure a woman gets home alright if he's interested in her. I wasn't exactly sure what was going on, but I figured it had very little to do with you. He seemed harmless enough, so I just sent him on his way."

"You never told me that."

I can feel him shrug behind me. "We weren't exactly on the best of terms in the early days."

"Well, you hiding things from me doesn't exactly put us on the best of terms now," I grumble but there's no heat to my words.

He ignores my interruption and continues. "Then there was the fact that Violet kept *disappearing,* your words, not mine. That's when I first got the inkling that they might be together."

"That seems pretty thin, Detective."

"Yeah, but when I set up my security system, I caught her climbing into his truck a few times late at night. I figured it wasn't for work."

"I can't believe you didn't tell me." I say twisting around to look him in the eyes. I mean, he had visual proof and didn't say a god-damn word to me.

"Back up, Sparky. I didn't know anything for sure and it wasn't my business. I don't really know either your father or Violet and everything I had was circumstantial. If you had wanted to see what was going on, you would have figured it out yourself, but I think you were firmly living by the ignorance is bliss creed."

I turn back around in his lap and grumble to myself again. He's probably right. I had even more pieces than he did, and I hadn't put it together. I can't believe I was trying so hard to get Mom and Dad to reconcile. Things seemed to be progressing on Mom's end, but Dad told me several times to back off. I guess I should have listened. It's just, sometimes when I get these ideas in my head, it's hard for me to let them go.

Besides, I was honestly worried about him. I haven't seen him date in twenty years. Not since their divorce. I was a little worried that maybe he had been pining away for her all these years. Obviously, that isn't the case. I just didn't want him to be alone forever like I was going to be. Then again, as I feel Carson firmly holding me to his chest and I can see Oliver's slightly open door down the hallway, I wonder if maybe I won't be alone after all. It's a dangerous way to think but I'm already past the point of protecting myself. My heart is firmly involved already. It doesn't matter if we stopped seeing each other now or if he rejects me once he finds out about my health issues, the results will be the same. I'll have a heart that will be broken beyond repair.

"I know it was probably shocking finding them that way, I'm sure you want to rub your eyes out with soap—"

"Bleach," I correct.

He lets out a low chuckle. "Okay, bleach. But what's really upsetting you about this? Do you not want them to be together?"

It's a good question. I've been running on shock since I left Dad's and dropped Mom at her new place. She'd been ranting and raving the entire ride, acting about ten times worse than Oliver ever has, and I pretty much just blocked her out. I haven't really had time to assess what my issue truly is.

"I guess I'm mostly mad that they lied to me, and I'm hurt that they thought they couldn't tell me the truth."

"If they had told you the truth before you walked in on them, what would you have said?"

"I... I'm not sure. But I wouldn't have acted the way I did tonight." Suddenly I'm realizing how badly I behaved. I basically stood there yelling at Dad and ignored Violet for most of the confrontation. I was so angry at my father that the nasty things Mom was saying to Violet didn't even register with me until much later. I'm going to need to have a few words with my mother about that. Nobody should say those things to other women, let alone Violet, one of the sweetest people in the world.

While I'm thinking about Carson's question my phone buzzes violently in my purse. I'm almost scared to know who's calling but let out a sigh of relief when I see it's Hollie. I try to pull myself off Carson's lap to take the call but he holds me firmly to him. "You can talk in here."

I shrug, I was just trying to not be rude. "Hey, Hollie."

"What the hell is going on over there, Bianca?"

"I see you've spoken to Violet." I let out a sigh. Hollie will be a neutral third party. Of the three of us she's always been the most pragmatic and has always been good at reading people.

"Yeah," she says more softly. "I just got off the phone with her. She's kind of a mess. She's worried she's lost you and that you're going to hate her forever."

I can immediately feel myself deflate. I may be angry for the moment, but she hasn't lost me. "I don't hate her," I practically whisper.

"I know you don't, sweetie. She's just scared and upset right now. You know you and I are the only real family she has."

I close my eyes and take in a deep breath letting the guilt wash over me. She's right. I may have a family support system, but Violet doesn't have that. Her parents are social climbing pieces of shit who don't care about her unless she conforms to the mold they want to put her in. Hollie and I are all she has.

"You know she would never hurt you on purpose right, B? She was scared of how you'd react, and I think she's been really happy with Dante. I think you should talk to her."

"I know, you're right. Thanks for the call, Hollie. What would I do without you?"

"Oh, just fuck up all the relationships in your life. So if you want to tell me about that cop—"

"Goodnight, Hollie." I say loudly, ending the call. I surreptitiously move my eyes to look at Carson and see if he caught that last part, but his face is inscrutable as he strokes my hair.

"You gonna go talk to Violet?"

"Yeah, I think I need to. I know she's worried and I don't want to make her have to wait until morning. Plus, I have a few questions of my own that need to be answered."

"Just take it easy on her." I must have given him a *what the hell are our you talking about* look because he continues on. "I know you're a spitfire, Sparky. But you have one of the kindest, most generous hearts I've ever seen. You just don't always show it. I think Violet needs that big heart of yours right now."

I give him a quick peck on the cheek and quickly push off his lap, heading towards the door without turning around. I don't want him to see the moisture that's gathered in the corners of my eyes. How can this man see me so clearly? I know I put up a tough as nails, carefree, don't give a fuck front, but the people I love? I care about them deeply and would do anything for them. I guess Carson can see it because he and Oliver are among those people now.

"Have a good night," I say softly, closing the door behind me.

Chapter Seventeen

Bianca

"Bianca."

Margot barks out my name from the stair landing. "In here, please." She turns and goes back into her office leaving the door open for me. I'm really not in the mood for this today. I'm glad to have everything resolved with Violet and I plan to talk to Dad after work, but I barely got any sleep last night. I guess falling asleep has become difficult without Carson fucking me into exhaustion first.

I quickly climb the stairs and enter Margot's inner sanctum. "Have a seat," she says, indicating the chair in front of her desk. God, I hope she's not firing me or something. "I notice you haven't brought me any more of your work to look at."

The tension leaves my body as soon as I realize I'm not about to get a verbal pink slip. "I haven't come up with anything I thought was good enough yet." That's a lie. I've done plenty of pieces lately that I thought Margot would like. The problem is my subject matter.

All my paintings, whether they're portraits, abstracts, or anything in between seem to bleed Carson and Oliver. It doesn't matter what I set out to make, it always ends up being them. Even if it's not one of their direct likenesses, it's something that reminds me of them.

I know it's emotions I'm not dealing with coming out in my work and that scares the shit out of me. Even if they are some of the best pieces I've ever done.

Carson keeps asking to see what I've been working on, but I've been putting him off. I can't let him see me open and exposed on the canvas. The second he looks at it I know he's going to see how I feel about them. About him. I just can't face it yet.

"Aren't you painting every day?" She asks, pushing her large red framed glasses back to the bridge of her nose.

"Yes, every chance I get." I assure her.

"And you haven't come up with anything you think is *good enough* for me to look at." She uses air quotes when she says good enough and it makes me want to snap at her. I don't need her making fun of me right now.

I just shake my head. I honestly thought she had forgotten about telling me to bring her something else to look at. It's not like she doesn't have anything else to do.

"I find that hard to believe, Bianca."

I open my mouth to say something but just end up snapping it closed again. What is there to say?

"Next week bring me the most recent piece you've created whether you think it's *good* or not." I really don't want to but what can I do? She's my boss so I just nod and make for her office door. "Bianca, you show a lot of talent. Don't hide your emotions, let it drip down the canvas for us all to see."

"Thanks, Margot." I hope she can't hear the lack of enthusiasm in my voice.

These stupid fucking shoes.

I've gone through more pairs of high heels lately than I care to admit. I love heels, they make me feel sexy and powerful. I wear them every day to work even if I'm running around setting up a show. But today, these shoes can suck it.

Just as I was walking to my car after work my heel caught in a crack in the sidewalk, and I went crashing to the ground, skinning my knee. What was worse was the heel broke off my favorite pair of Betsey Johnsons.

I stopped at Dad's on the way home to talk to him about Violet and now I'm scanning the street for a parking space. I see Violet's car parked in the driveway already and realize I'm going to have to hunt down a spot. I can't believe she and my dad are dating. They seem to truly have feelings for each other. Is it a little weird? Of course. But it's not like I have any reason to be mad about it.

Sure, I was trying to set my parents up, and maybe for a fleeting moment I thought it would be cool if they were together again, but I just wanted them both to be happy. Especially Dad since he seemed so lonely lately.

Well, it looks like Violet took care of that problem for me. I'm not much of a romantic by any stretch of the imagination, but I do have spectacular taste in friends, and if Dad can find happiness with one of them, then more power to him. He honestly couldn't do better than Violet.

I finally find a spot several houses down and grab my destroyed shoes from where they've been sitting in the passenger seat. I carefully navigate the sidewalk barefoot, keeping my eyes down so I can avoid any rocks, twigs, or in one case a line of ants on the way to do whatever it is ants do.

Because I'm so focused on where I'm stepping, I don't notice the door to the house is wide open until I've almost reached it. I call out "Hello," and stick my head inside, then let out a gasp.

The living room looks like it was hit by the Tasmanian Devil. The chairs and end tables have been knocked over, their contents strewn across the room. But what really draws my eye is the coffee table that's shattered into pieces and is covered in blood. Now that I've spotted it, I also see blood in other places, a small patch against the far wall, a few drops in the entryway, and most terrifying, a long trail in the hallway leading to the bedrooms.

I can hear a man's voice coming from deep in the house, but I can't make out what he's saying. If this was a few months ago, I would have rushed in without a thought and probably gotten myself killed. Now I have Carson drilling into me that I've been taking too many liberties with my safety, and I know he's right. There's a fine line between being brave and being stupid. What I'm looking at right now is something that I have no way of handling.

Suddenly, I remember Violet's car parked in the driveway. Unless she went somewhere and left her car, she's in there. My heart catches in my throat and I freeze, not knowing what to do.

Crash.

The sound of glass breaking from deep in the house seems to snap me out of my indecision. I immediately drop the heels in my hand, along with my purse, and take off at a sprint across the lawn. I don't stop running until I make it to Carson's front door. It sounds like Oliver's got that obnoxious kids' station turned up to eleven, so I pound frantically on the door.

"Carson! Carson, please open up! Carson!" It feels like it's years before the door opens, but logically it was probably more like fifteen seconds. The door swings in and I'm filled with relief at the sight of his concerned face.

"Bianca, what's wrong? Are you hurt?" He moves his hands over my arms, presumably looking for injuries, but I shake him off. I don't have time to catch my breath but manage to gasp out, "The door was open. Everything's broken. There's blood. So much blood. Please." His face morphs from concern back to his serious cop face, and it calms me down. He pulls me inside quickly, scanning the street behind me.

"Please, you have to hurry," I beg. "I think Violet's in there."

"Fuck." He turns to the small safe he keeps by the door and punches in a code before pulling out his badge and a heavy looking black gun. I can't take my eyes off it. What if something goes wrong, and he accidentally hits Violet? What if the guy in there has a gun and Carson gets shot? Either of them could get killed. I feel like I'm going to throw up.

He bends over slightly so we're eye to eye, forcing me to look away from the gun in his hand. "Bianca, listen to me. I need you to stay here with Oliver. As soon as I walk out of here, I want you to lock all the doors and windows, then call nine-one-one and tell them what's going on. Take Oliver to the playroom in the middle of the house. Don't open the door for anyone but me, understand? Can you do all that for me, Bianca?"

I just nod my head and look out his window back toward my house. This is taking too long. "Bianca, do not leave this house. I'll go get Violet."

"Please. You have to make sure she's alright. She has to be okay." I clutch his sleeve, but he just nods his head at me, then walks out the front door, moving towards my house as quickly as possible with his head swiveling back and forth, gun held low.

I do as he's instructed and make sure all the doors and windows are secure. I go to grab my cellphone but quickly realize it's in my purse that I dropped outside. I say a silent prayer of thanks that Carson is one of the few people left in the world with a home phone and quickly dial nine-one-one. I'm so out of it I'm not even sure what exactly I told them because honestly, I have no fucking idea what's going on over there. I remembered to tell them that there's a police officer in the house though so at least they won't shoot him. Right?

Fuck. Fuck. Fuck.

I'm tempted to sit and stare out the window to find out what's happening, but I know that if there's shooting, a window is a dangerous place to be. If something is wrong with Violet, Carson is the best chance I have of saving her, and he doesn't need to be worried about me doing something stupid. Plus, I need to find Oliver and make sure he's safe, away from the windows, and if possible, oblivious to the chaos that's happening next door. I head toward his playroom and again hope that Violet isn't in the house after all.

The cordless phone is still in my hand, and I can hear the emergency operator telling me to stay on the line but I don't have time to sit there on the phone with her, I've got to make sure Oliver is safe. Once I've found him I try to paste a smile on my face so he won't know anything is wrong.

"Hi Bianca!" He runs over to me and wraps his arms around my legs. I reach down and return his hug while trying to keep my hands from shaking. "You don't have any shoes." He's practically shouting over the radio that's playing but I don't want to turn it down. I don't want him to hear anything that's happening next door.

Oh god, I really think I might throw up.

I slowly lower myself to the floor and ask him to show me what he's playing with. He goes off on a long tangent about his new set of construction trucks Carson bought him.

"That's awesome, kid." I don't know what he's saying to me, I'm just glad he's distracted. I've never been so scared in my life. When people talk about having an out-of-body experience I wonder if it's like this. I'm here, sitting in the room with Oliver, but I feel like my heart is next door. I can't seem to focus on any one thing.

Oliver's looking at me funny again and I don't know what to say so I just give him my best fake smile and stare blankly at the wall. A few seconds later I hear two sharp cracks and my breath catches in my throat.

A scream almost escapes me, but I hold it back for Oliver's sake. I think up until this very moment I wasn't entirely convinced there was anything really dangerous over there. At the very least, I was in a deep denial, but the sound of gunshots cracking through the air have brought everything into sharp focus.

209

Oliver just continues to play with his toys, not even seeming to have heard the sounds that caused my heart to stop dead in my chest. I can't just wait here, I have to go out and see what's happening. What if Carson and Violet are hurt and they need my help?

"Oliver, I want you to stay in this room, okay?"

He shrugs at me like it's no big deal. "Okay."

"I'm serious about this Oliver. You stay in this room and only come out if your Dad or I come to get you, understood?" His eyes are big, and I know it's because I never speak to him this way, but this is important. I'll apologize for my tone later. He nods and I slip out of the room, closing the door softly behind me.

I just make it to the kitchen window when I hear sirens approaching. You would think they would be a comfort to me but I'm just stressing over the fact that nobody has come out of the house yet. It's taking everything inside me to stop myself from throwing the front door open and sprinting over there, but I promised Carson I would stay put. That I would take care of Oliver. Oh god, what if something's happened to him? What if those shots were someone shooting him and not the other way around? I'll never be able to forgive myself for sending him in there.

Two squad cars come screeching to a halt in front of my place, one halfway up the driveway and the other right in the middle of the street. Officers exit both cars, guns drawn low, and running in a crouch towards the front door. It's only then that I hear Carson's voice shouting. He's stepping out of the front door, his badge held high and his other hand up in the air.

He's saying something to the other officers but I can't hear any of it because all I can see is the red splashed across his shirt. Fortunately, he's standing and he doesn't seem hurt. The other officers are rushing past him into the house, if he was hurt they would be stopping to help him, right? That's when I remember Violet.

Where the fuck is Violet? Shouldn't she be with him? I clutch the window frame so tightly I'm afraid that I'm going to splinter the wood. It's then that Carson sees me standing in the window and he jogs over to me.

"Are you okay?" I get out, though the words are thick in my throat.

"I'm fine," he says. I can't help but put my hand against the glass wishing I was close enough to touch him but knowing he wants me to stay right where I am. He reaches out and places his hand over mine and I swear I can almost feel his warmth reach me through the glass.

"Violet?" I sob. His mouth turns into a straight line, and he looks like he's searching for the right words. "No!" I shout, sure he's going to tell me she's dead. I feel dizzy and I'm pretty sure I'm swaying on my feet.

"Bianca," he snaps at me, pulling me out of my spiral and getting my eyes to focus on him. "They're going to take Violet to the hospital. Will you please call Gloria to come watch Oliver?" I nod emphatically at him. "I'm going to ride with her in the ambulance, alright? Once Gloria gets here, come meet me at the hospital. You should probably call her parents and your dad too."

"Is she going to be okay?" I ask, truly afraid of the answer.

He closes his eyes for just a moment before opening them and staring deep into mine, making sure I'm paying attention to what he's saying. "Right now, all I know is that she's unconscious but she's breathing."

I just nod my head, trying to not let any tears fall. I have to be strong for Violet. "I'll go call Gloria." I turn to find where I dropped the phone, but Carson calls out for me to stop.

He reaches into his back pocket and holds up an ID for me to look at. I squint because it's smudged with blood and he brings it closer to the window.

Tyler Crosson. I let out a gasp.

"Do you know who this is?"

"It's the guy she dated a few times, but she dumped him. I don't think she was really into him, and he was acting like a creep at my birthday party. Where did you get that? Is he in there?"

He looks over at the two ambulances pulling up and the cops that are coming in and out of the house. He looks like he's contemplating what he should tell me, but he should know by now I'm going to get the information I want.

"He was attacking Violet when I went in there." I forget to breathe for a second. I guess the second he showed me the ID I knew what had happened, but it's a whole other thing to have it confirmed. It's only then I remember the sound of the gunshots. "Is he..." I can't even bring myself to ask the question. Carson looks pained but shakes his head. Tyler's dead. Carson had to kill him. This is a fucking nightmare.

"Thank you. Thank you for saving, Violet." He doesn't say anything, just jerks his head in a nod at me then takes off towards the ambulances, shouting instructions at the EMTs on where they can find Violet inside.

I find the phone in the playroom where Oliver is oblivious to all the horror and chaos that's going on next door. "Hey, kid." I say with a slightly shaky voice. "Gloria is going to come watch you for a while. Your dad has to work, and I need to take care of some things, is that okay?"

"Do you think she'll order me pizza?"

I'm not sure if I want to laugh or cry. "Yeah, I think she will." I head into the kitchen and fill Gloria in on what's happened. She's on her way to get Oliver and she's going to take him home with her since I don't know how long Carson is going to be tied up with this. I take a deep breath and feel a single tear fall down my cheek which I quickly wipe away. I don't have either of Violet's parents' numbers with me but I do have one memorized that I need to call. I steady my hands and dial the number to Dad's cell.

CHAPTER EIGHTEEN

CARSON

The white of my knuckles is almost the same color as the porcelain sink I've got a death grip on. If I let my fingers loosen, I know my hands will start shaking. An extremely weary man is looking back at me from the dirty mirror. This was not how I intended my day to go.

I wash my hands in the scalding hospital bathroom water one more time, making sure I've gotten all the blood out from under my fingernails and any stray spots that might be on my arms. I do my best to avoid getting water on the blue scrub top the hospital gave me to wear since the shirt I came in with was covered in blood and is currently in an evidence bag with the OPA, or Office of Police Accountability, along with my gun. It's standard operating procedure after any officer involved shooting and I don't expect there to be any issues. It was a good, clean shoot. I've handed over all the evidence I quickly collected at the scene to Rafe, and he's going to take over from there. He told me to go home and get some rest but I need to get my head on straight first.

Walking into Bianca's house and seeing all the blood and destruction had my gut twisted in knots. Not because of the state the house or the danger lurking inside, but because Bianca could have been home, or more likely, knowing her, she could have rushed in there without thinking of the consequences in order to save her friend. That's the kind of person, friend, she is.

When I found the young man leaning over a beaten and unconscious Violet, I called out and identified myself as SPD. When he looked up at me his eyes were wild and I spotted the large knife clutched in his hand. I tried to get him away from Violet as quickly as possible because from where I was standing, I couldn't tell if she was breathing or not. I told him to drop the knife, raise his hands, and step away from her slowly. That's when he came running at me.

I did what I had been trained to do and took the shot, hitting him with one in the shoulder and one in the chest. It wasn't the first time I'd killed someone on the job, working in the gang and narcotics unit in Los Angeles is a dangerous and life-threatening assignment, but it's certainly not something I take lightly either.

My entire body feels exhausted as I drag my hand through my hair and over my face, trying to wake myself up as my adrenaline crashes. On the edge of the sink, my phone lights up again and makes an annoying buzzing sound against the porcelain. I don't even need to look to know it's from Bianca.

She started messaging and calling me as soon as she made it to the hospital and they wouldn't let her back to see Violet. Her father somehow talked his way inside and I've already spoken to him, telling him what I could about what happened. The man looked destroyed, like he'd aged ten years since the last time I'd seen him, and I can't say I blame him. If it were Bianca instead of Violet in that hospital bed I would be just as wrecked, maybe worse. Though I thought it best to not share that information with him.

I've always been so careful. I never tried drugs, I don't drink to excess, I avoid anything that could spin me out of my perfectly crafted control. I've never been addicted to anything in my life. That's changed now. Bianca's my addiction. The one thing I can't shake. And to be honest, I don't want to.

The phone lights up again and I snatch it off the sink, shoving it down into my pocket. I know I need to message her back. But what do I say? Pacing the small space of the bathroom back and forth, I try to get my thoughts in order, my emotions under control.

I haven't spoken to Bianca yet because my first instinct is to scream at her. She could have been hurt. That could have been her I found lying on her bedroom floor, body beaten and bloody, which is crazy because she's literally done nothing wrong. She did exactly what she was supposed to do. She ran to me for help.

I'm certain if this had been the Bianca I met a few months back she would have run into that house without a second thought and gotten herself killed. Maybe all my browbeating her about being more careful about her personal safety can be credited for that.

Still, it feels like there's a band around my chest and it's slowly tightening, making it harder and harder to breathe. This entire situation has made me realize one thing, I'm not just falling for Bianca Moreno, I'm undisputedly, full on cliched, head over heels in love with her.

I know she feels *something* for me. She has to. I can see it in her eyes during her most vulnerable moments when she doesn't think I'm paying attention. When she's watching me from across the room, when I'm playing with Oliver, when I'm deep inside her and she can't tell where one of us ends and the other begins. Why does she keep hiding from me?

I've been waiting, trying to be patient, but I've had enough. It's time she understood that she's mine and I'm hers. Hell, I've been hers for a while now, she just hasn't realized it. And if she doesn't think she's mine, well, she's dead wrong.

I've been letting her run me in circles, stopping me from taking what I—what we both—want just because I worried it would scare her away. Well, I'm done waiting and tiptoeing around. It's time she gets on board with what's happening between us. I don't plan on giving her any other option.

Even though I'm certain she has feelings for me, I know it in my gut, I'm still worried. Those walls she has are tall and they're thick. I just hope I've been chipping away at them enough to finally get them to crumble to the ground. Bianca isn't someone who will be backed into a corner. She's not going to like that I'm giving her an ultimatum. What else can I do? Stay and be held at arm's length until she tires of me and moves on to someone else?

I won't tell her today that I'm in love with her, I'm not a stupid man. Pushing her to admit we're in a relationship and not just some dirty secret she keeps from her friends and family is going to be hard enough. If I throw up my feelings all over her, she'll be gone so fast it would make my head spin. No, it's better to just get her to give us a real chance and ease her into it. Of course, that's what I thought I'd been doing all these weeks, and it hasn't gotten me anywhere. Oh well, one step at a time.

The only problem is I'm not sure what to say to her. How do I approach this so she'll agree to give a relationship between us a chance? Then there's always Oliver to worry about. What if this scares her off for good? Oliver would be absolutely crushed if he never saw Bianca again. I knew from the very start I didn't want to introduce a woman into our lives that wasn't going to stick around, but Bianca somehow slipped in so seamlessly that by the time I noticed, he was already attached. Hell, so was I. My life has gotten exponentially more complicated than when it was just me I had to worry about.

If she's going to bail, I guess it's better to get it over and done with now rather than later when she's even more ingrained in our lives. I mean, hell, she goes to every art class, she picks him up from Gloria's when I'm working late, she even knows his full bedtime routine. For someone who proclaims to hate children, she sure seems to have a bond with mine, but then again, Oliver is easy to love.

I finally bite the bullet and pull out my phone. There are five missed calls and fourteen unread texts from Bianca. I don't even bother going through them one by one, from the looks of it, most of them are her berating me for not getting back to her. Guilt floods my system. I know I should have responded before now. I was just so overwhelmed, not only with the situation, but with all the feelings that were swarming my head and my heart.

I shoot her a quick text letting her know that the doctor says Violet is going to be alright, but I figure her dad has probably already filled her in.

As I exit the restroom into the sterilized, off-white halls of the hospital, my phone buzzes in my hand again.

Bianca: Where are you???

I suppose my silence justifies three question marks.

Me: Getting ready to leave the hospital

Bianca: The gatekeeper of hell out here won't let me back there to see Vi so I might as well go home. Need a ride?

I lean against the wall thinking over my options. On the one hand, I really don't want to speak with her until I've worked out what I'm going to say, but on the other, I'm craving her closeness after such a close call. Plus, I do need a ride home. I arrived via the ambulance carrying Violet, so it's hitch a ride with Bianca or get a rideshare.

I weigh my options for about a half a second before my need to be near her wins out.

Me: Please. I'll meet you in the ER waiting room.

A few minutes later I make my way through the swinging emergency room doors and it only takes me a second to spot my statuesque beauty among the masses of people waiting to be seen. As soon as she sees me approaching, she runs straight into me like a lineman trying to sack the opposing quarterback.

I wrap my arms tightly around her, holding her body close to mine and close my eyes, just soak in the feeling of her pressed against me. I take a deep breath and inhale that sweet and spicy scent that's all Bianca and tuck her head under my chin while she's chattering away about something. I don't hear any of it, I'm just relishing this moment where I get to hold her here in front of everyone. How could she not want this? Not want us? I have to make her realize she wants this as much as I do.

"Carson, are you even listening to me?" Uh, actually no, I wasn't.

"Of course, what were you saying?" She gives a little huff of annoyance and then asks me to confirm Violet's going to be alright. I do my best to reassure her while we head out to the parking lot.

Just as we reach her car, she stops me with her hand on my forearm. I see a look I rarely get from her. One that's full of affection, gratitude, and something else that I haven't been able to figure out yet.

"I don't know how I'll ever be able to repay you for what you did today, Carson."

I shake my head at her. "You don't owe me anything, I was doing my job."

"You could have died." The tiny shake in her voice is the only thing betraying the emotions she's holding back. I know once she's alone, she's going to break down and let everything out. I wish she felt safe enough to do that with me.

"I'm fine, babe. Everybody who matters is fine." I tilt my head down until her forehead is resting against mine. "Thank you."

"What are you thanking me for?" She tries to pull away and look up at me, but I keep her pressed firmly to me.

"Because you didn't go into that house. You came and got me. If you had gone in there and something had happened to you, I don't know what I would have done." I press my lips to the crown of her head and give her a kiss while squeezing her tight.

She gives a little sniffle and buries her face into my scrub top. Bianca isn't good with the mushy feelings stuff, at least not with me. She'll go on and on about her family and friends. I hear her on the phone telling them she loves them all the time. But when it comes to us, she pulls away from anything that even borders on emotional. Since I've decided we're not playing this game anymore, she might as well get used to this. I won't shove down my emotions because they make her uncomfortable. I'm going to make her feel so loved and safe she won't have any choice but to return my feelings.

I give her one last squeeze and release her. "C'mon, let's go home."

She averts her eyes from me and tries to cover them by letting her hair fall over her face, but I can see the wetness in the corners wanting to spill over. I'll let her hide it. For now. As soon as we have our talk, there won't be any more hiding.

The drive home is quiet. She doesn't seem to have anything to say, and I don't want to start an important conversation in the car. After we've driven along in quiet for a few minutes, she puts on some music to cover the awkward silence.

CHAPTER NINETEEN

BIANCA

I don't even bother trying to go to my place once we get home. It's covered in crime scene tape and is crawling with cops. I don't know how long they're going to be over there or when I'll be able to go home.

I want to pack a bag to bring to Violet in the hospital. Maybe Carson can help me get some stuff out of the house. God, am I going to have to hire one of those crime scene clean-up crews? I thought there was a lot of blood in the living room, but according to Carson, the real carnage is back in Violet's bedroom. I can't stop the shudder that runs through my body just thinking of Tyler in there, attacking her, and what could have happened if Carson hadn't come to save her.

The ride home from the hospital was oddly silent. Usually Carson and I don't have any trouble finding things to talk about, but he seemed deep in his head and I had my own thoughts to deal with. I was scared shitless today. To be honest, I'm still scared. This is the stuff Carson deals with every single day. What's going to stop him from going to work one day and never coming home to me? The thought made my heart rate pick up and I had to make a concentrated effort not to spiral out into some kind of panic attack.

Even now that we're back in his house, the mood remains subdued. Carson clatters around in the kitchen while I take a seat on the sofa and wrap myself in the throw that normally lives on the back cushions. It's only when my eyelids feel heavy that I realize how tired I am. Between the adrenaline dump my body has gone through and the hours that have passed since I got home, I feel myself starting drift off.

I feel the weight on the other end of the couch and open my eyes to see Carson sitting there, holding out a glass of wine to me. Quickly extracting my arms from the blanket, I reach out and take the stemmed glass from him, sipping the deep red liquid. "You're not having any?" I ask when I notice he doesn't have a glass in his hand.

"Not right now. Bianca, we need to talk." He says seriously.

Fuck. He wants to have the *we need to talk* conversation? I usually dip out long before this happens. It's basically my signature move. My heart starts rapidly beating in my chest again. He's going to tell me he doesn't want to be with me anymore because I almost got him killed. Or maybe it's because I'm too reckless. I want to vault over the couch and make a run for the door but instead I make sure my voice is steady as a rock when I ask nonchalantly, "Oh? What about?"

He runs his hand back and forth over his short blonde hair like he always does when he's nervous and my heart sinks. Whatever he has to say isn't going to be good. I place my glass down on the coffee table and turn towards him, waiting for the other shoe to drop.

"We've been... sleeping together for a while now." He's speaking slowly and choosing his words carefully. "And the way things have been going... well, this just isn't working for me any longer."

Ouch. I'm getting the break-up speech and I haven't even told him what usually sends guys running for the hills. Good one, Bianca. Nicely done.

I start to get up off the couch; I know I can't go home but I obviously can't stay here when he's telling me to get lost. Dad's still at the hospital so I guess I can go over to his place for the night.

Before I can even stand up fully Carson's hand is gripping my shoulder and pulling me back down. "Jesus Bianca, sit. Will you let me finish?"

"First, don't tell me to sit like I'm some kind of dog." I snap. "I think you calling me Sparky all the time is getting you confused. Second, I get it. You don't need to give me some big, long explanation. We aren't really anything to each other anyway, just neighbors with benefits. If you want to end things between us it's no big deal, I'll get out of your hair so you can enjoy the rest of your evening." The words spewing from my mouth taste bitter and don't come close to how I'm feeling inside. Not a big deal? Then why does it feel like the sky is falling? But I can't stay here and listen to how I'm not good enough for him.

"Bianca, will you listen to me for just a minute?" His hands come up and cup both sides of my face, his voice gentler now. I nod my head, but still can't bring myself to look at his face. I'll listen to what he has to say and then I'll go. If he has some things he wants to get off his chest, I guess I can hear him out.

His thumbs lightly stroke my cheeks, his gentle touch confusing not only my brain but my body as well, as my nipples immediately harden in response. God, why am I like this? "Baby, when I say this isn't working for me anymore what I'm talking about is you sneaking out of my bed every night. You hiding us from your friends and family. You not making a commitment to me. I want us to be together for real. No more of this neighbors with benefits bullshit or whatever you want to call it. I want to wake up with you in my bed every morning. I want to meet your friends and your parents. I want everyone to know that I'm yours and you're mine."

I think my jaw about hits the floor. That was obviously not anywhere close to what I was expecting him to say. I finally manage to pull my eyes up to look deeply into his green ones, and I can feel the sincerity there. He really means it. He wants to be with me. I start to smile and for the briefest of moments my heart soars before everything comes crashing back down.

He only wants to be with me because he doesn't know. I should have gotten out of this before my feelings got involved like. I knew this was a huge mistake and now I'm going to pay for going against my every instinct that was telling me to run before I got too attached. As soon as I tell him, that look of sincerity in his eyes is going to turn into one of disappointment. Maybe even pity. I've seen it again and again. This time it's nobody's fault but mine.

Leaning back, I effectively pull my face from the gentle hold of his hands. I avert my eyes and start to nervously pick at the blanket covering my lap, trying to figure out what to say.

"Bianca? What's wrong?" The concern in his voice nearly does me in and I can feel the tears burning behind my eyes, begging to be unleashed, and to fall freely down my face. But I'm Bianca Fucking Moreno. I don't cry over some guy. *That's right Bianca, keep telling yourself he's just some guy.*

"You don't want to be with me, Carson."

He lets out a deep rumbling chuckle that even now makes my stomach do a tiny flip. "I'm pretty sure I'm saying the exact opposite of that."

"You know I don't like kids."

He rolls his eyes at me. "You haven't exactly been shy about that. Do you like Oliver?"

My head rears back in surprise. "How can you even ask me that? You know I love Oliver. I don't even think of him as a kid, more of a kindred spirit or something."

His eyes and face soften when I talk about his adopted son, the corner of his mouth ticking up in a smile. "Then I don't see the problem."

I let out a huff of frustration. I'm doing a shit job of explaining this, but I can't bring myself to come right out and say it. "Look, you know how I told you I was on birth control? Well, I lied. I haven't been."

He's looking at me in confusion before his eyes go wide. I think he's understanding what I'm getting at before he asks, "You're pregnant?"

"No, no, no." I reassure him quickly. "That's not what I'm trying to say."

"Oookay. You're going to have to help me out here Bianca because I'm not getting it."

I take a deep breath and let it out. "I can't have kids."

He just shrugs at me, still looking confused. "That's fine, I know you don't want kids."

I realize he still doesn't understand what I'm trying to tell him and now I'm getting frustrated. "No, Carson. I mean, yes, I don't want kids." My voice is laced with annoyance at having to spell this out so clearly. Not only do we not seem to be on the same page with this conversation, it's like we're reading completely different books. "It's not just that I don't want kids. It's that I can't have them, hence the reason I don't need birth control. There's no changing my mind later, children aren't a possibility for me. That car accident I was in? You know, the one that gave me my scars?" He nods his head and his eyes widen with understanding. "You shouldn't have to give up having a family just to be with me."

He leans forward and grabs my waist, lifting me up before settling me on his lap with both of my legs straddling his. Our faces are so close together there's no escaping his penetrating gaze. "Bianca, have you ever heard me say that I want kids?"

I try to think back and realize that no, he's never explicitly talked about having kids other than Oliver. "Not that I remember."

"I never really planned on having them. True, it wasn't something I had made a conscious decision about, but I had zero plans of having a family. Hell, I thought I would probably be single forever. I don't care that you can't have children. It's a non-issue for me."

I want to believe him so badly. I really do. But experience tells me he'll change his mind. "You say it's fine now, that you don't care, but eventually you'll resent me for being the reason you don't have a family of your own."

He reaches up and runs his fingers through my long hair. I want to lean into his touch but resist the temptation. Barely. When he finally speaks, his voice is almost a whisper. "Is that what's had you so scared this whole time, baby? You think I care that much about having kids? I already have Oliver. I love him like he's my own and I don't need another one. You're not a kid person and that's fine with me. As long as you love Oliver, I don't give a fuck. I don't need some hypothetical future child. I'll tell you what I do need though. I need you. You make every single thing in my life better. You clear out all the darkness that I see every day and fill it with your own personal brand of sunshine. Do you think I would give you up just because you can't have kids? That I *could* give you up?"

"Everybody cares," I whisper.

"What are you talking about?"

"Every guy I dated in college who found out, dumped me or just wanted to be my fuck buddy. They didn't want to put in the effort of a relationship if it was just going to end because I couldn't give them the family they wanted. I don't even blame them. Eventually, it just became easier to avoid relationships altogether. I was doing just fine until you came along. Now you want to tell me it doesn't matter? That it's no big deal? How am I supposed to believe that?" I lean back and turn my head away, studying his strange, color-coded bookcase, trying to give myself a chance to reel my emotions back in.

One of his hands tangles in my hair pulling me back to face him while the other starts to gently stroke up and down the side of my body, barely grazing the side of my breast. I bite my bottom lip as my body responds to his touch.

"Those boys you dated in college? They were just that. Boys. They were weak. Someone as beautiful and strong as you needs a man, not a boy. Even though I'd like to beat the shit out of them for hurting you, I'm still thankful for those little shits, otherwise you might not be here right now with me and that would be the tragedy of my life."

Before I can say anything else, he tugs on my hair, pulling my mouth to his and softly presses his lips against mine. What starts as a gentle kiss quickly burns out of control. I open my mouth to his probing tongue and let him in, sucking gently on him gently and bringing out a low moan that immediately floods my panties.

He breaks the kiss to yank my shirt over my head, then he's right back to kissing me breathless. His hands are all over my body, my face, my stomach, before landing on my breasts. He pulls each one out of the cups of my lace bra and ends our kiss, leaving me dizzy and gasping for air. He balances each breast carefully in his hands. My arousal is making them extremely sensitive and when he lowers his mouth and gently traces one nipple with the tip of his tongue, I let out a gasp. My hands try to steer his head to take the entire thing into his mouth, but he won't be rushed.

He moves to my other breast, and I let out a whine that's full of needy annoyance. My skirt is hiked up around my hips and my panty-clad pussy is pressed firmly against the bulge in his jeans. I rock back and forth, hoping the pressure of the zipper against my slit can give me some relief but before I can even get started, he grabs my hips, stilling them.

"Are you feeling needy tonight, baby?" He asks me with that smirk I want to wipe off his face, but the only thing I can bring myself to do is beg.

"Please Carson, stop playing."

"But I love to play with you. You're my favorite girl." Damn. A whole new wave of wetness comes flowing out of my channel when he says I'm his favorite girl. It shouldn't feel that good.

"Don't tease," I whine while trying to rock my hips into him again. He takes a hold of one of my nipples and gives it a sharp tweak causing me to cry out.

"Don't I always give you what you need?" I tilt my head and glare at him, but he just lets out a laugh. "Well, I give you what you need when you're a good girl." I moan again, letting his words wrap around my body like a caress and heat my skin.

His lips trail up my neck alternating between kisses and licks until he gets to my ear and gently bites down. Fuck, he knows exactly what I like. My nails dig into his shoulders and my entire body feels like one raw nerve. "You said you were going to give me what I need."

Suddenly his fingers are brushing up against my wet slit through my panties and my entire body jerks. I try to lean into his fingers, needing more pressure, but he pulls them away from me. "I'm not sure yet if you should be rewarded for how careful you were today, or if I should punish you for thinking I wouldn't want you," he whispers, his breath hot in my ear, sending shivers through my heated body.

"Rewarded," I grind out. This man loves to tease and edge me to extremes I've never imagined possible. I would never take this type of commanding attitude in the bedroom from anyone else. I'm used to being in charge of my own pleasure, probably because most of the men I've been with couldn't find a clit or g-spot if their lives depended on it. But when I'm with Carson, I easily hand that control over to him. I'm held captive by his sexual will and that means I don't always get what I want right when I want it. But when he finally lets me come? God, it's like nothing I've ever experienced before. There are times I have to beg him to stop because the pleasure is too much for my body to handle.

His hands slide under my ass and he lifts me into the air like I weigh nothing. Squealing, I hold on to him like a spider monkey, arms around his neck, legs wrapped tightly around his waist. I take the opportunity to run my tongue into the hallow of his neck and smile when I feel his body shudder against me. He may be in charge of my orgasms but I'm in charge of his pleasure too.

As soon as we're in his bedroom, he tosses me into the center of the bed and starts ripping off his clothing. I join in and I've soon discarded my skirt, bra, and panties to the side of the bed. When Carson's done stripping down, his clothes are laid neatly on the chair across from the bed. I'd roll my eyes at him if I could take them off his turgid, dripping cock. I reach out for it, but he dances away from my grasp.

"On your back, legs spread for me." I immediately follow his instructions putting myself on full display for him while he climbs onto the bed, looming over me on his knees. His big hand grips his rigged and angry cock, slowly stroking it from root to tip and back again, his gaze wandering lazily over my body.

"What are you waiting for?" I ask with a groan. I'm so turned on and desperate for his touch that my breath is coming out in little puffs.

"Give me a minute to look at what's finally mine." His words make me whimper and I'm pretty sure my entire body blushes from head to toe. Is that even possible?

"Well, if I'm yours then you're mine." I counter. Even when my body aches for him I still can't resist giving him shit. His eyes have darkened to that deep emerald color again and his hand is moving faster along his hard length.

"You've got that right. I'm yours and you're mine. Just like this is your cock." The hand that's not currently occupied with jerking himself off moves to my pussy and he runs two fingers down my slick lips before letting them both slide smoothly inside me, making me gasp. "And this is my tight wet little cunt. Isn't it, baby?"

I can't stop myself from grabbing his wrist, trying to draw his fingers deeper inside me. All I can do is nod my head and jerk my hips. He immediately pulls his hand away from me, leaving me gasping and feeling so empty I could cry. "I want to hear you say the words, Bianca."

My brain short circuits when he brings his fingers up to his mouth and slowly sucks my cream off them until they're clean. He closes his eyes, and a deep rumble of satisfaction emanates from his chest at my taste. Whimpering, I reach out for him, but he dodges my hands, staying out of reach.

What does he want me to say again? I'll say anything if he'll just let me come. When I can't take it any longer, I reach my hand down and rub my clit in furious circles while I watch the pre-come steadily drip from the tip of his cock, marking the sheets.

The pleasurable sensations have just started to build when he smacks my hand away. I cry out, not from any pain but out of pure frustration. I feel like I'm a rubber band pulled tight, and the slightest thing is going to cause me to snap.

"That's my orgasm too, baby. It belongs to me. When you're desperate to come from now on, you come to me and I'll decide what you need. Now, tell me who's tight needy cunt this is."

"Yours!" I shout, desperate for what he's only ever been able to give me. "My cunt is all yours, Carson."

With a growl he lets go of his cock and covers me with the length of his body. He balances his weight on his forearms on either side of my head, so he doesn't crush me. I can't help but writhing underneath him until I feel the head of his cock notched at my entrance. He holds it there, teasing me all over again.

"Look at me, baby." It's not until I hear the deep timber of his voice that I realize my eyes are screwed shut, waiting for him to plunge deep inside me. As soon as they're open, I see his face hovering right over mine. "All of you is mine. Every single piece of you. Nothing is ever going to change that, you understand me? You're perfect the way you are."

Don't cry Bianca. Don't you fucking cry.

I bite down on my lip to keep the tears at bay and nod and give him a nod. Could what he's saying possibly be true? Could he really be the only man that has ever been able to truly accept me the way

I am? All my experiences tell me it's not possible, he'll change his mind someday and leave me devastated and alone. I want to believe him. With every fiber of my being, I want what he's telling me to be true. He might just be worth taking a chance on. The thoughts going through my head are overwhelming. Then he pushes his cock all the way inside me in one hard thrust and I'm not capable of thinking anything anymore.

From the very start our pace is wild and frantic, his thrusts so hard they're sliding me up the bed. I grab onto his ass as he moves inside me and hold on for dear life. He's rutting into me like an animal and I'm urging him to go harder, faster.

He grabs one of my legs and throws it over his shoulder, changing the angle he's entering me and now I can feel every inch of him rub back and forth against that spot inside me. I'm no longer urging on his pounding into my body, I'm not sure I'm even breathing. Leaning down, with my ankles practically bent back to my head, I can feel his hot breath on my face.

I'm not sure how he's done it, but with the control he's had over my orgasms these past weeks he must have somehow trained my pussy to come on command, because as soon as he whispers into my ear, "Come on my cock now, perfect girl," an orgasm slams into me out of nowhere. It's deep, and it's intense and leaves me scrabbling to hold on to something while I cry out his name.

Carson's rhythm becomes choppy and his thrusts erratic before he quickly pulls out of my pussy, leaving me to cry out at the empty feeling he's left me with. He's sitting back on his heels and pumping his cock hard and fast, his gaze transfixed on my dripping slit. It's one of the hottest things I've ever seen. His hand is moving so quickly it's like a blur and I can see his lips continuously moving. It takes me a moment before I realize he's repeating the word *mine* over and over. The words make my walls clench and a whimper escape my throat.

I'm not sure if he lets out a roar, or it's the sound of blood rushing in my ears but his body stills as spurt after spurt of his sticky white come lands on my body. He's coating me in it, his spend so hot it feels like it's burning my sensitive skin. His orgasm seems endless, and I wonder if he's ever going to stop. He's coated my pussy and my thighs, I can see white streaks of jizz sliding down my slit. When he's finally empty, his hand starts to slowly and almost reverently rub the come into my skin. "Carson, what are you doing?"

"You're mine now so I'm marking you. I want you to feel me all on your skin, to smell like me. I want any motherfucker within a ten-foot radius to smell my come and know you're mine."

"There's nobody here but us."

"Good, that just means I won't have to beat the shit out of someone for getting close enough to smell your pussy."

He's acting slightly—okay, completely—unhinged right now. This display of possessiveness should freak me out but all it does is make me feel cherished and wanted. He wants me enough to mark me as his. I chew my bottom lip then bring my finger down to my wet pussy. I run my fingertip from my hole up and over my sensitive clit, which makes me groan, and when my finger is covered in our combined fluids, I pop it into my mouth.

I close my eyes and let out a little moan. It shouldn't taste as good as it does. It should be dirty, filthy, wrong. And it is those things. But it's also extremely erotic and the taste of both of us together is something I want to remember.

He's watching me clean both of our come from my finger intently, an inscrutable expression on his face. "See? You're fucking perfect."

He collapses onto the bed next to me and pulls me into his arms, spooning my body while cupping my come covered pussy possessively with his large hand. I'm about to drift off to sleep when I hear him ask, "You'll be here in the morning?"

I don't even have to think before I give him my answer. "Yeah, I will."

He tucks my head under his chin and gives my pussy a squeeze, reminding me who it belongs to. I feel his chest rise and fall in a steady rhythm that's lulling me to sleep, and I put all my worries and insecurities to the back of my mind.

He thinks I'm perfect.

I know that I'm not, but maybe I could be perfect for him.

Chapter Twenty

Carson

The early morning light is streaming in through the bedroom window and falls across my face waking me before my alarm goes off. I was so wrapped up in Bianca last night, I forgot to close the blinds. Worth it.

Yesterday was a long and tough day but it was all worth it because I finally made Bianca mine. Now I just have to get her to fall in love with me, then get her to stay with Oliver and me forever. Baby steps.

Her lush body is currently pressed up against me, her curvy ass pressed into my groin. My cock's already standing at full mast in the cradle of her ass. I slowly stroke down her stomach and hip, over the scar tissue she once played off so casually to me. My pushing her yesterday made her finally reveal why she had been holding me at arm's length for so long.

I still can't believe she thought I wouldn't want her just because she can't have children. Though I suppose if I had been rejected for the same reason repeatedly, I might be weary of who I told as well. I just hope I was able to assuage her fears last night. I truly don't give a flying fuck if she can have kids. Hell, I already knew she didn't want them, it wasn't like I planned to push her into having a child she didn't want. Even if Oliver had never come into my life, Bianca would be more than enough for me. Getting to have her in my life far outweighs any kind of paternal need I could ever have.

When I said that having a family wasn't something I ever really thought about, I wasn't lying. I was always too busy. I was caught up in trying to take care of my mom and sister. Then when they were both gone, I threw myself into my job. I was relentless in my pursuit of putting away the trash that filled the LA streets and helping those who seemed to actually want my help, unlike my sister. My focus was almost single-minded. I would put up goal after goal and time and time again I would knock them down, sometimes with dire consequences to those around me, but my tunnel vision wouldn't let me see anything else, let alone allow thoughts of starting a family. And now it's not something I need when I already have the woman who lights up my every single day by my side.

When I brought Oliver to Seattle, I was full of fear and guilt. Our last days in Los Angeles had been dark, and it was the perfect time for the both of us to make a fresh start. Even with having Gloria here I figured it would take us both quite a while to acclimate to our new city. Then, out of nowhere, on the very first day in our new home I meet a woman who both drives me crazy and cracks my heart open. Without even trying, she somehow rearranged everything in my life and slotted herself in perfectly. She didn't even want to be there, but now that I've got her, I'm sure as fuck not letting her go.

Bianca makes a little sighing sound in her sleep that goes straight to my dick and makes it twitch against her ass. God, I'm always hard when I'm around this woman. Though it's sometimes inconvenient, I wouldn't have it any other way. Finally waking up with her in my bed, bathed in the early morning light makes my heart twist in my chest and my cock swell.

I bury my nose in her hair and breathe in my favorite scent in the world. Fuck, if I could somehow bottle her smell I'd be able to make a fortune, but I'm not sure I'd be able to share it with anyone else. All of her belongs to me now, even her smell.

I slide her leg up and back so it's draped over my own, opening up her sweet pussy to me. She makes these cute little mumbles in her sleep, but she doesn't wake up, only burrows herself further into the blankets.

I reach down and spread her lips, unable to suppress a smile when I see she's already wet. Even in her sleep she's ready for me. I told her the truth last night. She's fucking perfect.

I position my cock at her entrance and slowly, steadily push forward burying myself inside her. She's so goddamn tight in this position I have to grit my teeth to keep from coming the second I'm buried fully inside her. I slowly work my cock in and out of her tight hole and the sounds of her little whimpers fill the room making a spurt of come shoot out of my tip. Her nipples are puckered, tight, and too much of a temptation for me not to play with. The second I do, she's awake, her head rolling back to look at me.

She's beautiful like this, sleepy, rumpled, and arousal already darkening her deep brown eyes. I lean down and take her mouth in a deep and passionate kiss.

I make love to her slowly with languid movements, whispering sweet nothings into her ear, and letting the pleasure build slowly between us until both our bodies are slick with sweat. I move my hand from her tit down to her waiting pussy and slide her swollen nub between two of my fingers, giving it a steady and firm squeeze. I can feel her body erupt in pleasure, shuddering in my arms. The feel of her clenching tunnel triggers my orgasm and milks out every last drop of come until my balls are empty.

We're quiet for a long while, just enjoying being in each other's company. Eventually the sun rises higher in the sky and even though I'd love to laze in bed all day, fucking her brains out, I know there are things I need to take care of. I grab my phone off the nightstand and start shooting off texts to some of my colleagues. Bianca, apparently unwilling to start her day, ignores me and piles more blankets over the top of herself making me smile. Hell, she can stay in my bed all day if she wants to. In fact, maybe I should tie her to it so she can't leave. That's a thought I'll have to tuck away for another day.

The first order of business is to find out if they've released the crime scene next door so she can get into her house. I don't expect them to hold it much longer if it's even being held at all anymore. While I'm waiting for a response on that, I reach out to a local forensic cleanup crew and schedule them for later this morning. I get a message back from Rafe saying they've released her house and pay a rush fee to get the cleaners here sooner. I know Bianca is going to want to get inside as soon as possible to get a change of clothes but I don't want her to have to deal with the mess.

"Babe, do you want to go with me to get Oliver from Gloria's? He has class this morning."

She lets out a yawn and rolls over so she's facing me. Goddamn she's beautiful in the morning that I can't help but lean down and place a kiss on her forehead. She looks good in my bed. Like she belongs here. "I can't. I need to pack a bag for Violet then go to Dad's and pack one for him too before I head to the hospital. But if I'm done before his class is over, I'll meet you there."

"Sounds good to me." I toss my phone back onto the nightstand and crawl out of bed. "They've released your house, but it hasn't been cleaned. I've got a company coming to take care of everything within the hour and I'll let them in."

"You didn't have to do that," she says giving me a little frown.

"Hey, cut it out. Of course I didn't have to, I wanted to. That's what this is." I point back and forth between the two of us. "I take care of you, and you take care of me. We're a team now. Right?"

She's eying me a bit skeptically but I don't let her off the hook, I stand there and wait for her to answer me. I'm not letting her back away after the progress we made last night. "Yeah, okay."

"Good," I say with a smile. "Now get your ass up. We're going to take a shower then I'll run next door and grab some things for you and Violet." She looks like she's going to argue with me, so I just hold up my hand to stop her before she starts. "I don't want you going over there until its all been cleaned up. There's blood and glass everywhere. Just let me get the stuff for you."

She lets out a little huff. "You're pretty bossy, you know that?"

"So my girlfriend's told me."

Bianca slides off the bed and sidles up to me in all her naked glory, hips swaying seductively, and tits bouncing. "So, I'm your girlfriend now?"

I try not to swallow my tongue as I take her in. "Definitely."

"What kinds of perks comes with that title?" She wraps her arms around my neck and presses her tits against my chest.

"I thought I showed you those last night... and again this morning."

"Those are some definite perks. What else do I get?" She glides her lips down the side of my throat, making my mouth go dry and my cock start to firm up again.

"How about I get Gloria to watch Oliver tonight and I take you out on our first proper date?"

She pulls back slightly and looks up in surprise. "You want to go on a date?"

"Hell yes I do. The only problem is going to be trying not to drag you into a dark corner, fuck you up against the wall, and let everyone in the restaurant hear how I make you come."

I notice the flash of arousal in her eyes and the way she rubs her nipples against my chest, seeking friction. So, my girl likes the idea of getting fucked hard and dirty in public. Noted.

"Can I go see Bianca?" Oliver asks as he climbs out of the backseat of the car. I glance over at the house next door but there's no sign she's home. She texted me earlier letting me know she wouldn't be able to make it to Oliver's class. I know she felt bad about it, but I told her she needed to take care of Violet and her dad who spent the entire night in the hospital with her. That Bianca loves Oliver and feels bad about missing even one of his classes means so much to me, it makes my chest feel tight.

"Not right now, she's out helping her friend remember?"

"Oh, yeah."

"You're going to hang out with Gloria for a while tonight then we'll pick you up and the three of us are going to spend the day together tomorrow, so you should think about what you want to do."

We're headed up the walkway towards the door and he's chattering away about all the things we could do together tomorrow, making me smile. I can't help but imagine Oliver, Bianca, and I functioning like a little family. Hell, I even fantasize about the mundane things like her picking him up from school and me cooking dinner for the three of us, lazy Saturday's spent barbecuing in the backyard, going to the movies together. All those things don't seem quite so boring when the three of us are doing them together.

I'm pulled out of my daydream as I approach the porch and realize Oliver is no longer speaking. Instead, he's holding up a big manila envelope, inspecting it like maybe he can see through the outside to its contents. "What's that, bud?"

He gives me his signature shrug. "It was on the ground."

"Why don't you give that to me and you can put your painting away in your room? Then I'll make us some lunch."

I open the door and he hands me the envelope before rushing down the hallway to his room. I close and lock the front door before arming the alarm then taking a seat at the kitchen table.

There's nothing on the front of the envelope except my name. I'd know that block lettering anywhere. This is from the person who's been harassing me, but they've never delivered notes in envelopes of this size before. It's always been small, letter sized envelopes stuffed with single sheets of paper. This feels thick, like there's something more substantial inside.

I go to the cabinet and fish out the evidence baggies and gloves I've been keeping in case a new letter showed up, then carefully open the envelope, doing my best to not tear it, smudge any prints, or wipe away any DNA. I slide out the contents and realize that these aren't pieces of paper. The envelope is stuffed with eight by ten photos. I flip through the stack slowly, trying to decipher what exactly they are. It takes me a minute because there are large portions of every photo that is scratched and crossed out so deeply and repeatedly that the photo is almost unrecognizable. In a few cases, there are even portions that have been gouged out.

My breath hitches in my chest when I realize that every single photo is of Bianca and Oliver. There are photos of them walking down the street together, at the store, in the park, there's even a few of them walking from her car to our front door. Although every photo is different, the consistency is that in each one, both of their faces have been obliterated.

The very last photo has a message scrawled across it in red.

I'LL TAKE YOUR FAMILY LIKE YOU TOOK MINE

My heart is pounding and I swear I'm seeing red. I flip through the photos again and again, hoping there's something that will identify who's been following my family, but it's useless. This guy has been smart every step of the way. All the letters have been filled with vague, benign threats focused exclusively on me. This is a significant escalation. The utter obliteration of their faces, occasionally straight through the paper, shows a rage he doesn't seem to be able to contain any longer.

I quickly take out my cell and call Rafe to meet me at the house. He agrees without question and says he'll be here in five minutes. I shove the photos back into the envelope and force myself to start on dinner while I wait. My world may be in upheaval, but I still have a kid to feed. I've dumped everything into the baking dish for a chicken and rice casserole and shove it into the oven just as Rafe shows up.

"Shit," he mutters while sifting through the photos. "Who's the chick?"

"It's my neighbor, Bianca. We've been seeing each other. You met her that night at the convenience store robbery."

His eyes light up with recognition. "Right. I shouldn't be surprised you've been hitting that with how you two were all over each other."

A low rumble that sounds suspiciously like a growl comes from my chest. "I'm not *hitting that*. She's my girlfriend."

He looks up from the photos and gives me a grin. "Good for you, man. I'm happy for you."

"Thanks." I run my hand over my face, trying to wipe the worry away. "Unfortunately, it looks like all I've done is put her in this psycho's crosshairs. Don't we have anything to go on yet?"

"Sorry man, there's just nothing there. The guy always seems to wear gloves and you know how long DNA takes, but if he's been careful about leaving prints I doubt he'd be stupid enough to leave DNA behind."

"You're probably right." I pace the small kitchen with Rafe's eyes following me as he sits at the table.

"I think it's time for you and I to sit down and go through your old cases and try to pinpoint anyone that could have done this. We've been brushing this off until now but he's obviously not going away and now he seems to be escalating. It's time we examine anyone that could possibly want to hurt you."

"I know. You're right. It's just that there are so many people it could be. You know how it is being a cop. And I worked with drug addicts and gang members back in LA. The list could be a mile long."

"Well, we'll start by looking at the last six months and go from there. What did the video show?"

"Shit. I forgot about the video." I pull out my phone and with a few taps I've got the feed from the front of the house pulled up. I run it back until I see a dark figure then let it play out. The person is tall and bundled up tight with a distinctly male shape which is what I suspected, but this is the first time I've been able to confirm it. Rafe steps over and crowds around my tiny phone screen.

"Hat on, head down, it's like he knows there are cameras. Don't think we'll get much from this. Forward it over to Criminalistics anyway. They may find something we're missing. What do you plan to do about Oliver and your girlfriend?"

I want to slam my fist into the wall. That this guy can just walk right up to my front door like it's nothing is making me crazy. How am I supposed to protect them when this asshole knows where I live and can come and go with impunity?

"I'm going to have to keep them both away from me until we figure this out. Maybe if he doesn't see either of them with me, he'll lay off and refocus his attention on me instead."

"How do you plan on accomplishing that?"

"I'll have Oliver stay with Gloria for a while. I don't want to freak them out, so I'll just tell them I'm going to be working a lot of overtime and it'll be easier if he stays with her. She'll understand and I'll get over there and visit when I can."

"And your girlfriend?" He asks with a raised brow.

"I'm just have to tell her the truth. That it isn't safe for her to be around me right now, that it's too dangerous." Rafe barks out a sharp laugh and I narrow my eyes at him. "What's so damn funny?"

"You think the girl who attacked a gunman with a high heel shoe because he was mean to an old man is going to just go into hiding because you think she's in danger?"

Fuck. I let out a groan. "You might be right."

"Of course I am. Haven't you learned yet? I'm always right."

"You're also a modest motherfucker, anyone tell you that?"

"All. The. Time." He says, deadpan. He reaches over and carefully slips the photos back into their envelope before easing the entire thing into an evidence bag. "Look, I'll take these down to the station and get the lab to work on them. You sort out your family situation then meet me there. We have to go over your list of possible suspects."

He leaves taking the offending photos with him. The first thing I do is make a call to Gloria to ask about Oliver staying with her a while. Thank God she seems thrilled by the idea of having him with her. It's just another of those times I'm reminded that I absolutely made the right choice by moving to Seattle. Gloria loves Oliver whole heartedly and would do anything for him. I feel a little guilty not telling her the full story but there's no reason to worry her. Besides, if this guy knew who she was he probably would have included a picture of her as well. I'm guessing he's only been lurking around my place and saw Oliver and Bianca coming and going then followed them.

A shiver runs down my spine. I really don't like the idea of this crazy motherfucker being close enough to get pictures of them. Who knows how long he's been following them because those photos were obviously all taken on different days. It's a major relief that I have some place to stash Oliver while this gets resolved. Hopefully, we'll have this wrapped up in a week, two tops. If we can't pinpoint who it is through my suspect list, we'll have to do something to flush this guy out. I'm not going to live on pins and needles because of him.

My real problem is Bianca. Rafe is absolutely right, if I tell Bianca the truth, there's no way she'll take it seriously. I know her. In fact, when she hears that someone was following her it's more likely to piss her off than scare her, then Lord only knows what she would do.

I go back to pacing the kitchen, trying to think of the best way to handle this. I need to keep her safe. The thought of something happening to her causes a sharp stabbing pain in my chest and I can't help but reach up and try to rub away. She and Oliver are my entire world.

This isn't the FBI, it's not like I can stash away in some safe house. Even if it were a possibility, she would never be okay with that. Bianca doesn't let anybody scare her off from anything. But I need her to stay far away from me. Maybe if this guy thinks she's out of my life, he'll leave her alone. Before I can even think, my frustration comes flying out and I slam my fist into the granite countertop causing pain to shoot up my arm.

"Goddamnit," I hiss as I rub my knuckles, knowing they'll bruise but that seems fitting. I know I'm going to deserve it because in order to save Bianca, I'm going to have to hurt her.

CHAPTER TWENTY-ONE

BIANCA

I'm still in surprisingly good spirits considering how long of a day it's been. Well, maybe it's not so surprising. Not after everything that happened with Carson yesterday and the way he woke me up this morning. I can't help the smile that crawls along my face whenever I think of him. God, not even twenty-four hours of having a boyfriend and I've already turned into a sappy goon.

When I left his place this morning, I took the bag he had grabbed for me of Violet's things and then headed over to Dad's to pack a bag for him as well. I don't know how long Violet is going to need to be in the hospital, but I'm pretty sure he won't want to be away from her. When I got there and saw them together, I realized how right I was. From the look on his face whenever his eyes landed on my best friend, he wouldn't be leaving that hospital without her. The way they looked at one another made my heart happy for the both of them.

I was shocked when I could finally see Violet, but Dad kept reassuring me she looked much worse than she actually was. Good thing because she looks like hell. I think he needed to keep saying it to reassure himself she was going to be alright. If Carson hadn't of already killed Tyler, I would have. Nobody hurts my friends like that.

Especially not one as sweet and gentle as Violet. Just the thought of it is enough to fill me with rage.

When I left the hospital, there wasn't time to make it to Oliver's art class so I headed home, happy to find that the cleaning crew Carson scheduled had already come and gone. I didn't see any remnants of blood in the house, but it still needed some TLC. The base that once held the now shattered glass top of the coffee table stood in the middle of the living room and there were broken pieces of chairs piled against the wall. I dragged most of the junk to the back patio, hoping Carson would help me take it out on trash day.

After that was finished, I went into Violet's room to survey the damage. The place was a mess and gave off a bit of a creepy vibe that I didn't want Violet to feel when she came home. I spent the next hour straightening up her room, washing the clothes that had been strewn about, and trying to erase any hint that something nefarious had taken place there. I know it wasn't much, but at least I felt like I was doing something to help her. Though, judging by the possessive glint in Dad's eye at the hospital, I'm not sure how much longer she's going to be living here anyway. I have a feeling he's going to whisk her away to his place the second he gets a chance.

I'm not looking forward to living alone now that Hollie is gone and Violet seems to be on her way out. But who knows, maybe with Carson and I making things official, I won't be here long myself. Hell, pretty soon my dad could have his property back to rent out.

The thought of me moving in next store makes my heart beat faster. It's not something I ever would have let myself think about before but now... well, anything's possible.

My date with Carson isn't until later this evening so after I've put Violet's room back into some kind of order, I decide to get some of my own work done. It's drizzling outside, so I set up my easel in the living room and prep a brand-new canvas. I'm not sure exactly what I'm going to paint so I just kind of let myself go.

Unsurprisingly, the painting takes shape in the form of Carson's face. It's not the first time I've painted him over the past weeks. Hell, I seem to paint him no matter what I set out trying to paint. However, this time, instead of holding back like I've always done in the past, I let my feelings for him pour out of me. I let every emotion that I'd been holding back for weeks out onto the canvas. Before I'm even halfway done, I know that I'm going to be showing this one to Margot. Who knows, maybe I'd even show this one to Carson himself.

I've been hiding my paintings from him, knowing that as soon as he saw the sheer volume of work dedicated to him and Oliver, he would know exactly how I felt about him and I couldn't have that. But somehow, beyond all odds, it seems he feels that same way about me. I shouldn't be ashamed of showing him how he looks through my eyes. If anything, I get the feeling that he'll love seeing it. That he'll appreciate how much time and effort I've put into creating pieces that are distinctly... him.

I'm about to put a few finishing touches on the piece, marveling to myself how I could have gotten so much done in just a few scant hours, when there's a knock at the door. I set down my brush and try to rub some of the paint off of my hands but as usual, it's in vain. I'm going to have to get some paint thinner out to really do the job before our date.

Opening the front door, I'm surprised to see Carson standing there. I turn and look behind me at the clock on the wall confirming he's early. Very early.

"Hey, I thought we weren't leaving until seven. If you want to come on in and wait, I can start getting ready." I open the door wide for him and move to head back inside, my mind occupied with how quickly I can get ready, I'm not exactly known for speed in this area, when I'm stopped by his hand resting on my shoulder.

When I turn around, I take a moment to actually look him over, something I neglected to do when I first opened the door. He doesn't look exactly thrilled to be here. His shoulders are slightly hunched, and his chin is tilted downward. The lines of his face are stern and harsh, not a trace of a smile anywhere. What worries me the most are his eyes. They somehow look both cold and hesitant at the same time.

"What's going on, Carson?"

He runs his hand over his face in that gesture he makes when he's overwhelmed or frustrated and it causes alarm bells to ring in my head. I don't know what's wrong but whatever it is, I know it's not good. "Can we go inside for a second?" he asks.

I step away from the door, holding it wide open in response and let him walk inside before closing the door behind us. I can feel the negative emotions coming off him in waves, but don't have any idea what could be wrong. Heading back into the living room, I take a seat on the couch. I expect him to sit next to me, or at least take the chair across the room, but he remains standing, looking over my shoulder.

"Are you going to sit?" I ask, not liking how he's looming over me.

His face hardens before he brings his eyes to mine, and when he finally does, it sends chills through my body. Not the good kind of chills either. "I think it's better if I stand. This won't take long."

"Okaaay." What is going on with him? He's got my anxiety ratcheted up to ten, my heart is slamming against my chest, when suddenly a thought occurs to me. "Oh my God, is Oliver alright? Did something happen?"

His body gives a little jerk, and he looks deep into my eyes. I can sense his body relax for just a second before the tension runs through him again, stringing him as tight as a bow. "Oliver's fine."

I let out a sigh of relief and sag a little against the back of the couch. If Oliver is okay, at least it can't be anything too bad.

"I think I've made a mistake," he says, his voice cold.

"A mistake?"

"When we spoke last night. I think I was too quick to invalidate your concerns. I'm going to need some more time to think about them."

"My concerns? What are you talking about?"

He takes a deep breath like he's trying to steal himself to say what he needs to say. "Your concerns about not being able to have children. I think that maybe... that might matter to me. I'm not sure. I need more time to think about it."

I can feel my body freeze up. Every shitty thing every ex has ever said to me about my condition comes screaming into the forefront of my mind.

You didn't think this could actually lead somewhere, did you?

Look, it's okay for right now but someday I'm going to want a family.

Face it Bianca, you're a lot of fun but you're not exactly wife material.

I feel like everything is coming crashing down around me but I carefully school my features into a mask of indifference. My ability to project an *I don't give a shit* attitude has been my armor over the years and it's the first thing I pull out when I'm under attack.

"So, what you're saying is, you've changed your mind."

For a second, he looks lost for words and I'm not sure why. This is one hundred percent his choice. He doesn't get to look lost right now. Not when he let me believe that there could be a future for the two of us. Hell, for the three of us.

Just as I'm about to lay into him his features harden up once again so I can't read what's going on behind his eyes. "Yeah, I guess I changed my mind."

I give him a jerky nod, not trusting my voice. I think if I say anything it might waver and give away how much he's gutting me right now. Jumping off the couch I hustle to the door, flinging it open, silently telling him it's time to get the fuck out of my house.

"Look, Bianca I—"

"You don't owe me an explanation," I cut him off. What I want to do is scream at him that maybe he should have thought it through when I told him I couldn't have kids instead of telling me he didn't care. But no, he had to give me false fucking hope that maybe I could have a great love like my friends. But ranting and raging at him would give him all the power. I'll never show him how much this hurts me. In fact, if I never see him again, it will be too soon.

Suddenly, I feel an additional pain in my chest and I can't help but ask, "What about Oliver? Are you going to keep me away from him?" I may not want to see Carson, but that doesn't mean I want to lose Oliver too. He didn't do anything. Hell, he's an innocent little kid.

There's a look of surprise on Carson's face. I'm not sure if he's surprised that I actually care about his son—which really pisses me off—or if he just didn't consider that Oliver is going to be losing me as well.

"Of course not, Bianca. I would never keep you away from Oliver, but..." he trails off mid-sentence, his expression turning into one of regret. I stand there, patiently waiting for him to continue. "It's just that I'm not sure how much he's going to be around right now."

I can feel myself growing increasingly cold. It's obvious he doesn't want me anywhere near his kid. It's one thing to reject me, but it's quite another to keep me away from Oliver. He knows I care about him and no matter what he says, he can't convince me that Oliver doesn't care about me. Instead, he's going to make up some lame excuse about Oliver not being around? What kind of bullshit is that? This, more than anything else, tells me right where I stand with him.

"Right," I say. "Got it. I think you better go."

Carson heads for the open front door but then stops and opens his mouth looking like he wants to say something. Well, whatever it is, I don't want to hear it.

"Goodbye, Carson."

"Bianca, I—"

"Goodbye." The word is thrown from my throat, clipped and harsh. I want him out of my house right this second before I do something stupid like beg him to reconsider. He merely nods his head at me and walks outside.

It takes every ounce of strength I have not to slam the door. Instead, I close it gently, letting the door click softly behind him. I won't give him the satisfaction of slamming the door and letting him know how much this conversation's affected me.

I collapse back onto the couch and cover my face with my hands, making a concentrated effort to steadily breathe in and out. I will *not* cry about this. The first thing I want to do is call Violet. She always has a way of making me feel better, but I can't bother her while she's in the hospital recovering.

I don't know how long I've sat at the same place on the couch, watching the shadows stretch across the living room, but when I finally pull out of my funk, it's dark outside. I can't help but peek out the window and see several of the lights in Carson's house are on.

I let out a sigh and pick at the paint on my hand. I can't even be mad at him. Not really. After all, I knew this was going to happen. It's my own stupid fault for thinking I could have love when my life experience has shown me it just wasn't in the cards for me. It's my fault that I let myself believe for even the briefest of moments that someone could love me, could look past the one thing I could never bring to the table, and this is what happened.

Actually, I can be a little mad at him. That fuck face made me believe for a second that I could have someone to share my life with, then less than twenty-four hours later he changes his fucking mind? Well, fuck that and fuck him. And fuck me too. I don't know what I'm doing here moping on the couch. It's not my style. I'm not going to sit in this empty house all alone when I can practically *feel* him right next door. I'm going out. Who knows, maybe I'll even meet somebody that will get my mind off Carson and his wishy-washy ass.

I shoot texts to both Jenna and Hollie before I jump in the shower and by the time I'm out both have responded that they'll meet me at Vinnie's tonight. I paw through the clothes in my closet, hell bent on wearing the absolute skimpiest outfit I can find. It's not long before I've settled on a crop top that barely covers the bottom of my breasts and a high-waisted skirt that will surely flash my thong anytime I bend over. I've never been known for my conservative party outfits, but this is a bit much for even me.

Fuck it. I'm the good time party girl, right? It's not like I'm dressing to find a guy of any substance. I'm out looking for a hookup and this will definitely get the job done, I think while looking myself over in the mirror one more time.

I finish loosely piling my hair on the top of my head and doing some light makeup, it's not like I'll need much with this outfit. I may be a mix of confusing emotions and on the prowl tonight, but I'm not stupid. I leave my car at home and slip inside a rideshare headed out for a night on the town.

I'm on my fourth—or is it my fifth?—drink and both Jenna and Hollie are eying me with concern. I'm not totally unaccustomed to the look from Hollie, but this is new for Jenna. Hell, when I let loose, that girl is usually three steps ahead of me. I'm always the one reeling her back in.

"Don't you think you better slow down?" Hollie asks while sipping on a vodka soda. I'm pretty sure it's the same one she's been nursing since she arrived.

"Why?" But even I can hear the slight slur in my voice. "Amelia!" I shout once I spot the tiny redhead behind the bar. "I'll take another, please."

Amelia stops stacking the glasses behind the bar and eyes me skeptically. I put on my most sober smile and she lets out a sigh. "Look, drink this and I'll get you another." She slides a glass of water across the bar towards me and I wrinkle my nose at it. "No water, no drink," she says firmly.

I let out a groan and snatch up the water, chugging it down like I'm in a frat party drinking contest. Before Amelia's even had time to move down the bar to other customers I'm slamming the empty glass on the wood, letting her know I'm ready for another drink.

I see her eyes skip to something behind me but before I can turn to see what it is I hear her say, "You want to get your friend under control here, Jake?"

I furrow my brow at her. "I'm not out of control."

"Well, you're something." She mumbles under her breath and takes off to the other end of the bar where more sober patrons are seeking her attention.

Jake's hulking mass settles on the barstool next to me and I hear Hollie mutter, "Thank fuck," under her breath. I shoot her a scathing look, but her face is all innocence. Instead of saying anything back to her, I grab the drink out of her hand and down it in one gulp. "Hey!" she yells indignantly.

"Come on, you know I need it more than you do right now. You with your perfect boyfriend who gives me presents worth tens of thousands of dollars."

Hollie just rolls her eyes and turns to Jake. "Can you watch her for a second while I use the restroom?" He nods and she takes off, leaving Jake and I alone.

"So, what are you doing here?" He asks.

"What does it look like I'm doing here? Letting loose. Having fun. Enjoying the single life. I think the better question is, what are *you* doing here?" I lean forward to poke his chest with my finger and almost fall forward out of my seat. He grabs me and straightens me on the stool.

"Can't a guy come out and get a drink?"

"Yeah, but I thought you were on the straight and narrow. Doesn't that mean no hanging out in bars by yourself looking for tonight's hookup?"

"Who says I'm looking for a hookup?" I notice his eyes track Amelia as she works her way from one end of the bar to the other before she approaches us again. She places a beer in front of Jake without him having to ask and slides another vodka soda over to me which I promptly pluck off the bar and begin drinking. Though from the taste of it, I'd say it's almost all soda.

"What's going on, Bianca? I'm not sure I've ever seen you so determined to get plastered so quickly before."

"Nothing's going on. I've just decided your whole idea of settling down is idiotic. You'll realize it soon enough too. Don't say I didn't warn you."

"And why is that?"

"We're just not built that way, you and me. We're two sides of the same coin."

"I don't think that's the way it needs to be, Bianca." I see his eyes go back to our bartender and I want to slap some sense into him. He might think he has a chance with her, but she'd crush his heart soon enough. Believe me, I know.

"I think we better go, B. You have to work in the morning, and you know how Margot is. If you come in too hungover to work, she's going to be pissed." Jenna gently pries the drink from my hand and settles it on the bar before pulling me off the stool.

"I'll have Archer come give us a ride home," Hollie says as she returns from the bathroom. I'm not exactly thrilled with the three of them trying to tell me what to do but at least I don't have to put the effort in to keep up conversation.

"It's okay, I'll take her home," Jake offers. I just shrug my shoulder. I don't care how I get home. In fact, I'd rather stay here. At least here there isn't a certain somebody in the house next door that's happy to be rid of me.

"Thanks Jake. If you take her home, I'll make sure her tab gets settled." He nods to Hollie then he and Jenna help me outside to his truck. Jesus, maybe I had more to drink than I thought because walking is suddenly a very difficult task. They both help me into the passenger side of the lifted truck, and I manage to crawl in without flashing anybody. I think. They close the door and I lean my cheek against the cool glass of the window. The last thing I remember is their hushed voices whispering outside.

Chapter Twenty-Two

Carson

"Let's go over them again." Rafe paces back and forth in front of my desk in the bowels of the substation.

"This is bullshit. It's not getting us anywhere," I bark at him. It's been a week since I received the photos and we're not any closer to finding out who's been threatening my family. I feel like I'm about to snap.

"We'll keep going over them until something makes sense." I didn't mean to snap at Rafe. He's been right here with me every day trying to figure out what's going on. It feels like he's almost as invested in this as I am. We've gone back six months and come up with a few incidents that could motivate some kind of vengeance plot against me, but none of them quite fit. "We've got Oscar Mendoza, the eighteen-year-old kid you witnessed committing a murder that's been put away for twenty to life."

"It's not Oscar. Well, it's not his family at least. He's got a grandmother but she's on the bad side of seventy, the only real family he has is the Rolling Sixties and this isn't their style. If they wanted to get back at me for putting one of their members away, they'd just come after me, maybe do a drive by. There wouldn't just be one guy and he definitely wouldn't be hiding from my cameras. They'd want me to know it was them. These kinds of cat and mouse games just aren't them. Plus, they're too comfortable operating in Los Angeles, they wouldn't travel all the way up here for a vendetta relating to one of their footmen. Mendoza had barely even joined up. He certainly wasn't high up enough in the organization for the big dogs to care about what happened to him."

"Okay, so it probably doesn't have anything to do with Mendoza. Who's next?"

I let out a sigh and sift through the papers on my desk. "Janet Howard."

"That was your CI, right?"

"Yeah." The thought of what happened to Janet still makes my stomach turn. She's one of the major reasons I was happy to leave Los Angeles far behind me. "She was a good kid but got involved with a guy named Darryl Brown, the head of the Shoreline Crips. He was an unscrupulous son of a bitch, didn't care that he or his guys were dealing to kids. He got Janet hooked on crack and she couldn't get out. When she approached me wanting to help put Darryl away, I was skeptical at first, but eventually my eagerness to take him down won out against my common sense. She was young, too young. I shouldn't have let her become an informant, but I'd been after Brown for months and couldn't see any other way. She fed me a ton of info on not only her boyfriend but the entire supply line for Shoreline. I don't know exactly what happened, and I probably never will. All I know is that she must have slipped up somehow because they slit her throat and dropped her body off on the steps of my precinct."

The memory of her lifeless eyes and her throat cut from ear to ear still haunt me. If I had known it was going to end that way for her, I never would have taken her help, but she reminded me of my sister and I wanted to not only get her out, but put the man behind bars that got her addicted to crack and used her body as a bargaining chip. Maybe I was no better than him, using her the way I did for information.

"And you don't think this has anything to do with her?"

I just shake my head, brining myself out of the painful memories. "There's no reason for Shoreline to come after me. They killed my informant and left her in public for me to find. As far as they're concerned it's over. Plus, when I spoke to her about becoming a CI, I made sure she didn't have any family. It's part of my intake process. There's nobody who would come after me for anything that had to do with her."

Rafe continues pacing the shitty linoleum floor, his fingers tapping against his side. The guy is almost as on edge as I am. Rafe is just like me; he doesn't like to lose. They couldn't have pared me with a better partner.

"And the last thing you can think of was that shipment for the Valley Boys?"

"Yeah, I got a tip about a shipment that was coming in from a cartel down south. We intercepted the truck and confiscated a shit ton of cocaine, meth, fentanyl, and a stash of weapons. But there were a ton of cops involved in that bust, I don't know why anyone would focus in on just me. And again, the pictures, harassment, and threats really aren't the gang's MO. They're more likely to walk up to me on a crowded street and shoot me in the back of the head than they are to stalk and threaten my family. I'm telling you, none of these fit." I slam my fist down on my desk and immediately regret it when I see a couple of guys look over at us from across the bullpen. I shoot them an apologetic look before turning back to my partner.

"We're in the same place we were a week ago. Hell, a month ago. I've got to catch this guy, Rafe."

"I know, man. We'll find him." He claps my shoulder with his oversized hand and finally settles into the chair at his desk that's facing mine. "We're going to have to go back further than the past six months. Let's take it back a full year."

A frustrated sigh escapes my lips. I want to scream at him that this is a waste of time but there's no point in taking my frustration out on him. He's doing everything he can to help. He just doesn't understand how hard this week has been for me.

I wasn't joking when I said Bianca had become my addiction. A week without her and I'm completely on edge. It feels like I'm going through withdrawals. I can't sleep, I've lost my appetite, every thought I have that's not focused on finding this psycho is consumed by her.

It's not helping that I see her leave her house every goddamn night, dressed to the nines. I know she's going out with her friends, probably in an effort to forget all about me and it's my own fucking fault. But what if she actually meets someone? What would I do then?

The first night she went out after I called things off I sat and waited by the window until she rolled back in well after midnight. The problem was that she wasn't alone. Some guy pulled up in a too big truck, hopped out, and helped her inside. My girl could barely fucking walk in a straight line. I wanted to rush out my door and beat his face in for daring to touch her, even if it looked like all he was doing was helping her get inside but that wasn't my right anymore. I had taken care of that.

I saw her face when I was breaking up with her. All that work I dide to get her walls to fall had been swept away in a moment. As I spoke, I could see her face shuttering, her walls climbing back up to the sky before my eyes. But I know it will all be worth it when we catch this guy and she's safe. God, it better be worth it.

The mystery guy was inside the house with her for about three minutes before I couldn't stand it any longer and I jumped out of my chair, headed to the front door. Luckily, it was then that he exited the house, locking the door behind him before jumping back into his enormous truck—that frankly had to be compensating for something—and driving away. The entire situation left a foul taste in my mouth but there wasn't anything I could do about it.

That became my routine for the rest of the week. I would go to work during the day then head over to Gloria's afterward to spend some time with Oliver. God, I missed him. With both him and Bianca currently being kept at a distance, my life felt hallow and lonely. How did I live like this before and never even realize how sad my existence was?

After dinner with the two of them I would head home, sort through my personal files, and wait, my body barely concealed behind my curtains. I watched Bianca go out every night this week. She was a bit of a party girl before me but this seemed excessive. I tried to stay away from that window. To stop myself from inflicting my personal torture that was watching her get dressed up and head out to tease and flirt with other men, but what choice did I give her?

No, I had set her free, and she was doing what any other single girl would do in her position. I couldn't expect her to sit at home and pine for me after I'd broken her heart in the only way I knew how. But if I had seen her bring another man home, all the reasoning in the world wouldn't have stopped me from beating him to a bloody pulp. It was a good thing for all our sakes when she showed up home, alone every night.

I check the time on my watch and say goodbye to Rafe so I can catch dinner with Oliver. Rafe's going to stay here and speak to the lab about anything they might have been able to pull from the security footage. I can't thank him enough for how much time and effort he's been putting into this. With him working alongside me, at least I get a few brief hours with my kid every night even if it doesn't feel like enough. I keep telling him he doesn't have to stay and do this, but he brushes me off, reminding me he's single with no kids and it's better than sitting at home alone. I'd argue with him, but I know exactly what he means.

Throughout dinner I dodge questions from Gloria about when my schedule is going to ease up. I know it's not because she doesn't want Oliver with her. In fact, she seems thrilled to have him around. It's more like she's worried about me working too hard. I still haven't told either of them why I really have Oliver here, but I feel much better with him staying with her. She owns a house in a fancy gated community that's filled to the brim with security personal. I've also spoken to the head of security for the community. It turns out he's an ex-cop which makes me feel better. I didn't tell him all the details, but I gave him enough information that he knows he needs to keep an extra eye on them and any suspicious characters that may be hanging around. I couldn't have found a better place for Oliver to stay.

By the time I get home, I'm mentally and physically exhausted. Between wracking my brain to find this guy and staying up to watch Bianca leave and come home every night, it's all taking a toll on me. I make it to my porch when I see Bianca's car pulling to a stop at the curb in front of my house. I'm confused for a second on why she would park on the street but then I look over and see Violet's car in their driveway. She must be home from the hospital.

I know I should head inside and pretend like I didn't see her, but I'm rooted to this spot. No matter how much I tell my feet to turn the fuck around and go, they remain firmly planted on the porch, pointed in her direction.

It's obvious she hasn't spotted me when she turns and reaches into her back seat to pull out a few canvases she was transporting. She stacks them in her arms, closes the car door with a bump of her hip, and starts heading towards her own home.

This is the closest I've been to her in a week and before I give my body any sort of conscious command I'm calling out, "Bianca," and striding across the grass.

Her head whips up, startled, and she looks around a moment before she spots me heading towards her. The second she sees me her eyes narrow disapprovingly. I'm not going to lie, it hurts like a motherfucker.

"I swear to God, Carson, if you say something about me being parked too close to your driveway, I will beat you to death with one of these canvases."

Her sass is such a surprise that it forces a bubble of laughter out from between my lips. That laugh quickly dies when her face conveys she's dead serious. There's no warmth in her eyes, not even that challenging fire I love so much. I need to find this guy quick because judging by her reaction to me, I'm going to have a hell of a time getting her to forgive me.

She turns to leave when a canvas drops out of her hand. She leans forward and tries to scoop it up without dropping the others, but I rush forward and save it from the ground before she loses any of the others that are barely held in her arms. I'm handing it back to her when I notice the painting is of me. Well, of Oliver and I together. It's not photorealism, but it's obvious it's us. The colors are bright, warm, and vibrant. Frankly, it takes my breath away.

"This is amazing, Bianca. You've never showed me one of your paintings before. I don't know much about art but it's obvious to even me that you have a true talent." I place the painting back on top of the stack of others and I suddenly want to go through them all. How many of them are us and our family? Is that what she's been painting? Why she would always avoid showing me what she'd created? All of my warm thoughts turn to ash when her cold, lifeless voice reaches my ears.

"Yeah, well, I did these before. Now they belong in the garbage with all my other work that's just not good enough."

I physically flinch at the tone of her voice. She doesn't sound sad or even angry. She sounds disgusted. With me. Like having to be near me is distasteful. Like I mean nothing to her, I never did and never will again. It scares the shit out of me. I want to shake her and scream that I'm doing this to protect her, but I know I can't do that yet.

Hell, I probably shouldn't even be talking to her right now just in case someone's watching, but I can't seem to help myself.

"Bianca..." I don't even know what I'm going to say, what I can say to make this right.

"What? Are you going to tell me you changed your mind *again*? Suddenly, having a family and a child of your own doesn't matter to you anymore?"

What can I possibly say to that? I can feel my mouth opening and closing but not a single word makes it out.

"Yeah, that's what I thought." She lets out a laugh that's cold and hollow, nothing like the Bianca I know and love. Instead of looking at me, she clutches the canvases tightly to her chest and starts walking away without a backward glance.

"Bianca," I try again. This time grabbing her arm so she'll turn and look at me. She wrenches it out of my grasp and looks at me with icy dead eyes.

"What the fuck, Carson? I'm not somebody you can play games with. You think you can still have some fun on the side with me while you go out and find the woman you can settle down and have babies with? I don't fucking think so." Her face is turning red, and I can feel the rage coming off her in scalding waves, so much so that I have to take a physical step back from the vitriol in her voice. "Don't you touch me ever again. You don't have the right, understand?"

She stands there, clearly waiting for an answer from me and all I can do is nod my head at her then watch as she turns and slowly walks away with her head held high. Every step she takes further away from me feels like miles she's putting between us. Miles I pray to fucking God she'll let me cross some day when all of this is over.

We need to find this motherfucker right now before I lose her for good.

CHAPTER
TWENTY-THREE

BIANCA

I'm chewing on my bottom lip. It's a nervous gesture that Margot Gault brings out in me. Every time she looks at a piece of my work, I feel like I'm a bug under a microscope and she'd be all too happy to crush me under the heel of her shiny leather boots.

She's been staring intently at the two paintings I've brought in for her to critique for the last five minutes. She hasn't said a word about either one and it's starting to make me anxious. She'll occasionally make a humming noise and tilt her head to the right and then the left before facing them straight on again. I honestly have no idea if that means she likes them or not.

I was nervous about bringing these to her. I know they're good. Well, at least I think they are. But these are two of the most raw and emotional paintings I've ever done. Though they're both the same subject, the emotions provoked by each couldn't be more different. The first is the portrait of Carson I did the day we decided to give our relationship a real chance. The piece feels surrounded by love and full of hope, all the feelings that were bursting straight out of my chest and onto the canvas. It's full of pinks, yellows, and blues with just the faintest splash of red here and there. The only other color is his moss green eyes. Those fucking eyes that still haunt me in my sleep no matter how I try to shake him.

The second painting is one I did a few days ago. It's still a portrait of Carson but the emotions radiating from it are entirely different from the first. This canvas is filled with black, reds, and purples. Not even the moss green of his eyes survived this one. No, his eyes are steady, unyielding black holes of despair. The lines of his face that in the first painting make him seem so handsome, appear cruel and severe here. I fucking hate this painting. But again, I know it's good. I wanted to burn the fucking thing as soon as I finished it, but why waste such an amazing piece when it could help me get into one of Margot's shows. It's not like Carson would concern himself with how I portray him. If he cared about what I thought of him, he wouldn't have treated me how he did.

I'm completely lost in my morose thoughts when Margot slides those signature glasses from the tip of her nose back to the bridge before turning to me and smiling. "I always knew you were capable of this, Bianca. I wouldn't have hired you if I didn't think this was the kind of work you could produce."

"You really like them?" I ask, a bit stunned. I mean, sure, *I* thought they were good but my opinion is a far cry from Margot Gault's.

"Like them? They're spectacular. You can feel all the love and hope in this one," she indicates the first painting. "Then you can see it ripped away from you. This man betrayed you and left you a shell of your former self." She's staring at the second painting again, nodding up and down.

Jesus. Is that what it looks like? I'm a shell of my former self? I guess I should just be happy she likes them. I certainly left everything inside me on both canvases.

"I see you've found your muse," she says, like it's as plain as day.

"Well, I don't know about that." I mumble. The thought of Carson being my muse makes me a little sick to my stomach. I don't want to need him for anything, let alone for him to be the reason I can finally create a piece of art that's worthy of Margot.

"Don't be silly, of course you have! Now, don't let this gentleman get away. I can only imagine the great things you'll create with him by your side to draw out these kinds of emotions."

"Well, that's the thing, I painted this one after we broke up." Margot has her hand on her chin and is nodding at the painting as she studies it with a critical eye once again.

"Yes, I can see that. But there's so much emotion here. You don't plan on letting him get away, do you? I've been with many men in my life and only a handful have been able to provoke such a powerful reaction from me it's shown through into my work."

This conversation is getting distinctly uncomfortable. I just wanted to show her my pieces, I didn't want to go over my dating history. "Well, that's going to be a problem. He broke up with me. It's not like he's waiting in the wings to inspire my next work."

Margot crosses her arms over her chest. "Hmmm well, that could be a problem. I have a spot open for the next exhibition that's happening in two months and I was planning to offer it to you. It would be these two paintings and then two more. But if you don't think you can create something of the same caliber, then I may have to rethink it."

"No!" I shout, immediately embarrassed at my outburst. "I mean, no, that's totally alright. Just because I'm not seeing him anymore doesn't mean I can't produce something similar. I mean, the emotions are all still there, right?"

Margot eyes me skeptically before slowly nodding her head. "Well, they shouldn't be exactly the same, but they need to all tie in together. Look, I'm going to need to see the other pieces before I commit to giving you the spot. Can you have them for me to review in three weeks?"

"Three weeks?" I squeak out. That's not much time. Sure, when I'm on a roll I can really pump out the pieces but if she's expecting something like these two, it's not exactly going to be easy to bring those kinds of emotions to the surface.

"Maybe you're not ready yet." Margot turns away from me and starts sorting through the stacks of paperwork on her desk that are piled so high they're threatening to fall over.

"No, Margot. I can do this. I swear. Three weeks and I'll have them for you to look at. I won't let you down."

She looks up at me with her eyebrow slightly arched. "Don't make me regret this, Bianca. Do you know how many young artists would kill for this chance?"

"I know and you don't have to worry. You're going to be blown away."

"Let's hope so."

I pull up to the heavy security gate with a guard shack and give them my name. The guard examines the list and asks to see my ID which I hand over. It feels a little excessive, especially because I've been here a handful of times before. He hands back my ID, and the gate opens allowing me to drive on through.

I pull into Gloria's long driveway and shut off the engine. I was about to leave the gallery for the day when I saw Gloria's name lightening up my phone. Apparently, she's tweaked her back again and wanted to know if I could take Oliver for a couple hours while her muscle relaxer kicks in, and she can get some rest. I'm happy to help her out. It's been way too long since I've seen Oliver and I've been missing him terribly.

I walk along the carefully placed stone path that's surrounded by perfectly manicured hedges and approach the oversized house. I'm not sure my one woman needs this much space, but it's a beautiful place.

I wrap my knuckles against the heavy oak door and stand there and wait. Nervous anticipation causes me to shift my weight from one foot to the other. What if Oliver's angry at me for not being around? I wanted to be, I really did, but it wasn't what Carson wanted. In fact, I'm pretty sure that Gloria hasn't even bothered to run this by him or else he would have shut it down immediately.

Well, it's not my problem. They're his family. He should be the one to tell them we're no longer together, it's not my responsibility. Plus, I'll take any time with Oliver I can get.

After a minute I hear a little voice call out from the other side of the door. "Who is it?"

I can't help but smile as I call out "Bianca" in response. The door gets jerked open and a little blur of color charges into me, wrapping himself around my legs. I squat down so we're on the same level and take Oliver in my arms, squeezing him tightly. I haven't seen him at all since Carson and I ended things and I'm surprised by how much I've truly missed him. There's an ache in my chest as he pulls away and he leads me inside.

"Where's your Aunt Gloria?" I ask. He leads me into the living room where I find Gloria stretched out along the length of the sofa, her face tense with pain.

"Thank you so much for coming, Bianca. I know how busy you are."

"It's not a problem," I reassure her. "I'm happy to look after Oliver for a while. But what about you? Is there anything I can do to make you more comfortable?" The woman is tough, but she definitely looks like she's in pain.

"I'll be fine, I've just wrenched my back again. I'm waiting for these dang muscle relaxers to kick in so I can move but I'm not comfortable being confined to the couch when Oliver might need me."

"I totally get it. He can hang with me this afternoon, then I can drop him off at home later on when Carson is back from work."

"Actually, would you just bring him back here in a few hours? I'm sure I'll be feeling better by then and Oliver's been staying with me. Carson's hours have been crazy for the past week, and it's just been easier if he stays at my house until everything settles down."

I know I don't do a good job of hiding the shock on my face. "Really? That seems odd, doesn't it?" I guess that's one reason I haven't seen Oliver lately. I guess he's been here with Gloria, but it's not like Carson separate himself from his son, even when he's busy. Then again, I obviously don't know Carson as well as I thought I did.

Gloria just shrugs at my questioning. "He seems very stressed and if keeping Oliver here with me can help I'm more than happy to do it. Besides, I wouldn't want to spend my days any other way than hanging out with my great-great nephew." She shoots Oliver a smile. "Why don't you go gather up a few things so you can play with Bianca and by the time you're back I'll be up and have dinner ready for you?"

Oliver rushes off down the hallway, presumably to grab a few things while I eye Gloria skeptically. "Are you sure? Maybe we shouldn't be leaving you alone."

She waves off my concerns. "Don't be silly. I've taken a muscle relaxer, I'll have a nice little nap, then I'll have something delivered for dinner. You're free to join us you know. Sometimes Carson comes over after his shift and has dinner with us too."

That bit of information makes my shoulders stiffen. No matter how much my soul is crying out to see him, to spend any amount of time I can with him, I know it's for the best that I don't. It will only make things harder for me in the long run. Frankly, I'm still embarrassed by how I handled my run in with him yesterday. I wanted to be the calm, cool, you mean so little to me that your breaking my heart didn't affect me at all, Bianca. Instead, seeing him touched a hurt I felt so deeply I couldn't help lashing out at him. I was angry and I know that I've shown my hand. I've let him see how vulnerable he makes me and for that, I'm extremely angry at myself.

No, I'll just watch Oliver for a few hours and then drop him right back here. If I'm lucky, Carson will be nowhere in sight.

"Well, if you decide you need anything while we're out, don't hesitate to call and I can pick it up for you on our way back."

"Thanks darling, you're truly a lifesaver. Carson and Oliver are so lucky to have you." Emotions clog my throat until I feel like they're blocking my breathing. I try my best to swallow them down, but they want to come bursting out. They want me to sit and cry and tell Gloria everything. Not that I ever would. That's not how I operate. Instead, I give her a forced smile, grab Oliver's hand, and quickly exit the apartment.

I'm perched on the concrete lip that surrounds the sandbox in Oliver's favorite park, freezing my metaphorical nuts off. Out of all the places we could have gone, of course he wanted to go to the park. I watch him climb the ladder and throw himself down the slide again and again as I blow my warm breath into my hands and rub them together, trying to stave off the cold.

"Five more minutes, Oliver! It's cold out here and it's getting dark." I can see him jut out his bottom lip at me in a pout, but he doesn't argue which makes me suspect he's getting just as cold as I am. I bet if I look, I can find some kind of indoor playground for him. With us quickly heading into winter and this being Seattle and all, there has to be places where kids can run around and play, right? I think about looking into it when I get home but realize it's not my problem anymore. This will probably be one of the last times I watch Oliver, especially with how cagey Carson was when I asked if I could see him.

Then again, he didn't say I couldn't see him, just that he wasn't going to be around much. Now I find out he's spent the past week at Gloria's. I'm not exactly sure what's going on with them, but something just doesn't seem right.

I grab my purse that's been sitting next to me and start sifting through the contents, looking for my keys and my cell phone, before shoving them down into the pocket of my coat. I call Oliver over and let him know it's time to leave. He only argues with me for about thirty seconds before giving in and we're walking towards my car in the parking lot, his hand clasped in mine.

Oliver is happily chatting away at my side, telling me about all the things that happened in school this week and what he's working on in the art classes I've missed. There's a stab of guilt in my gut for missing so much, but there isn't really much I can do about it. Maybe I'll talk to Carson next time I see him and push to be more involved with Oliver. It's probably not my place but I don't particularly care. Oliver and I are friends. Just because Carson changed his mind about wanting to be with me doesn't mean that both Oliver and I should suffer for it.

We're about twenty feet from my car when a large white van with no windows comes screeching to a halt right in front of us. I instinctively take Oliver's arm and jerk his tiny body behind me, out of the path of the carelessly driven vehicle. The driver pops out of the front seat and comes rushing towards us.

"Hey man, what the fuck do you think you're doing? You could have killed—" my mouth immediately slams shut when the man driving the van stands in front of me with a gun pointed directly at my chest. I can't stop staring at the gun that's clutched in his slightly shaking hand. Carson's gun is large and black while the gun this man is holding is much smaller and silver. I wish I knew anything at all about guns, the only thing I know is that it's pointed straight at Oliver and me and that's not good.

Oliver keeps trying to look around my legs and is calling out my name. "Stay right where you are, Oliver," I bark at him. I can feel him flinch at my tone, but he stays behind me, clutching at my thigh.

My heart feels like it's about to pound out of my chest and it takes me a minute to realize that the man is yelling at me. I peel my eyes off the gun in his hand and finally look at the rest of him. He's dressed in disheveled and wrinkled clothing, his brown hair is dirty and unkempt, sticking out every which way from under his stained baseball cap. He looks like he's somewhere in his mid-fifties but it's difficult to tell with the layer of dirt caked over him.

It's then I realize I've seen this man before. It's the same man that was lurking in the trees weeks ago when Oliver and I were playing in the park. Was he watching us the entire time or are we merely targets of convenience right now? It takes a minute but my ears finally home in on what he's saying. "You stupid bitch, what are you deaf? Get in the fucking van or I'll blow your brains out."

He wants us to get in that van? Not fucking happening. I watch Dateline. As soon as Oliver and I got in there, nobody would ever see us again. My eyes dart around the parking lot but this late in the day there's nobody near enough to us to see what's going on. There's a group of parents sitting at some picnic tables but those are at least a hundred yards away. There's nothing they can do to help us right now.

"We're not getting in that van with you," I say with a lot more conviction in my voice than I'm currently feeling at the moment.

"Did you not hear the part where I said I was going to blow your fucking brains out?" He's getting steadily angrier and my mind searches for the right thing to do. The only thing I know for certain is that if Oliver and I get into that van we're fucking dead. And that's if we're lucky and not sold into slavery or something even worse.

EVE STERLING

Surprisingly, I don't seem to give a shit about myself. My mind is solely focused on Oliver and getting him out of this situation. I'm not letting this psycho touch him. "Look man. The kid and I are not getting into that van with you, so you've got two options here." The rage of me speaking back to him is turning his face purple so I keep going before he does something we'll all regret. Like shoot me in the face. "Like I said, we're not getting in that van. So, you can shoot me right now. Between the sound of the gunshot and how fast this kid can run it will alert everyone in the park to what's happening. They'll see you, they'll see your van, and you'll be caught before you even make it to the highway. That's your shitty option number one."

He looks back and forth between us and the groups of people interspersed around the park. "Your option two is letting the kid go." I continue on, my voice deceptively steady. "You let him go right now and I'll go with you myself, no arguments, no struggle. Then you've got a nice cooperative hostage. If you're lucky, nobody will even see you."

"What about the kid?" He asks skeptically. Frankly, I'm a little surprised he's even considering my suggestion. Obviously, this guy isn't an experienced criminal. That's going to work heavily in my favor.

"Are you kidding me? He's five. He won't remember what you and your car look like. Even if he did, who would believe him? Unreliable witness and all that." The man is looking around again, his hands shaking. There's even a split second where I think I might be able to wrestle the gun away from him, but I'm too worried that it might go off and hit Oliver. The entire reason I'm agreeing to go with this guy is to keep Oliver safe and out of danger so that's an unacceptable risk.

His face settles back into one of determination. "Give me your phone and your purse," he snaps. Fuck. I was hoping he would forget about my phone. Like I said, he doesn't seem like this is his kind of thing, and with how badly his hands are shaking, I figured

272

he might not think about it. I hand over my purse and dig my phone out of my pocket before handing them over to him.

He starts pawing through my bag. I'm not sure what he's looking for but in no time at all, my receipts, makeup, and wallet are strewn across our little corner of the parking lot. The next thing he does is take my phone and hurls it against the ground, shattering the screen. I flinch a little when he draws back his foot and smashes his heel into the phone grinding it against the concrete, ensuring its destruction. Maybe this guy isn't as clueless as I first thought. "Now get in the fucking van!" He snaps at me through clenched teeth.

Before I make a move to follow his command I turn and gather Oliver into a tight hug. "It's going to be okay, Oliver. You understand me?"

Tears are running down his cheeks, gutting me. "But why are you going with that man?"

"It's going to be fine. I just have to go with him for a little while. You go find some grown-ups and tell them to call your dad, okay?" He looks like he wants to argue with me but he just nods his little head. I take my hands and rub them up and down his arms in a slow, soothing gesture before leaning forward and quietly whispering a simple "Shhhh," into his ear. His eyes are wide, and he nods his head at me in understanding.

"Enough of this shit, let's go." The man grabs my arm and yanks me away from Oliver but not before I bury my clenched fist down into the bottom of my coat pocket. I wrench my arm out of his grip, hold my head up high, and climb into the van without any assistance.

"Go find a grown-up Oliver, remember?" He nods his head, tears streaming down his face, and takes off in a sprint across the park toward the group of people sitting at the picnic tables across the field. He's scared and confused and doesn't understand what' going on. I wish I could hold him and comfort him, but I've already accomplished my main objective. I've gotten him away from this psycho with a gun. As I'm watching him, the door to the van slides closed, blocking my view, and the man crawls through the interior until he's back in the driver's seat.

"What the fuck do you want, anyway?" I ask, unable to help myself.

"Just keep your fucking mouth closed and I won't have to break your jaw, bitch." I narrow my eyes at him but stay silent. He's still got the gun gripped in one hand as he awkwardly puts the van in drive and peels out of the parking lot.

I don't know where he's planning on taking me and I don't know what the fuck he wants with me. I decide my best move is to stay quiet and closely watch where he's going, mentally logging turn after turn, just in case I'm able to escape. Then at least I'll have some idea of where I am. I keep my hand buried deeply into the bottom of my coat pocket as I desperately clutch the GPS tracker I was able to slide off Oliver's hand when I was hugging him. Hopefully, he'll remember to tell Carson I took it. The man is now constantly shaking and talking to himself though I can't make out what he's saying. I'm worried that this tracker in my hand is the only thing that's going to get me out of this situation.

Chapter Twenty-Four

Carson

I check my watch and notice the time is long past when I promised Gloria I would be by for dinner. I know she'll understand, I just don't like missing any of the little time I have to spend with Oliver right now. The week without Bianca has been hard but the only thing that's kept me going is getting to see my son every day, even if it's only for a few hours.

Rafe and I have been going through old files the LAPD sent over for the past few hours and my eyes are starting to blur. No matter how many I go through them, it just feels like I'm grasping at straws. That we haven't been able to find a single viable suspect, added to the lack of any additional clues from the perpetrator himself, and I feel like I'm spinning in circles.

I'm about to tell Rafe that we can pack it in for the evening when my desk phone lets out a shrill ring. "Detective Turner," I say cradling the receiver between my ear and shoulder while I close the files on my desk.

"Detective, this is Shirley at the front desk."

"What can I do for you, Shirley?" I try to keep the irritation out of my voice. It's not her fault I'm tired and ready to go home.

"We just got a call from dispatch. Apparently, they received a call from someone that claims to be with your son."

"What?" I practically shout. What is she talking about? Oliver is tucked safely away with Gloria. At least, he's supposed to be.

"He's currently at Alterman Park. I'm not sure of all the details. Do you want me to put dispatch through to you?"

I snatch my keys off my desk and catch Rafe's attention who is looking at me questioningly. "Can you put them through to my cell? I'm heading to the park right now."

"Of course," she says and disconnects the call.

"What's going on?" Rafe asks.

"I'll explain on the way." I throw on my coat and head toward the back exit where all our cars are parked just as my cell rings with the requested call.

The car comes skidding to a halt and I'm not even positive I have it in park when I jump out the door and start sprinting towards the small group of people gathered around a cluster of picnic tables in the evening haze.

As I get closer, I spot Oliver standing sandwiched between a uniformed officer and an older woman who seems to be stroking his back comfortingly. He jerks around to face me as I shout out his name. I can see the tears streaming down his cheeks and the second he spots me he takes off in a run. I scoop him up into my arms and hold him tightly to my chest, trying to assure myself he's here in my arms and that he's alright.

"I'm sorry, Dad. I'm sorry." He's practically wailing in my arms, and I know I need to get him calmed down if I'm going to get anything useful out of him.

"It's okay, Oliver. You didn't do anything wrong, you understand me?"

I don't bother turning my head but can feel Rafe step up beside me. "I'm going to talk to the unis and see what they have so far." I just nod my head as he moves over to the small group of people who all seem to be speaking at once. I can't stop running my hands over his limbs and across his body, doing my best to assure myself that he is indeed unharmed.

I didn't get much out of dispatch, just that there was a kidnapping attempt, but that Oliver hadn't been taken and was asking for me. They didn't have much other information in all the confusion but they said he was unharmed and safe which was the only thing playing over and over in my head as I sped towards the park. "Where's Gloria?" I ask, clutching him to me tightly while scanning the crowd for her. I know that wherever Oliver is, she is sure won't be far behind.

"She wasn't with us, Dad," he says on a hiccup. I look down at him, confused.

"What do you mean she wasn't with you? How did you get here? Who were you with?"

"Bianca." He lets out on a sob before breaking down into tears again. The relief I was feeling at knowing Oliver was safe has evaporated instantly. I look around and don't see Bianca anywhere.

"What do you mean you were here with Bianca?" I'm doing my best to keep my voice level, but I don't think I'm doing a very good job of it. I want to drill him with questions until I get the full story and he tells me where Bianca is, but I manage to restrain myself. I see he looks just as distraught as I feel and I pull him into me, hugging him tightly. I take a deep breath and start again, trying not to let my sense of urgency leak through to my voice. "Why were you here with Bianca? I thought Gloria was watching you."

"Aunt Gloria hurt her back and called Bianca so she could watch me while she took a nap. Bianca didn't want to go to the park. I made her. I'm so sorry." He's back to crying and I rub his back in what I hope is a soothing manner.

"That's okay, buddy. Tell me what happened at the park with Bianca."

"We were walking to the car to leave cause it was cold, and a man stopped his car in front of us. Bianca pushed me behind her so I couldn't see but I took a peeked and he had a gun. Was he a bad man or was he a good guy like you?"

I take a deep breath trying to calm the rising panic in my chest. There's only one reason a man would pull a gun on Bianca and Oliver, and it definitely wasn't because he was a good guy. "I'm not sure, buddy. What happened after that?"

"He told us to get in his van and he was yelled at Bianca to hurry. Then he called her bad words but she wouldn't go. I was really scared. He was waving the gun around and Bianca kept saying to stay behind her."

"You did the right thing by listening to her. I'm really proud of you. What happened after that?"

"I didn't understand everything, but Bianca said she would get into the car if he left me here. That if he tried to take us both there would be loud and people would hear, but if he just took her, she would be quiet. Why would she go with him, Daddy?"

I knew exactly why Bianca would go with him. She was trying to do everything she could to keep Oliver out of danger. My breathing is coming fast now as I try to stave off my panic. "Did you recognize the man?"

"No, he was all dirty."

"Okay, you did great buddy." I call Rafe over to me and he extracts himself from the group of bystanders and comes jogging over while I hand Oliver off to a female uniformed officer and ask her to call Gloria.

"He has Bianca."

Rafe's eyes turn steely. "I thought he might. One of the parents over there mentioned that Oliver kept talking about a woman who got into the car. Why wouldn't he take both of them? He had them all alone and from what I could tell, they were too far from anyone else in the park for them to be a problem."

"It sounds like she convinced the guy she would go quietly if he let Oliver go."

"Smart girl," he says while nodding. While I'd love to agree with that sentiment, I can't think of anything other than getting her back right this moment.

"We need to put a trace on her cell ASAP."

Out of the corner of my eye, I see Oliver pull away from the officer I've handed him off to and he comes running back towards me. "I have her phone, Dad." He lifts it up to me and I swear when I see its crushed state. While this guy certainly isn't a professional—or else he wouldn't have been talked into giving up one of his hostages—he has some idea what he's doing.

"Did she leave anything else?" I ask. He runs to the table and comes back with Bianca's purse. He must have made her ditch the entire thing just in case, even after obliterating her phone.

"God-fucking-damnit," I roar. I know how upset Oliver is when he doesn't even bother calling me out on my cursing. I drop to a knee in front of him and take him by the shoulders. "I need you to think really hard for me, Oliver. Did the man or Bianca say anything about where they might be going? Anything at all that can help us find her?"

He scrunches his face up like he's concentrating hard then suddenly his features light up. "My watch!"

"What are you talking about?" I ask.

"She gave me a hug before she left and she pulled the watch off my arm. I almost cried because she didn't loosen it when she pulled it off my hand, but she told me to *shhhh*. I don't think the man saw it, he was looking behind us and didn't say anything when she put it in her pocket."

I want to let out a whoop of joy knowing that Bianca had the wherewithal to grab the tracker, but of course, that doesn't mean he didn't find it later or that he hasn't done something to her already. "You did a great job, buddy." I try to reassure him.

"Is Bianca going to come back?" He asks, his eyes once again welling with tears. The truth is that I don't know what's going to happen. I don't know where exactly Bianca is, what's happening to her, or even what this guy's plans are for her. But I can't tell Oliver that. Instead, I give him the best smile I can muster and squeeze his shoulder.

"Uncle Rafe and I are going to go get her right now. I promise."

He nods his head solemnly, like he believes every damn word that's coming out of my mouth and I only hope I can live up to the promise I just made.

I quickly jog with Oliver back to the officer and am informed that Gloria is on her way to come get him from the park. With a sigh of relief, I thank her and quickly dig my phone out of my pocket, pulling up the tracking app for Oliver's watch.

"What have you got there?" Rafe asks, peering over my shoulder.

"It sounds like after he ditched her phone Bianca grabbed Oliver's tracker so with any luck, I should be able to pull it up on here and find out where she is."

"So, what you're saying is, not only does your girl have balls of steel, she risked herself to save your kid, and then was smart enough to give us a way to track her down?"

I try to tamp down the pride I feel at his words because now is not the time to think about what an amazing woman Bianca is, but I can't help letting a, "You're damn right she is," slip out.

"Fuck, when this is all over, you're going to have to help me find a girl like that for myself." I barely hear his words because I'm staring so intently at the screen on my phone. How long is it going to take this damn thing to load? All it does is flash *Connecting*.

"Goddamn it!" It's all I can do to not fling the thing across the park.

"Calm down for a second, Turner. Just give it a minute. She could be in a place with crappy reception." I grumble under my breath but still don't pull my eyes away from the screen.

Connecting... Connecting... Connected.

I nearly let out a whoop but tamper down my excitement. The dot is still and not moving which means that it was either ditched somewhere or they're no longer on the move. I see it's about five miles away from our location but I don't know very much about the area so I shove the phone towards Rafe so he can have a look at it.

"Okay, this is down by one of the old waterfronts. Lots of abandoned houses and warehouses there. It would make sense that he would be holed up in one of these."

"C'mon, let's go." I grab my phone back from him and start jogging towards my unmarked cruiser, Rafe close on my heels.

"Don't you think we should call in for some backup?" He asks.

"You can call them on the way. I won't let something happen to her while I'm sitting here on my ass. Hell, something could have happened to her already."

"You can't think like that," Rafe chides as we slide into the car. I don't even bother saying anything back to him. We've both been on the job long enough to know she could very well be dead already, he's just trying to keep my hopes up. The only thing that's really keeping me going is the thought that this guy is obviously obsessed with not only me, but with making me pay for whatever it is he thinks I've done to him. I doubt he'd just kill Bianca and leave her in some abandoned building for me to find. No, he wants me to see what he's going to do to her.

It's that thought that has my foot pressed solidly on the floor of the car as we speed out of the parking lot, tires squealing as Rafe gets on the phone to call in our destination.

We park one house down from a dilapidated clapboard two-story house. To say the place has seen better days would be an understatement. The windows all appear to be broken out, there's so much paint peeling off the exterior that I can only faintly tell it was a white or gray color at one point. The porch has collapsed in on itself and the eaves above it are sagging so low they're almost blocking the door that looks like it's barely hanging onto its hinges.

I glance at my phone again to confirm that this is indeed the house that the signal is originating from.

"You're sure this is the right place?" Rafe asks.

I don't even bother looking at him, my eyes transfixed on the house. "As sure as I can be."

"You think we should wait for backup?" This time I tear my gaze away from the collapsing house and train my eyes on him but don't bother saying a word. He lets out a sigh. "Yeah, that's what I thought."

We both exit the car, guns drawn and held low as we creep up to the building from the side. There's an old, beat up, white service van tucked into the overgrown driveway on the side of the house and I'm more certain than ever that this is the place we're looking for. I signal for Rafe to head towards the front of the house while I circle around to the back.

As I approach the blown-out windows on the back porch, I can hear voices coming from inside. One is a male I don't recognize, and the other is distinctly Bianca. My body wants to sag in relief that she's alive and talking but I know that she's not out of danger yet. I need to keep complete focus if I'm going to get us all out of here alive. I slowly inch closer and closer to the back door that's only being held on by a single set of hinges at the top of the frame, letting me get a better sense of what's going on inside.

"I don't know what you're hoping to accomplish with this," I hear Bianca's voice loud and sure. "If you're expecting Carson to give a fuck that you've taken me, you've made a big miscalculation, asshole. Carson dumped me. You'd have had a better chance of getting him out here if you'd taken one of his lawn decorations."

"Is that so?" The man asks, his voice has a slight shake to it. He doesn't sound anywhere as confident as Bianca does. "I've been watching you two and that brat of his for a long time. How fucking stupid do you think I am?"

"Pretty fucking stupid, actually. Like I said, he broke up with me. He doesn't want anything to do with me anymore. I don't know what your plan is, but if you think Carson's going to come running in here to save me, you've got another thing coming. He only cares about his kid, and you let him go." She lets out a hysterical laugh, and that's the only sign I have that she's way more frightened than she's letting on to this guy.

"Shut the fuck up!" He yells at her before I hear the sound of flesh hitting flesh. I have to take a deep breath to stop myself from running in there half-cocked, getting the both of us killed.

"Did anyone ever tell you, you hit like a fucking girl?" Bianca asks. I almost laugh at that but remain focused on the job at hand. I creep closer to the window and peek inside.

Bianca is tied to a rickety old kitchen chair and a man I only vaguely recognize from my security camera is pacing back and forth in front of her, one of his hands running agitatedly through his hair while the other holds onto a revolver that's currently pointed at the floor. If he had any idea Rafe and I were outside, he definitely would have the gun up and at the ready because once I get my hands on him, I'm going to tear him limb from fucking limb.

I quickly shoot a text to Rafe who's at the front of the house. Not thirty seconds later I hear a large crash, causing the man to spin towards the sound, his gun raised high and pointing toward the front door.

Before he can turn back to Bianca, I ram my shoulder into the old rickety door. I'm surprised by how easily it crumbles away and almost end up sprawled onto the floor. I'm able to catch myself right in time and level my gun at the man holding the love of my life hostage.

"Drop the gun and get on the ground," I shout.

Unfortunately, he doesn't heed my warning and closes the two feet that are between him and Bianca, grabbing her by the hair, almost causing the chair to topple over, and holds the gun against her head.

Fuck.

"Nice of you to join us, Detective Turner."

"You have me at a disadvantage, you seem to know who I am, but I don't have any idea who you are." I keep my gun steadily on him, hoping that there will be an opportunity for me to get a shot. Unfortunately, he's crouched down too closely to Bianca at the moment for that to even be a consideration.

"It's nice to see you care about this bitch when you didn't care about my daughter." He yanks on Bianca's hair, and I can see her grit her teeth in an effort to not cry out.

I want to pull his attention away from her the best I can. The more erratic he gets the more likely he is to shoot her, either on accident or on purpose. "Why don't you tell me your name. I don't think we've met."

"Of course we haven't met," he spits out. "My name is Daniel Howard." The name is like a punch to the gut but I try not to let it show.

"You must be Janet's father," I say as calmly as possible. As far as I knew, Janet didn't have a father. In fact, I asked her outright if she had any family and she told me she didn't. Whenever I used confidential informants that were as deep in as Janet was, I wanted to make sure there were no family members out there who could have any kind of blow-back on them.

There are tears welling up in his eyes, but his grip hasn't loosened at all on Bianca. "Of course I'm her father, and you got her killed! You used her like some piece of trash and when she couldn't help you anymore you just tossed her to those fucking wolves. She trusted you!"

"Mr. Howard, I can't tell you how sorry I am about what happened to Janet—"

"You're not sorry! Don't you dare say you're sorry! You didn't give a shit about her!"

I can feel him losing control but at least his focus seems to be focused on me now and not Bianca. He's obviously unstable and if Janet was the last thing he had to live for, he won't hesitate to go down shooting. There's no way I can let that happen.

"Janet didn't tell me she had a dad. I promise you, I asked. In fact, Janet was the one that came to me. I didn't go seeking her out."

"Why would she say she didn't have a dad?" The gun is shaking in his hand now and I'm hoping I can get him to set it down.

"I don't know. Maybe because she knew that if I found out she had family, I wouldn't have used her. I'm notorious for not using CIs with close family. But Janet came to me. She hated Darryl and didn't see a way out. He had gotten her addicted to drugs and was selling them to kids. Janet was desperate and didn't want what he did to her happen to anybody else. She wanted to help."

"She could have come to me!" His voice reverberates around the empty house and behind him I can see the outline of Rafe slowly closing in. I just have to keep him distracted for a little longer and maybe he can disable him before the situation devolves into flying bullets.

I raise my hands up in the air, pointing my gun at the ceiling, trying to show him I'm non-confrontational but also knowing that Rafe is slowly edging up behind him. "I don't know why she didn't come to you or why she told me she didn't have a father. What I can tell you is that she helped so many people. All the information she fed me about Darryl's operations, about the drops, the money exchanging hands, they all helped us put some terrible people away. I wish I could have done more to help her Mr. Howard, I really do. When she was murdered, it devastated me. It was one of the reasons I left Los Angeles."

"You left because you're a coward."

"Look around you. Do you think Janet would be happy with what you're doing right now? You're hurting another woman who's just as old and innocent as she was." Howard glances around the room and for the first time seems to notice the death grip he has on Bianca's hair. Even though she's doing her very best to be silent and inconspicuous, I can see the big intake of air she draws in when he lets go of her.

"You know I'm right, Mr. Howard. Janet wouldn't want you to hurt anyone, she wanted to help people. Even when she was hurting and didn't know what to do for herself, she still wanted to help people she didn't even know. She wouldn't want things to end like this."

The shaking gun falls out of his hands, and he drops to his knees as he begins to cry out "My little girl! They killed my little girl!"

As soon as the gun hits the floor Rafe leaps out from the shadows and tackles him to the floor, though it doesn't look like he's struggling. I'm in front of Bianca within two seconds and reach behind her, working to untie the binds that have her to the chair. She's sucking in air in big gulps like she can't seem to get enough of it.

"I've got you, baby. I'm here. Nothing bad is going to happen to you, I swear."

The second she's untied she launches herself at me and has me down on my butt on the dirty kitchen floor, her body wrapped tightly around mine. I'm whispering how sorry I am and any other nonsensical thing that comes out of my mouth in an attempt to comfort her when I finally hear the sirens in the distance. I'm smoothing down Bianca's hair and watching Rafe kick away the revolver before cuffing Daniel Howard's hands behind his back.

I hold her tightly against me and breathe her in. Hell, this feels like the first time I've been able to breathe in a week let alone the past few hours.

Suddenly, she pulls away from me and starts frantically looking around. "Where's Oliver? Is he okay? Oh God, I didn't want to leave him Carson, I swear I didn't, but I couldn't let him get into that van. I had to leave him there. I'm so sorry."

She won't stop talking and I try to calm her fears. "Oliver is fine, baby. He's more worried about you than anything. You did the right thing. Well, I'd have preferred if neither of you got into the van, but you did good by getting him to let Oliver go."

"You promise he's fine?" She asks looking up at me with concern painted all over her face.

"I promise. And thank God you took his tracker. That was really smart. I don't know how I would have found you without it."

"I wasn't even thinking. I just knew when he smashed my phone there would be no way for you to find me. I hugged Oliver, and I felt it and I pulled it off him. I hope I didn't hurt him, but I didn't have time to undo the band."

"He's fine, Bianca, I swear. He's going to be so happy to see you."

"Hey, I don't mean to interrupt this happy reunion, but we've got officers incoming," Rafe calls out to us from the doorway.

I pull myself up off the floor and help Bianca to her feet but keep my arm firmly wrapped around her, not ready to let go yet. I swear, I've lost a good ten years off my life today.

"Who is he?" She asks while warily eying Daniel Howard's face down on the dirty ground.

"He's someone from my past back in Los Angeles that apparently followed me up here to Seattle. It's a long story but basically, he's been stalking and harassing me for months."

She looks up at me with confusion written all over her face. "Months? Why didn't you say anything? I had no idea."

"I didn't want you to know. I didn't want to scare you." Grabbing her chin, I bring her face close to mine so she can't look anywhere but directly into my eyes. "Last week he sent me a package of photos. They were all of you and Oliver."

I can feel a shiver run through her body. "Me?" She almost squeaks out.

"He's been following you and threatened the both of you. I didn't know what to do to keep you safe."

She's quiet, her eyes searching my face while I can practically see the wheels in her brain turning. "That's why Oliver has been staying with Gloria and why you broke up with me out of the blue."

"Yes, exactly. I didn't know how else I could keep you safe."

"It wasn't because I can't have kids?" She asks quietly while diverting her gaze.

"Hey," I say softly until her deep brown eyes are locked with mine again. "Of course not. I told you I don't care, and I don't. I just want you, Bianca. I knew if I told you this crazy guy was following me and making threats you wouldn't have cared. You're fierce and you're brave. While I love those things about you, they also scare the shit out of me. I know you wouldn't let him scare you off. You understand, right?"

"Yeah, I understand," she says with a small, sad smile. Something still doesn't feel quite right with her but that could be any number of things. Hell, she just got fucking kidnapped and had a gun held at her head, of course she's not acting like her normal self. Now there's about a dozen officers streaming through the house and we're being pulled in different directions to give our statements. I'll feel much better when I have her out of here and home with me, where she belongs.

CHAPTER
TWENTY-FIVE

BIANCA

The ride back home is quiet. I keep catching Carson staring at me out of the corner of his eye. I want to snap at him to keep his eyes on the road, but I don't have the energy. I know I'm not acting like my normal self and he most likely thinks it's some kind of aftereffect of this evening's trauma. Don't get me wrong, I was scared out of my mind. Up until I got into that van with him the only thing I could think of was getting Oliver as far away from him as possible. It wasn't until I was alone with him that the fear truly set in.

But that's not why I'm being quiet. Not really. I have a lot of things on my mind.

I understand what Carson did, and I understand why he did it. Hell, even if I wasn't being hunted down by some misguided grief filled father our breakup was inevitable. I should thank the man.

For a split second I believed that I could have the same thing that everyone else did. I'd trained myself for years not to expect anything from a man. A relationship, a family, a future. I had learned not to want those things. Then in comes Carson, like a bull in a china shop and he blew away my carefully constructed defenses, making me believe those things were possible, that they could be within my

290

reach. Really, I'm thankful for the cold hard dose of reality that took it all away from me.

Oh, I absolutely believe Carson thinks he wants me. He's a good man. How he handled this situation is enough to see that. He cares about me now, he might even love me a little, but that's why I have to let him go. Someday he'll realize he wants those things I don't want, and even more importantly, *can't* give him. That look of affection in his eye will turn to one of resentment. I don't want to be there to watch the feelings he has for me slowly turn to those of hate for taking his choices away like they were taken from me.

It's best for everyone if I go back to living my life the way it was before he and Oliver came into my life. Then they can both move on. Maybe find a woman who has more to give than I do. One that will expand their family beyond three.

I feel his hand grip my thigh and I'm deep in my thoughts and it causes me to jump so high I practically hit my head on the roof of the car. "Hey, you okay over there?"

"Yeah, great," I say giving him a smile I'm not positive I'm pulling off.

"I spoke to Gloria before we left. Oliver is already passed out at her place so it's just you and me tonight."

I cover his hand with my own and give it a squeeze. "That sounds perfect." And it does. I can give myself one last night with him. Sure, it's probably a little selfish of me but I'm giving him up for his own good. I can have this one thing for myself, can't I? Besides, it's not like he won't be getting anything out of it.

We pull into his driveway, and I've barely stepped a foot outside of the car before he's grabbing my hand and dragging me behind him towards the front door. I let out a laugh as he pulls me inside. "Somebody is a little eager."

"Can you blame me? I haven't been inside you in a week. It's been fucking torture." Before I can answer his lips are moving against mine. It's somehow both rushed and unhurried at the same time. Almost like he's sipping deeply from my lips.

I let out a little gasp and his tongue quickly swipes inside my mouth, barely making contact with my own. My tongue tries to chase his back into his mouth, but he pulls away causing me to let out a whimper of frustration. His lips move down the column of my neck and my head falls back giving him greater access, as my entire body starts to warm and tingle in anticipation.

My hands move down to his waist, and I quickly pull out the tucked in tails of his shirt, slipping my hands underneath so I can feel his hot skin on my fingertips. I can feel the growl deep in his chest and before I know it, his shirt is gone, discarded somewhere on the floor. Just as I'm about to continue my exploration with my hands, he drops to his knees in front of me and starts tugging my pants down.

I can hear the little sounds of anticipation I'm making but I'm unable and unwilling to stop them. His face is pressed against my cotton covered mound and I can hear him inhale deeply, taking in the scent of my arousal. Every time he does this, I know I should feel embarrassed but when I look down and see him licking his lips, anticipating the taste of me on his tongue, I can't feel anything except blood rushing to my core, plumping up my clit for him.

"Please, Carson," I can't help but beg. God, I've missed this. Has it really only been a week?

"Tonight, baby, you don't need to ask for anything." With that promise he swiftly pulls on my panties, causing them to rip, and leaving a stinging sensation on my hip and thighs that only turns me on more. "You're so fucking wet for me. You need this as much as I do, don't you, baby?"

"Yes." The word is an answer and plea combined. I can feel my wetness covering my thighs and he hasn't even touched me yet. It's always like this with him. With just a look, he can make my pussy gush like it never has before.

He doesn't dive into my slit like I expect him to, instead he gently licks me from my entrance up to my clit and back again. As soon as he hits my bundle of nerves, my hips give an involuntary jerk and push into his skilled tongue. He kisses my wet pussy like he's kissing my mouth, gently darting his tongue in and out, swiping left and right, driving me out of my mind.

I grab onto the short hairs at the top of his head and do my best to pull him closer into me. He stiffens his tongue and uses it to rub my engorged clit, causing me to hold on to his hair tighter and ride his face, rubbing my pussy firmly up and down his face, using his tongue to fuck myself.

While I'm riding against his face with abandon, he grabs my ass cheeks and pulls against him even more tightly. I can hear the wet and sloppy noises his mouth is making against my dripping cunt and between the sounds and his tight grip on my ass I'm getting so close to the edge I'm not sure I can hold back.

"Carson, I'm gonna come."

He doesn't say a word, only redoubles his efforts, this time sucking my clit fully into his mouth before batting it back and forth with his tongue. I'm so close but I just something more to get me there. As usual, Carson senses what I need and gently bites down on my swollen clit.

I let out a scream I'm sure the neighbors will hear and feel a release of more of my juices escape my core straight into his mouth. Carson doesn't slow down but continues to eat me through my orgasm while I simply hold on to his hair for dear life while all I can see are stars.

When I finally come back to my senses, I realize we've moved to the bedroom, and I have absolutely no recollection of how I got here. Carson's now naked, his cock so hard it's practically pointed straight up in the air and it's shiny with pre-come. My mouth waters and I can't take my eyes off it while he reaches behind me and unsnaps my bra.

I quickly push him backwards until the back of his legs hit the bed, and he's forced to sit.

"Wha—" he starts to ask but gets the picture pretty quickly once I'm on my knees in between his outstretched legs. I lean forward but he quickly stops me by cupping my chin with his hand. "You don't have to do this tonight, baby. I want this to be about you."

I give him my best pout. "I thought you said I don't have to ask for anything tonight."

"Fuck." His hand falls away from my face and I lean forward, practically attacking his cock with my mouth. This isn't a slow seduction, this is me hungry to get him inside me, to have the taste of him fill my mouth. I swirl my tongue over the helm of his cock and take him deep in my mouth, sucking as I pull him back out again. His fingers are tangled in my hair and his eyes look wild when he says, "You're so fucking beautiful when you have my cock in your mouth like it's the best thing you've ever tasted."

I let out a moan I know he can feel up his shaft when he tightens his hands in my hair. I love it when he talks dirty to me. I continue to suck him into my mouth, running my tongue across his length repeatedly, driving him crazy. Once saliva collects in my mouth and running out of corners, coating him fully, dripping down to cover his heavy balls, I can't hold back any longer and I bring my hand between my legs to play with my swollen clit. You'd think I'd be satisfied from the orgasm I'd had just minutes ago but the taste of him in my mouth is too much.

Carson looks down and catches my hand buried in my cunt. "Shit, are you so fucking horny you can't even wait for me? You've got to play with that horny little pussy while you suck me off?"

All I can do is nod my head and hum my confirmation while I continue working him up and down. I reach up with my free hand and tug on his balls, heavy with his come.

That seems to be his breaking point. He lets out a roar and pulls my head back and off him before grabbing me under the arms and settling me onto the middle of the bed, positioning himself between my thighs, his pulsing cock resting against my drenched slit.

Wrapping my legs around his hips, I try to draw him inside me where I need him most but instead, he starts to gently fondle my tits. His fingers slide down the sides of each one so lightly it's almost more of a tickle than a caress before he pushes them together, alternating sucking on one sensitive peak at a time. My fingernails dig into his back of their own accord, asking for more without words which causes him to lightly nip at my hardened tips, causing a surge of pleasure directly between my legs.

Pulling back slightly, he ignores my imploring hands so he can look straight into my eyes. God, I could get lost in those moss green eyes of his. I've painted them so many times it's almost embarrassing, but now I'm realizing I've never been able to capture this look he's currently giving me. They're filled with heat, passion, and something else I can't quite describe, let alone put on canvas.

"You're so fucking beautiful, Bianca. I don't know how I got lucky enough to make you mine but now that I have you, I'm never letting you go."

I try to look away but can't. His eyes have captured me. I swear they're seared on my soul. I'm just thankful those eyes can't read my mind since it's a jumbled mess of arousal, longing, sadness, and reluctant acceptance.

Instead of saying anything in return, I grab his face and drag him back to my mouth for a passionate kiss, doing my best to put every emotion, every sentiment that I can't express to him, into our mouths molding together. The kiss quickly turns wild and out of control, sloppy, and full of teeth clashing.

Carson pulls back and we both try to catch our breaths. He smooths the hair that's plastered to my forehead with sweat away from my face and gently kisses my collar bone.

"Slow down, baby. Let me make love to you," he whispers in my ear.

I take a shaky breath trying to keep my emotions in check. I don't want him to make love to me. I need a hard and punishing fuck from him tonight. I need him to fuck me like he hates me because that's exactly how he's going to feel in the morning. If he does that, maybe then I won't feel so guilty for letting myself indulge in the pleasure of his body this one last time, but I don't know how to convey that to him without saying the words that would cut us both so deeply.

He flexes his hips, causing his long hard member to run down the center of my warm and wet slit. I let out a gasp when the head of his cock nudges against my clit.

"Please Carson, I need you tonight. I need to feel you inside me." He knows how much I hate to beg and he promised me I can have what I want tonight. Well, what I want is him. And I want him right now.

"How can I resist when this tight cunt needs me so badly? You know I'll always be here to give you what you need, don't you?"

All I can do is nod emphatically while he notches the head of his cock into my entrance. Before I can ask again, he enters me in one smooth thrust seating himself deeply inside, causing me to suck in air.

His strokes are long and forceful. I try to urge him to move faster with the raising of my hips against his, but he's determined to take this at his own excruciating pace while peppering my face and chest with the sweetest of kisses. I eventually give up on the hard fuck I'm craving and let myself sink down into the slow and languid pleasure he's providing me.

His hands are all over me, like he's trying to memorize my body through his fingertips. They're on my face, my stomach, my breasts, each movement heightening my pleasure. My arms wrap tightly around his shoulders, holding him to me and bringing his mouth back to mine. Our kisses have turned slow and sensual while he rocks his body into mine, bringing me higher and higher.

It's painfully obvious that he's right, this is making love. While Carson's always been the best sex I've ever had, I've never experienced anything that's even come close to this feeling. Of course, there's that bone deep, toe curling, bliss that's always between us when we come together. But tonight, there's undeniably something more. There's a closeness, a surging of emotions that almost has me blurting out those three words that I can never say to him.

He's continually whispering in my ear, telling me how beautiful I am, how talented and passionate, how he can't live without me. I have to block all of that out of my brain or I won't be able to do what I know needs to be done. Instead, I focus completely on the sensations he has running through my body.

His movements are becoming jerkier, less controlled, and I can feel his impossibly hard cock somehow swelling even larger inside me. The stretch is almost too much to take as I toss my head back and arch my hips causing each thrust inside my pussy to drag the base of his cock against my needy clit.

"I'm going to fill you up with my come, beautiful. I'm going to mark you as mine from the inside out." His whispered words are apparently the last thing I need to push me over the edge into oblivion. My entire body tightens before bursting into waves of rolling pleasure as I call out his name.

My orgasm triggers his own and I can hear him roaring my name into my ear and feel hot jets of his come fill me deep inside. Every additional stream seems to keep my orgasm going, and it's not until much later that I feel myself finally coming back to my senses.

Carson is lying next to me with one arm and leg thrown across my body, holding me down to the bed, like he somehow knows I'm going to make my escape. While I lay there, trying to get my breathing under control and feeling his come leaking out from between my thighs, all I can think is that I don't want to go. I don't want this to be over. But I know I don't have a choice. If I don't end it now, it will just hurt us both more in the long run.

I can feel tears silently streaming out of my eyes and down my cheeks. I turn my head, trying my best to hide them away from him but it's no use. "Are you alright?" He asks gently.

"Yeah, it's just been a crazy emotional day. I'll be fine. Promise." I quickly wipe away the tears and pat his arm in what I hope is a reassuring manner. He nuzzles my ear and places kisses along my neck just where he knows I love them. I close my eyes in an attempt to quiet the emotions swirling inside me.

After a few minutes pass I hear him whisper softly against my ear, "I love you." That almost sends me into a fresh wave of tears but I do my best to pretend I'm asleep in his arms. The need in my chest to tell him I love him too feels almost violent, but I manage to tamp it down. Instead, a few more tears slip past my iron control and slide down my face, landing on the pillow. I stay there, as still as I can until I finally feel Carson's breathing even out behind me. I wait another thirty minutes in frozen silence before I slip out of his bed and out of his life.

Chapter
Twenty-Six

Carson

"Bianca?" I call out as I walk through the house, first checking the bathroom, then the living room and kitchen, before making it all the way to the other end of the house, finding it empty. I'm not really sure why I'm calling for her and doing a thorough search. As soon as I woke up and she wasn't tucked into my side, I knew she was gone. Her absence in my space had an almost physical feeling to it.

I peek out the side window and don't see a car in her driveway. Still, I quickly slide on some sweatpants and a tee shirt and head over to her place, banging on the door. Again, I'm not surprised by her lack of answering.

I could tell there was something wrong last night, I just couldn't place what it was. I let myself believe her brush offs about it being an emotional day was the reason for her distance, but deep down I knew there was more going on. There has to be or else she wouldn't have snuck out of my bed like a thief in the night. I can't decide if I'm angry with her for leaving without a word or if I'm just plain worried about how she's handling the events of yesterday. It's probably a bit of both.

I check my watch and see that I need to head out and pick up Oliver. After yesterday's insanity I'm planning on spending the day with him, especially since I haven't seen him much this past week, Bianca doing a runner on me isn't going to change that. Still, it doesn't stop me from scooping up my phone and firing off a text.

Me: Why did you leave this morning? Is everything okay?

I finish getting ready for the day and check my phone, noting that my message has been read but that there's no response. Now I'm legitimately getting annoyed. She can't even take a moment to text me and let me know she's alright?

Me: I'm planning on spending the day with Oliver. I know he'd love to see you. If you want to meet up with us, let me know.

I realize I'm bringing out the big guns by telling her that Oliver wants to see her but it's not like it isn't true. He would be thrilled to spend the day with her.

If I thought that would push her to respond I was sorely mistaken when the message almost immediately shows read, but again, I get no response. I let out a sigh and grab my car keys. Perhaps she just needs some time and distance. I can't imagine how she's feeling today, I just wish she would let me in so we could talk it out. I'm sure I'll hear from her later in the day.

Except that I don't. I send her multiple texts throughout the day, some just checking in, some letting her know what Oliver and I are doing, and I get nothing but radio silence from her. At this point I'm past annoyance and am just confused. Why won't she speak to me? She's obviously getting my messages.

When Oliver and I get home, I make a quick stop at her house again but the place is completely dark and there's no answer when I bang on the door. By the next morning I still haven't heard from her and I'm getting the distinct feeling that I'm getting blown off. If she thinks that after everything we've been through, she can get rid of me by just ignoring me, she's sorely mistaken.

Then the thought seeps into my head that maybe I've been wrong about everything. Maybe she doesn't feel about me the same way I feel about her. I told her I loved her last night, but she was already asleep and didn't respond. I'd like to think that if she was awake, she would have repeated those words back to me but maybe I've just been kidding myself. Is it possible that I've been nothing more than a place filler for her?

No, that's not possible. After our heart to heart about her not wanting or being able to have children, she seemed just as enthusiastic about being in a relationship as I was. There was no way I read that wrong. Something must have happened between then and now. I know I broke up with her, but I explained how that was to keep her safe. She said she understood, and I think the fact that she was actually kidnapped could only strengthen the truth of my words.

The fact of the matter is that I just need to get her to speak to me. That's the only way I'm going to be able to figure out what's wrong and fix it.

The next day dawns with still no word from Bianca and as I drop Oliver off at school, I'm more determined than ever to get her to speak to me. Since I'm currently on paid leave because of what happened with Daniel Howard, I head home and spend the rest of the morning cleaning the house from top to bottom while keeping one eye glued to the kitchen window that faces Bianca's house.

At around eleven a.m. I see her car pull into the driveway and watch as she hurries into the house without even sparing a glance in this direction. I immediately leave the dishes I've been washing in the sink, change my shirt, and head over to her.

My heart is pounding at an unreasonable rate as I approach her door. I tell myself there's no reason for me to be nervous, but my body doesn't seem to agree. I'm on edge and feel like I'm about to go into battle which can't be a good sign.

Knocking on the door doesn't bring any response. I can't even hear any movement from inside. In fact, if I didn't see her walk inside not five minutes ago, I would assume she was still out. I pound on the door again, harder this time. "Bianca, open the door. I saw you come home. I'm not leaving until we talk."

The door quickly opens like she's been standing right behind it the entire time and I pause just a moment to take her all in. She's wearing a pair of sleep shorts and a tank top that is barely containing her breasts which immediately gets me half hard. I tell my body to behave itself, but my dick has a mind of its own when it comes to Bianca. Her hair is piled high on the top of her head in a messy bun with tendrils falling all around her face that my fingers itch to push back behind her ear. Surprisingly, her face appears to be make-up free. It's not often I see Bianca without makeup, usually it's just before she goes to sleep or after she gets out of the shower. She always looks gorgeous, whether she's made up or not, but there's something about her fresh faced that makes her appear younger, more vulnerable.

"What's up, Carson?" I'm so surprised by her nonchalant attitude and the slight tone of impatience in her voice that it takes me a second to answer.

"What's up? What do you mean, what's up? Where have you been, Bianca? I know you've been getting my messages."

She glances behind her, then over my shoulder. I get the feeling she's trying to look anywhere but into my eyes. "I'm sorry, I've been busy."

"You've been busy." I say, deadpanned. "You haven't been home. Where have you been?"

"I've been staying at Dad's. You know, helping him take care of Violet. I'm only home to grab some stuff then I'm headed back over there." Well, at least that makes sense. It makes me feel slightly better knowing why she hasn't been home, but it still doesn't explain why she snuck out of my bed and why she's been ignoring my texts.

"Okay. Well, do you want to come over for dinner tonight?" She shifts her weight from one foot to the other in a nervous gesture I'm not used to seeing from her.

"I don't think that's a good idea."

My brow furrows as I watch her closely. "Well, what would be a good idea?"

Finally, her eyes pull up to meet mine. Unfortunately, there's no warmth in them at all. They look flat and cold, and it sends chills down my spine. "I don't think we should see each other anymore, Carson. It was fun while it lasted but I think you had the right idea when you ended things a week ago."

I have to make a significant effort to not bend over because it feels suspiciously like I've just taken a baseball bat to the gut. "What are you talking about, Bianca? I told you why I did that. I was only trying to protect you. I thought you understood that."

She takes a deep breath but keeps her eyes steadily locked with mine. "I do understand why you did it. Believe me, I appreciate how you looked out for me. But that doesn't mean you were wrong to do it."

"What are you talking about?"

"God, do I have to spell this out for you?" Her voice has risen an octave and I do my best not to flinch. "You were right, you deserve the choice of whether or not you want to have a family. I'm not the right girl for you. I'm sure you'll find someone new in no time. But you and me? We're over."

It's this exact moment I realize how badly I fucked up. When I broke up with her, I let her believe it was because of her medical issues because it was easy. Convenient. I never should have done that. I should have made up something else. Hell, I should have told her the truth. I made the monumental mistake of letting her greatest fear come true. I rejected her because she couldn't have children. I'm the one that planted that seed of doubt in her mind and all it's done is grown unchecked for the past week.

She takes a step back and tries to close the door on me, but I put my hand out to stop it. "Bianca, we already talked about this. I don't need kids. I have Oliver. All I need is you, I thought you understood that."

"Look Carson, you're a good guy. I even think you honestly believe that. But one day you'll change your mind. You'll resent me for keeping you from having a full life. I'm not going to be the person that keeps that from you."

"If I have you, I'll have a full life. If I don't have you, I'll have nothing. You have to believe me when I tell you that I don't give a care about having children. I just want you. What can I do to make you believe me?"

"There's nothing you can do, Carson. It's already over. Please, I just want you to go."

"But I love you, Bianca, and I know you love me too. I love you more than anything."

If I expected my declaration to soften her, to loosen her resolve I couldn't have been more wrong. I see her face harden into a mask of indifference right in front of me. "You'll get over it," she says in a voice as cold as ice.

I'm so taken aback by her reaction to my declaration of love that I let my hand fall away from the door and she takes the moment to close it firmly in my face. I don't know how long I stand there on her porch, my eyes staring blankly at her closed door, but I know a considerable amount of time has passed when the alarm on my phone goes off telling me it's time to leave so I can pick Oliver up from school.

I don't want to leave. I want to find something I can say, something I can do, that will make her believe me, but I'm coming up blank. Instead, I concentrate on turning and putting one foot in front of the other so that I can go pick up my son.

It's been a week since I've seen Bianca, but it's not for a lack of trying on my part. I've been keeping a close eye on her place, but it doesn't look like she's been home since my last confrontation with her. When she mentioned she was going to stay at her father's and help with Violet, I didn't imagine it would be for this long.

Of course, I considered she was trying to avoid me, but I hoped that wasn't the case. However, it was made apparent that avoiding me was exactly what she was doing when three days ago Hollie showed up to her place and came back out with her easel, some canvases, and other miscellaneous art supplies.

I haven't given up though. I'm not sure I'll ever be able to. Every day, I text her. Several times a day. They run from the mundane *Good Morning* text to bad jokes I've heard around the precinct sprinkled around pleas for her to listen to me and give me another chance. Every text is met with a stony silence.

I may have abused my police access the tiniest bit by pulling her father's address from the system. I figured since it's concerning my future wife and father-in-law it can't be all that bad.

Rafe didn't agree with that reasoning either.

I don't know much about getting the love of your life to come back to you, I've never been in love before. Hell, I've never been in a serious relationship before. Rafe told me all women love flowers, so I started with those, but I didn't know what flowers where her favorite. So I've been sending a different bouquet to her father's house every single day. I still haven't heard a word from her but at least the flowers haven't been dumped on my porch in a twisted mess of petals and stems. That's giving me a bit of hope.

I know, I know. Just let me grasp at straws here.

Now that it's been a full week and I'm truly at a loss for what to do, I've decided to go to one of the only people who might be able to help me. Her father. Believe me, he wasn't my first choice. I would have approached either Hollie or Violet before going to him but since it doesn't look like either live next door anymore, I think Dante Moreno might be my only hope.

When I knock on his door I'm half hoping, half dreading that Bianca will be here. Of course I want to see her, I'm like a man dying of thirst and she's the only source of water within a hundred miles. But I know that if she's here, I'll get thrown out on my ass immediately. I'm hoping the fact that it's the middle of the day will work in my favor and she'll be at the gallery.

Less than a minute after I ring the doorbell the door opens, and Violet is standing in front of me. Well, below me. I've only met her in person that one time and I obviously was a little too preoccupied to notice she's over a foot shorter than I am. Her face is still covered in bruises, but they've faded from red and blue to those deep yellow and brown tones. There's still a bandage on her hand but I'm happy to see she's out of the hospital and looking like she's on the mend.

"Violet, right?" I ask, not sure she even knows who I am. The only time I've ever been in the same room as her, she was unconscious.

"Carson Turner?" Her eyes go wide and before I realize what's happening, she's thrown herself at me, wrapping her arms around my waist. "I never got the chance to thank you for what you did for me. Thank you so much. I wouldn't be here if it wasn't for you."

She pulls herself away from me and blesses me with a smile. I'm a little thrown off by the warm welcome. Not that I'm not thrilled she's happy to see me, I was just expecting a stern and angry Dante answering the door.

"Of course, I was just doing my job." Giving the standard answer I always provide when somebody thanks me lets me feel like I'm getting my feet back underneath me, but Violet just rolls her eyes.

"Yeah, well, *just doing your job* saved my life."

I open my mouth to respond when I hear a deep voice from behind her. "Who's at the door, baby?"

She turns towards Dante who's just joined us. "It's Carson." She looks back over at me and seems to suddenly realize I'm still standing outside on the porch. "Oh gosh, I'm so sorry. Please come in, come in." Before stepping inside, I shoot a brief glance at Dante since it is in fact his house but he's already walking towards a large open room when Violet grabs my wrist and drags me inside.

Once we make it to the living room, I sit on an overstuffed love seat with the two of them side by side on a couch facing me over a wooden coffee table. I'm trying to figure out where to start when Dante dives headlong into the conversation.

"I'm glad you're here, Detective Turner. That entire day was kind of a blur for me, but I know you saved Violet and I'm not sure I properly thanked you at the hospital." He throws his arm over Violet's shoulder, dwarfing her as she looks up at him with adoration in her eyes, and pulls her closer into his side. I'm about to do my standard deflection of thanks once again but before I can get the words out of my mouth he continues. "I also heard about how you saved Bianca last week. I can't thank you enough for what you've done for this family."

"It's not a problem, sir. She wouldn't have even been in any danger if it wasn't for me."

"Nonsense. You didn't do anything but love her. It's not your fault what happened to her any more than it's my fault what happened to Violet." I'm not sure that's true, but I decide it's probably in my best interest at this point to not argue with the man that can help me get the love of my life back.

"I'm just glad everything worked out and nobody was hurt. Actually, I was hoping I could speak to you about Bianca."

"I thought that's why you might be here."

Violet gives me a look that's laced with sympathy and pops up from the couch. "I'm going to let you two talk. There's some work I need to get done upstairs in the office."

"Are you sure, baby?" Dante asks her.

"Yeah, I think this is a talk the two of you should have and I should stay out of it." As she walks past me towards the stairs, she gives me a pat on the shoulder. "I'm rooting for you, Carson Turner."

I'm not sure if I should be happy about the fact that one of Bianca's best friends is rooting for me or deflated that she feels the need to tell me she is in the first place. I decide I'll stick to the happy feeling and hold on tight.

"So, you and Bianca, huh?" Dante seems to search my face looking for the slightest sign I don't have the purest of intentions when it comes to his daughter. At least I know in that regard, he won't find anything to disappoint him. I only want what's best for Bianca. It just so happens that I'm what's best for her.

"She's an amazing woman. But I've messed things up between us and I'm hoping you can give me some advice."

"I'm not going to sugar coat it. Bianca is as stubborn as they come. In fact, if she knew you were here talking to me, she would be pissed at us both." I open my mouth to respond but he holds up a hand stopping me. "I'm not going to tell her you were here. I'm completely loyal to my daughter and I'll always do what I think is best for her, even if she and I disagree on what that is."

I merely nod my head, letting him continue. "Bianca has been happy for the last few months. Happier than I've seen her in a very long time. It wasn't until recently that I learned that was in large part due to you and your son. Are you too old for her? Maybe." His eyes wander to the stairs that Violet just disappeared up. "But who am I to judge something like that? As long as you care about each other I'll be happy for the both of you."

Hearing that I have her father's blessing should feel like a weight lifted off my shoulders, but unfortunately, I don't have Bianca's blessing yet. "Thank you, I really appreciate that. But I've messed up. I tried to do the right thing, but I went about it the wrong way and now she thinks we aren't right for each other. That I'm going to tire of her. She's completely shut me out and I don't know what to do about it."

Dante leans forward, resting his forearms on his thighs and clasping his hands together while watching me closely. "Bianca has one of the biggest hearts there is. Even I didn't know how loving and thoughtful she was until she accepted Violet and me with barely a fight. The one thing she never talks about, not even to me really, is the accident and her infertility. Until the two of you broke up, she hadn't even told Violet or Hollie about it."

I flinch a little at that. I obviously knew this was her biggest insecurity. But she had never even told her closest friends about it? The size and scale of my fuck up keeps growing and growing.

"When she came over here a week ago, asking if she could stay until I found her a new place, I basically forced her to tell me what was going on."

"She's moving?" I almost shout the words but manage to calm myself down. No matter how bad things got I could always comfort myself with the fact that she was right next door, I still had a shot as long as she was within arm's reach. I figured this stay at her father's was just a short-term thing to help with Violet and maybe get a little break from our forced proximity. I wasn't expecting her to move.

"The house she's living in is one of my rentals and she wants to switch to a different one, but I don't have anything else available right now. There's one that's under construction and should be ready sometime next month but for now she's stuck there."

My level of desperation just shot up significantly. I'm going to need Dante's help more than I thought I would. "Look, I'm not used to asking for help, but I need yours here. I don't know what to do. I can't even get her to talk to me, let alone give me another chance. There has to be some way to get through to her, to make her understand."

"Once Bianca makes up her mind, *really* makes it up, I'm not sure I've ever seen her change it. I can tell you love her."

He goes silent then, still watching me closely, waiting for a confirmation I have no problem giving. "She's the love of my life. I want to be with her forever. I don't care that she can't have children, all I want is her."

Dante nods his head like I'm confirming something he already knew. "Honestly, I've already tried encouraging her to rethink her position on this but she seems determined to stand by her decision." I try not to let this piece of information deflate me, but if she won't listen to her father, I'm not sure what hope I have of getting her to listen to me. "I don't think she's going to be persuaded by words. You're going to have to think of a way to show her how serious you are about her."

"I'm getting that feeling. It doesn't seem like anything I've said is getting through to her."

"Like I said, you're going to have to find a way to show her. I don't know how but I honestly hope you do. Otherwise, I worry she may stay alone for the rest of her life."

The thought that the men she's dated, myself included apparently, may have damaged her psyche so much that she'd stay alone forever is enough to make me feel like a villain. Dante is right, I have to find some way to show her how much I love her. That she's the only person in the world for me.

After thanking him and leaving, I get in my car and drive aimlessly for a while, letting my thoughts drift. How can I show Bianca how much I love her? Obviously, daily texts and flowers aren't the way to go. I'm not rich like Archer Clarke, I can't buy her some expensive painting, though to be honest, I don't think Bianca is the type to be swayed by that type of thing, anyway. Hell, she has the painting he gave her for her birthday hanging above her bed for her own enjoyment, it's not even out on display for others to see. No, she doesn't need an expensive gesture; she needs something big but intensely personal.

My mind is stuck in a loop of ways to show her what she means to me, but I discard every idea as soon as it comes to mind. Nothing seems good enough, big enough, to show her she's the only thing I want, that I'll ever want. To be honest, the thought of having kids with someone who isn't Bianca makes me slightly nauseated.

There's one idea that I've been kicking around in the back of my mind for several days. I think it might be the only option I have left. My big Hail Mary. If I do this, and she still won't take me back, then I'll know it's really over. I'm just a little worried she might think I've gone too big, too crazy. But maybe it's time I take a page out of Bianca's book and be a little reckless. If I can get her back, it will be worth it.

CHAPTER TWENTY-SEVEN

BIANCA

It's been two weeks since I've last laid eyes on Carson and almost a full week since I've heard from him at all. I should be happy. Thrilled even. The constant texts were annoying. And all those flowers? I mean, what was I going to do with them anyway? They were currently dotted around Dad's house, most of them wilting away and dying but for some reason I stop Violet every time she tries to throw one of the older bouquets out. I think I just enjoy the aesthetic.

Like I said, I should be thrilled he's given up. I guess I just didn't expect for him to give up so soon. I know that probably makes me sound like a hypocrite. I love Carson, so of course I'm going to miss him. It's because I love him that I don't want to hurt him in the long run. I'm saving him from himself. I'm being rather selfless really.

When Violet told me he came by to see Dad last week, I don't know what I expected to happen. I can tell you I *didn't* expect him to cut off contact with me and completely give up. If I had a less stubborn soul, I would corner Dad and demand he tell me what the hell he said to Carson to make him go away for good. But I won't. This is what I wanted after all.

The first week after the breakup I would go out and party every night, dancing and drinking away all my pain. Well, at least I tried to.

I mostly just ended up with sore feet and terrible hangovers. Now Jenna keeps trying to persuade me to go out, but I haven't been able to muster the energy. As of a few days ago it seems like she's finally given up and is letting me sulk, which I appreciate.

I've been staying at Dad's place, not willing to go home and have to see Carson's daily comings and goings. There's plenty of room here and Dad assures me he and Violet—who it seems has taken up residence here as well—don't mind that I'm here. I know they're telling the truth but I'm sure they want some alone time now that they're officially together.

A few days after I essentially moved in, they sat me down and told me Violet was pregnant. I'm honestly happy for them and excited at the prospect of being a big sister for the first time. Yeah, it's a little weird that my dad and my best friend are engaged and having a baby, but they're both so disgustingly happy and obviously in love that I'd have to be a truly bitter soul to give them a hard time about it. Okay, so I might call Violet my step-mom from time to time, but she deserves me giving her a little bit of shit considering she hid their relationship from me for so long. While I'm overjoyed for them both, it's still a stark reminder of why I'm alone and not with Carson.

So while I'm comfortable here, I know it's time for me to head home, give them their space, and get back to my normal routine. Dad is going to let me know as soon as a property is available so I can move and in the meantime I'm going to get back to working on my paintings. Margot is still waiting on the two other pieces I promised her so I really need to be concentrating on that instead of what Carson is or isn't doing.

The bags I've been essentially living out of the past few weeks are packed and sitting by the front door, waiting to be loaded into my car, I'm just not ready to leave quite yet. Instead, I grab a bottle of wine from the fridge and pour myself a large glass before sitting at the table and taking three large gulps. I shouldn't be so nervous about going home. I don't have to see Carson. If he's outside, I'll just circle the block until he's back in his house and I can safely park and scurry away into my place. Luckily, since he's stopped reaching out to me, I don't have to worry about him barging over and demanding to have some kind of conversation about "us" again. God, when did I turn into such a fucking coward? I'm so much stronger than this. I guzzle the last bit of wine in my glass and refill it again, hoping for a little liquid courage though not so much that I can't make it home.

Violet comes wandering into the kitchen, distracting me from what was about to be a serious wine binge. "How you doing?" She asks. She's basically been treating me with kid gloves since I've been staying here and it's rather odd since she's usually the more sensitive of the two of us.

"I'm just getting ready to head back home. I've got a lot of work to do and if I keep showing up to the gallery in the same three outfits, I think Margot's head is going to explode."

"It looked to me like you were drinking a bottle of wine all by yourself."

"Well, I would offer you some, but my little brother has taken away my drinking buddy." I jokingly glare at her stomach where she's not even showing in the slightest. In fact, I'm pretty sure she wouldn't even have realized she was pregnant yet if it wasn't for her recent stay in the hospital.

"Hey, it could be your sister. We don't know yet." She laughs and places a hand protectively on her stomach with a dreamy look on her face. I smile and realize that it's not just lip service. I really am happy for her. All Violet has ever really wanted in life was to be a mother. Looking at her now, you'd have to be a real monster for resenting that. I'm many things but I'd like to think that a monster isn't one of them.

"Well, my only experience with is with boys so I'll just have to keep my fingers crossed," I say taking another sip. My mind drifts to Oliver and my smile disappears from my face. Sure, I miss Carson, but I miss Oliver too. The worst part is that he's too young to understand why I've disappeared. I wonder what Carson's told him about why I'm not around anymore.

Violet must be able to read my troubled thoughts because she comes over and hugs me from behind while I stay seated at the kitchen table. "You know, I'm sure you could go see him. Carson seems like a reasonable guy. I don't think he would keep you away from him, especially if Oliver likes you as much as you say."

I shrug my shoulders, effectively removing her arms from around me. "Who knows, maybe I made our relationship into a bigger thing than it was. I mean, how do I know how kids behave around people? I was probably just another random adult to him."

"You don't really believe that, do you?"

"It doesn't really matter what I believe, does it? The fact of the matter is that things between Carson and I are over. Keeping any entanglements with Oliver will just make things messier than they need to be."

She pulls out the chair next to me and takes a seat. "Hey, life is messy. Look at me. I have parents that want nothing to do with me and I'm engaged to my best friend's dad who's not only much older than me, but who also knocked me up. I mean, it doesn't get much messier than that."

"Jesus Christ, you're a fucking mess, Vi," I say jokingly. "When you lay it all out like that, it does sound like a bit of a mess."

She gives me one of her signature soft smiles. "It is, and I couldn't be happier about it. And then look at Hollie falling in love with her grumpy bosshole. I mean, who would have ever believed things would work out for the two of them after all that crazy stuff with her mom *and* her dad? That was a pretty big mess too. I don't know, maybe you should try being a little messy."

I return her smile with one of my own but don't answer her with words. There isn't really anything to say. Things aren't as easy as she wants to make them out to be. Sure, everything worked out for her and Hollie, but what are the chances of that? One in a billion? More? No, despite what fairytales say, we don't all get our happy ending, and I accepted that a long time ago. I was just stupid enough to forget that for a short time.

I cough and wave my hand to disperse some of the dust particles out of my face. How the fuck did this place get so dusty after only a few weeks? I swipe the shelf containing my paints with the dust rag again but am smart enough to turn my head this time. I let out a groan when I realize that whether I'm here or in the new place Dad finds for me, I'm going to be the person doing all the cleaning now.

I mean, I'm not a slob, but the deep cleaning stuff was never my forte. I never seemed to have to worry about it either. It must have been something that Violet or Hollie just took care of without telling me about it. Maybe, I should think about getting a new roommate who can help me out with my newly increased list of chores. The thought makes my mood dampen considerably so I push it to the back of my mind and simply continue setting up my station so it's ready for me to get some painting done.

As soon as I got home, I chucked my bags into my bedroom, not really bothering to put anything away. My fingers were itching to get to work and let some of this emotion that's been brewing inside of me out onto the canvas. I quickly changed into an old pair of jeans and an already paint splattered shirt, then quickly tied my hair up into a messy bun at the top of my head.

Standing in front of the blank canvas, I'm not really sure what I'm going to create. I normally sketch what I'm going to paint out of the canvas before I start but this time, I immediately dip a medium-sized brush into the mauve and start making broad, bold strokes.

I've only been working for about twenty minutes when the doorbell rings, breaking me out of my trance. My stomach immediately drops to the vicinity of my feet. I'm not expecting anybody. I glance at my phone that's sitting on the workstation next to me and don't see any calls or texts. Most everyone I know would reach out to me via phone before just coming over. That really only narrows it down to one person. How can you want so deeply to not see a person but desperately need to at the same time? I feel like a crazy person.

I set down my brush and slowly make my way to the front door then just stand there. Maybe he's left and I can just go back to painting. I'm about to turn around when the bell rings again. Instead of standing there a moment longer in this torturous limbo I wrench the door open.

"Carson." The word escapes me on a breath. I'm not even sure I said it loud enough for him to hear me. He's got on a pair of loose-fitting jeans that are sitting low on his hips and a faded, plum colored polo shirt. His hair is getting just a little long on the top and I barely resist the urge to reach up and run my fingers through it. How the hell is it fair that he looks so good when I know exactly how I look in my old, paint-stained clothes and messy hair.

"Hey, Bianca." He gives me one of his little smirks and I want to melt on the spot but I remind myself that he shouldn't be here, and I shouldn't be talking to him. Not if I ever plan on getting over him. Okay, getting over him is a stretch, I'm not sure I'll ever be able to do that, but I would like to limit the number of times I think of him a day from about three hundred to a nice manageable ten or so.

"You're not supposed to be here, Carson. I thought I made that clear."

The smile leaves his face and I hate that I'm hurting him, but I know I'm doing the right thing. Right?

"I know you don't want to see me, but will you please let me in for just a minute? I have something I want to say and if you don't like it then I'll walk away and leave you alone. Forever. I just need a few minutes of your time."

The thought of him leaving me alone forever shouldn't feel like such a stab to the heart. "There's absolutely nothing you could say that would change how things are between us, Carson. I think it's best that you go." I start to swing the door closed, but he places his hand out and stops it.

"I don't just have things to say, I have something to show you too. Will you at least let me show you before you send me away?" His voice has a tinge of desperation to it and my guilt comes rising up. I know I put that desperation there. What's the harm in seeing what he has to show me? Plus, I could talk to him about seeing Oliver sometime. Maybe I could take him to his art class a few times a month.

I step back from my place in the doorway, creating plenty of room for him to pass by me. "Fine, five minutes and that's it."

"That's all I need, Sparky." He passes so close to me I can smell his soap and it causes a tingling between my legs that I immediately shut down.

"I hate it when you call me that," I mumble.

"No, you don't." That smirk is back and instead of making me melt it makes me want to smack it off his face. I lead him into the living room and sit in the chair that's facing the couch, that way he won't be able to sit next to me. There's no use in tempting fate.

He perches on the edge of the sofa, resting his forearms on his knees and clasping his hands together. The look in his eyes is so earnest and pleading it makes my chest ache. We're silent for a long minute, just staring at one another in the stillness of the house.

"You had something you wanted to show me?" I prompt him to move this along. I look and notice he didn't bring anything with him so I'm not sure what he possibly has to show me, but his presence is making me feel claustrophobic.

"I do. I just want to say something first." I open my mouth to tell him I don't want to hear it, but he forges on before I can get the words out. "I know I've told you I don't care about having kids, Bianca, and I know you don't believe me. I understand where your mistrust comes from. If I had experienced the same kind of rejection for something I had no control over, I'm not sure what I would do. But I know how I feel about you and even though you don't believe me, I know what I want. It's you, Bianca. I'm not going to change my mind about that. I know that words don't mean much to you, that they can be twisted and rescinded. But I'm not willing to lose you over this so I did something that will hopefully show you I'm committed to you no matter what. Whether you can or can't have children doesn't matter to me. Hell, even if you could have them, I know you don't want them and I'm fine with that." He lifts slightly from the couch and reaches into his back pocket, pulling out a folded piece of paper that's slightly crumpled, before holding it out to me. "I did the only thing I could think of that would give me even a chance of you believing me."

I stare mutely at the piece of paper. Almost afraid of what it could be. I want to believe him, I really do.

I just don't.

I guess that's not true; I believe he feels that way right now, I just think that odds are his feelings will change in the future and he'll either feel stuck with me or he'll leave me, shattered and broken. I don't know how a simple piece of paper could change all that, but I want it to. I really do, but I'm terrified it won't change a thing and that will be it. We'll be done and over.

"Go on, look at it," he says gently after I make no move to take the paper from him. I reach out slowly and slide it out of his hand. I can feel his eyes on me, like a weight, while I slowly unfold it.

I don't know what I was expecting, but it wasn't this. It's some kind of official looking form with a couple of pages stapled behind it.

My eyes scan down the first page and I'm more and more confused the longer I look at it. That is until my eyes catch on one word.

I can feel my jaw drop and my eyes go big. I quickly look over at Carson who's just sitting there and I notice how he's nervously fidgeting with his hands.

"You got a vasectomy?!" Even though I didn't really mean it to, the question comes out as a shout. I don't know what to think. I'm feeling a little stunned.

"I told you it was the only thing I could think of to get you to believe me I don't need to have children."

"Are you crazy?" I'm pretty sure I yelled that too. I can't seem to stop. Or pick my jaw up off the floor. He gets off the sofa and moves over to where I'm sitting, pulling me up out of my chair and wrapping his arms around my waist.

"I'm absolutely crazy, but you have to take some responsibility for making me this way."

"Are you trying to say you getting a vasectomy is my fault?" I ask incredulously. That's just what I need. Before, I worried he would regret that he didn't have kids because of me, now I have to worry that I made him get an entire medical procedure on one of the pieces of his anatomy I love the most.

He cups my face with his hands. "God, no Bianca. It's not your fault, it's not anybody's fault. The thing is, it doesn't matter. I love you so much the thought of having a child with anybody else is physically repulsive to me. If I was going to have children, which I'm not, it wouldn't be with anybody except for you. So whether I got this done or not, it doesn't matter. I'm not having kids. Shit, I hope that doesn't mean my insurance company isn't going to deny it for not being medically necessary."

He gives me a grin, causing me to smack his chest in response. "This is not the time to be joking," I say while trying to hold in a laugh. It was a little funny.

"Babe, it didn't matter how many times I've told you I loved you and only needed you and Oliver to be happy. Your mind wasn't going to let you believe it and unfortunately for me, I don't seem to be able to live without you. The only thing that's ever really scared me, I mean truly terrified me, was the thought of losing you. I'm not just talking about when you were taken, I'm talking about these past weeks without you. I knew I had to find some way to show you how I felt. Pretty words weren't going to cut it. This was the only thing I could think of."

"The only thing you could think of was getting a vasectomy? I think you need to crack open a book, maybe get some more education. That is completely insane, Carson."

"Yeah, but did it work?"

He's looking at me with such hope and love in his eyes while stroking my cheek. Is he crazy? Abso-fucking-lutely. Who gets a medical procedure to convince a woman to be with you? Apparently Carson, that's who. And I'm the woman he did it for. If I ignored this and just sent him away, I'd be almost as crazy as he is. Almost.

"Look, this doesn't give you carte blanch to go off and do something stupid every time I'm mad at you but... yeah, it kind of worked," I say with a smile.

He wastes no time in bringing his lips down to mine. I sigh into his kiss and my body easily melds against him. I've really fucking missed him these past weeks. As he deepens the kiss, I wonder how I even considered trying to live the rest of my life without him. There would have been no way.

I pull back from him and try to catch my breath. "I love you too, you know."

"Yeah, I know," he says with a smile.

"You know?"

"Of course I know. Well, at least I strongly suspected it. Do you think I go around letting doctors slice into my package for just anybody?"

"I would certainly hope not." I smile and slide my hands underneath his shirt, feeling the warm skin of his stomach on my fingertips. "So, did the doc give you the all clear to, uh, get back in action?"

That smirk that always makes me either want to smack him or kiss him appears. "I don't know, why don't we go find out?" I squeal as he hoists me off the ground and over his shoulder, carrying me back to my bedroom.

"Put me down you Neanderthal."

"Nope." He merely smacks me on the ass and keeps walking. This man drives me absolutely crazy. Apparently as crazy as I drive him. And I wouldn't have it any other way.

Epilogue

Carson

Six Months Later

"Now?"

"Not yet," I tell her. She lets out a moan of frustration that only serves to bring a smile to my face. I grip the fabric that's bunched at her hips tighter and continue the steady pace of my swollen dick moving in and out of her tight pussy. She pushes back against me, trying to get me to move faster so she can get the orgasm that's just within her reach, but I make her wait for it. I know it will be better if I make her wait.

It feels like she's strangling my dick as I plunge one hand down the front of her dress and inside her bra, squeezing her tit and making her gasp. "Jesus fuck, please Carson."

I run my lips up the side of her neck, nipping then kissing every spot along the way. The shiver that I can see run down her spine fills me with male satisfaction. I may get to control when my woman comes, but she's always satisfied, always desperate for me. I see her hands grip the edge of the sink tighter as she tries to suppress her cries of pleasure that my cock is providing her every time it slides against that spot deep inside her.

"What do you say, baby?"

She grits her teeth, and I can see that spark of rebellion flash in her eyes through the mirror. It's short-lived though as she quickly lets it go in favor of the orgasm she's about to receive. I'm sure I'll pay for it later. I'm okay with that. "Please Carson, let me come."

"Do you deserve to come?" I whisper in her ear while keeping up my relentless pace.

"Yes," she bites out before realizing snapping at me isn't going to get her anywhere. "Yes, please. I deserve it. I'll do anything you say, anything you want."

"You'll give me whatever I ask for?"

"Yes. Just... please!" I doubt she'll even recall promising me that, but a little extra insurance never hurts.

"You better remember that later." I increase my pace until I'm pounding into her mercilessly. Her moaning is getting louder but I don't want anyone outside to hear us, so I put my hand over her mouth to contain the screams that are coming and bite down on her earlobe.

I feel her coming around my cock before I hear her muffled shout of ecstasy. The rhythmic pulsing of her coming pussy sends me over the edge and I spurt jet after jet of come deep inside her.

After a moment of us both catching our breaths, I reluctantly withdraw from her warmth and we take a moment to clean ourselves up, happy that we slipped away into a bathroom this time and not some closet. I help Bianca wipe up between her legs before I pull her panties back into place then proceed to straighten up my slacks and shirt.

"Look what you did to my hair," Bianca says, studying herself in the mirror and trying to shove a few stray strands back into the fancy knot she has at the back of her head.

"I think you look beautiful," I tell her, capturing her lips for a kiss.

"You always say that," she grumbles good naturedly.

"That's because it's always true."

She abandons her hair and turns around with a smile, wrapping her arms around my waist. "If I didn't know better, I'd think you were buttering me up for something?"

"That doesn't sound like me."

"You're right, it doesn't. Now I'm suspicious."

"Can't a man tell his girlfriend how beautiful, talented, and wonderful she is without her thinking something is wrong?" I place a kiss to her forehead, careful not to mess up her makeup any more than our impromptu quickie in the bathroom already has.

She's still looking at me a little suspiciously but then just shrugs her shoulders, brushing it off. "I would totally grill you, but we've been in here too long. Dad and Violet are watching Oliver and I'm afraid she's going to tip over any minute."

After one final kiss I open the bathroom door and usher her back into the employee break room of The Gault Gallery. She's right, we really do need to relieve Dante and Violet. They both took to Oliver as soon as they met him and offered up their babysitting services. When Oliver found out that Dante could show him how to build things the kid was all in. Even though Dante is already a dad I think they're both trying to get some kid time in since they have not one but two little ones on the way. Poor Violet is so tiny she looks like she's about to tip over with the twins and I'm sure chasing after Oliver isn't helping.

By the time we make it back to the gallery floor, hand-in-hand, the size of the crowd has grown significantly, letting me know we were gone longer than I thought. Bianca's first show was three months ago, and while she only had four pieces displayed they sold incredibly quickly and drew quite the buzz from the local art scene. This prompted Margot to invite her to take part in this show as well, but this time she gets to display eight paintings and if the small crowd of people clustered around the area her work is hanging is any indication, they're going to all have sold placards next to them before the night is out.

When she finally let me see her work all those months ago, she was surprisingly nervous and a bit abashed. I didn't understand it until she started pulling them out for me, one after the other. There were a ton that were just me. Some were me from the shoulders up, others just my face. There were even some with just an eye or an obscured body part. Besides me, there were quite a few of Oliver as well. Even though it was a little weird seeing myself on canvas, it was obvious that Bianca is incredibly talented. But I knew that from the sketches she used to draw around my place, before I even got to see her paintings. It's just now that everybody else is noticing it too.

I did feel a little awkward during the first show she had. I couldn't figure out why people were looking at me and whispering until I realized that several of my likenesses were hanging on a nearby wall. The thought of a painting of me hanging in somebody else's space was a little odd at first but I quickly got over it. If Bianca wanted to paint me, I would let her do it all day long and consider myself lucky for it. I knew it would be time to worry when she wanted to paint somebody else, though I'm counting on that day never coming.

"Bianca!" I hear Oliver before I even see him. Like a flash, he's dodging between people and heads straight at Bianca, ramming into her legs full force. I can't help but smile when she wraps him in a hug. She may not like kids, but she loves Oliver. She treats him just like he was her own and that's more than I could ever ask for. I'm only a little jealous that she seems to be his favorite person now. The two of them often disappear and go on adventures while I'm working late. Though I still insist they remain vigilant, and that tracker never leaves Oliver's arm, I'm glad that what happened hasn't stopped them from going out and experiencing the world. Even if I'd like to keep them both tightly ensconced in bubble wrap. I tried to get Bianca to wear a tracking watch as well, but she put her foot down and said I was going overboard. I'm still determined to get one on her someday.

Violet comes waddling over to us with Dante close behind her. "Sorry, he got away from me," she says while cradling her stomach.

"Honey, why don't you let me find you a chair so you can sit down," Dante says while hovering behind her. Not that I blame him, she looks a bit like she's wilting. I'll be surprised if they're still here in an hour which means I need to get this show on the road.

"I'm fine. The doctor said a little exercise was good for me."

"She also said you should rest," I hear him mumble grumpily which makes me smile.

"Thanks for keeping an eye on him, Vi. I just needed to talk to Carson about something for a few minutes."

Violet looks her up and down. "Yeah, I bet he wanted to *talk* to you."

Bianca doesn't even bother to deny the not-so-subtle accusation. There's no use. We're pretty notorious amongst our friends for slipping away and banging one out at any opportunity. "Have you seen Jenna?" She asks, looking around the room. "I've got to know who that painting belongs to. I can't get anyone who works here to tell me and any time I got within ten feet of it today to take a peek someone was there to usher me away. I don't get it."

I turn to the painting she's referring to that's hanging by itself on the far wall. It's currently covered by some kind of white fabric sheeting and there isn't a plaque next to it, indicating what it is or who might have painted it.

"That's weird, weren't you the person who set up most of the show?" I ask innocently.

"Exactly. Why keep this from me? It doesn't make sense."

"Well, let's walk around the room a bit, maybe we'll find Jenna and she'll be willing to tell you something about it." I wouldn't bet on it. I've sworn that girl to secrecy and I'm pretty sure I'll be fixing her parking tickets for the rest of my life for this one. "Besides, there are a group of people over there who look like they'd love to speak to the artist." With my hand resting on the small of her back I steer her towards the group of people clustered around her work.

Before we get there, we're stopped by a group of large men who look vaguely familiar and completely out of place, like they aren't quite comfortable in the nice clothes they've squeezed themselves into tonight.

"Oh my god, you guys came!" Bianca squeals. She rushes up to them and starts hugging one after the other. "I can't believe you guys are all here. Dad didn't tell me you were going to make it. You have no idea how much this means to me." I was about to lose my shit at her handsy greeting when I realize they're a group of men that work for her father. While it's not enough to stamp out my jealousy completely, it allows me to keep it in check for the moment. When she's done greeting each of them, I grab her hand and pull her back to my side making it very clear who she belongs to.

"Carson, this is Jake, Gabe, and Travis. They've all worked with Dad for years. Guys, this is my boyfriend, Carson."

After we all exchange greetings Bianca chats with them for a bit and I spot Margot not too far from me, conversing with a group of men and women in clothes that probably cost more than my car. She sees me staring and I give her a quick jerk of my chin which brings a smile to her face. Disengaging from her conversation, she makes her way across the gallery floor.

"I think your dad is calling us," I whisper into Bianca's ear. She says goodbye to the group of men, thanking them for coming once again, and we head over to where her father is standing with Violet tucked into his side in front of her paintings.

"What did you need?" She asks Dante. He looks over at her, slightly confused since he didn't actually call for her and he's about to respond when Margot claps her hands and her loud voice draws us all to attention. She's standing in front of the wall to our right where the mysterious covered painting that's been driving Bianca crazy is hanging, with Jenna by her side.

"Thank you all once again for joining us this evening. As you know, Gault Gallery has the honor of hosting Seattle's most premier artists. We take pride in providing our patrons with the best of the best. That being said, we also like to keep our ear to the ground and discover those up-and-coming artists that thrill and enchant us with their view of the world. You've seen some of those very artists hanging on our walls tonight."

Margot makes a sweeping gesture with her arm and there's applause from the room. I give Bianca a quick squeeze and look down to see her smiling. I know this has been her dream, to be recognized by her peers and art connoisseurs for her talent.

"Thank you, thank you," Margot says, quieting the crowd. "With all the pieces we've seen tonight, we still have one more to show you. Will the artist of this particularly extraordinary piece please come forward?"

I see Bianca's head swiveling back and forth searching the room just as I feel Oliver tugging on my pant leg. "Now, Dad?"

"You got it, buddy." I pat him on his back encouragingly. I'm worried about this part. Oliver is a shy kid. Standing up and speaking in front of a room full of strangers seems a bit terrifying, even for me. I told him he didn't have to go up there alone, that I would go with him, but he insisted on doing this part all by himself. Who am I to hold my kid back?

As soon as he moves forward and goes to stand at Margot's side, I hear a murmurer run through the room. "What's going on? What are you two up to?" Bianca questions. I know she hates being left out of what's happening so this has got to be killing her.

"Just watch," I say before leaning down and giving her a quick kiss. I can tell she wants to argue with me but we're in public and the room is quieting again after the initial upheaval and chatter that a five-year-old artist apparently causes.

I've been so focused on Oliver and his nerves, but it seems like all my worry was for nothing. He's insisted on practicing what he was going to say every day in the car on the way home from school and now he's standing there, at Margot's side, looking perfectly serene. Unfortunately, all that worry for Oliver seems to have turned towards me. I can feel my pulse in my ears as my heart pounds at a rate that can't possibly be healthy.

Has it been this hot in here all night? I undo the top button of my dress shirt to give myself a bit of breathing room.

"I've had the pleasure of meeting this young man a few weeks ago and had a chance to look at some of his work. He's an extraordinary developing talent and I have no doubt that one day many of his works will grace the walls of Gault Gallery. May I introduce to you all, Oliver Turner."

There's applause throughout the large room and Oliver gives a shy smile. Jenna holds out a microphone to him and he grabs it, holding it comically close to his mouth. In fact, I'm pretty sure his lips are all over that thing. I grimace slightly, hoping they cleaned it off before this.

"Thanks everyone and thank you Margot for having me." I can't help smiling like the proud father I am at how comfortable he seems. A few months ago, I doubt something like this would have been possible. From the corner of my eye, I can see Bianca looking back and forth between Oliver and me with a bemused expression on her face, so I squeeze her hand in a gesture that I hope conveys to her that everything is fine.

"My name is Oliver, and this is the first art gallery I've ever been to. I wanted to paint something special for one of my favorite people and I thought this would be a cool place to show her." The crowd gives a soft chuckle at that, but it seems to be with him and not at him which is good. "Before I show everyone, I want to thank Bianca." He points directly to her, and I can see her cheeks tinge just slightly pink. I'm not sure I've ever seen her blush before. Every head in the room has turned to look at the gorgeous woman at my side.

"She gave me my first sketchpad and pencils and told my dad where I could go for art lessons. Painting and drawing are my favorite things to do, and Bianca is the reason that I get to." He turns to Jenna who is standing right behind him. "Can you show it now?" He asks.

"Of course," she says with a look of affection.

"This is called *My Family*," he says as Jenna approaches the painting that's been the source of Bianca's curiosity and removes the covering over it. As the piece comes into view, there's a collective gasp throughout the room. I know most people are making that noise because they weren't expecting to see what's hanging there. Instead of some five-year-old's crude drawing there's a rather well-done portrait of myself, Bianca, and Oliver positioned in between us. It's not as refined as the paintings that are gracing these gallery walls but even I can tell it's good. It's better than any five-year-old should be able to do. Bianca recognizing his talent right away and nurturing it has certainly been a blessing. He's the one that wanted to call it *My Family* and we certainly look like one up on that canvas.

"Why don't you tell us about these people you've created, Oliver," Margot encourages. I wrap my arm around Bianca's shoulder's and draw her into my side. I can't bring myself to look at her yet. I'm not ready to see the look on her face and how she's taking all this because even if she looks less than thrilled, it's too late to back out now.

"This is my dad, and that's me, and that's my mom, Bianca." I feel her give a jerk against my side and I force myself to look down at her face. Her gaze is locked onto Oliver and if I'm not mistaken, there are tears in her eyes. She never even cried when she was kidnapped. I'm honestly not sure if this is a good or bad sign. I told Oliver that he didn't have to refer to her as his mom and that he may want to speak to her first, but he was insistent, there was really nothing I could do. She loves Oliver. It feels wrong to refer to her as his friend or his dad's girlfriend. She's so much more to him than that. Those two share a special connection that I can't even touch.

331

Oliver didn't practice anything to say after that, so for a moment he's just standing there, microphone in hand, shifting from foot to foot. That's my cue to take over. I use the back of my hand to wipe off the sweat that's suddenly accumulated on my forehead, drop my arm from around Bianca and move forward until I'm in front of Oliver. I lean down so we're eye to eye and say, "Good job, buddy. You killed it." He gives me his signature shy smile and hands me the microphone.

I brace myself and finally look at Bianca's face, hoping it won't be horrified. When I turn, her hands are clasped in front of her heart and there are tears now streaming down her face. She doesn't look ready to make a run for the exit, which I half expected to happen. Sure, she looks a little stunned, but she also looks... happy.

"If you could all indulge me just a moment longer," I say, "I have a few words for my girlfriend, Bianca." I can see her friends and father all giving me encouraging smiles, so I attempt to still my shaking hands and continue. For fuck's sake, I'm a police officer, this shouldn't be so goddamn frightening.

I level my eyes on her and attempt to remember everything I planned on saying, but it all seems to slip away now that the moments come so I guess I'm winging it. "Bianca, you're everything I never thought I needed in my life, but I was so wrong. From the very second you fought me over a parking space I knew you were what was missing from my life. Well, from our lives," Bianca lets out a stifled laugh. "Our love story wasn't easy, it had ups and downs, twists and turns, but it was absolutely, perfectly, us. Even when you were driving me crazy with your sass and attitude I never, not for a single moment, could conceive of a world where we weren't together."

I let go of Oliver and reach into my pocket, taking out the small box that's been sitting there like a lead weight all evening and get down on one knee. There's another round of gasps throughout the room accompanied by not so quiet whispers but I ignore them all.

My attention is glued to the most gorgeous woman in the world that's standing before me, looking at me with love in her eyes. I think that look is the only thing calming me enough to continue.

"Babe, you've made the three of us a family. You're the glue that holds us together. I went out and bought this ring the day after you agreed to come back to me. I've always known we were, I just had to wait for you to catch up, and now nothing would make me happier than if you would give me the greatest honor of my life and agree to be my wife and make us a family for real."

The entire gallery is so silent you could hear a pin drop. I wait a few heartbeats, but Bianca hasn't answered yet. She looks a little stunned and frozen to the spot, so I say the first thing that pops into my mind. "I'll even let you park in front of my driveway any time you want."

There's light laughter throughout the room and that seems to snap Bianca out of whatever thoughts she was lost in. She comes rushing towards me but stops to crouch down to Oliver's level. "You okay with this?" His face breaks out into a wide smile as he emphatically nods his head. She straightens back up and wraps her arms around my waist. "You promise, I can park in front of the driveway?"

I can't help but throw my head back and laugh. I should have known that even during my proposal she would give me shit. But that's one of the many reasons I love her. "Yeah, I promise."

"Then, yes. I'll marry you."

The knot in my stomach loosens. "You sure, Sparky?"

She groans and the nickname she secretly loves. "Don't give me a reason to change my mind."

Well, I don't want to do that. Instead of saying anything else, I capture her lips in a kiss and can vaguely hear applause and cheers from the people crowding the room.

I never would have thought the girl I fought with over a parking spot, with fire in her eyes, would end up being the love of my life and someone I could never live without. I silently vow to myself while my lips are on hers that I'll spend the rest of my life making sure she understands just how much she means to me and our family. There's nothing else I'd rather do.

THANK YOU FOR READING!

You can download an Extended Epilogue by visiting my website, evesterlingbooks.com

If you enjoyed this book, please consider leaving a review. As an indie author this helps me reach brand new readers and would be truly appreciated.

Yours In Seattle Series

By Eve Sterling

Unprofessionally Yours
(Hollie and Archer's Story)

Made To Be Yours
(Violet and Dante's Story)

Protecting What's Yours
(Bianca and Carson's Story)

ALL ABOUT EVE

Eve Sterling loves to write stories where the hero always falls harder. She was born and raised in the Southern California where she now resides after a brief detour to the San Francisco Bay Area.

After climbing the corporate ladder for many years, she decided to take a break and pursue her lifelong passion for writing. When Eve is not coming up with more book ideas than she could possibly ever write she enjoys reading, binge watching shows with friends, and hanging out with her two dogs.

Printed in Great Britain
by Amazon

24451238R00199